THE TITHE

CREATED BY

MATT HAWKINS & RAHSAN EKEDAL

PUBLISHED BY TOP COW PRODUCTIONS, INC.
LOS ANGELES

THE TITHE

MATT HAWKINS
CO-CREATOR & WRITER

RAHSAN EKEDAL
CO-CREATOR & ARTIST

BILL FARMER & MIKE SPICER
COLORISTS

TROY PETERI
LETTERER

RAHSAN EKEDAL & BETSY GONIA
COVER ART

BETSY GONIA
EDITOR

LINDA SEJIC
THE TITHE LOGO DESIGN

TRICIA RAMOS
PRODUCTION

Want more info? Check out:
www.topcow.com
for news & exclusive Top Cow merchandise!

THE TITHE VOLUME ONE. FIRST PRINTING. AUGUST 2015. COPYRIGHT © 2015 MATT HAWKINS, RAHSAN EKEDAL AND TOP COW PRODUCTIONS, INC. ALL RIGHTS RESERVED. PUBLISHED BY IMAGE COMICS, INC. OFFICE OF PUBLICATION: 2001 CENTER STREET, 6TH FLOOR, BERKELEY, CA 94704. ORIGINALLY PUBLISHED IN SINGLE MAGAZINE FORMAT AS THE TITHE #1-4. BY IMAGE COMICS & TOP COW PRODUCTIONS. "THE TITHE," ITS LOGOS, AND THE LIKENESSES OF ALL FEATURED CHARACTERS HEREIN ARE REGISTERED TRADEMARKS OF MATT HAWKINS, RAHSAN EKEDAL, & TOP COW PRODUCTIONS, INC. ANY RESEMBLANCE TO ACTUAL PERSONS (LIVING OR DEAD), EVENTS, INSTITUTIONS, OR LOCALES, WITHOUT SATIRIC INTENT IS COINCIDENTAL. NO PORTION OF THIS PUBLICATION MAY BE REPRODUCED OR TRANSMITTED, IN ANY FORM OR BY ANY MEANS, WITHOUT THE EXPRESS WRITTEN PERMISSION OF MATT HAWKINS, RAHSAN EKEDAL, & TOP COW PRODUCTIONS, INC. PRINTED IN THE USA. FOR INFORMATION REGARDING THE CPSIA ON THIS PRINTED MATERIAL CALL: 203-595-3636 AND PROVIDE REFERENCE # RICH – 632039. ISBN: 978-1-63215-324-1

"GIVING TO OUR MINISTRY DOES THE LORD'S WORK."

-JIM BAKKER, TELEVANGELIST OF THE 700 CLUB AND THE PTL CLUB (PRAISE THE LORD) CONVICTED OF FINANCIAL FRAUD IN 1989 WHO SERVED FIVE YEARS OF A FORTY-FIVE YEAR SENTENCE. HE WAS BACK ON TV IN 2003 WITH THE JIM BAKKER SHOW, WHICH STILL AIRS TODAY.

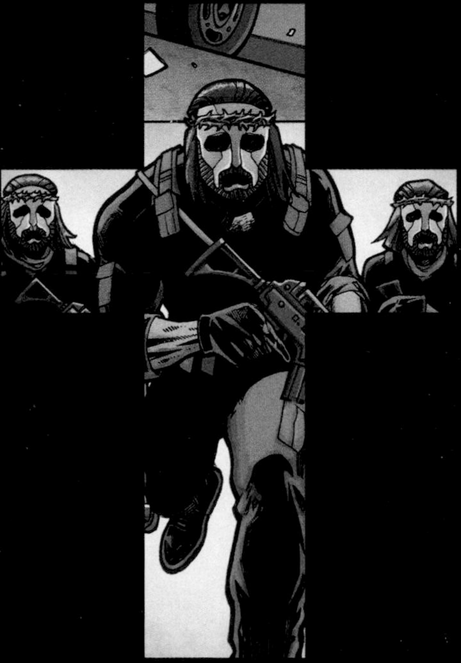

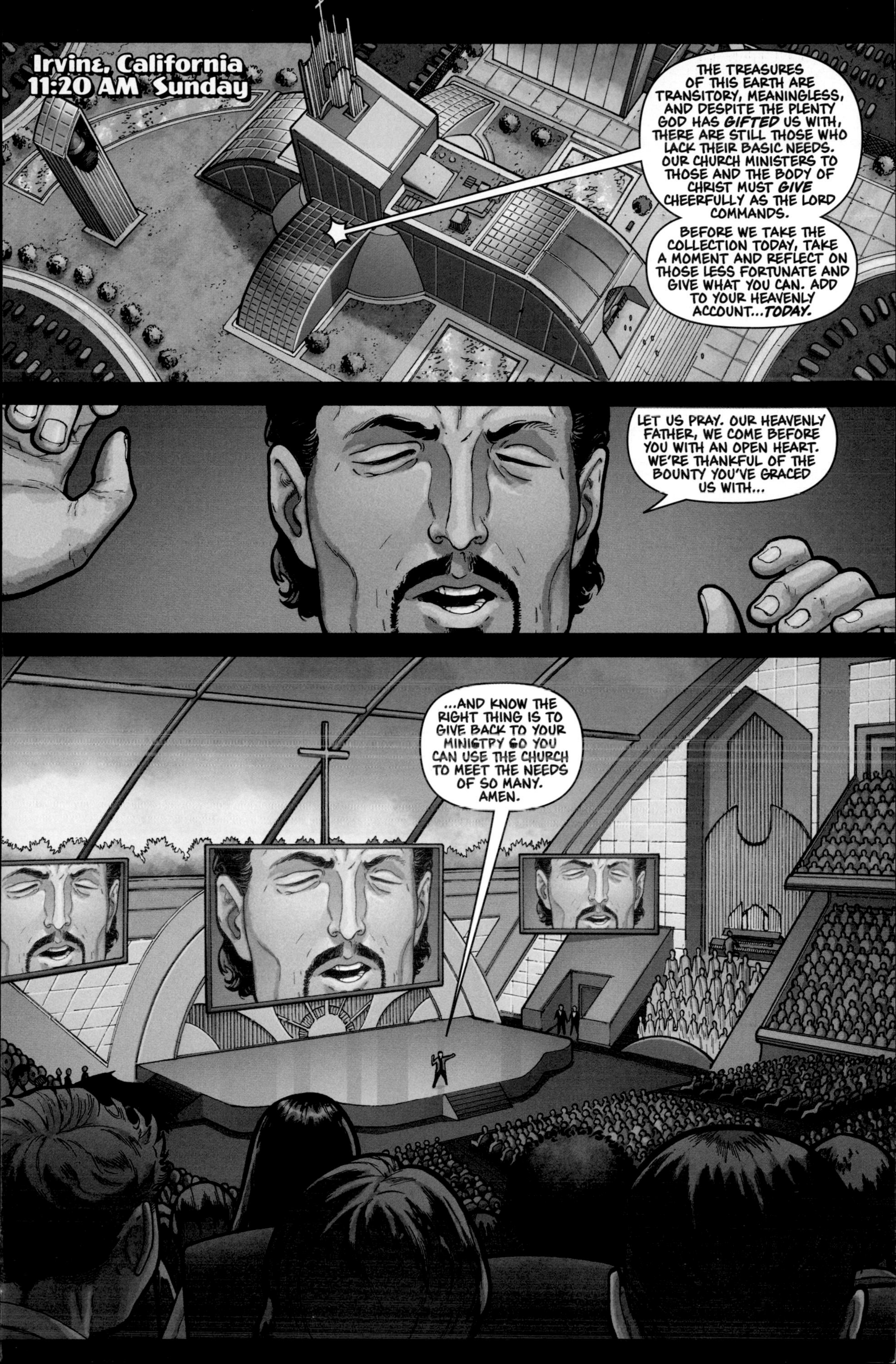
Irvine, California
11:20 AM Sunday
THE TREASURES OF THIS EARTH ARE TRANSITORY, MEANINGLESS, AND DESPITE THE PLENTY GOD HAS *GIFTED* US WITH, THERE ARE STILL THOSE WHO LACK THEIR BASIC NEEDS. OUR CHURCH MINISTERS TO THOSE AND THE BODY OF CHRIST MUST *GIVE* CHEERFULLY AS THE LORD COMMANDS.
BEFORE WE TAKE THE COLLECTION TODAY, TAKE A MOMENT AND REFLECT ON THOSE LESS FORTUNATE AND GIVE WHAT YOU CAN. ADD TO YOUR HEAVENLY ACCOUNT...*TODAY.*
LET US PRAY. OUR HEAVENLY FATHER, WE COME BEFORE YOU WITH AN OPEN HEART. WE'RE THANKFUL OF THE BOUNTY YOU'VE GRACED US WITH...
...AND KNOW THE RIGHT THING IS TO GIVE BACK TO YOUR MINISTRY SO YOU CAN USE THE CHURCH TO MEET THE NEEDS OF SO MANY. AMEN.

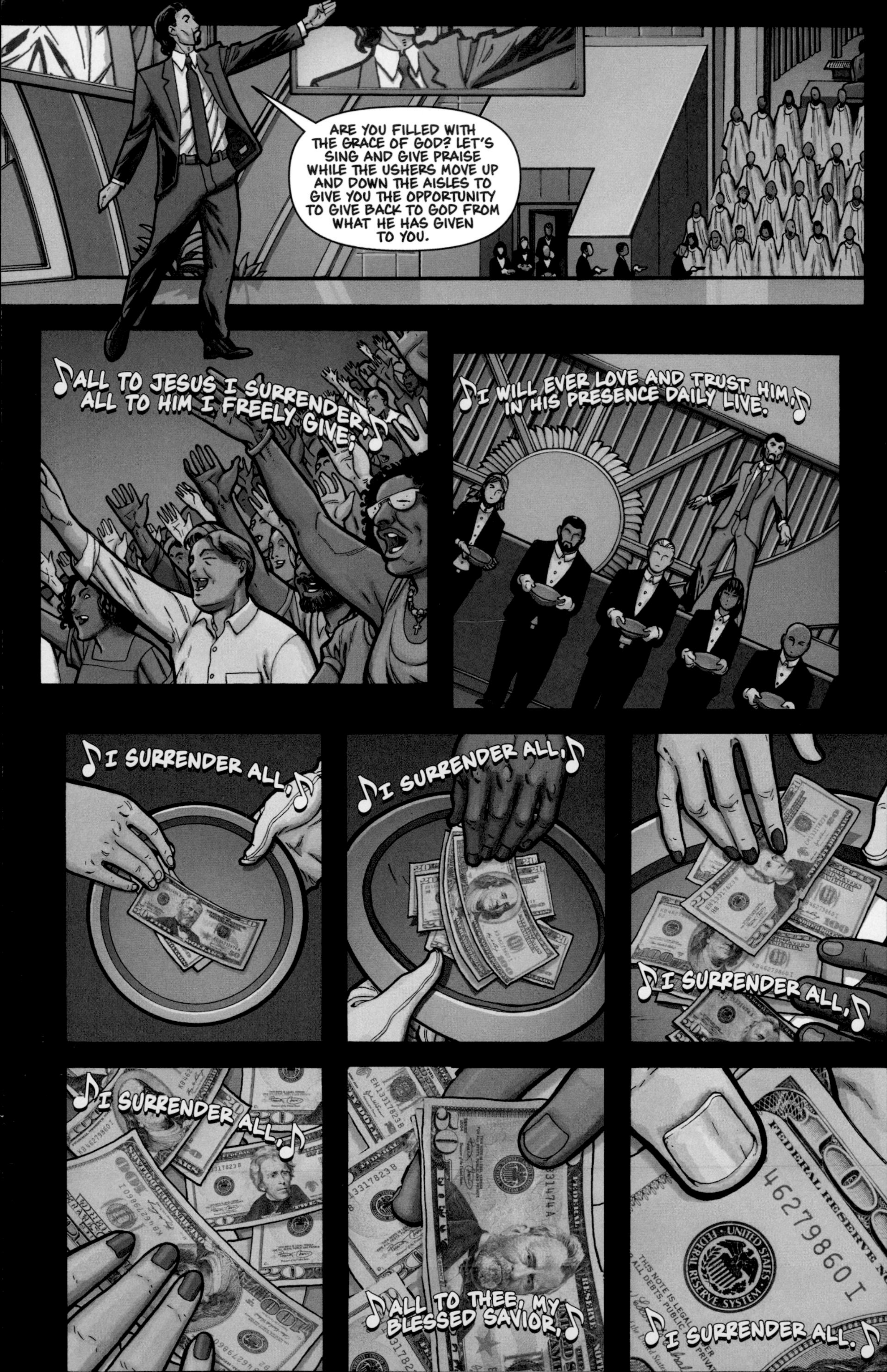

ARE YOU FILLED WITH THE GRACE OF GOD? LET'S SING AND GIVE PRAISE WHILE THE USHERS MOVE UP AND DOWN THE AISLES TO GIVE YOU THE OPPORTUNITY TO GIVE BACK TO GOD FROM WHAT HE HAS GIVEN TO YOU.
♪ALL TO JESUS I SURRENDER, ALL TO HIM I FREELY GIVE;♪
♪I WILL EVER LOVE AND TRUST HIM, IN HIS PRESENCE DAILY LIVE.♪
♪I SURRENDER ALL,♪
♪I SURRENDER ALL,♪
♪I SURRENDER ALL,♪
♪I SURRENDER ALL,♪
♪ALL TO THEE, MY BLESSED SAVIOR,♪
♪I SURRENDER ALL.♪

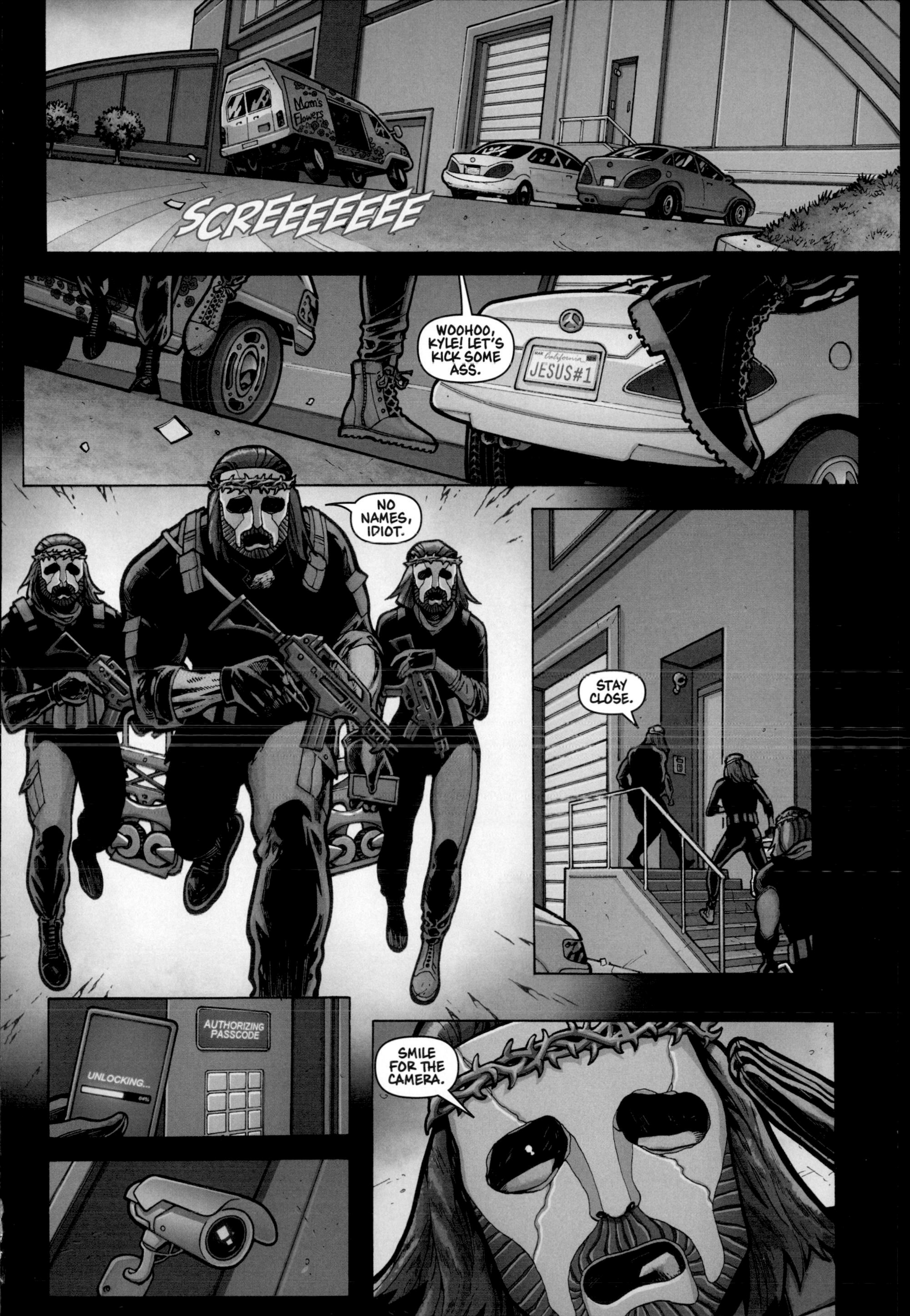

SCREEEEEEEE
WOOHOO, KYLE! LET'S KICK SOME ASS.
JESUS#1
NO NAMES, IDIOT.
STAY CLOSE.
AUTHORIZING PASSCODE
UNLOCKING...
SMILE FOR THE CAMERA.

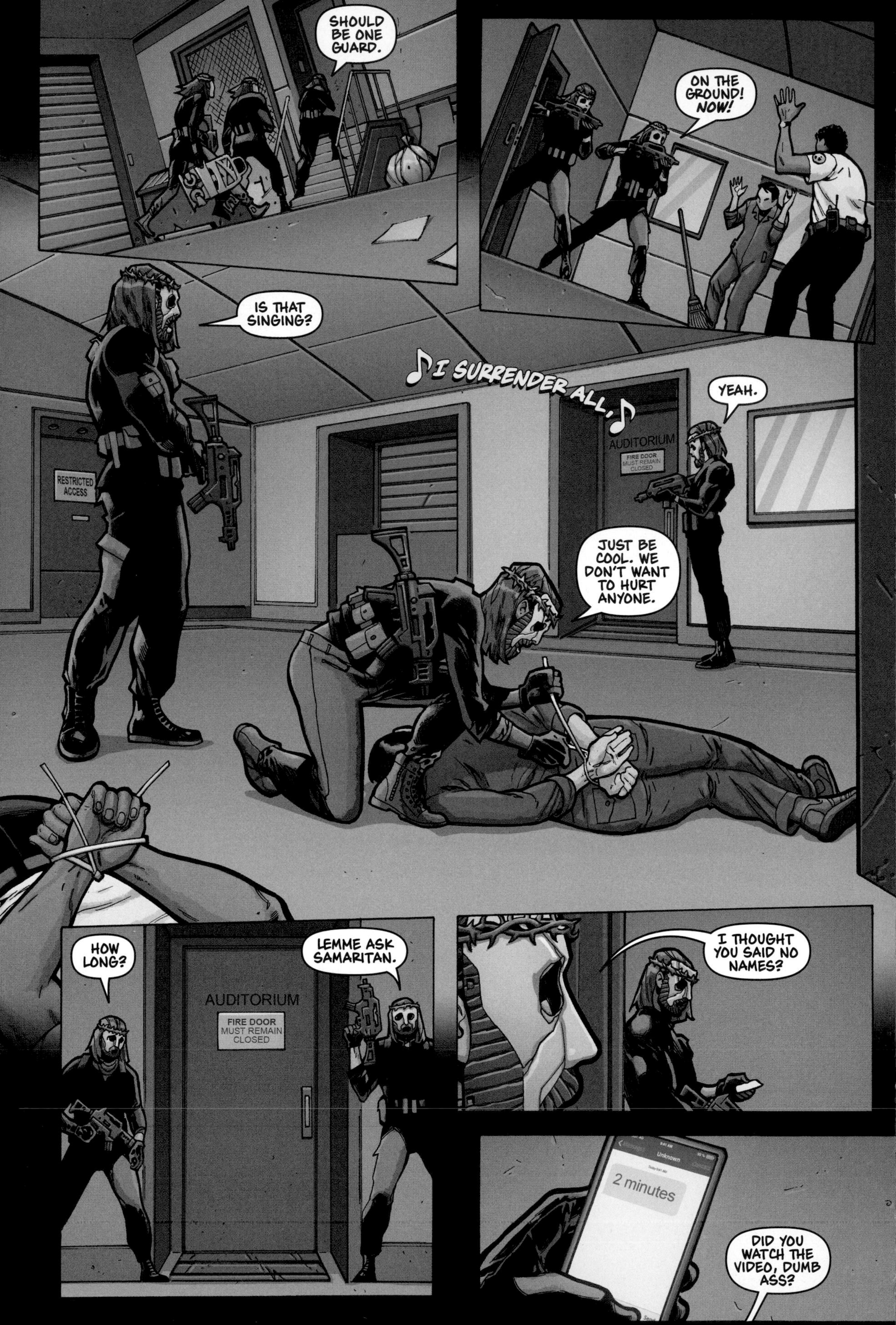

SHOULD BE ONE GUARD.
ON THE GROUND! NOW!
IS THAT SINGING?
♪I SURRENDER ALL,♪
YEAH.
AUDITORIUM
FIRE DOOR MUST REMAIN CLOSED
RESTRICTED ACCESS
JUST BE COOL. WE DON'T WANT TO HURT ANYONE.
HOW LONG?
LEMME ASK SAMARITAN.
AUDITORIUM
FIRE DOOR MUST REMAIN CLOSED
I THOUGHT YOU SAID NO NAMES?
Unknown
2 minutes
DID YOU WATCH THE VIDEO, DUMB ASS?

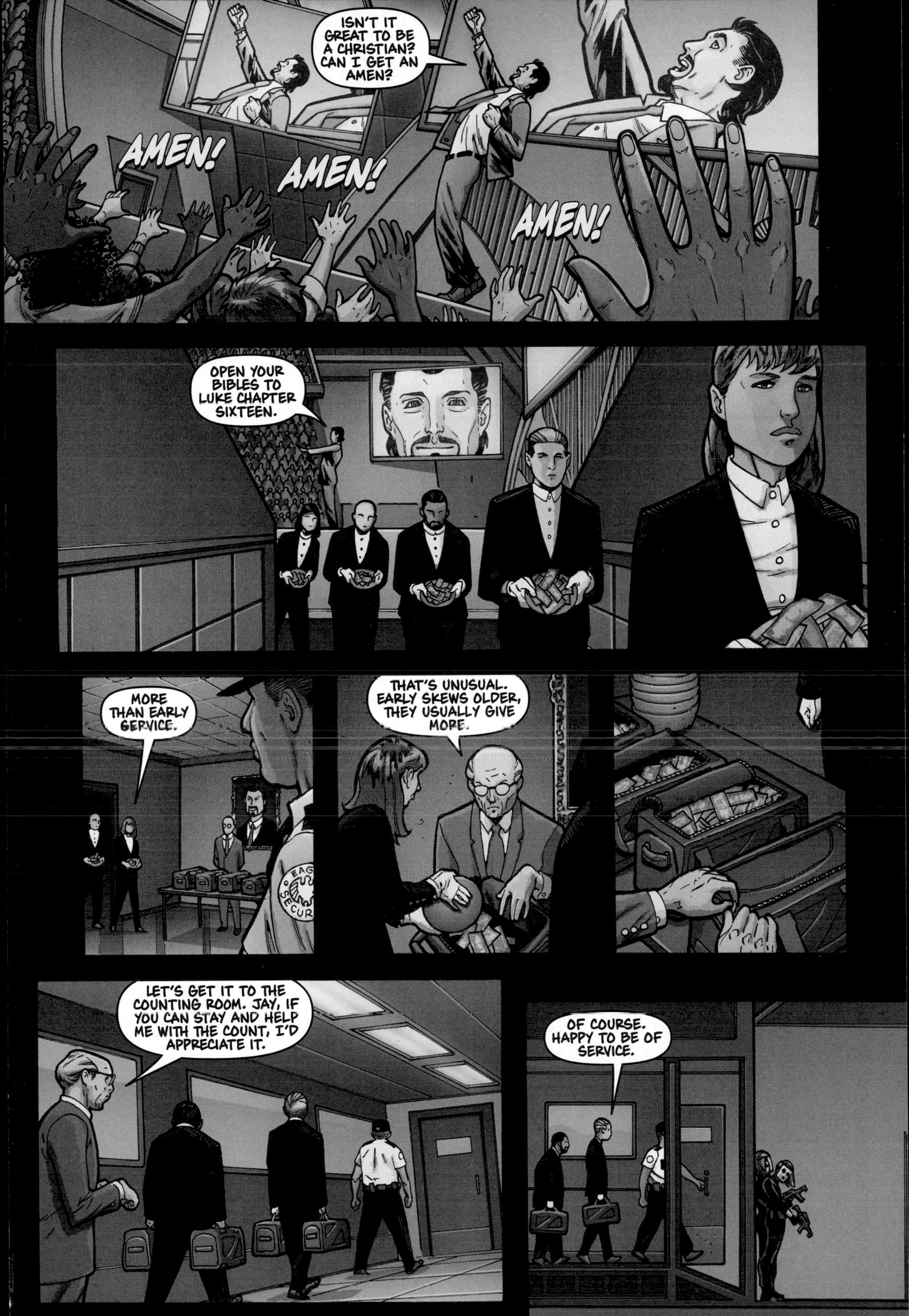
ISN'T IT GREAT TO BE A CHRISTIAN? CAN I GET AN AMEN?
AMEN!
AMEN!
AMEN!
OPEN YOUR BIBLES TO LUKE CHAPTER SIXTEEN.
MORE THAN EARLY SERVICE.
THAT'S UNUSUAL. EARLY SKEWS OLDER, THEY USUALLY GIVE MORE.
LET'S GET IT TO THE COUNTING ROOM. JAY, IF YOU CAN STAY AND HELP ME WITH THE COUNT, I'D APPRECIATE IT.
OF COURSE. HAPPY TO BE OF SERVICE.

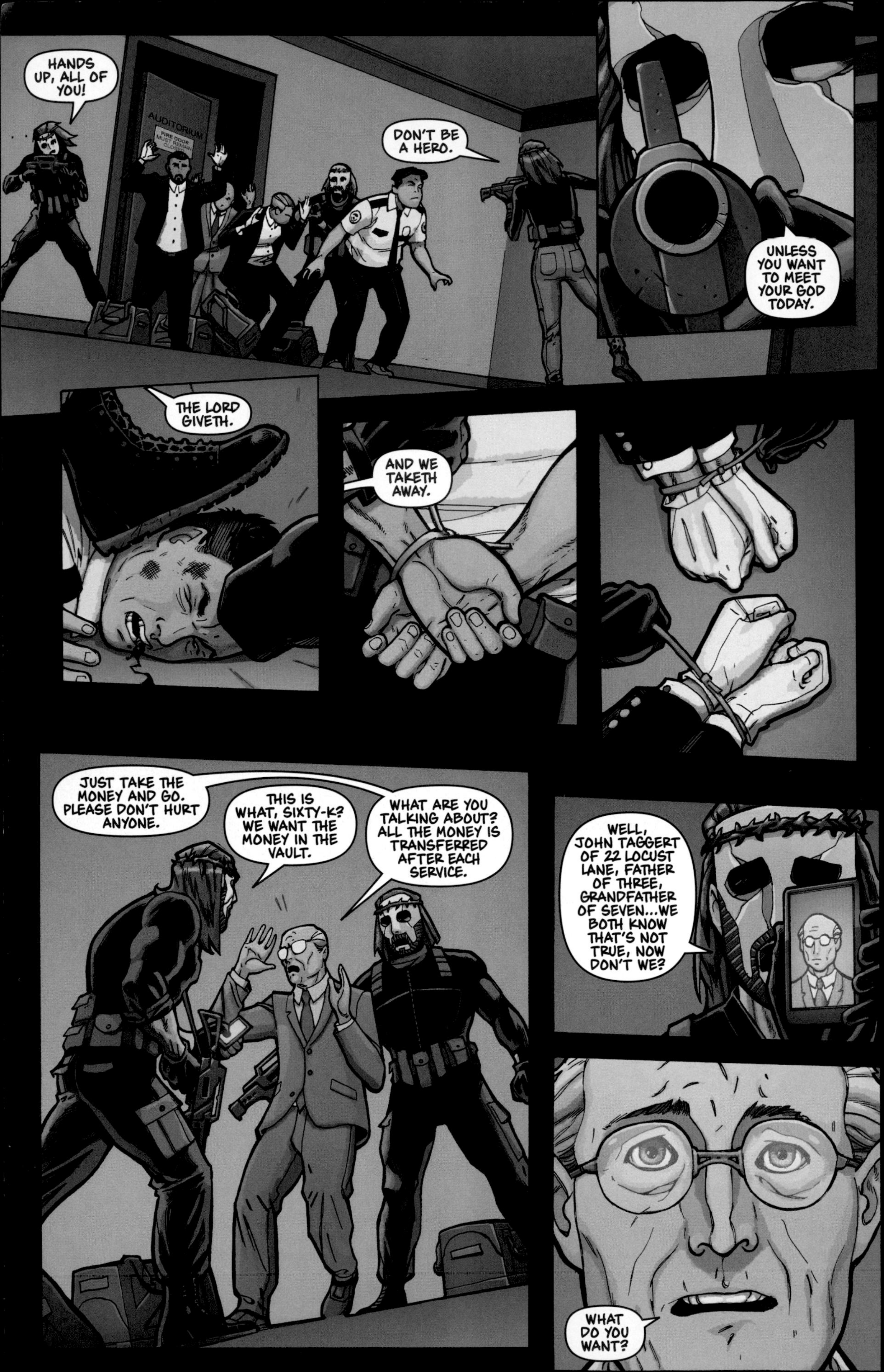
HANDS UP, ALL OF YOU!
AUDITORIUM
FIRE DOOR MUST REMAIN CLOSED
DON'T BE A HERO.
UNLESS YOU WANT TO MEET YOUR GOD TODAY.
THE LORD GIVETH.
AND WE TAKETH AWAY.
JUST TAKE THE MONEY AND GO. PLEASE DON'T HURT ANYONE.
THIS IS WHAT, SIXTY-K? WE WANT THE MONEY IN THE VAULT.
WHAT ARE YOU TALKING ABOUT? ALL THE MONEY IS TRANSFERRED AFTER EACH SERVICE.
WELL, JOHN TAGGERT OF 22 LOCUST LANE, FATHER OF THREE, GRANDFATHER OF SEVEN...WE BOTH KNOW THAT'S NOT TRUE, NOW DON'T WE?
WHAT DO YOU WANT?

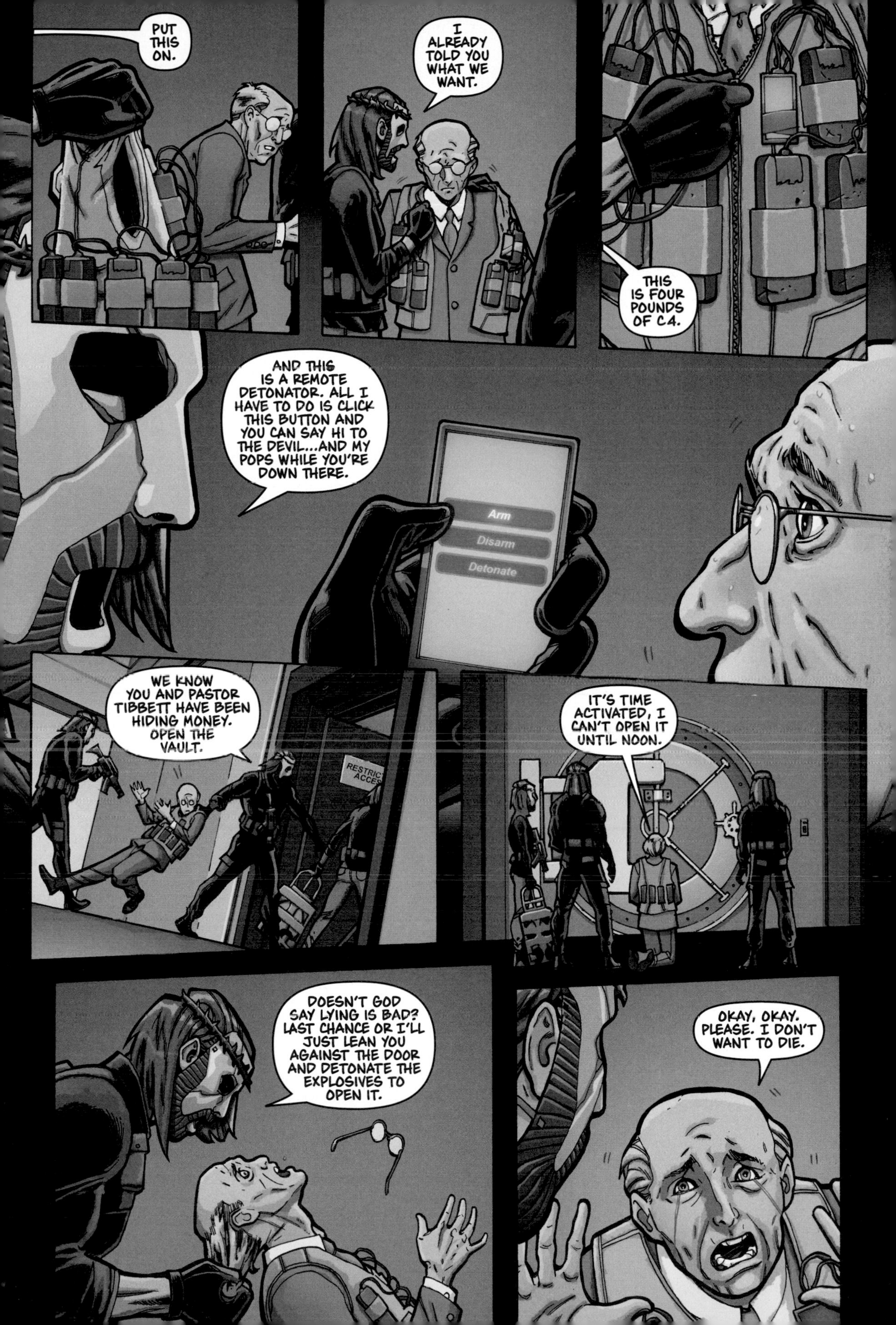
PUT THIS ON.
I ALREADY TOLD YOU WHAT WE WANT.
THIS IS FOUR POUNDS OF C4.
AND THIS IS A REMOTE DETONATOR. ALL I HAVE TO DO IS CLICK THIS BUTTON AND YOU CAN SAY HI TO THE DEVIL...AND MY POPS WHILE YOU'RE DOWN THERE.
Arm
Disarm
Detonate
WE KNOW YOU AND PASTOR TIBBETT HAVE BEEN HIDING MONEY. OPEN THE VAULT.
IT'S TIME ACTIVATED, I CAN'T OPEN IT UNTIL NOON.
DOESN'T GOD SAY LYING IS BAD? LAST CHANCE OR I'LL JUST LEAN YOU AGAINST THE DOOR AND DETONATE THE EXPLOSIVES TO OPEN IT.
OKAY, OKAY. PLEASE. I DON'T WANT TO DIE.

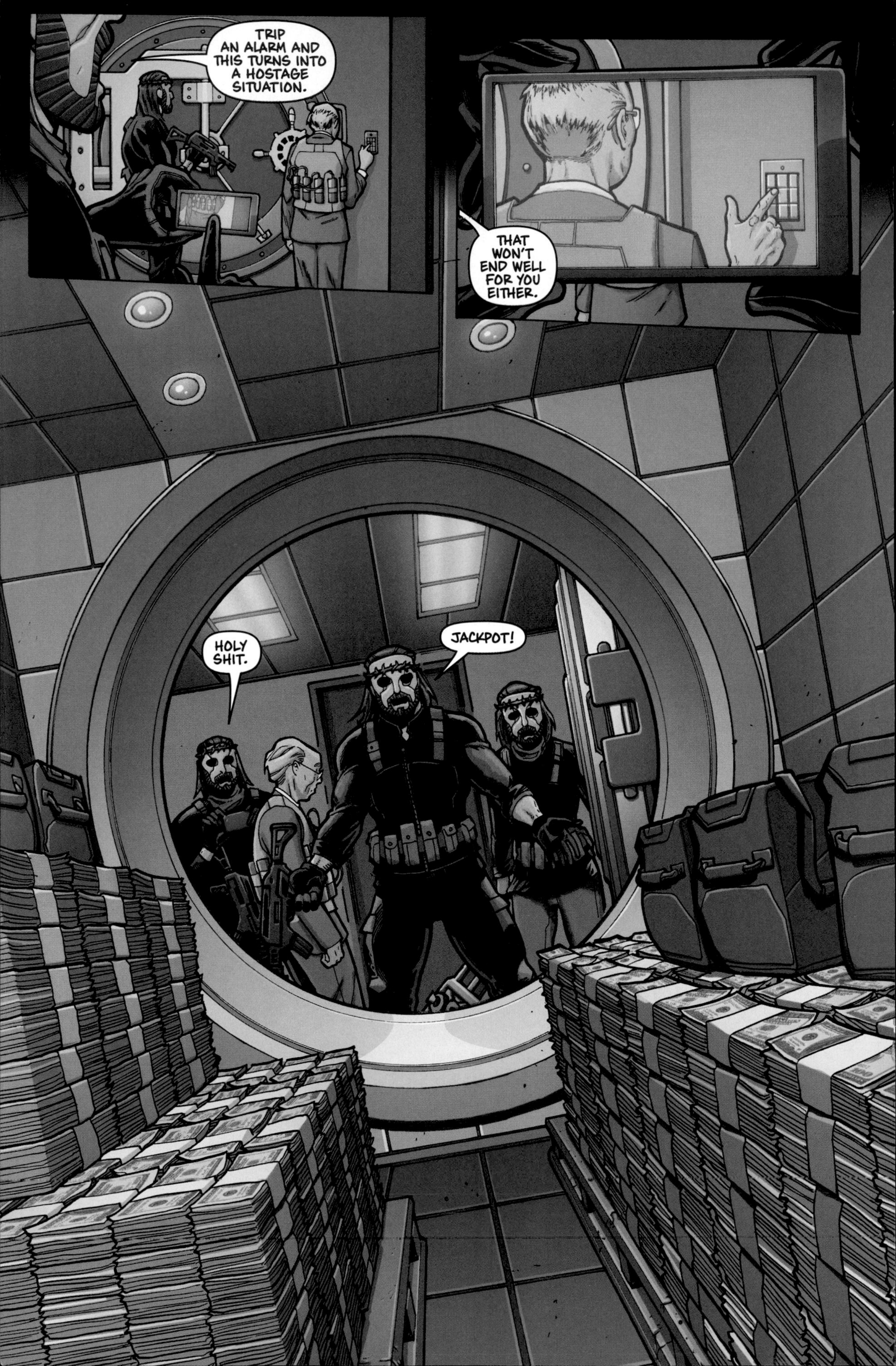
TRIP AN ALARM AND THIS TURNS INTO A HOSTAGE SITUATION.
THAT WON'T END WELL FOR YOU EITHER.
HOLY SHIT.
JACKPOT!

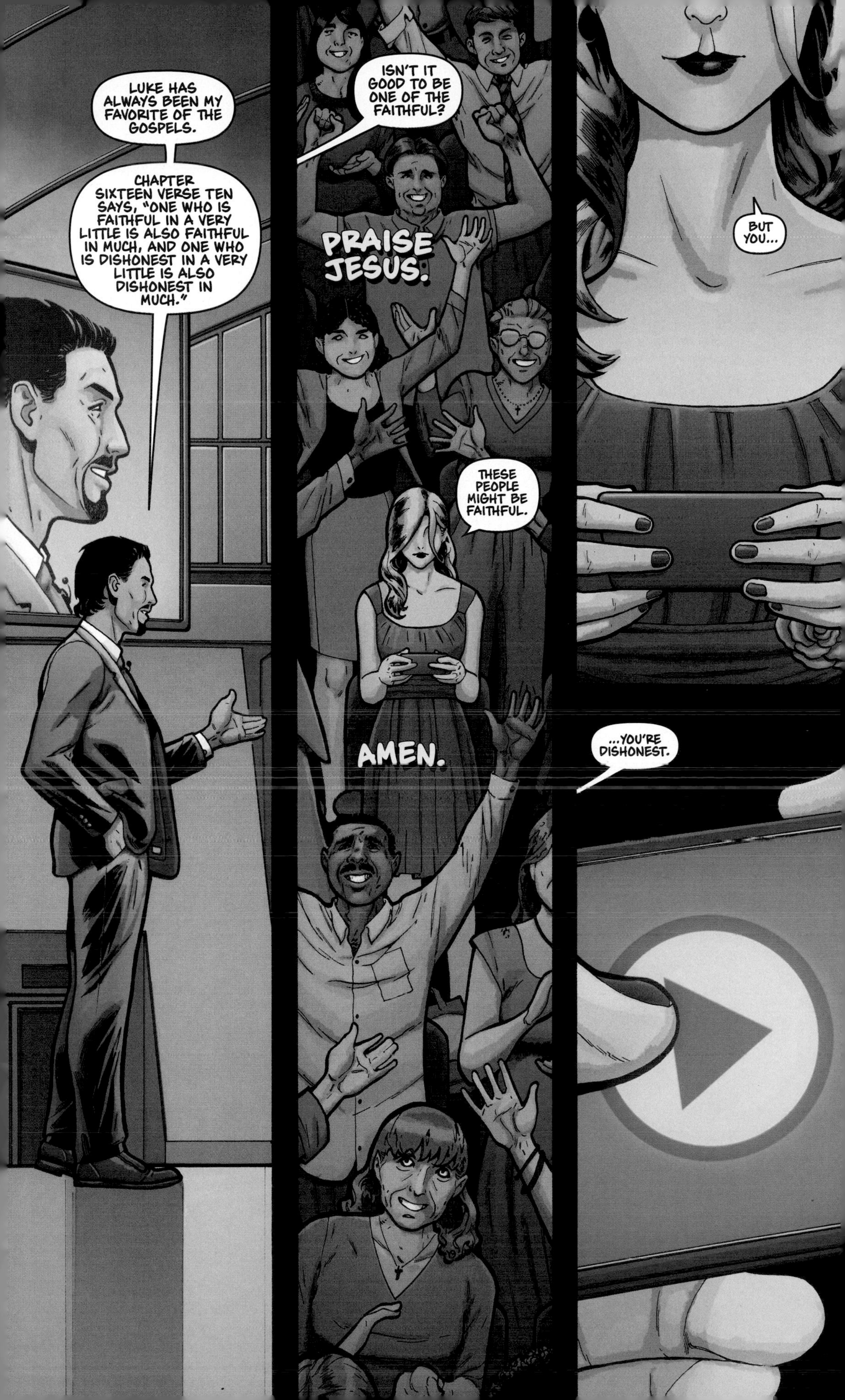
LUKE HAS ALWAYS BEEN MY FAVORITE OF THE GOSPELS.
CHAPTER SIXTEEN VERSE TEN SAYS, "ONE WHO IS FAITHFUL IN A VERY LITTLE IS ALSO FAITHFUL IN MUCH, AND ONE WHO IS DISHONEST IN A VERY LITTLE IS ALSO DISHONEST IN MUCH."
ISN'T IT GOOD TO BE ONE OF THE FAITHFUL?
PRAISE JESUS.
THESE PEOPLE MIGHT BE FAITHFUL.
AMEN.
BUT YOU...
...YOU'RE DISHONEST.

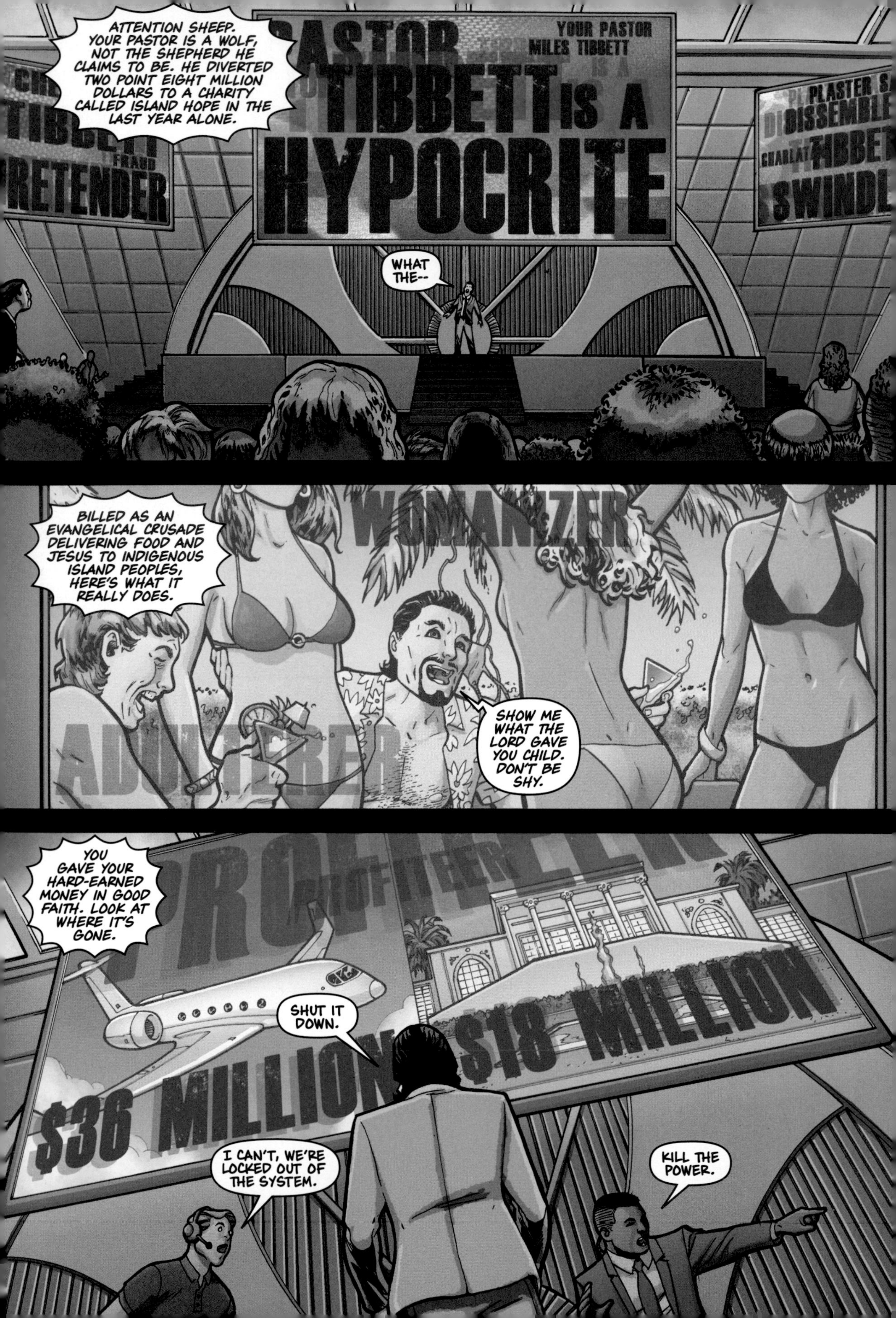
ATTENTION SHEEP. YOUR PASTOR IS A WOLF, NOT THE SHEPHERD HE CLAIMS TO BE. HE DIVERTED TWO POINT EIGHT MILLION DOLLARS TO A CHARITY CALLED ISLAND HOPE IN THE LAST YEAR ALONE.
PASTOR TIBBETT IS A HYPOCRITE
YOUR PASTOR MILES TIBBETT
FRAUD
WHAT THE--
BILLED AS AN EVANGELICAL CRUSADE DELIVERING FOOD AND JESUS TO INDIGENOUS ISLAND PEOPLES, HERE'S WHAT IT REALLY DOES.
WOMANIZER
ADULTERER
SHOW ME WHAT THE LORD GAVE YOU CHILD. DON'T BE SHY.
YOU GAVE YOUR HARD-EARNED MONEY IN GOOD FAITH. LOOK AT WHERE IT'S GONE.
PROFITEER
$36 MILLION
$18 MILLION
SHUT IT DOWN.
I CAN'T, WE'RE LOCKED OUT OF THE SYSTEM.
KILL THE POWER.

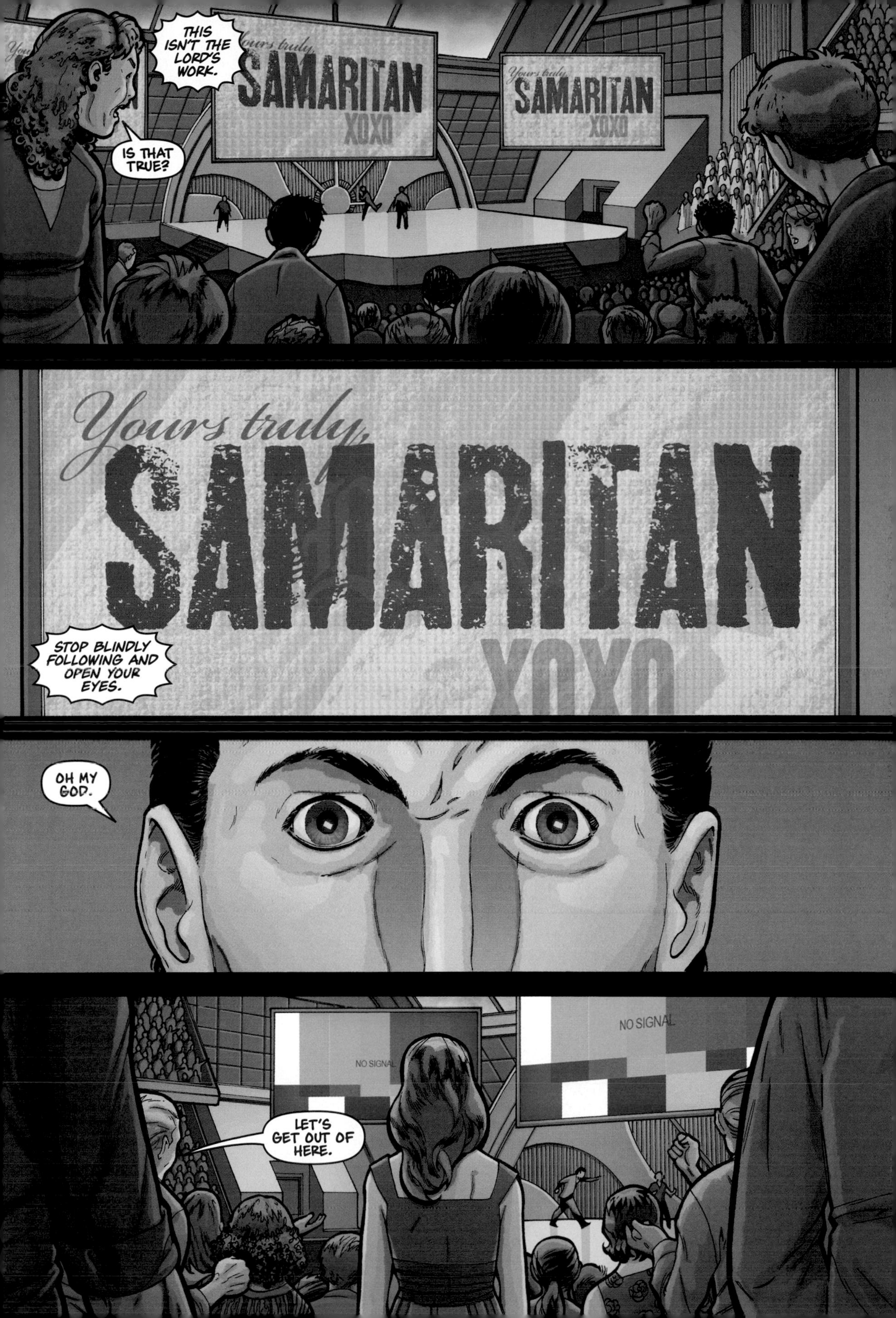
THIS ISN'T THE LORD'S WORK.
IS THAT TRUE?
Yours truly, SAMARITAN XOXO
Yours truly, SAMARITAN XOXO
Yours truly, SAMARITAN XOXO
STOP BLINDLY FOLLOWING AND OPEN YOUR EYES.
OH MY GOD.
NO SIGNAL
NO SIGNAL
LET'S GET OUT OF HERE.

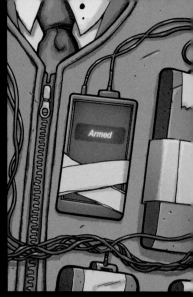

Armed

I KNOW PASTOR TIBBETT. HE'S A GODLY MAN. THIS IS ALL A LIE.

SHEEPLE, SIGH.

Arm

Disarm

Detonate

SOME OF THEM NEED A REAL SHOCK TO SEE THE WORLD FOR WHAT IT IS.

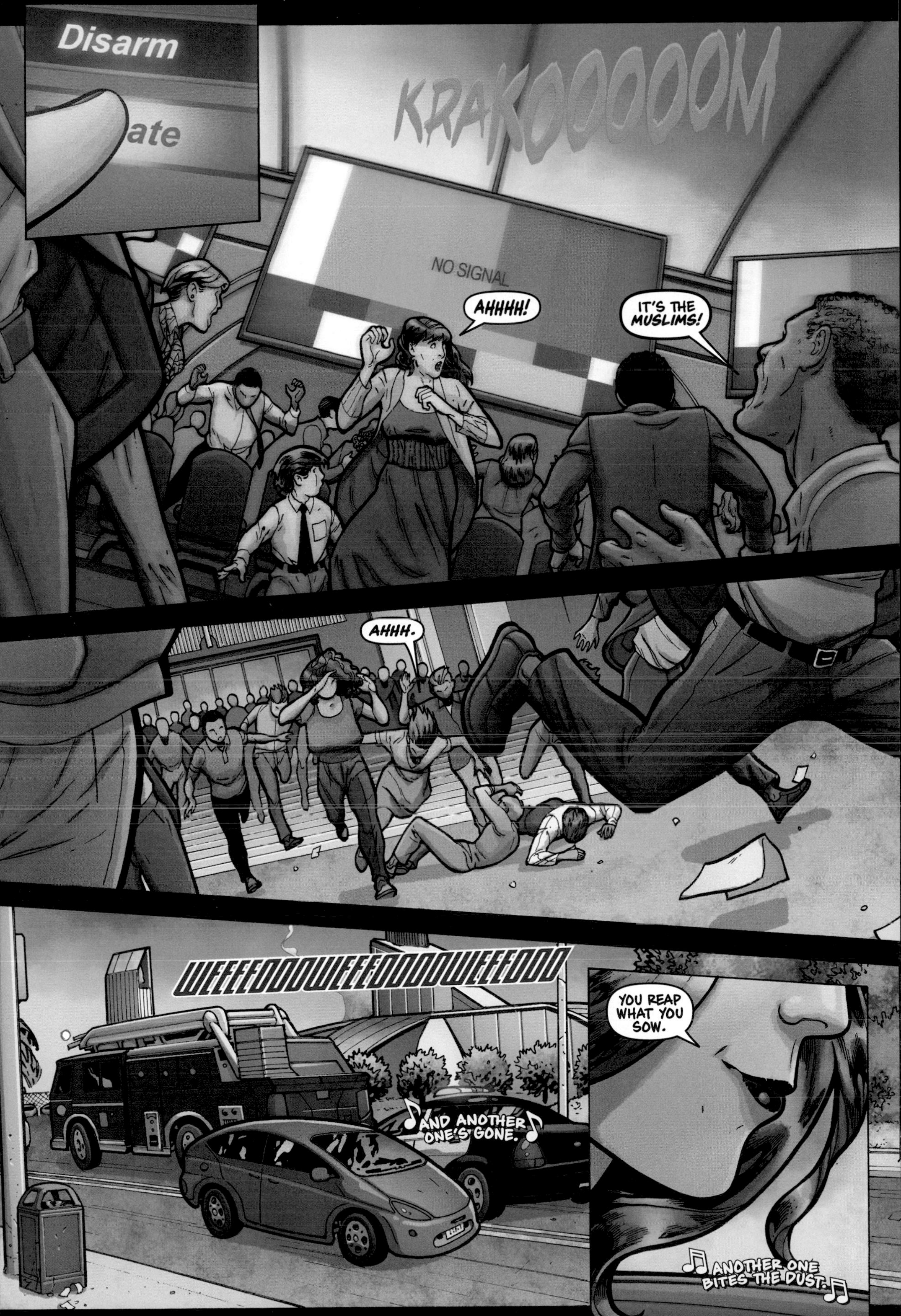
Disarm
ate
KRAKOOOOOOM
NO SIGNAL
AHHHH!
IT'S THE MUSLIMS!
AHHH.
WEEEEOOOWEEEOOOOWEEEOOO
AND ANOTHER ONE'S GONE.
YOU REAP WHAT YOU SOW.
ANOTHER ONE BITES THE DUST.

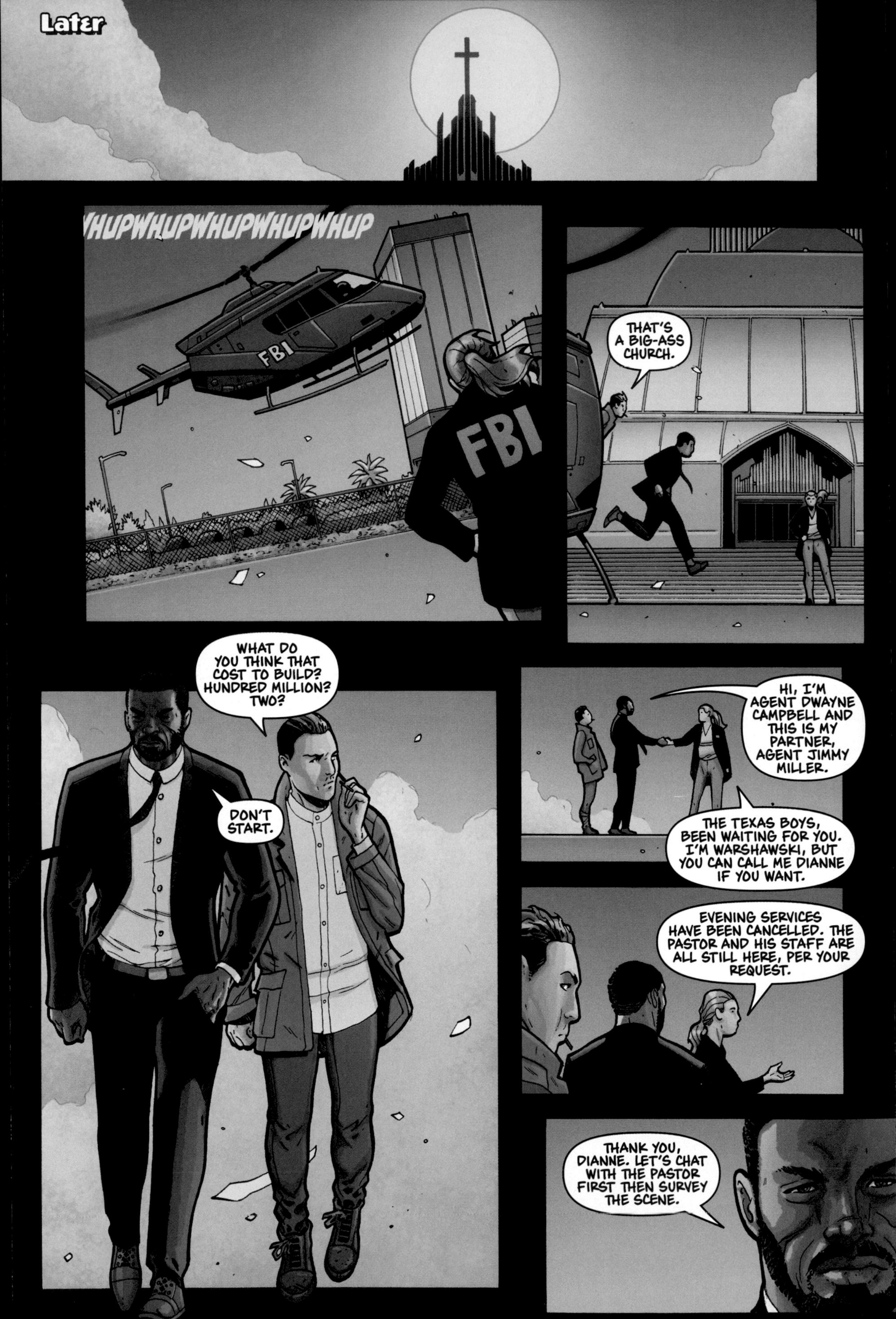
Later
WHUPWHUPWHUPWHUPWHUP
FBI
FBI
THAT'S A BIG-ASS CHURCH.
WHAT DO YOU THINK THAT COST TO BUILD? HUNDRED MILLION? TWO?
DON'T START.
HI, I'M AGENT DWAYNE CAMPBELL AND THIS IS MY PARTNER, AGENT JIMMY MILLER.
THE TEXAS BOYS, BEEN WAITING FOR YOU. I'M WARSHAWSKI, BUT YOU CAN CALL ME DIANNE IF YOU WANT.
EVENING SERVICES HAVE BEEN CANCELLED. THE PASTOR AND HIS STAFF ARE ALL STILL HERE, PER YOUR REQUEST.
THANK YOU, DIANNE. LET'S CHAT WITH THE PASTOR FIRST THEN SURVEY THE SCENE.

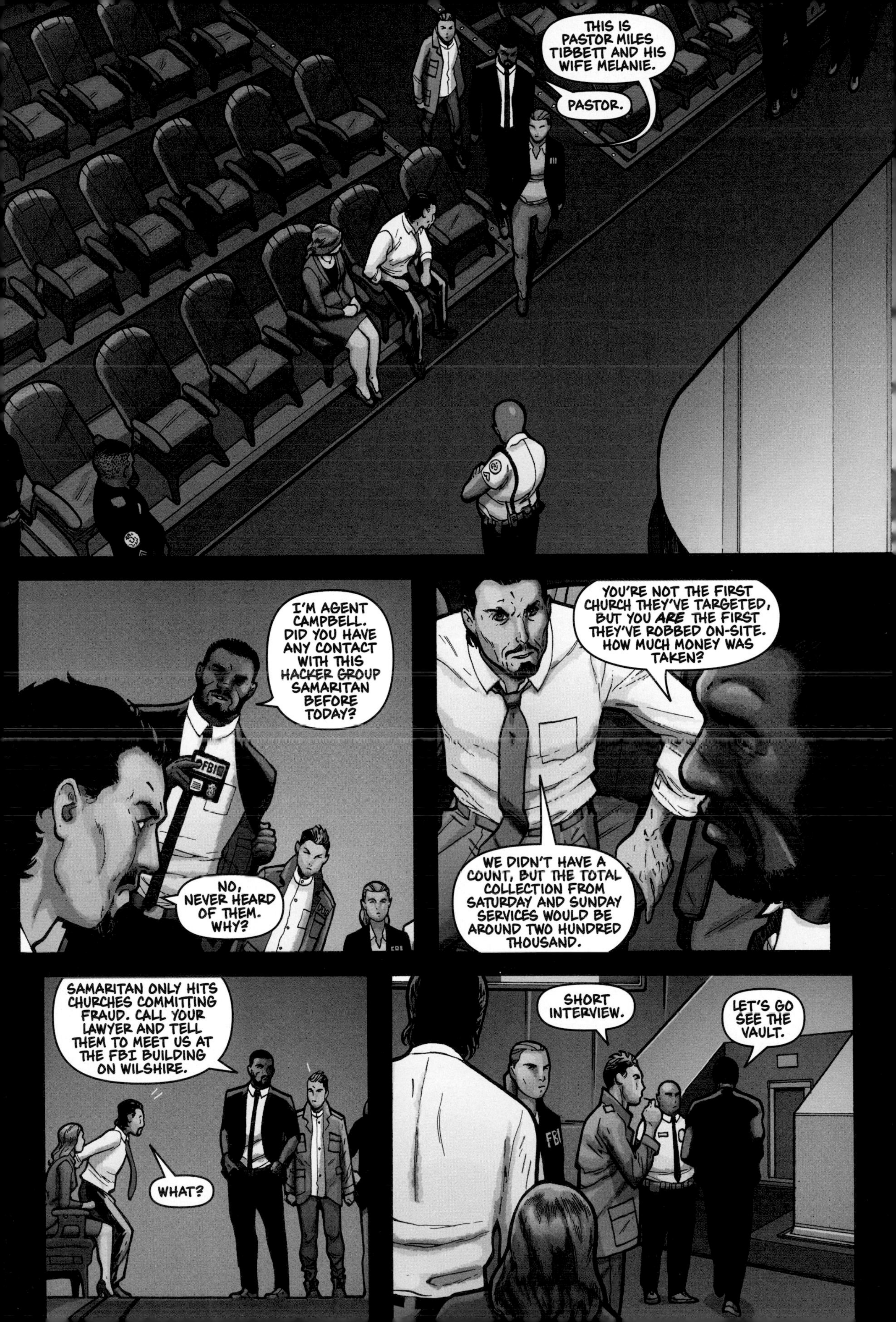
THIS IS PASTOR MILES TIBBETT AND HIS WIFE MELANIE.
PASTOR.
I'M AGENT CAMPBELL. DID YOU HAVE ANY CONTACT WITH THIS HACKER GROUP SAMARITAN BEFORE TODAY?
NO, NEVER HEARD OF THEM. WHY?
YOU'RE NOT THE FIRST CHURCH THEY'VE TARGETED, BUT YOU *ARE* THE FIRST THEY'VE ROBBED ON-SITE. HOW MUCH MONEY WAS TAKEN?
WE DIDN'T HAVE A COUNT, BUT THE TOTAL COLLECTION FROM SATURDAY AND SUNDAY SERVICES WOULD BE AROUND TWO HUNDRED THOUSAND.
SAMARITAN ONLY HITS CHURCHES COMMITTING FRAUD. CALL YOUR LAWYER AND TELL THEM TO MEET US AT THE FBI BUILDING ON WILSHIRE.
WHAT?
SHORT INTERVIEW.
LET'S GO SEE THE VAULT.

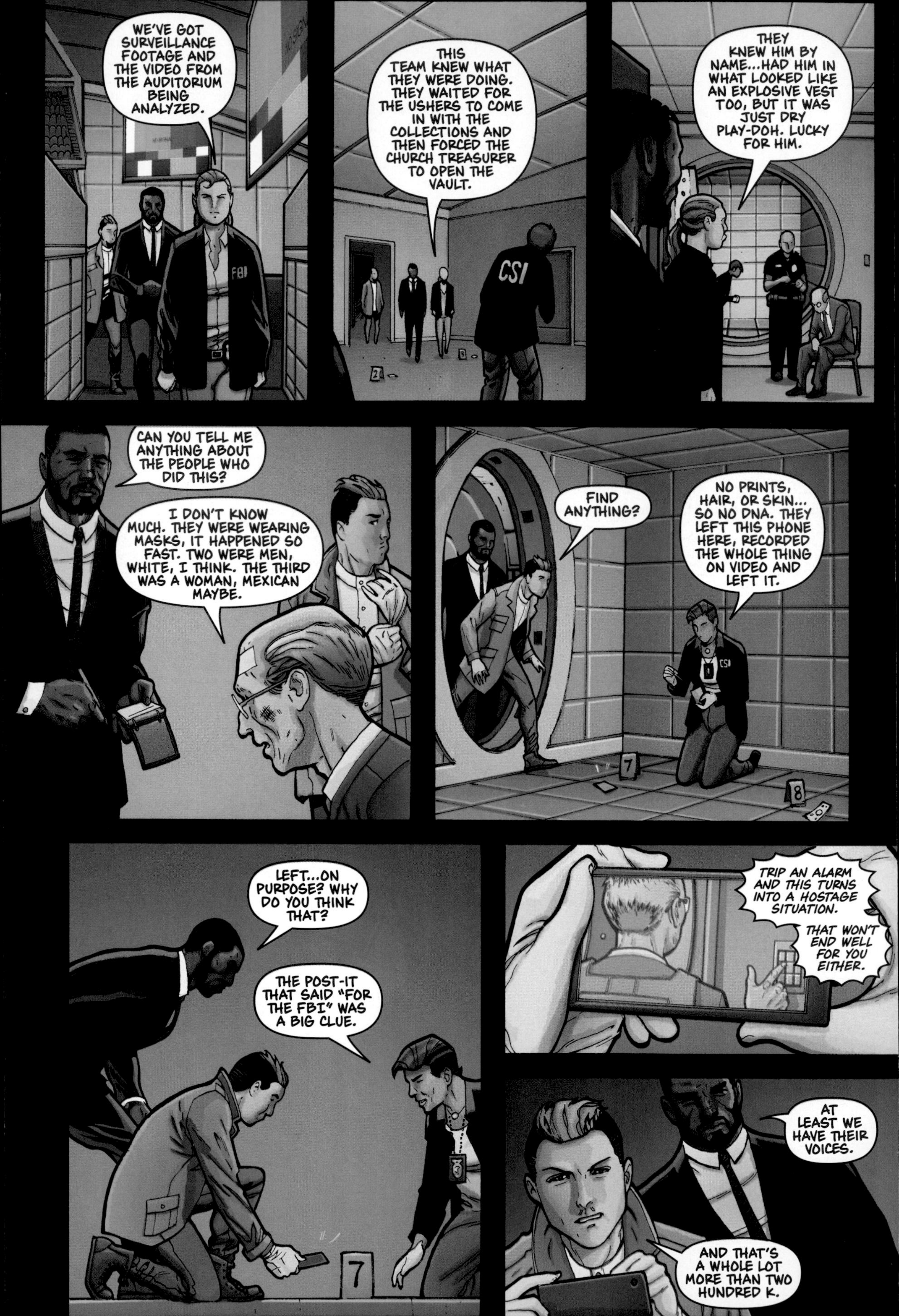
WE'VE GOT SURVEILLANCE FOOTAGE AND THE VIDEO FROM THE AUDITORIUM BEING ANALYZED.
THIS TEAM KNEW WHAT THEY WERE DOING. THEY WAITED FOR THE USHERS TO COME IN WITH THE COLLECTIONS AND THEN FORCED THE CHURCH TREASURER TO OPEN THE VAULT.
CSI
THEY KNEW HIM BY NAME...HAD HIM IN WHAT LOOKED LIKE AN EXPLOSIVE VEST TOO, BUT IT WAS JUST DRY PLAY-DOH. LUCKY FOR HIM.
CAN YOU TELL ME ANYTHING ABOUT THE PEOPLE WHO DID THIS?
I DON'T KNOW MUCH. THEY WERE WEARING MASKS, IT HAPPENED SO FAST. TWO WERE MEN, WHITE, I THINK. THE THIRD WAS A WOMAN, MEXICAN MAYBE.
FIND ANYTHING?
NO PRINTS, HAIR, OR SKIN... SO NO DNA. THEY LEFT THIS PHONE HERE, RECORDED THE WHOLE THING ON VIDEO AND LEFT IT.
LEFT...ON PURPOSE? WHY DO YOU THINK THAT?
THE POST-IT THAT SAID "FOR THE FBI" WAS A BIG CLUE.
TRIP AN ALARM AND THIS TURNS INTO A HOSTAGE SITUATION.
THAT WON'T END WELL FOR YOU EITHER.
AT LEAST WE HAVE THEIR VOICES.
AND THAT'S A WHOLE LOT MORE THAN TWO HUNDRED K.

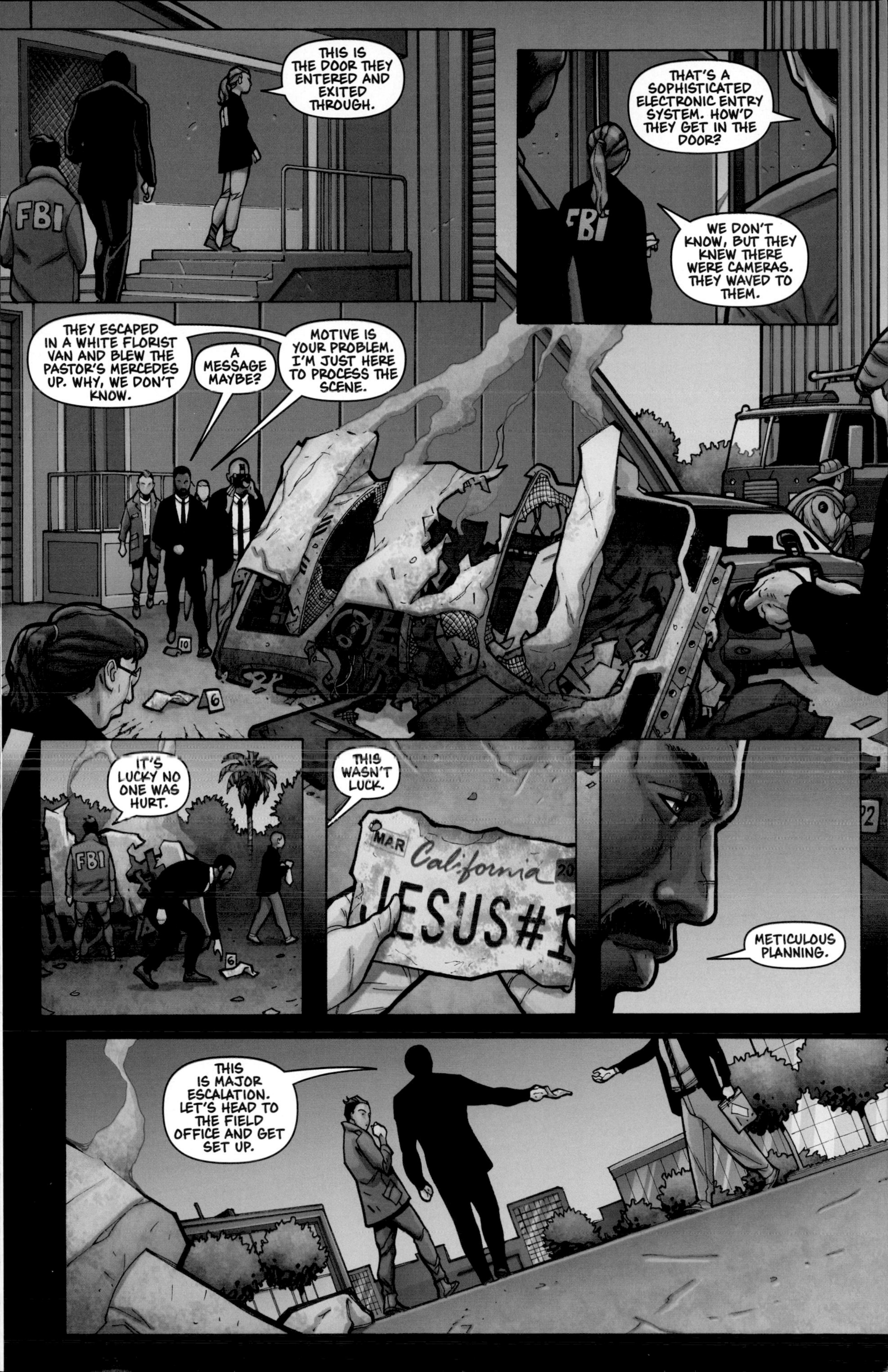
THIS IS THE DOOR THEY ENTERED AND EXITED THROUGH.
FBI
THAT'S A SOPHISTICATED ELECTRONIC ENTRY SYSTEM. HOW'D THEY GET IN THE DOOR?
FBI
WE DON'T KNOW, BUT THEY KNEW THERE WERE CAMERAS. THEY WAVED TO THEM.
THEY ESCAPED IN A WHITE FLORIST VAN AND BLEW THE PASTOR'S MERCEDES UP. WHY, WE DON'T KNOW.
A MESSAGE MAYBE?
MOTIVE IS YOUR PROBLEM. I'M JUST HERE TO PROCESS THE SCENE.
IT'S LUCKY NO ONE WAS HURT.
FBI
THIS WASN'T LUCK.
MAR California 20
JESUS#1
MEticulous PLANNING.
THIS IS MAJOR ESCALATION. LET'S HEAD TO THE FIELD OFFICE AND GET SET UP.

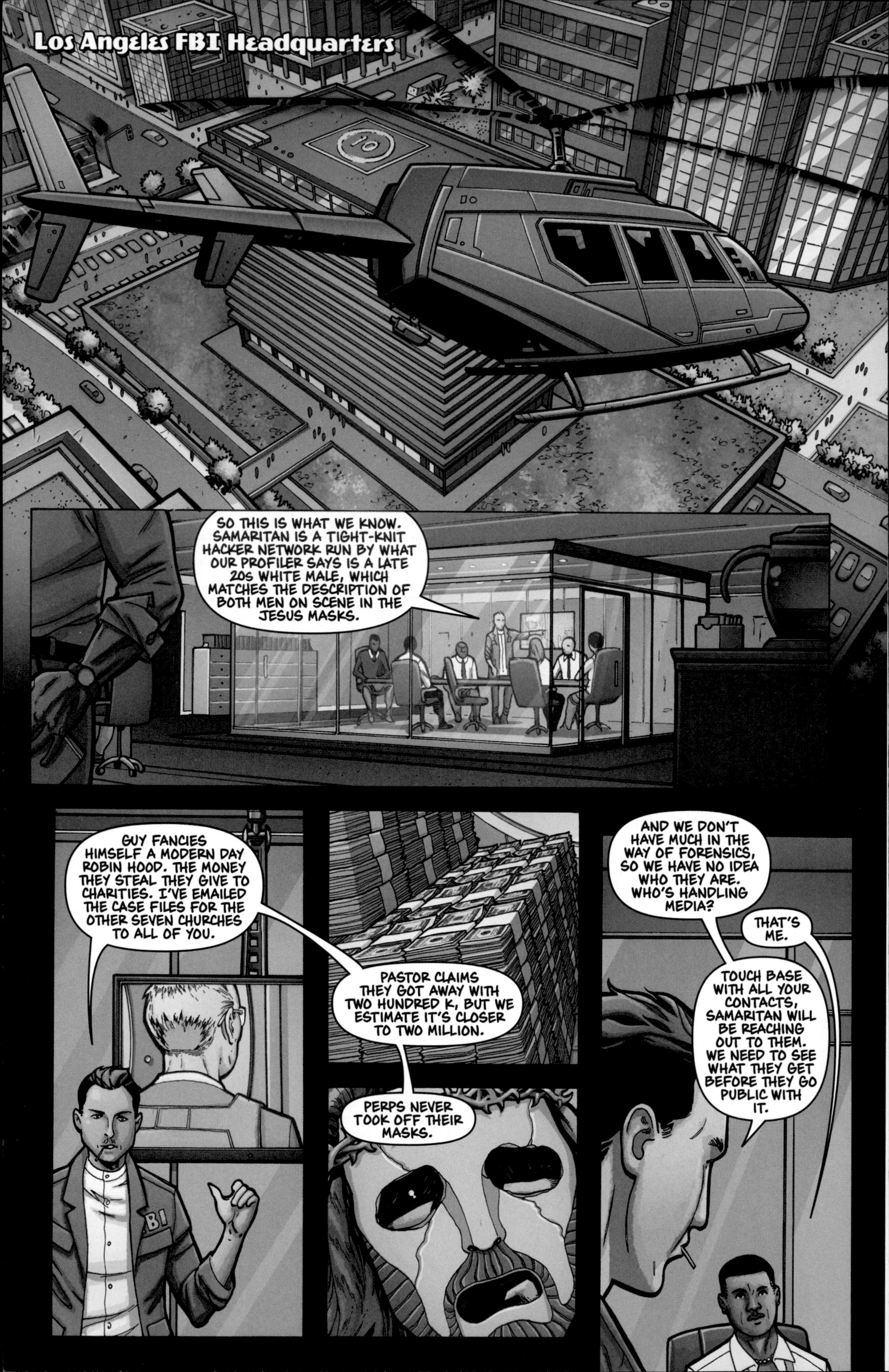
Los Angeles FBI Headquarters
SO THIS IS WHAT WE KNOW. SAMARITAN IS A TIGHT-KNIT HACKER NETWORK RUN BY WHAT OUR PROFILER SAYS IS A LATE 20s WHITE MALE, WHICH MATCHES THE DESCRIPTION OF BOTH MEN ON SCENE IN THE JESUS MASKS.
GUY FANCIES HIMSELF A MODERN DAY ROBIN HOOD. THE MONEY THEY STEAL THEY GIVE TO CHARITIES. I'VE EMAILED THE CASE FILES FOR THE OTHER SEVEN CHURCHES TO ALL OF YOU.
PASTOR CLAIMS THEY GOT AWAY WITH TWO HUNDRED K, BUT WE ESTIMATE IT'S CLOSER TO TWO MILLION.
PERPS NEVER TOOK OFF THEIR MASKS.
AND WE DON'T HAVE MUCH IN THE WAY OF FORENSICS, SO WE HAVE NO IDEA WHO THEY ARE. WHO'S HANDLING MEDIA?
THAT'S ME.
TOUCH BASE WITH ALL YOUR CONTACTS, SAMARITAN WILL BE REACHING OUT TO THEM. WE NEED TO SEE WHAT THEY GET BEFORE THEY GO PUBLIC WITH IT.

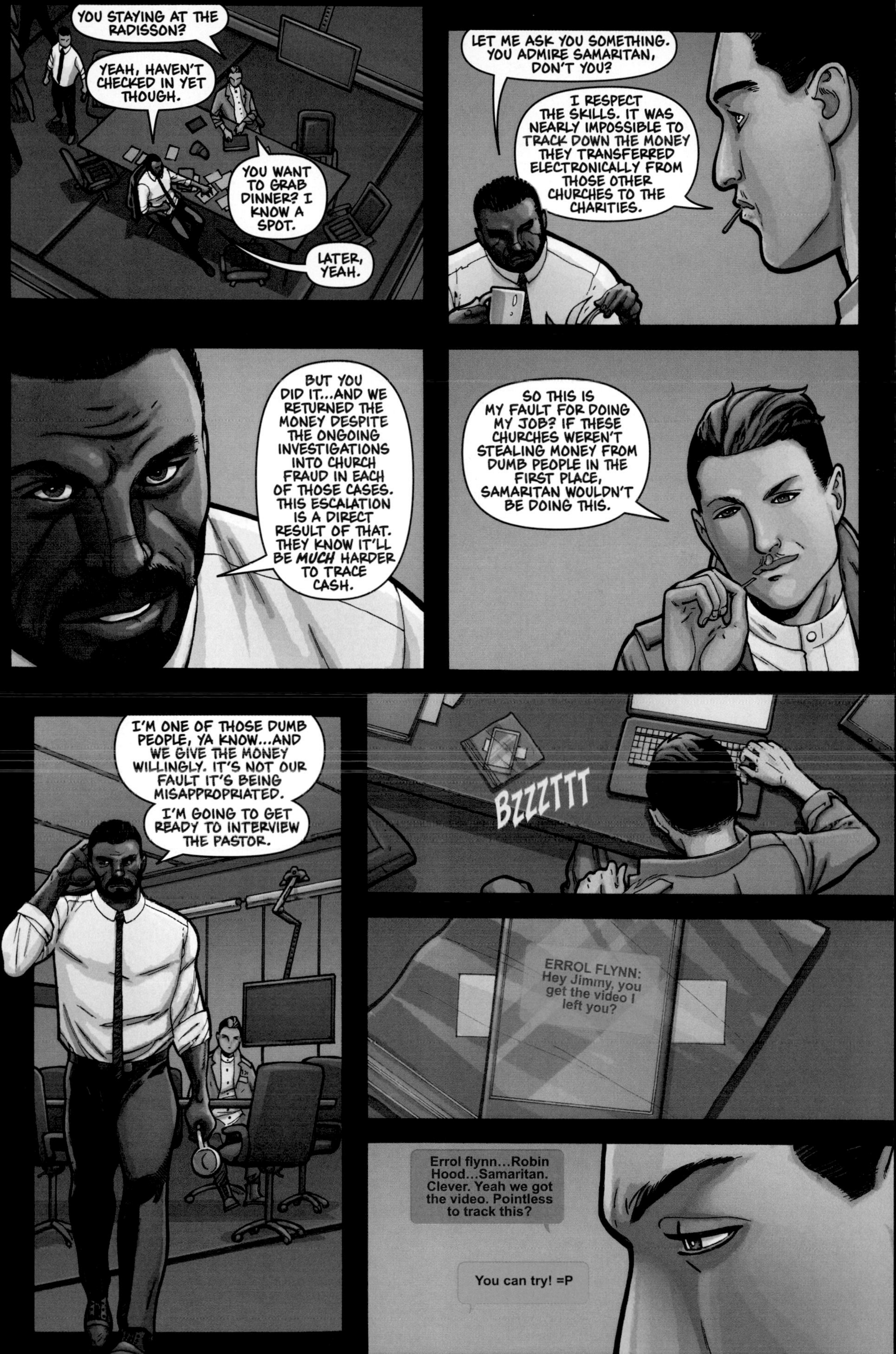
YOU STAYING AT THE RADISSON?
YEAH, HAVEN'T CHECKED IN YET THOUGH.
YOU WANT TO GRAB DINNER? I KNOW A SPOT.
LATER, YEAH.
LET ME ASK YOU SOMETHING. YOU ADMIRE SAMARITAN, DON'T YOU?
I RESPECT THE SKILLS. IT WAS NEARLY IMPOSSIBLE TO TRACK DOWN THE MONEY THEY TRANSFERRED ELECTRONICALLY FROM THOSE OTHER CHURCHES TO THE CHARITIES.
BUT YOU DID IT...AND WE RETURNED THE MONEY DESPITE THE ONGOING INVESTIGATIONS INTO CHURCH FRAUD IN EACH OF THOSE CASES. THIS ESCALATION IS A DIRECT RESULT OF THAT. THEY KNOW IT'LL BE *MUCH* HARDER TO TRACE CASH.
SO THIS IS MY FAULT FOR DOING MY JOB? IF THESE CHURCHES WEREN'T STEALING MONEY FROM DUMB PEOPLE IN THE FIRST PLACE, SAMARITAN WOULDN'T BE DOING THIS.
I'M ONE OF THOSE DUMB PEOPLE, YA KNOW...AND WE GIVE THE MONEY WILLINGLY. IT'S NOT OUR FAULT IT'S BEING MISAPPROPRIATED.
I'M GOING TO GET READY TO INTERVIEW THE PASTOR.
BZZZTTT
ERROL FLYNN: Hey Jimmy, you get the video I left you?
Errol flynn...Robin Hood...Samaritan. Clever. Yeah we got the video. Pointless to track this?
You can try! =P

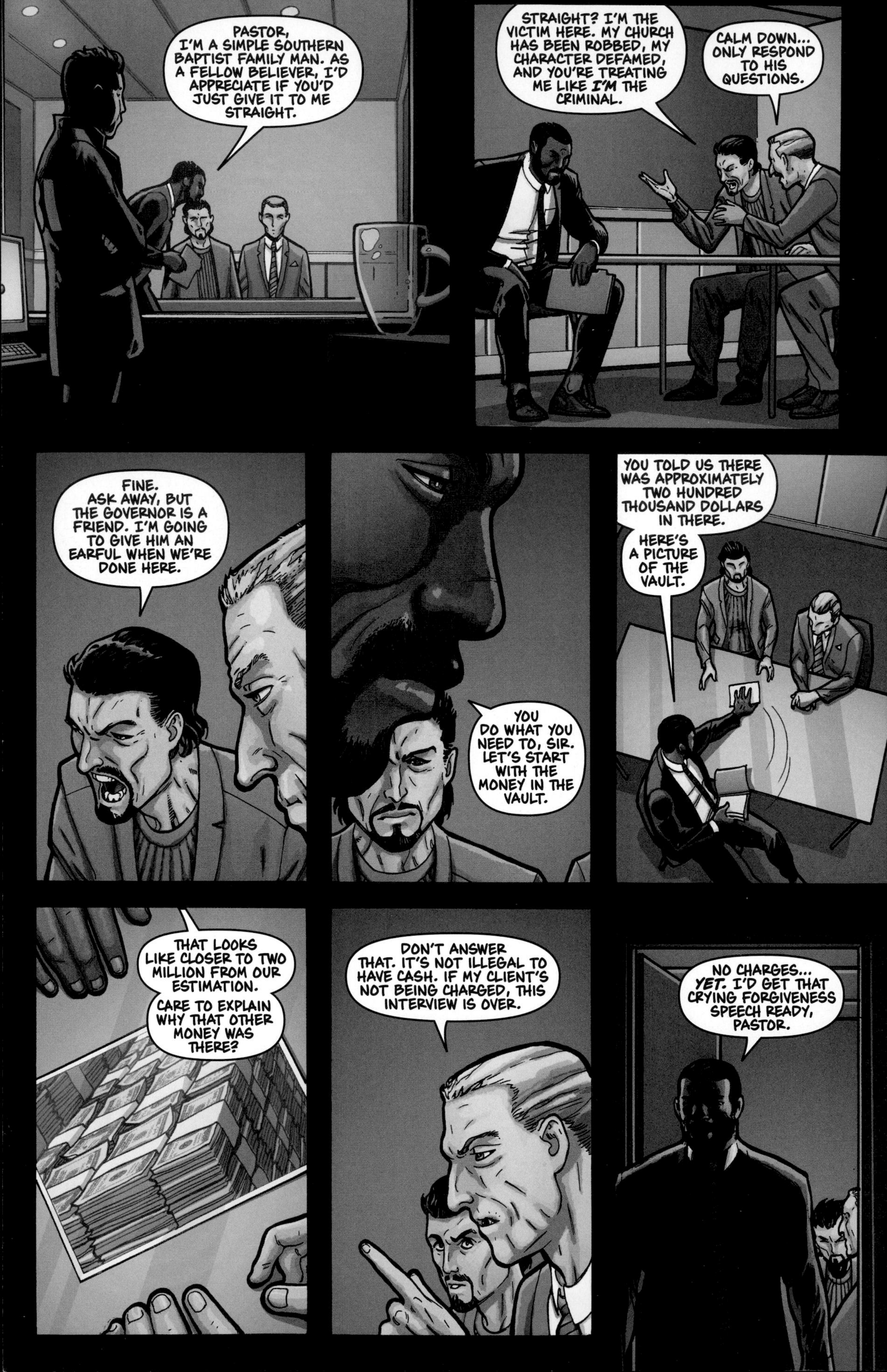
PASTOR, I'M A SIMPLE SOUTHERN BAPTIST FAMILY MAN. AS A FELLOW BELIEVER, I'D APPRECIATE IF YOU'D JUST GIVE IT TO ME STRAIGHT.
STRAIGHT? I'M THE VICTIM HERE. MY CHURCH HAS BEEN ROBBED, MY CHARACTER DEFAMED, AND YOU'RE TREATING ME LIKE *I'M* THE CRIMINAL.
CALM DOWN... ONLY RESPOND TO HIS QUESTIONS.
FINE. ASK AWAY, BUT THE GOVERNOR IS A FRIEND. I'M GOING TO GIVE HIM AN EARFUL WHEN WE'RE DONE HERE.
YOU DO WHAT YOU NEED TO, SIR. LET'S START WITH THE MONEY IN THE VAULT.
YOU TOLD US THERE WAS APPROXIMATELY TWO HUNDRED THOUSAND DOLLARS IN THERE.
HERE'S A PICTURE OF THE VAULT.
THAT LOOKS LIKE CLOSER TO TWO MILLION FROM OUR ESTIMATION.
CARE TO EXPLAIN WHY THAT OTHER MONEY WAS THERE?
DON'T ANSWER THAT. IT'S NOT ILLEGAL TO HAVE CASH. IF MY CLIENT'S NOT BEING CHARGED, THIS INTERVIEW IS OVER.
NO CHARGES... *YET.* I'D GET THAT CRYING FORGIVENESS SPEECH READY, PASTOR.

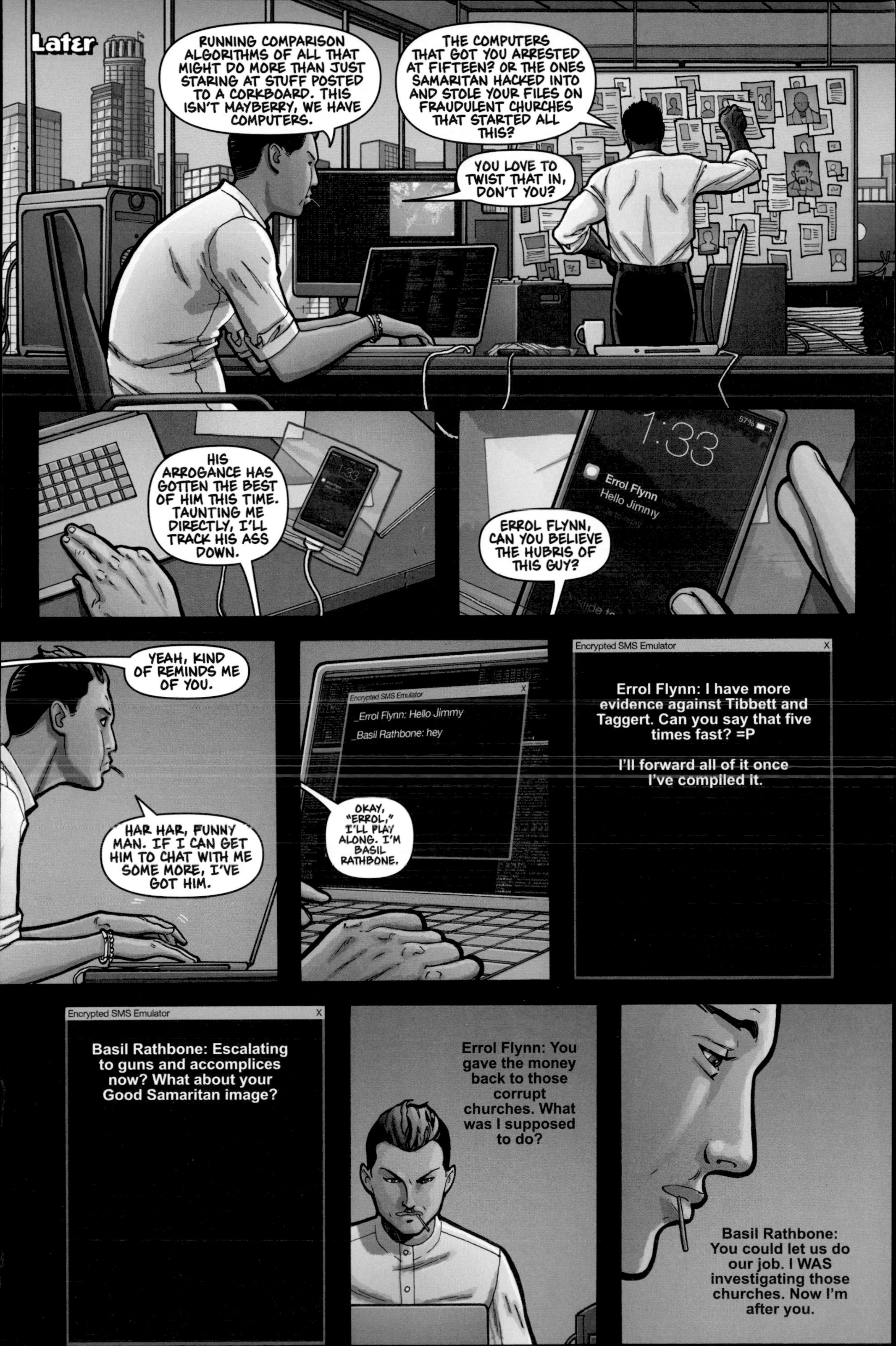
Later
RUNNING COMPARISON ALGORITHMS OF ALL THAT MIGHT DO MORE THAN JUST STARING AT STUFF POSTED TO A CORKBOARD. THIS ISN'T MAYBERRY, WE HAVE COMPUTERS.
THE COMPUTERS THAT GOT YOU ARRESTED AT FIFTEEN? OR THE ONES SAMARITAN HACKED INTO AND STOLE YOUR FILES ON FRAUDULENT CHURCHES THAT STARTED ALL THIS?
YOU LOVE TO TWIST THAT IN, DON'T YOU?
HIS ARROGANCE HAS GOTTEN THE BEST OF HIM THIS TIME. TAUNTING ME DIRECTLY, I'LL TRACK HIS ASS DOWN.
1:33
57%
Errol Flynn
Hello Jimmy
ERROL FLYNN, CAN YOU BELIEVE THE HUBRIS OF THIS GUY?
YEAH, KIND OF REMINDS ME OF YOU.
HAR HAR, FUNNY MAN. IF I CAN GET HIM TO CHAT WITH ME SOME MORE, I'VE GOT HIM.
Encrypted SMS Emulator
_Errol Flynn: Hello Jimmy
_Basil Rathbone: hey
OKAY, "ERROL," I'LL PLAY ALONG. I'M BASIL RATHBONE.
Encrypted SMS Emulator
Errol Flynn: I have more evidence against Tibbett and Taggert. Can you say that five times fast? =P
I'll forward all of it once I've compiled it.
Encrypted SMS Emulator
Basil Rathbone: Escalating to guns and accomplices now? What about your Good Samaritan image?
Errol Flynn: You gave the money back to those corrupt churches. What was I supposed to do?
Basil Rathbone: You could let us do our job. I WAS investigating those churches. Now I'm after you.

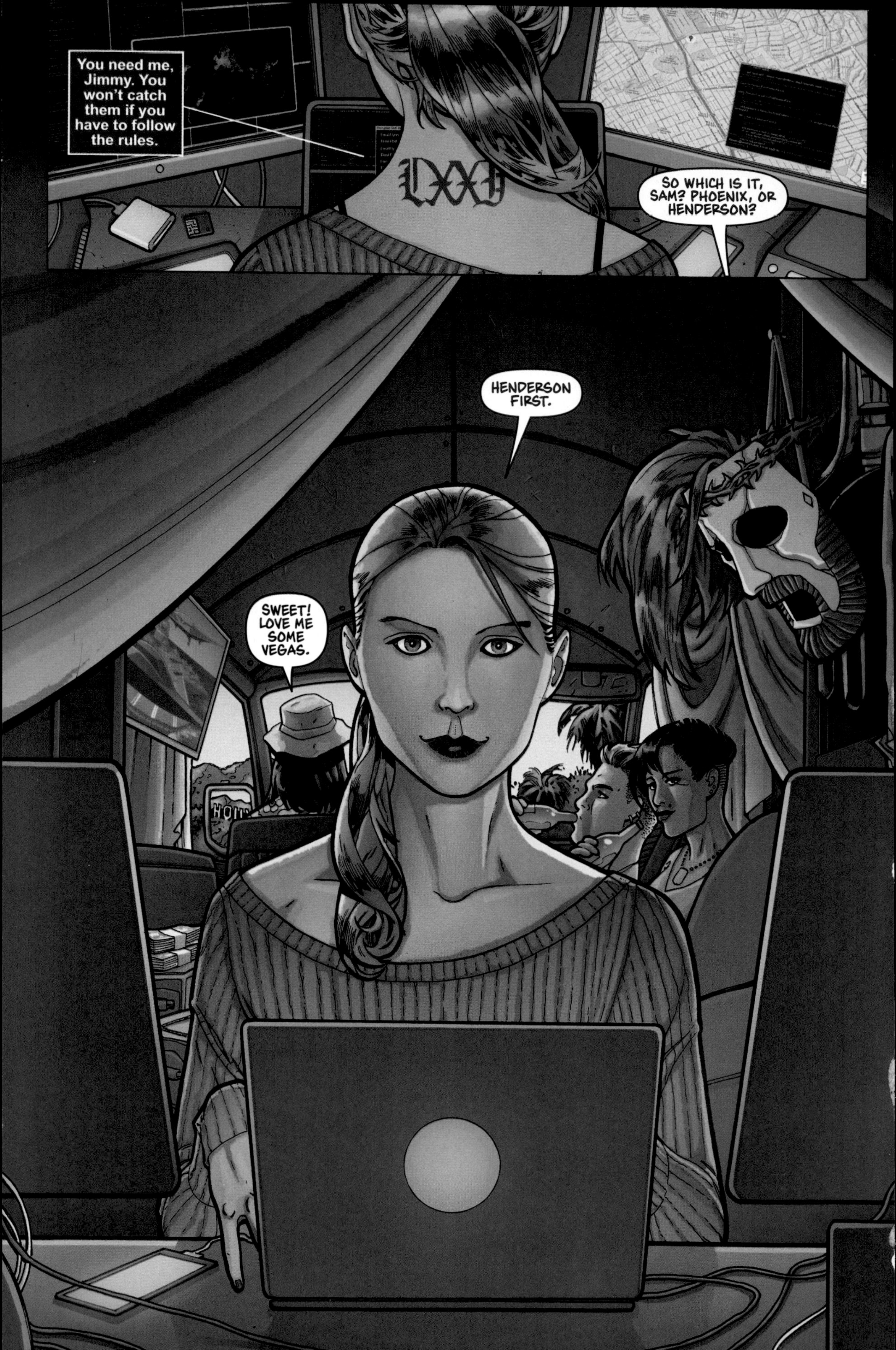

You need me, Jimmy. You won't catch them if you have to follow the rules.
SO WHICH IS IT, SAM? PHOENIX, OR HENDERSON?
HENDERSON FIRST.
SWEET! LOVE ME SOME VEGAS.

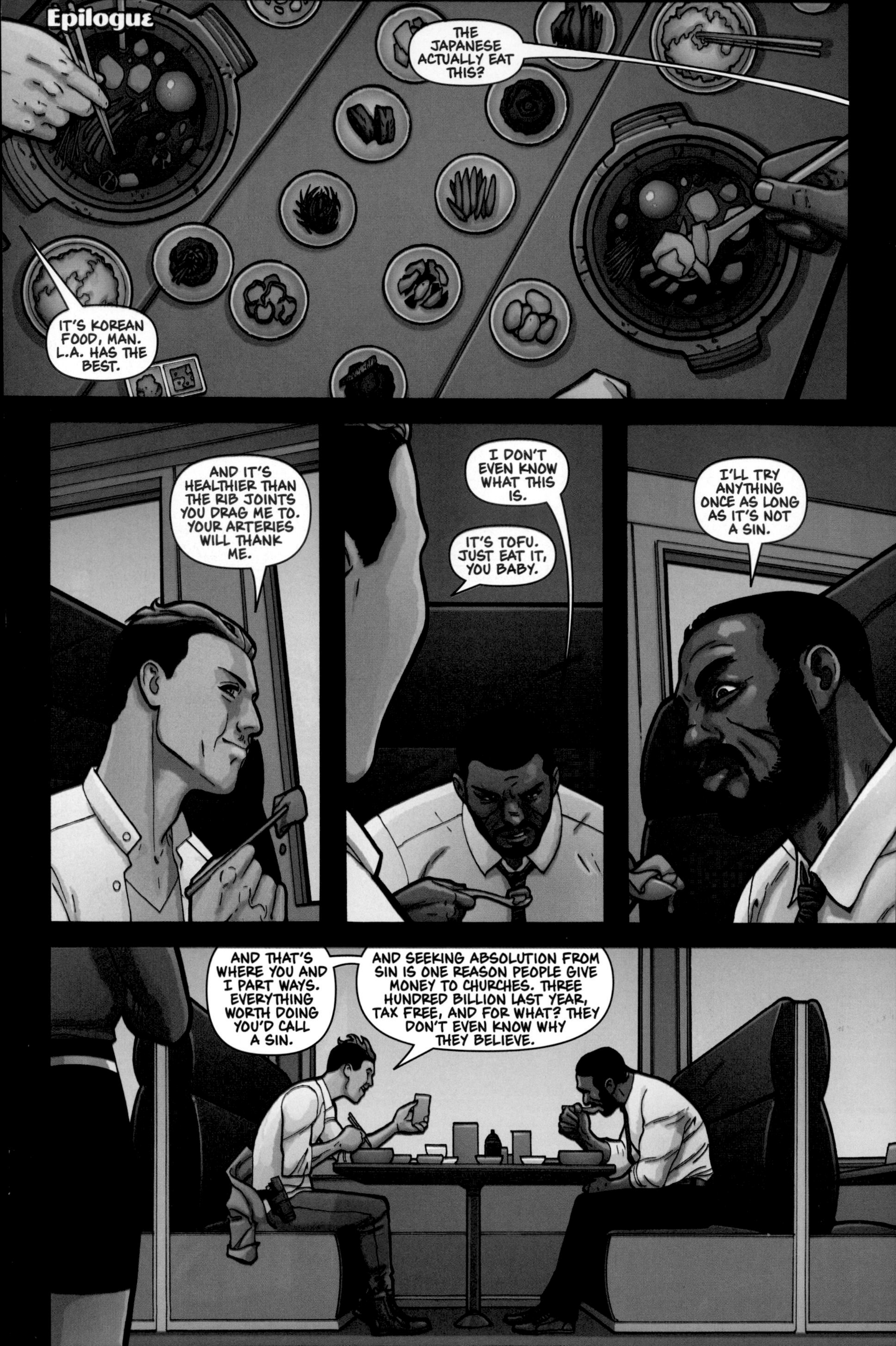
Epilogue
THE JAPANESE ACTUALLY EAT THIS?
IT'S KOREAN FOOD, MAN. L.A. HAS THE BEST.
AND IT'S HEALTHIER THAN THE RIB JOINTS YOU DRAG ME TO. YOUR ARTERIES WILL THANK ME.
I DON'T EVEN KNOW WHAT THIS IS.
IT'S TOFU. JUST EAT IT, YOU BABY.
I'LL TRY ANYTHING ONCE AS LONG AS IT'S NOT A SIN.
AND THAT'S WHERE YOU AND I PART WAYS. EVERYTHING WORTH DOING YOU'D CALL A SIN.
AND SEEKING ABSOLUTION FROM SIN IS ONE REASON PEOPLE GIVE MONEY TO CHURCHES. THREE HUNDRED BILLION LAST YEAR, TAX FREE, AND FOR WHAT? THEY DON'T EVEN KNOW WHY THEY BELIEVE.

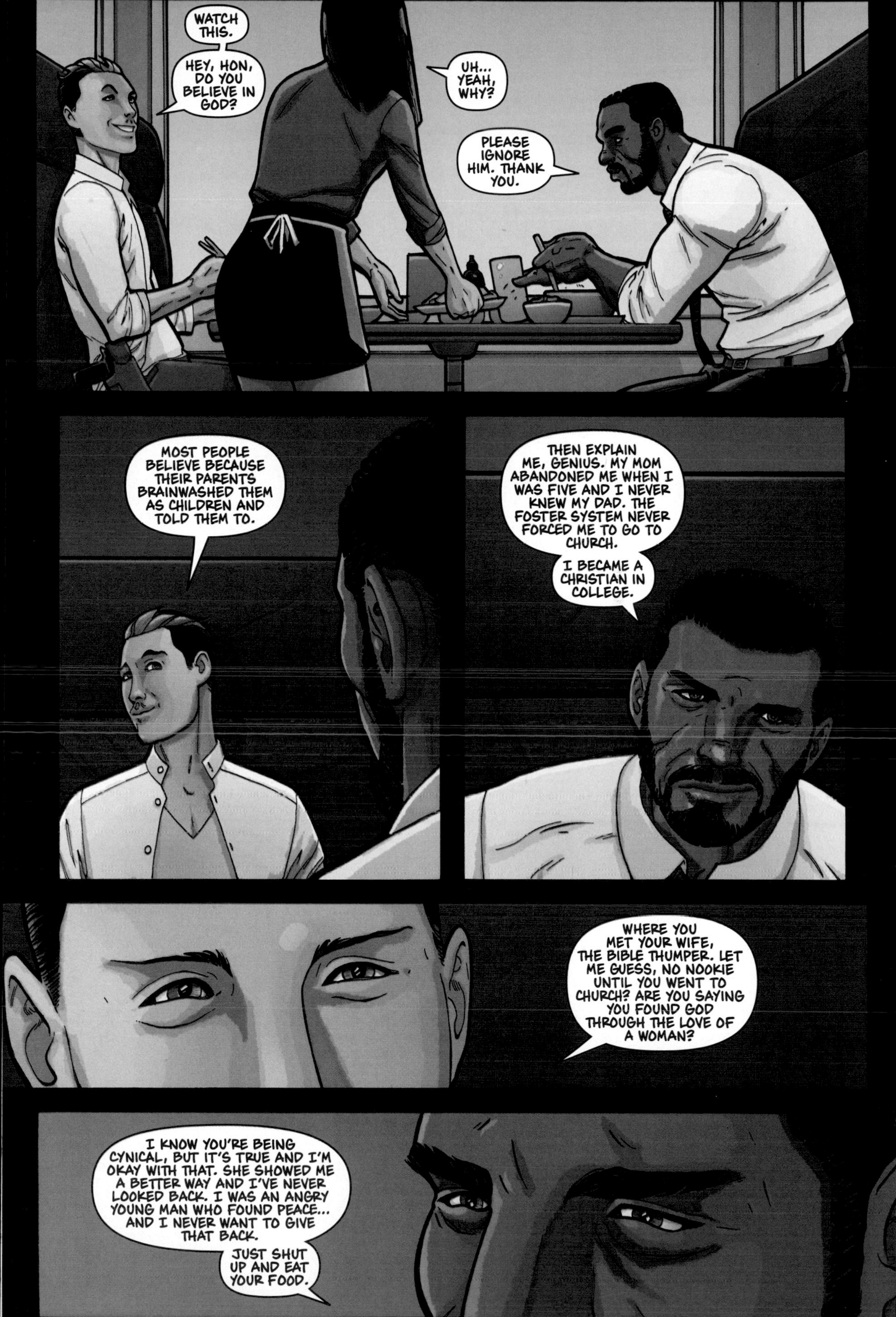
WATCH THIS.
HEY, HON, DO YOU BELIEVE IN GOD?
UH... YEAH, WHY?
PLEASE IGNORE HIM. THANK YOU.
MOST PEOPLE BELIEVE BECAUSE THEIR PARENTS BRAINWASHED THEM AS CHILDREN AND TOLD THEM TO.
THEN EXPLAIN ME, GENIUS. MY MOM ABANDONED ME WHEN I WAS FIVE AND I NEVER KNEW MY DAD. THE FOSTER SYSTEM NEVER FORCED ME TO GO TO CHURCH.
I BECAME A CHRISTIAN IN COLLEGE.
WHERE YOU MET YOUR WIFE, THE BIBLE THUMPER. LET ME GUESS, NO NOOKIE UNTIL YOU WENT TO CHURCH? ARE YOU SAYING YOU FOUND GOD THROUGH THE LOVE OF A WOMAN?
I KNOW YOU'RE BEING CYNICAL, BUT IT'S TRUE AND I'M OKAY WITH THAT. SHE SHOWED ME A BETTER WAY AND I'VE NEVER LOOKED BACK. I WAS AN ANGRY YOUNG MAN WHO FOUND PEACE... AND I NEVER WANT TO GIVE THAT BACK.
JUST SHUT UP AND EAT YOUR FOOD.

CHAPTER 2

MALACHI 3:8-12
NEW INTERNATIONAL VERSION (NIV)

8 "WILL A MERE MORTAL ROB GOD? YET YOU ROB ME.

"BUT YOU ASK, 'HOW ARE WE ROBBING YOU?'

"IN TITHES AND OFFERINGS.

9 YOU ARE UNDER A CURSE—YOUR WHOLE NATION—
BECAUSE YOU ARE ROBBING ME.

10 BRING THE WHOLE TITHE INTO THE STOREHOUSE, THAT THERE
MAY BE FOOD IN MY HOUSE. TEST ME IN THIS," SAYS THE LORD
ALMIGHTY, "AND SEE IF I WILL NOT THROW OPEN THE FLOODGATES
OF HEAVEN AND POUR OUT SO MUCH BLESSING THAT THERE WILL
NOT BE ROOM ENOUGH TO STORE IT.

11 I WILL PREVENT PESTS FROM DEVOURING YOUR CROPS, AND THE
VINES IN YOUR FIELDS WILL NOT DROP THEIR FRUIT BEFORE IT IS
RIPE," SAYS THE LORD ALMIGHTY.

12 "THEN ALL THE NATIONS WILL CALL YOU BLESSED, FOR YOURS
WILL BE A DELIGHTFUL LAND," SAYS THE LORD ALMIGHTY."

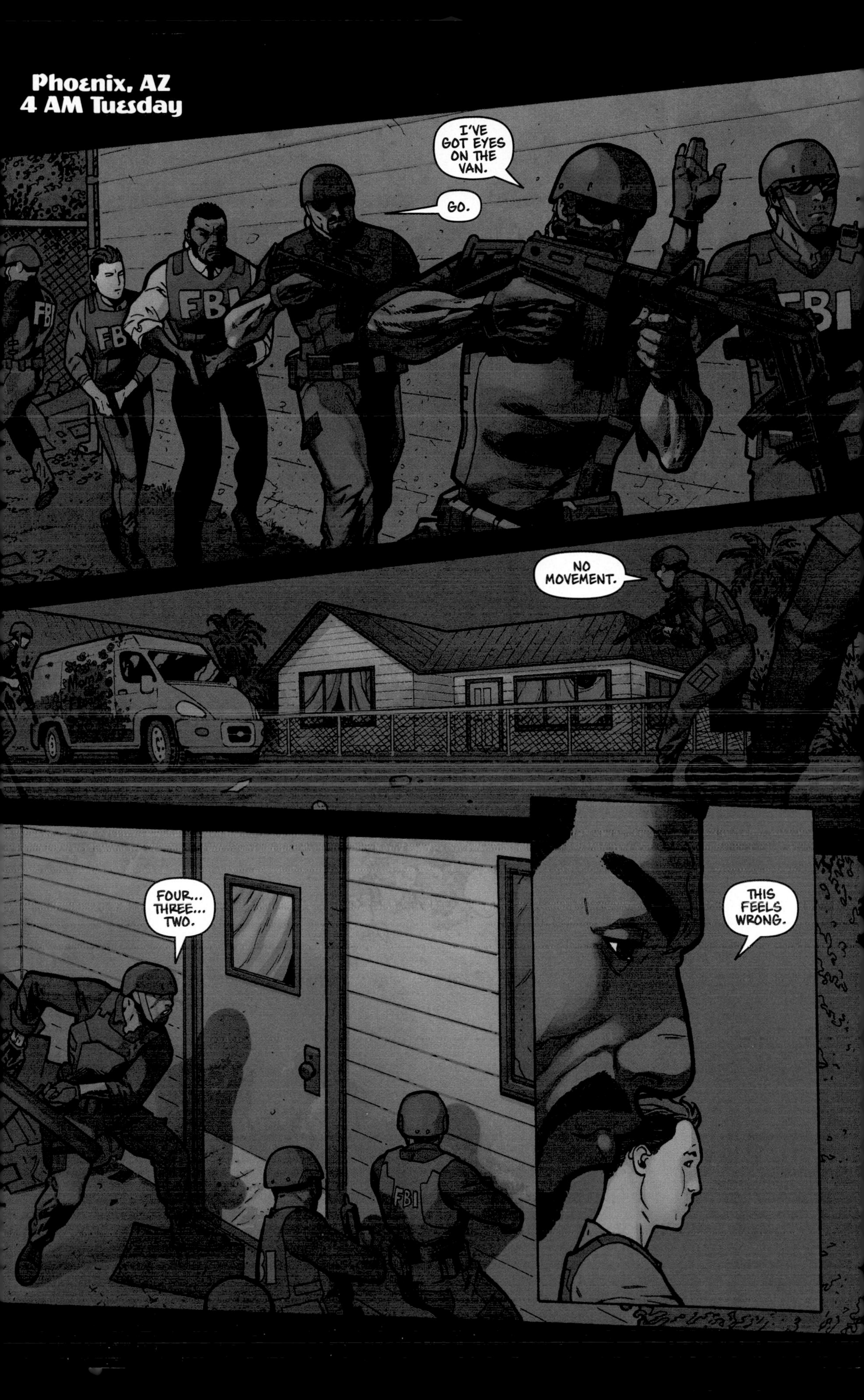
Phoenix, AZ
4 AM Tuesday
I'VE GOT EYES ON THE VAN.
GO.
NO MOVEMENT.
FOUR... THREE... TWO.
THIS FEELS WRONG.

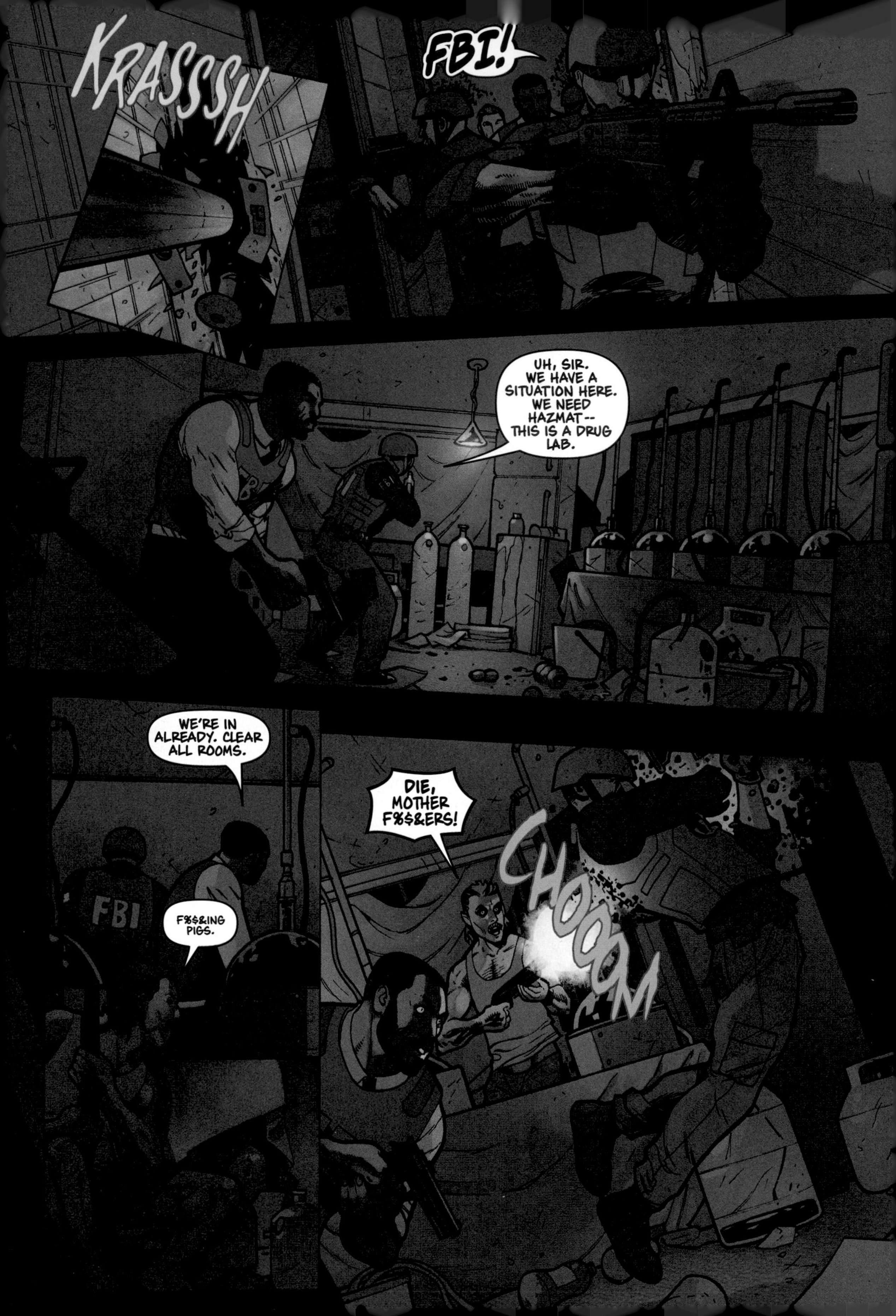
KRASSSH
FBI!
UH, SIR. WE HAVE A SITUATION HERE. WE NEED HAZMAT-- THIS IS A DRUG LAB.
WE'RE IN ALREADY. CLEAR ALL ROOMS.
F%$&ING PIGS.
DIE, MOTHER F%$&ERS!
CHOOOM

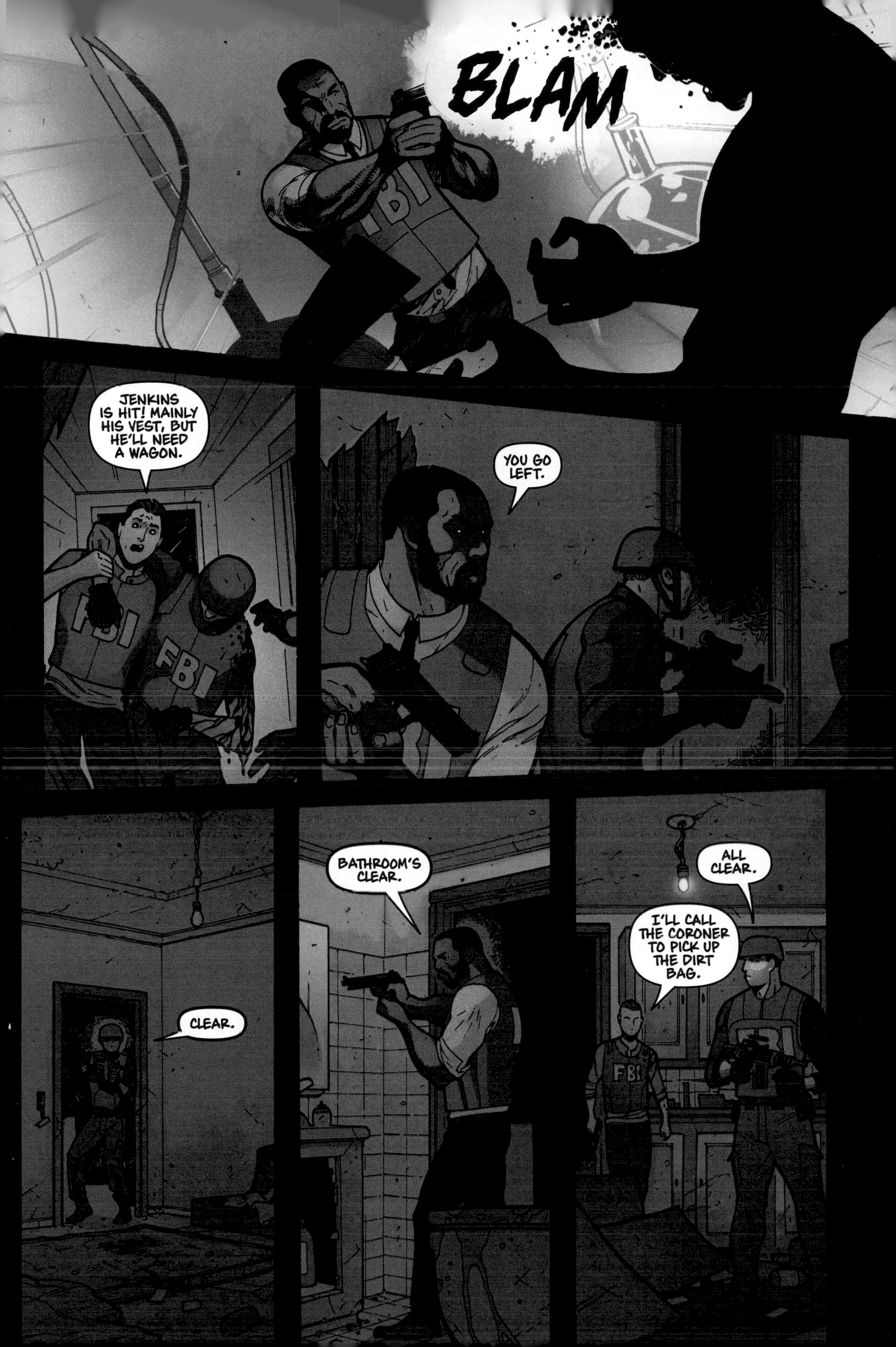
BLAM
JENKINS IS HIT! MAINLY HIS VEST, BUT HE'LL NEED A WAGON.
YOU GO LEFT.
CLEAR.
BATHROOM'S CLEAR.
ALL CLEAR.
I'LL CALL THE CORONER TO PICK UP THE DIRT BAG.
FBI
FBI
FBI
FBI
FBI

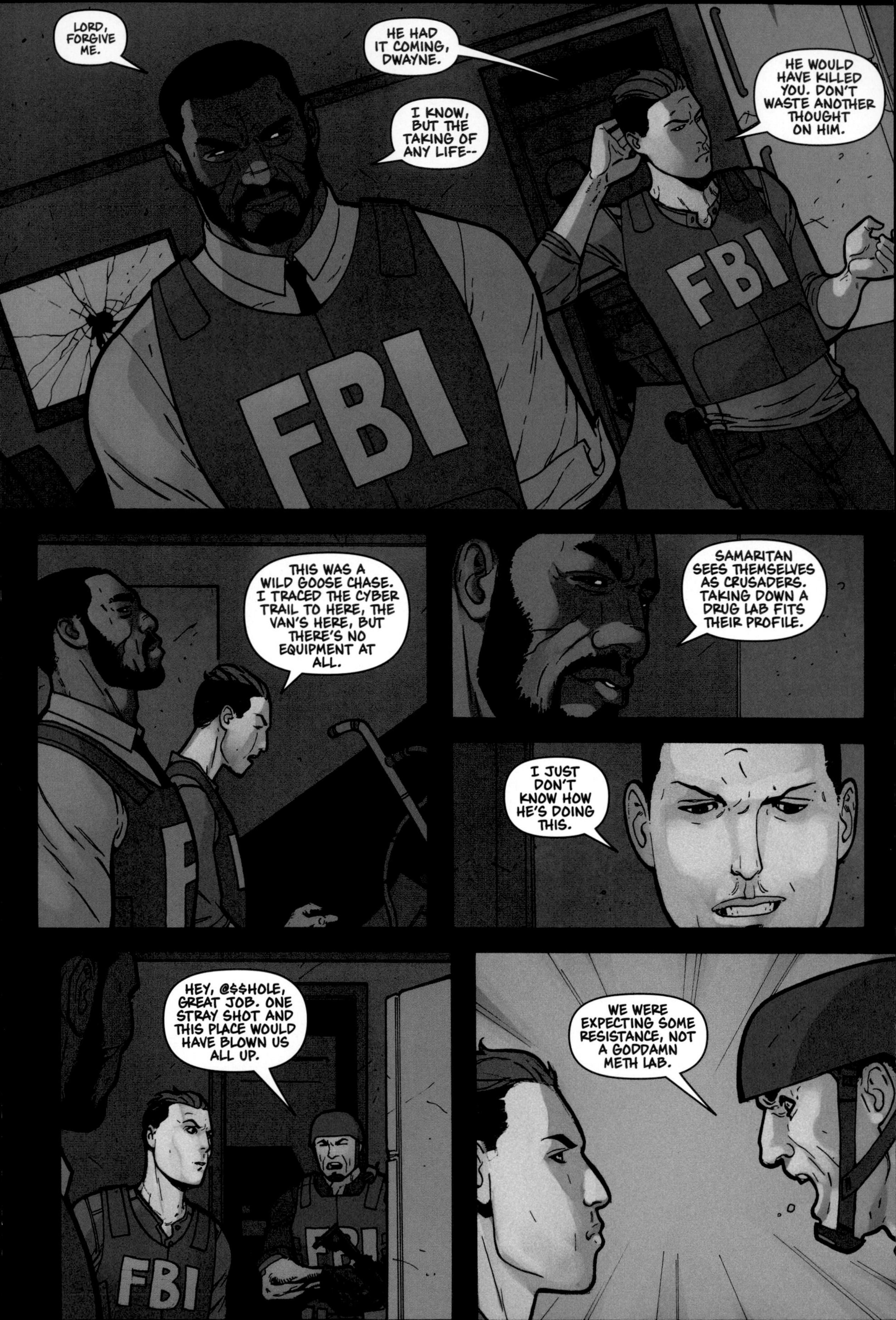
LORD, FORGIVE ME.
HE HAD IT COMING, DWAYNE.
I KNOW, BUT THE TAKING OF ANY LIFE--
HE WOULD HAVE KILLED YOU. DON'T WASTE ANOTHER THOUGHT ON HIM.
FBI
FBI
THIS WAS A WILD GOOSE CHASE. I TRACED THE CYBER TRAIL TO HERE, THE VAN'S HERE, BUT THERE'S NO EQUIPMENT AT ALL.
SAMARITAN SEES THEMSELVES AS CRUSADERS. TAKING DOWN A DRUG LAB FITS THEIR PROFILE.
I JUST DON'T KNOW HOW HE'S DOING THIS.
HEY, @$$HOLE, GREAT JOB. ONE STRAY SHOT AND THIS PLACE WOULD HAVE BLOWN US ALL UP.
FBI
WE WERE EXPECTING SOME RESISTANCE, NOT A GODDAMN METH LAB.

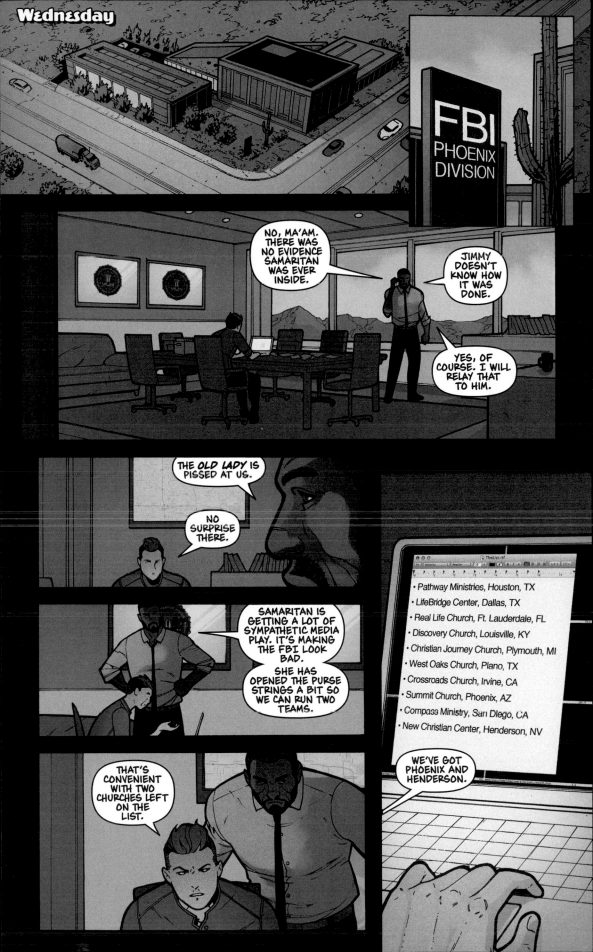

Wednesday

FBI
PHOENIX
DIVISION

NO, MA'AM. THERE WAS NO EVIDENCE SAMARITAN WAS EVER INSIDE.

JIMMY DOESN'T KNOW HOW IT WAS DONE.

YES, OF COURSE. I WILL RELAY THAT TO HIM.

THE OLD LADY IS PISSED AT US.

NO SURPRISE THERE.

SAMARITAN IS GETTING A LOT OF SYMPATHETIC MEDIA PLAY. IT'S MAKING THE FBI LOOK BAD.

SHE HAS OPENED THE PURSE STRINGS A BIT SO WE CAN RUN TWO TEAMS.

TheList.rtf

- Pathway Ministries, Houston, TX
- LifeBridge Center, Dallas, TX
- Real Life Church, Ft. Lauderdale, FL
- Discovery Church, Louisville, KY
- Christian Journey Church, Plymouth, MI
- West Oaks Church, Plano, TX
- Crossroads Church, Irvine, CA
- Summit Church, Phoenix, AZ
- Compass Ministry, San Diego, CA
- New Christian Center, Henderson, NV

WE'VE GOT PHOENIX AND HENDERSON.

THAT'S CONVENIENT WITH TWO CHURCHES LEFT ON THE LIST.

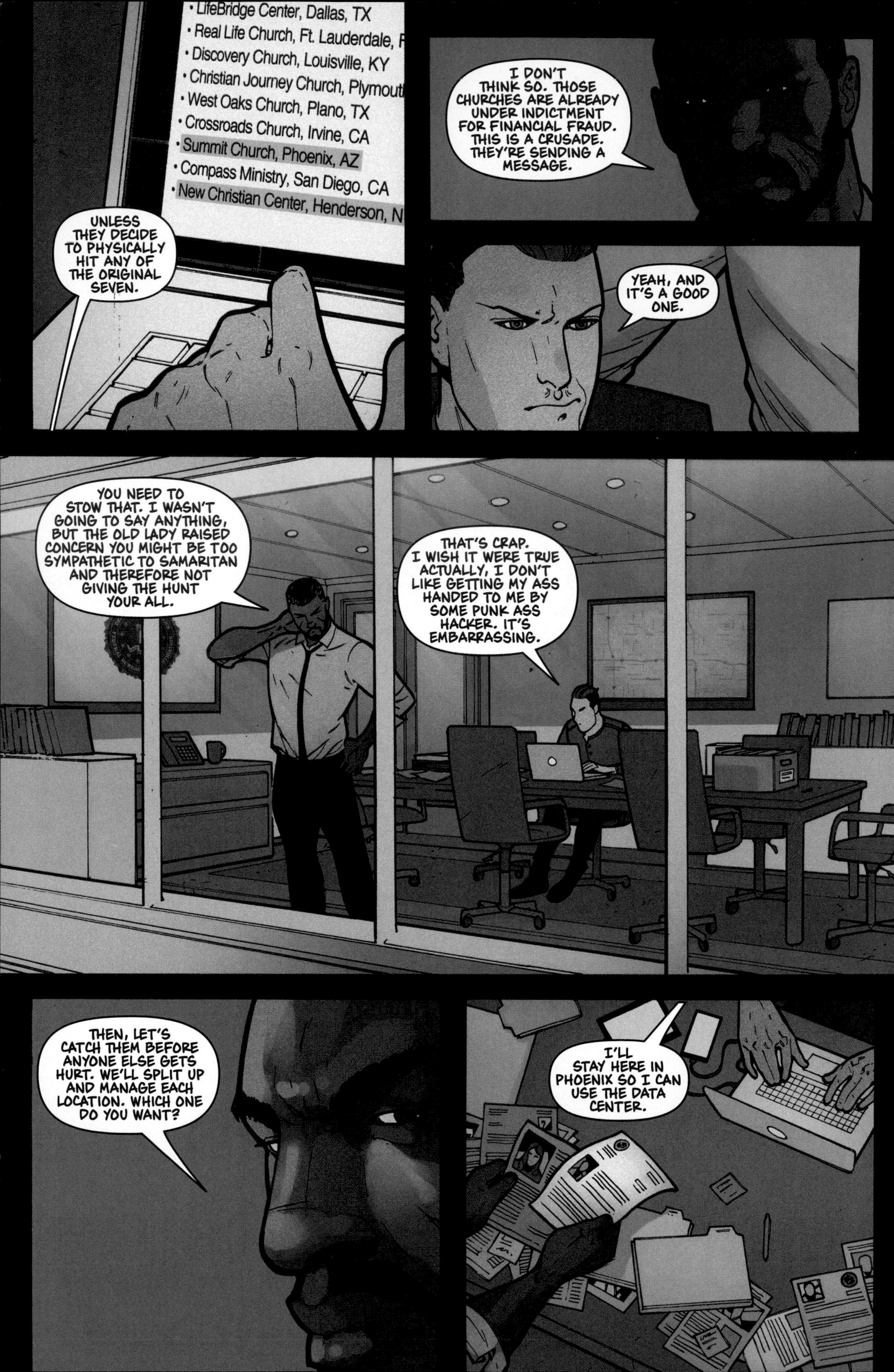

• LifeBridge Center, Dallas, TX
• Real Life Church, Ft. Lauderdale, F
• Discovery Church, Louisville, KY
• Christian Journey Church, Plymout
• West Oaks Church, Plano, TX
• Crossroads Church, Irvine, CA
• Summit Church, Phoenix, AZ
• Compass Ministry, San Diego, CA
• New Christian Center, Henderson, N
UNLESS THEY DECIDE TO PHYSICALLY HIT ANY OF THE ORIGINAL SEVEN.
I DON'T THINK SO. THOSE CHURCHES ARE ALREADY UNDER INDICTMENT FOR FINANCIAL FRAUD. THIS IS A CRUSADE. THEY'RE SENDING A MESSAGE.
YEAH, AND IT'S A GOOD ONE.
YOU NEED TO STOW THAT. I WASN'T GOING TO SAY ANYTHING, BUT THE OLD LADY RAISED CONCERN YOU MIGHT BE TOO SYMPATHETIC TO SAMARITAN AND THEREFORE NOT GIVING THE HUNT YOUR ALL.
THAT'S CRAP. I WISH IT WERE TRUE ACTUALLY, I DON'T LIKE GETTING MY ASS HANDED TO ME BY SOME PUNK ASS HACKER. IT'S EMBARRASSING.
THEN, LET'S CATCH THEM BEFORE ANYONE ELSE GETS HURT. WE'LL SPLIT UP AND MANAGE EACH LOCATION. WHICH ONE DO YOU WANT?
I'LL STAY HERE IN PHOENIX SO I CAN USE THE DATA CENTER.

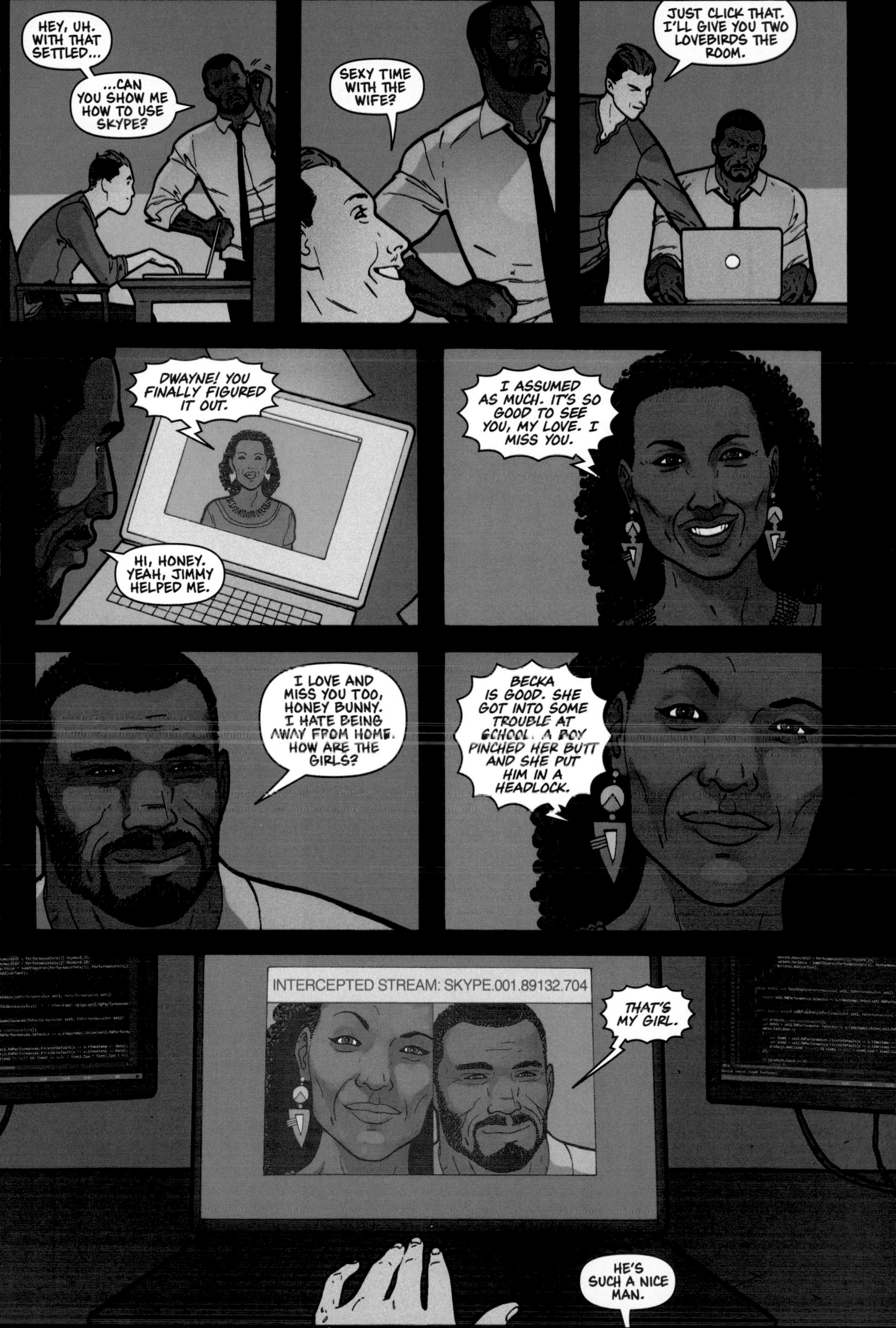
HEY, UH. WITH THAT SETTLED...
...CAN YOU SHOW ME HOW TO USE SKYPE?
SEXY TIME WITH THE WIFE?
JUST CLICK THAT. I'LL GIVE YOU TWO LOVEBIRDS THE ROOM.
DWAYNE! YOU FINALLY FIGURED IT OUT.
HI, HONEY. YEAH, JIMMY HELPED ME.
I ASSUMED AS MUCH. IT'S SO GOOD TO SEE YOU, MY LOVE. I MISS YOU.
I LOVE AND MISS YOU TOO, HONEY BUNNY. I HATE BEING AWAY FROM HOME. HOW ARE THE GIRLS?
BECKA IS GOOD. SHE GOT INTO SOME TROUBLE AT SCHOOL. A BOY PINCHED HER BUTT AND SHE PUT HIM IN A HEADLOCK.
INTERCEPTED STREAM: SKYPE.001.89132.704
THAT'S MY GIRL.
HE'S SUCH A NICE MAN.

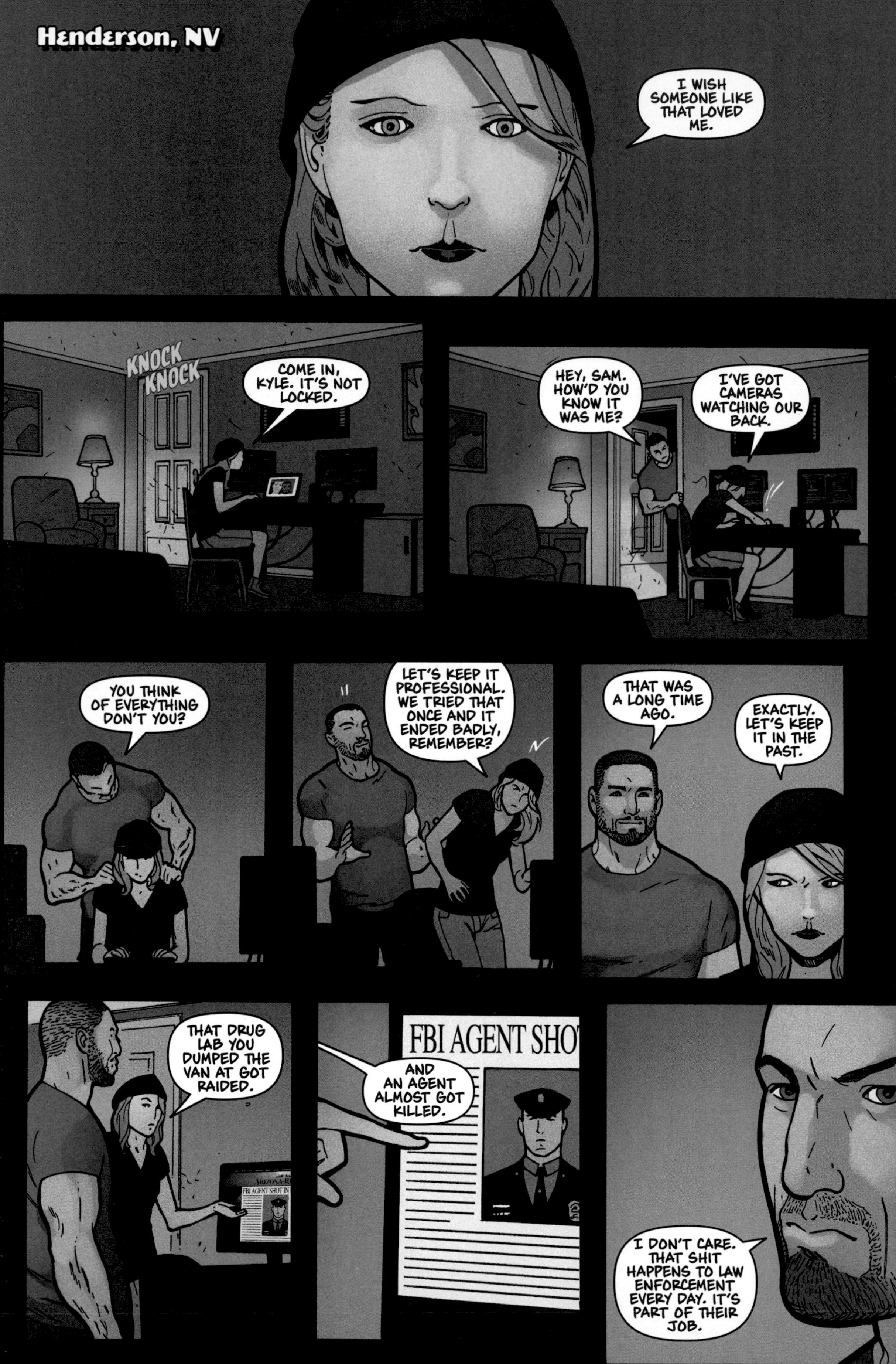
Henderson, NV
I WISH SOMEONE LIKE THAT LOVED ME.
KNOCK KNOCK
COME IN, KYLE. IT'S NOT LOCKED.
HEY, SAM. HOW'D YOU KNOW IT WAS ME?
I'VE GOT CAMERAS WATCHING OUR BACK.
YOU THINK OF EVERYTHING DON'T YOU?
LET'S KEEP IT PROFESSIONAL. WE TRIED THAT ONCE AND IT ENDED BADLY, REMEMBER?
THAT WAS A LONG TIME AGO.
EXACTLY. LET'S KEEP IT IN THE PAST.
THAT DRUG LAB YOU DUMPED THE VAN AT GOT RAIDED.
FBI AGENT SHOT
AND AN AGENT ALMOST GOT KILLED.
I DON'T CARE. THAT SHIT HAPPENS TO LAW ENFORCEMENT EVERY DAY. IT'S PART OF THEIR JOB.

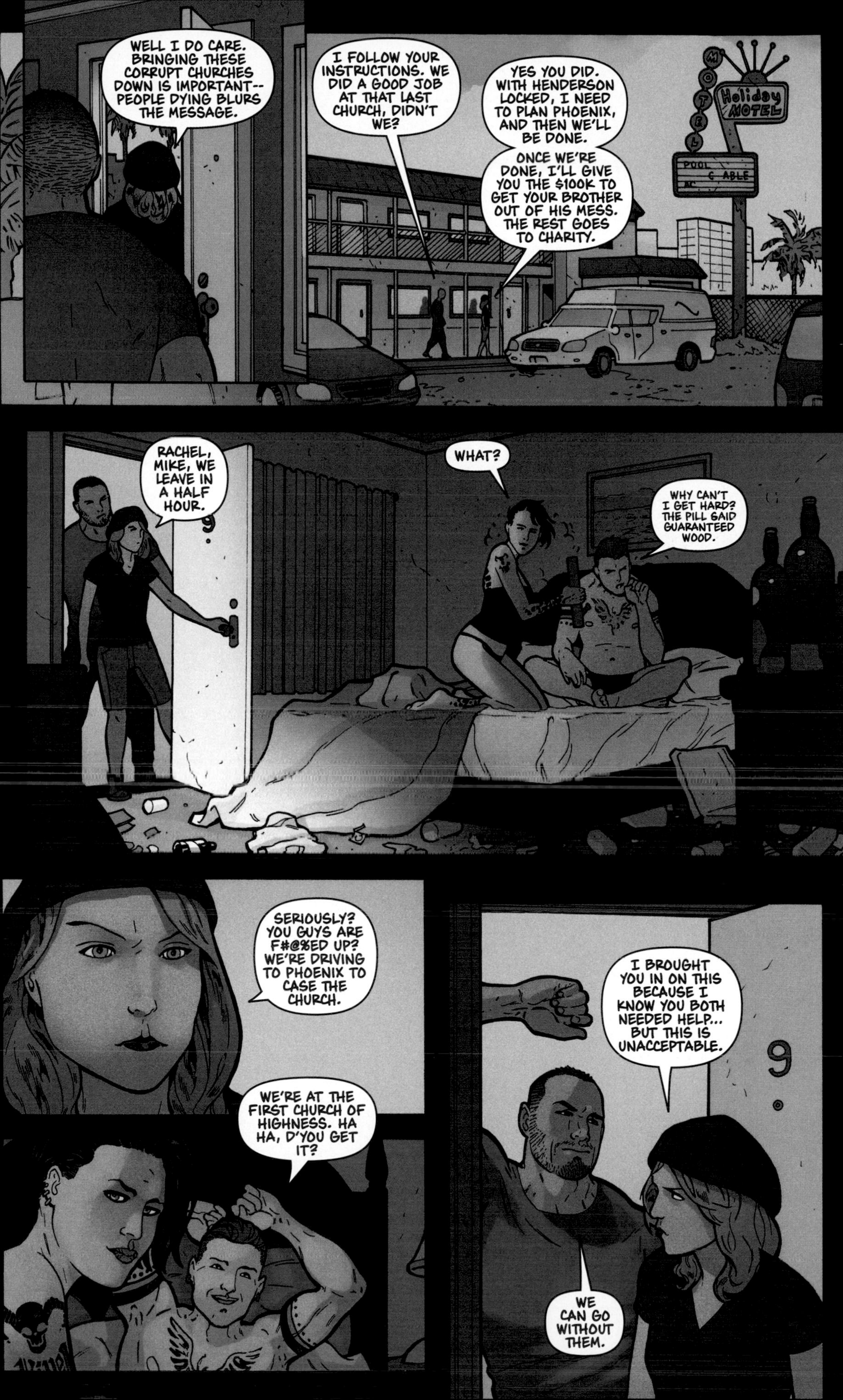
WELL I DO CARE. BRINGING THESE CORRUPT CHURCHES DOWN IS IMPORTANT-- PEOPLE DYING BLURS THE MESSAGE.
I FOLLOW YOUR INSTRUCTIONS. WE DID A GOOD JOB AT THAT LAST CHURCH, DIDN'T WE?
YES YOU DID. WITH HENDERSON LOCKED, I NEED TO PLAN PHOENIX, AND THEN WE'LL BE DONE.
ONCE WE'RE DONE, I'LL GIVE YOU THE $100K TO GET YOUR BROTHER OUT OF HIS MESS. THE REST GOES TO CHARITY.
MOTEL
Holiday MOTEL
POOL
CABLE
RACHEL, MIKE, WE LEAVE IN A HALF HOUR.
WHAT?
WHY CAN'T I GET HARD? THE PILL SAID GUARANTEED WOOD.
SERIOUSLY? YOU GUYS ARE F#@%ED UP? WE'RE DRIVING TO PHOENIX TO CASE THE CHURCH.
WE'RE AT THE FIRST CHURCH OF HIGHNESS. HA HA, D'YOU GET IT?
I BROUGHT YOU IN ON THIS BECAUSE I KNOW YOU BOTH NEEDED HELP... BUT THIS IS UNACCEPTABLE.
WE CAN GO WITHOUT THEM.

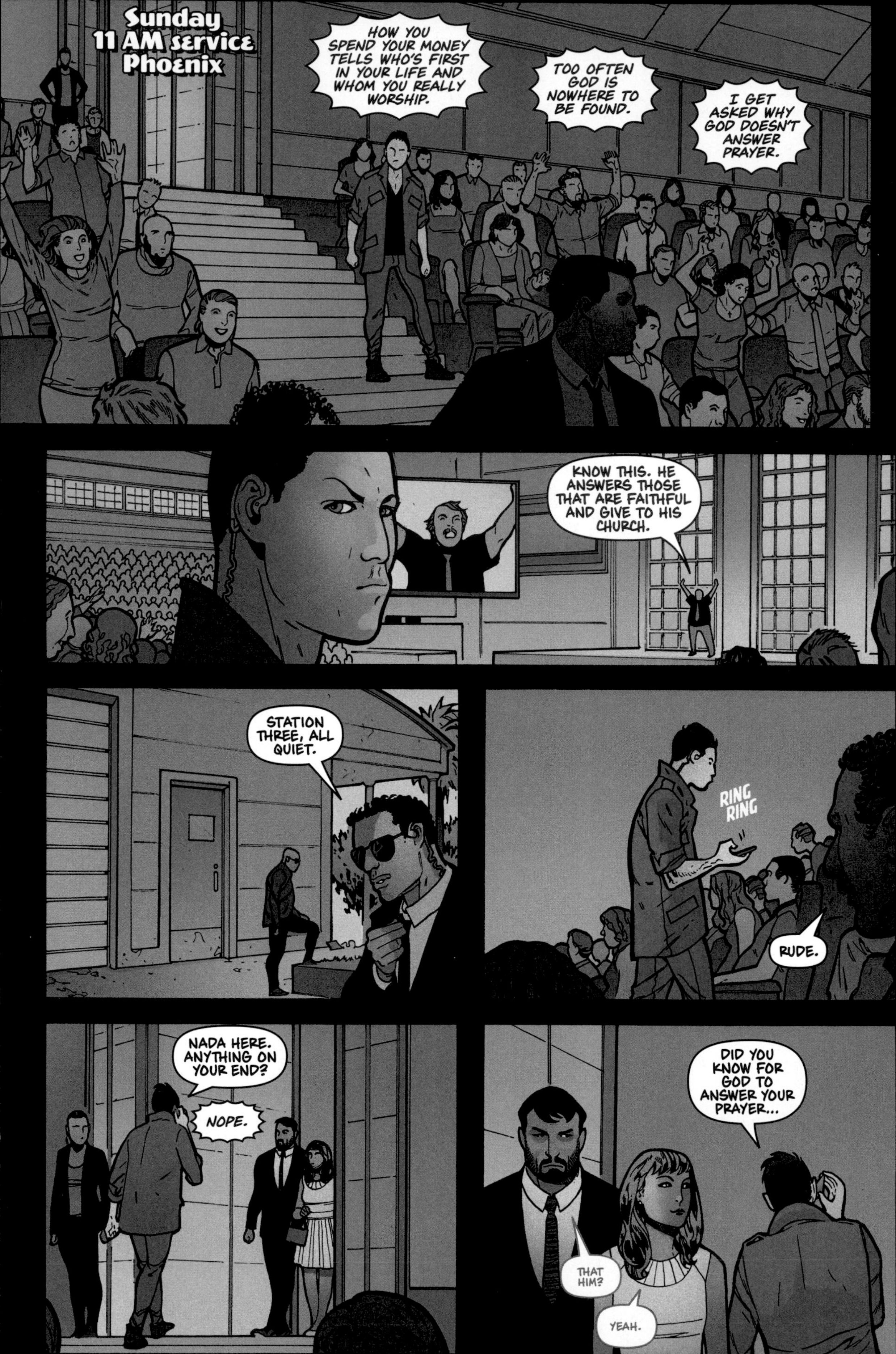
Sunday
11 AM service
Phoenix
HOW YOU SPEND YOUR MONEY TELLS WHO'S FIRST IN YOUR LIFE AND WHOM YOU REALLY WORSHIP.
TOO OFTEN GOD IS NOWHERE TO BE FOUND.
I GET ASKED WHY GOD DOESN'T ANSWER PRAYER.
KNOW THIS. HE ANSWERS THOSE THAT ARE FAITHFUL AND GIVE TO HIS CHURCH.
STATION THREE, ALL QUIET.
RING RING
RUDE.
NADA HERE. ANYTHING ON YOUR END?
NOPE.
DID YOU KNOW FOR GOD TO ANSWER YOUR PRAYER...
THAT HIM?
YEAH.

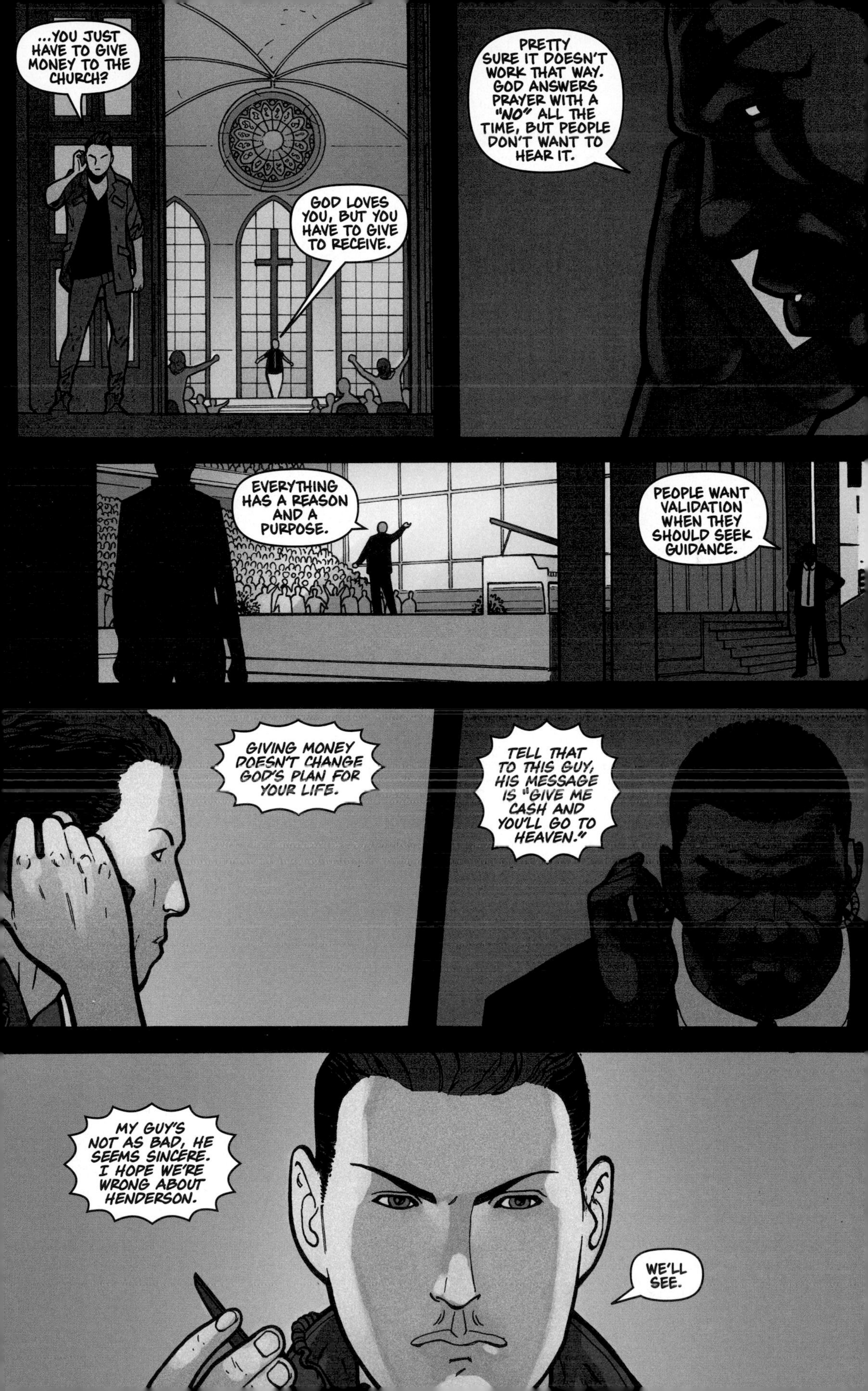
...YOU JUST HAVE TO GIVE MONEY TO THE CHURCH?
GOD LOVES YOU, BUT YOU HAVE TO GIVE TO RECEIVE.
PRETTY SURE IT DOESN'T WORK THAT WAY. GOD ANSWERS PRAYER WITH A "NO" ALL THE TIME, BUT PEOPLE DON'T WANT TO HEAR IT.
EVERYTHING HAS A REASON AND A PURPOSE.
PEOPLE WANT VALIDATION WHEN THEY SHOULD SEEK GUIDANCE.
GIVING MONEY DOESN'T CHANGE GOD'S PLAN FOR YOUR LIFE.
TELL THAT TO THIS GUY, HIS MESSAGE IS "GIVE ME CASH AND YOU'LL GO TO HEAVEN."
MY GUY'S NOT AS BAD, HE SEEMS SINCERE. I HOPE WE'RE WRONG ABOUT HENDERSON.
WE'LL SEE.

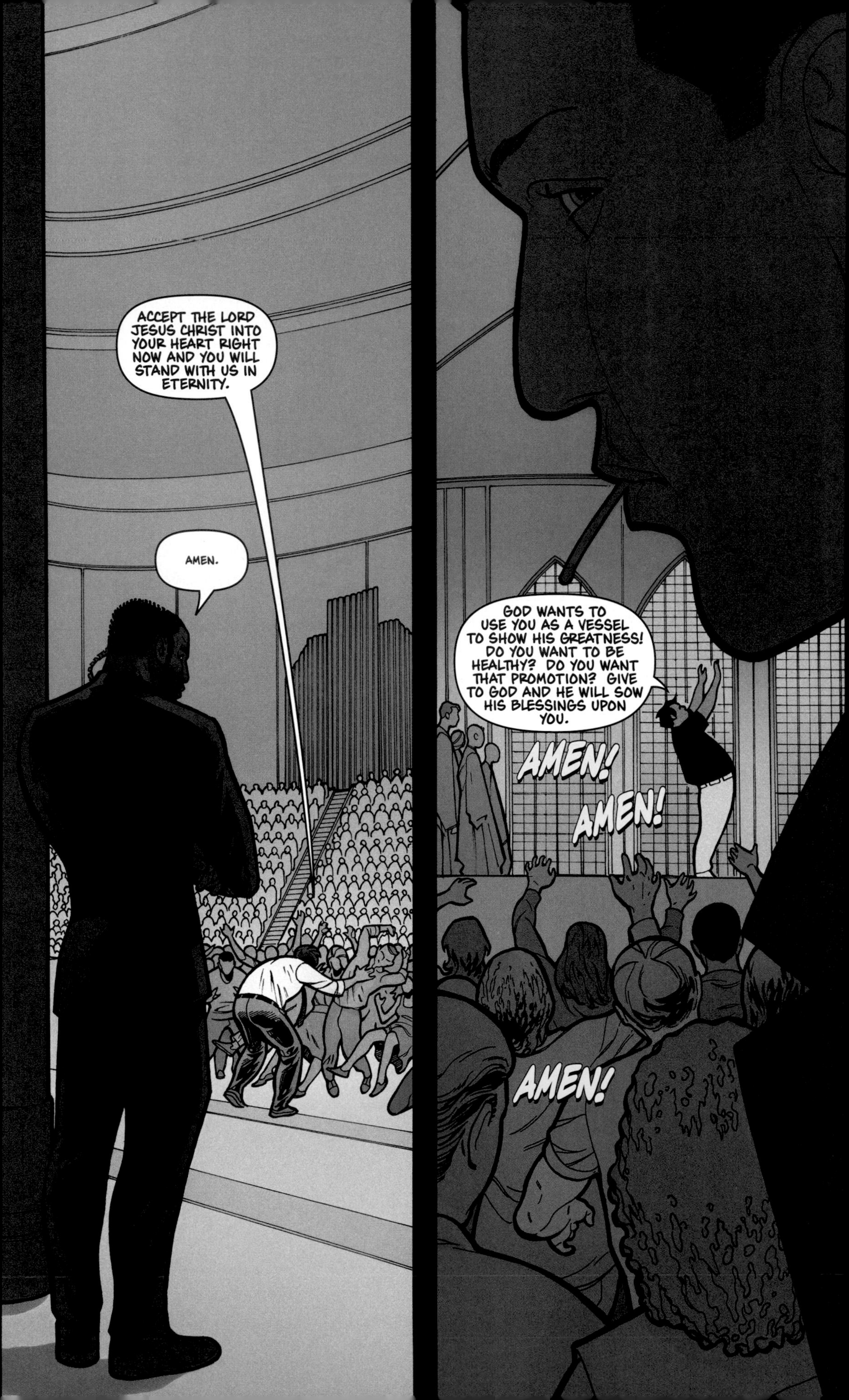
ACCEPT THE LORD JESUS CHRIST INTO YOUR HEART RIGHT NOW AND YOU WILL STAND WITH US IN ETERNITY.
AMEN.
GOD WANTS TO USE YOU AS A VESSEL TO SHOW HIS GREATNESS! DO YOU WANT TO BE HEALTHY? DO YOU WANT THAT PROMOTION? GIVE TO GOD AND HE WILL SOW HIS BLESSINGS UPON YOU.
AMEN!
AMEN!
AMEN!

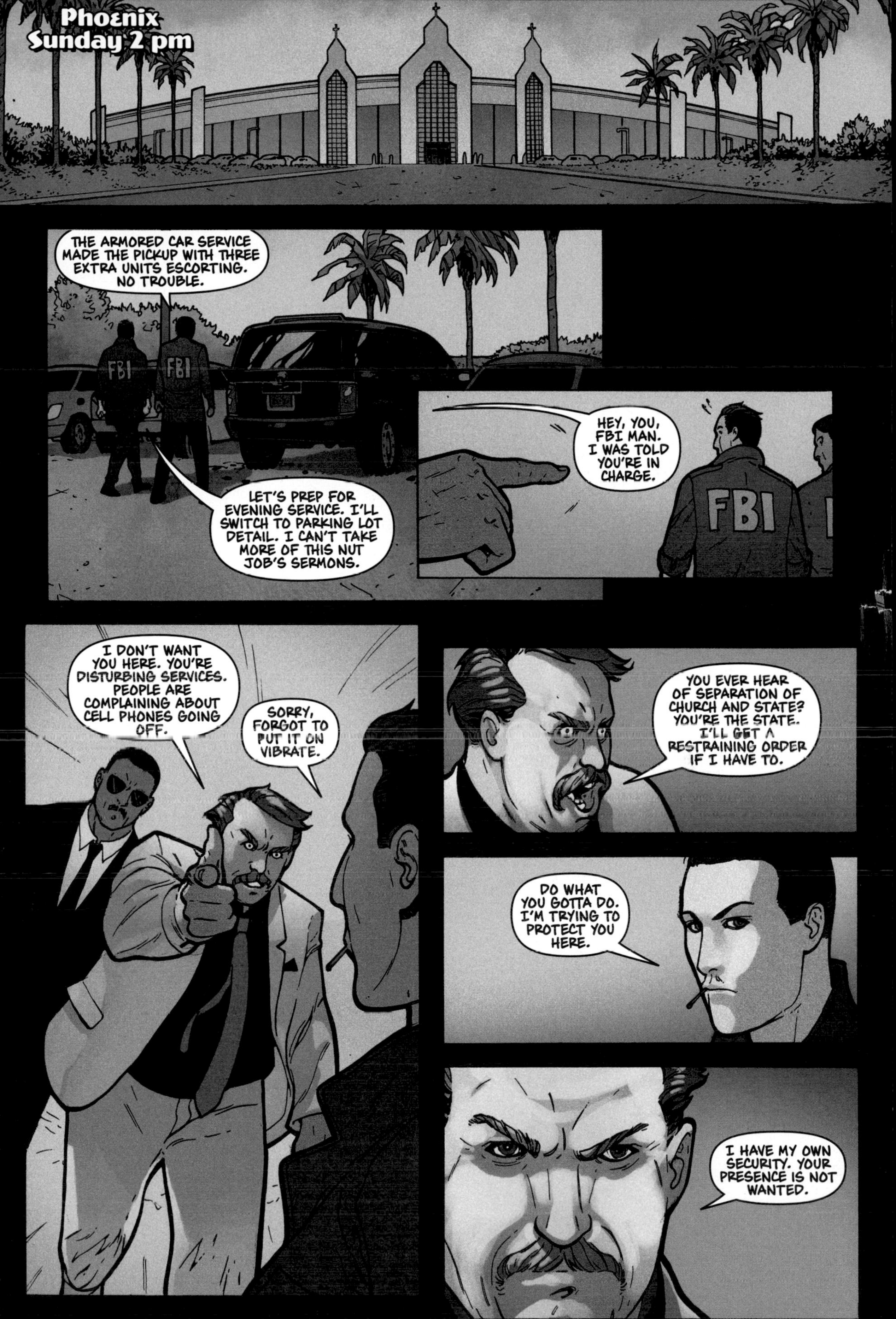

Phoenix
Sunday 2 pm
THE ARMORED CAR SERVICE MADE THE PICKUP WITH THREE EXTRA UNITS ESCORTING. NO TROUBLE.
FBI
FBI
LET'S PREP FOR EVENING SERVICE. I'LL SWITCH TO PARKING LOT DETAIL. I CAN'T TAKE MORE OF THIS NUT JOB'S SERMONS.
HEY, YOU, FBI MAN. I WAS TOLD YOU'RE IN CHARGE.
FBI
I DON'T WANT YOU HERE. YOU'RE DISTURBING SERVICES. PEOPLE ARE COMPLAINING ABOUT CELL PHONES GOING OFF.
SORRY, FORGOT TO PUT IT ON VIBRATE.
YOU EVER HEAR OF SEPARATION OF CHURCH AND STATE? YOU'RE THE STATE. I'LL GET A RESTRAINING ORDER IF I HAVE TO.
DO WHAT YOU GOTTA DO. I'M TRYING TO PROTECT YOU HERE.
I HAVE MY OWN SECURITY. YOUR PRESENCE IS NOT WANTED.

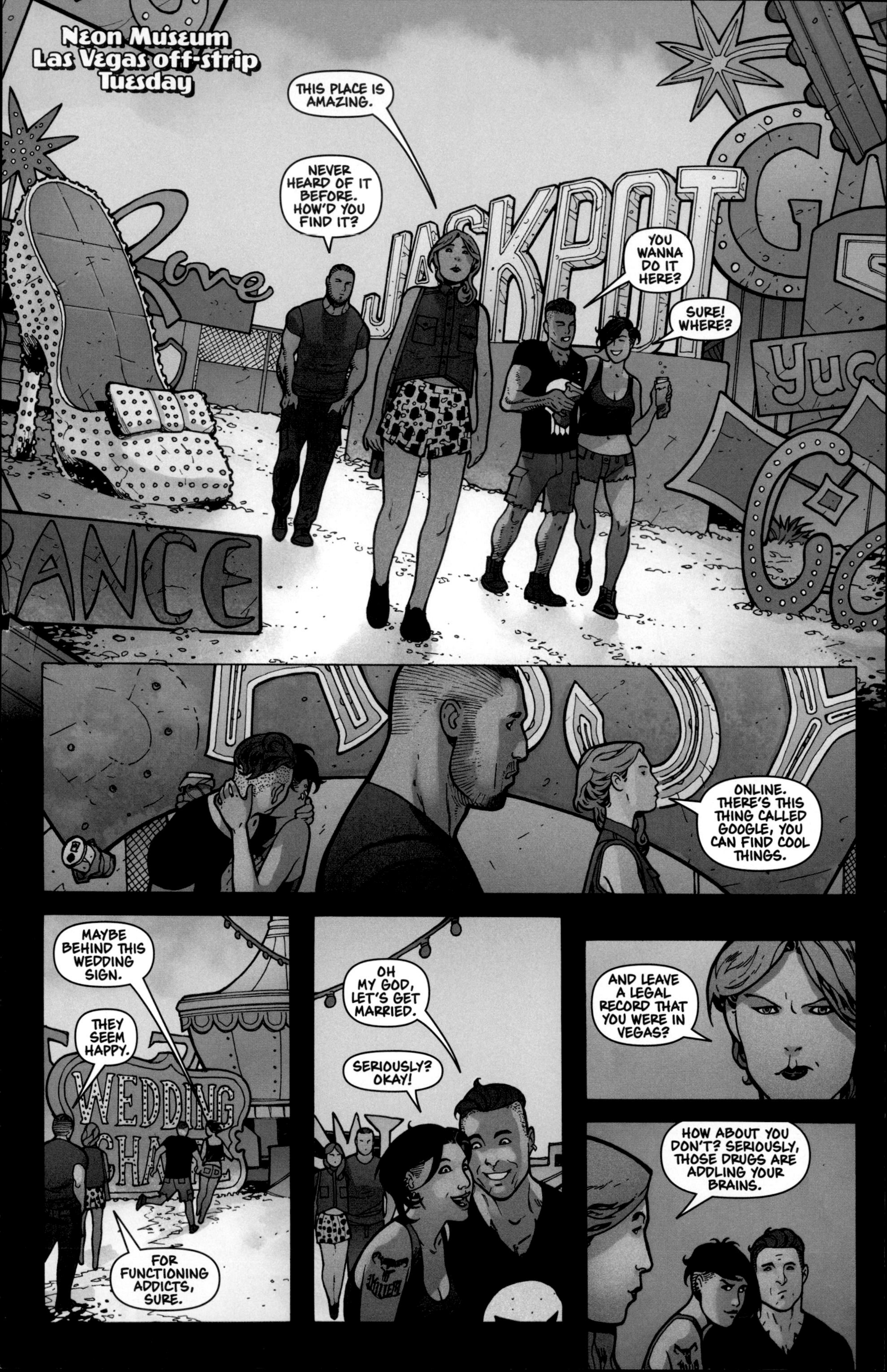
Neon Museum
Las Vegas off-strip
Tuesday
THIS PLACE IS AMAZING.
NEVER HEARD OF IT BEFORE. HOW'D YOU FIND IT?
YOU WANNA DO IT HERE?
SURE! WHERE?
JACKPOT
RANCE
ONLINE. THERE'S THIS THING CALLED GOOGLE, YOU CAN FIND COOL THINGS.
MAYBE BEHIND THIS WEDDING SIGN.
THEY SEEM HAPPY.
FOR FUNCTIONING ADDICTS, SURE.
OH MY GOD, LET'S GET MARRIED.
SERIOUSLY? OKAY!
AND LEAVE A LEGAL RECORD THAT YOU WERE IN VEGAS?
HOW ABOUT YOU DON'T? SERIOUSLY, THOSE DRUGS ARE ADDLING YOUR BRAINS.

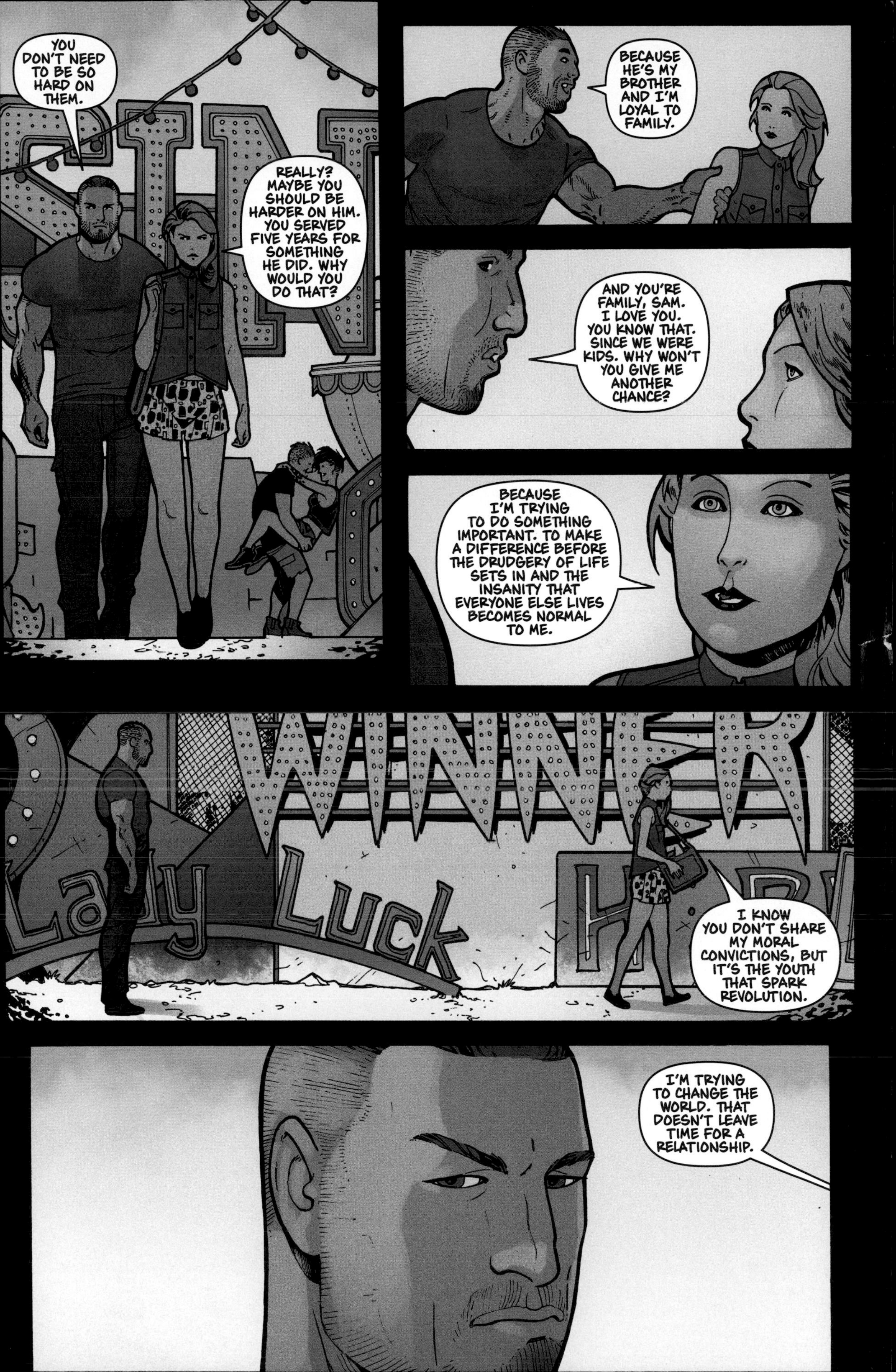
YOU DON'T NEED TO BE SO HARD ON THEM.
REALLY? MAYBE YOU SHOULD BE HARDER ON HIM. YOU SERVED FIVE YEARS FOR SOMETHING HE DID. WHY WOULD YOU DO THAT?
BECAUSE HE'S MY BROTHER AND I'M LOYAL TO FAMILY.
AND YOU'RE FAMILY, SAM. I LOVE YOU. YOU KNOW THAT. SINCE WE WERE KIDS. WHY WON'T YOU GIVE ME ANOTHER CHANCE?
BECAUSE I'M TRYING TO DO SOMETHING IMPORTANT. TO MAKE A DIFFERENCE BEFORE THE DRUDGERY OF LIFE SETS IN AND THE INSANITY THAT EVERYONE ELSE LIVES BECOMES NORMAL TO ME.
WINNER
Lady Luck
I KNOW YOU DON'T SHARE MY MORAL CONVICTIONS, BUT IT'S THE YOUTH THAT SPARK REVOLUTION.
I'M TRYING TO CHANGE THE WORLD. THAT DOESN'T LEAVE TIME FOR A RELATIONSHIP.

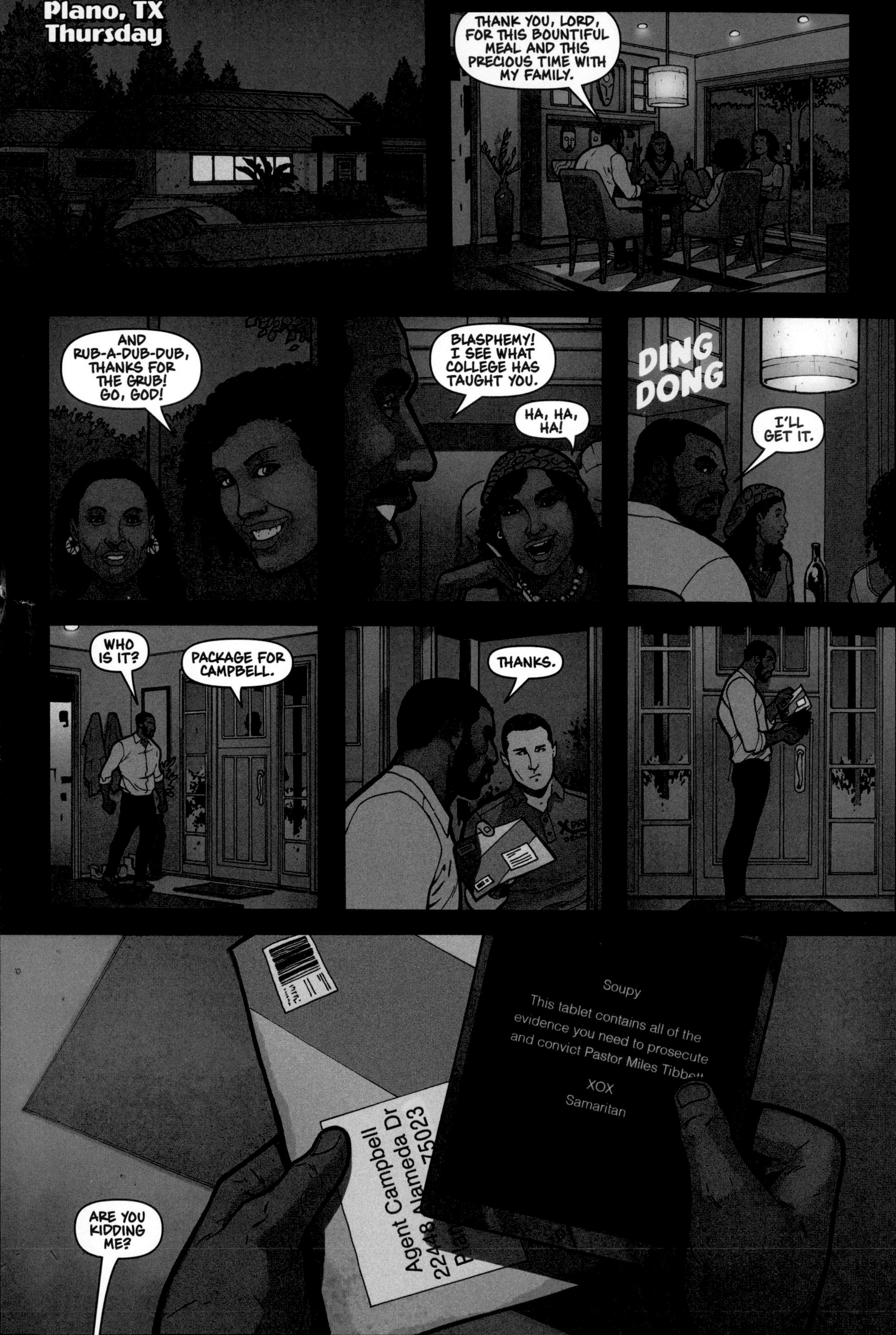
Plano, TX
Thursday
THANK YOU, LORD, FOR THIS BOUNTIFUL MEAL AND THIS PRECIOUS TIME WITH MY FAMILY.
AND RUB-A-DUB-DUB, THANKS FOR THE GRUB! GO, GOD!
BLASPHEMY! I SEE WHAT COLLEGE HAS TAUGHT YOU.
HA, HA, HA!
DING DONG
I'LL GET IT.
WHO IS IT?
PACKAGE FOR CAMPBELL.
THANKS.
Soupy
This tablet contains all of the evidence you need to prosecute and convict Pastor Miles Tibbe
XOX
Samaritan
Agent Campbell
22448 Alameda Dr
75023
ARE YOU KIDDING ME?

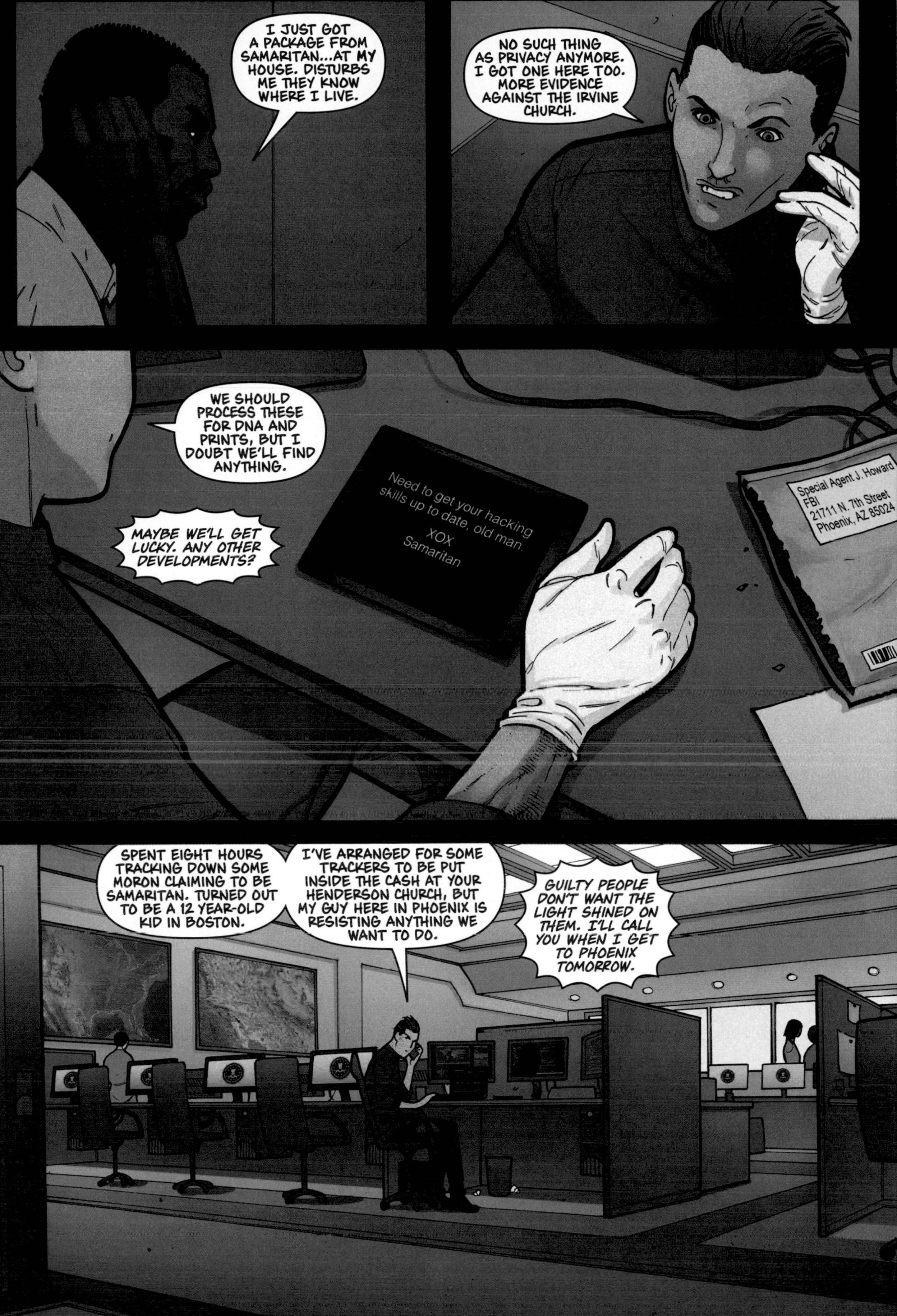

I JUST GOT A PACKAGE FROM SAMARITAN...AT MY HOUSE. DISTURBS ME THEY KNOW WHERE I LIVE.
NO SUCH THING AS PRIVACY ANYMORE. I GOT ONE HERE TOO. MORE EVIDENCE AGAINST THE IRVINE CHURCH.
WE SHOULD PROCESS THESE FOR DNA AND PRINTS, BUT I DOUBT WE'LL FIND ANYTHING.
Need to get your hacking skills up to date, old man.
XOX
Samaritan
Special Agent J. Howard
FBI
21711 N. 7th Street
Phoenix, AZ 85024
MAYBE WE'LL GET LUCKY. ANY OTHER DEVELOPMENTS?
SPENT EIGHT HOURS TRACKING DOWN SOME MORON CLAIMING TO BE SAMARITAN. TURNED OUT TO BE A 12 YEAR-OLD KID IN BOSTON.
I'VE ARRANGED FOR SOME TRACKERS TO BE PUT INSIDE THE CASH AT YOUR HENDERSON CHURCH, BUT MY GUY HERE IN PHOENIX IS RESISTING ANYTHING WE WANT TO DO.
GUILTY PEOPLE DON'T WANT THE LIGHT SHINED ON THEM. I'LL CALL YOU WHEN I GET TO PHOENIX TOMORROW.

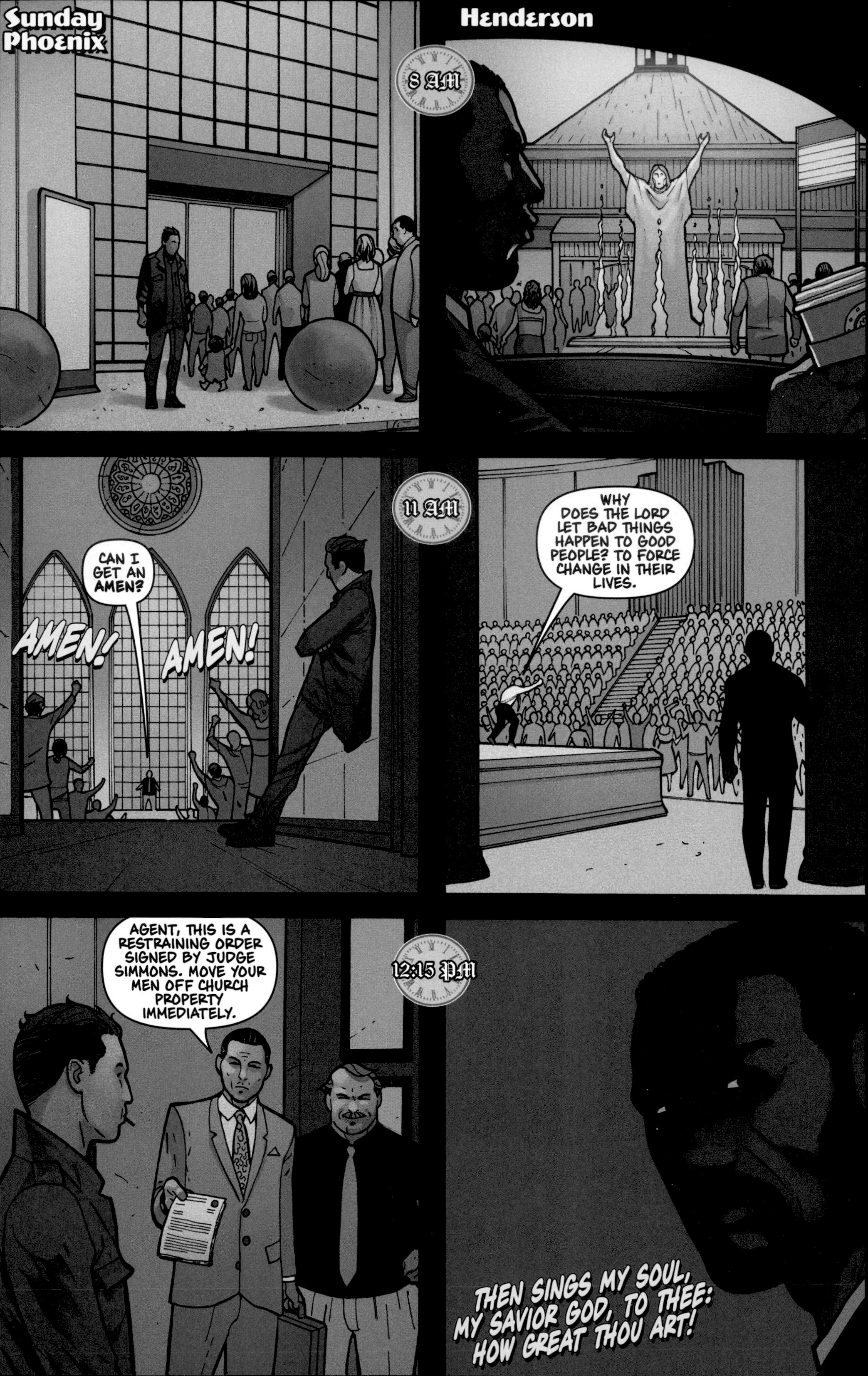
Sunday Phoenix
Henderson
8 AM
11 AM
CAN I GET AN AMEN?
AMEN!
AMEN!
WHY DOES THE LORD LET BAD THINGS HAPPEN TO GOOD PEOPLE? TO FORCE CHANGE IN THEIR LIVES.
12:15 PM
AGENT, THIS IS A RESTRAINING ORDER SIGNED BY JUDGE SIMMONS. MOVE YOUR MEN OFF CHURCH PROPERTY IMMEDIATELY.
THEN SINGS MY SOUL, MY SAVIOR GOD, TO THEE: HOW GREAT THOU ART!

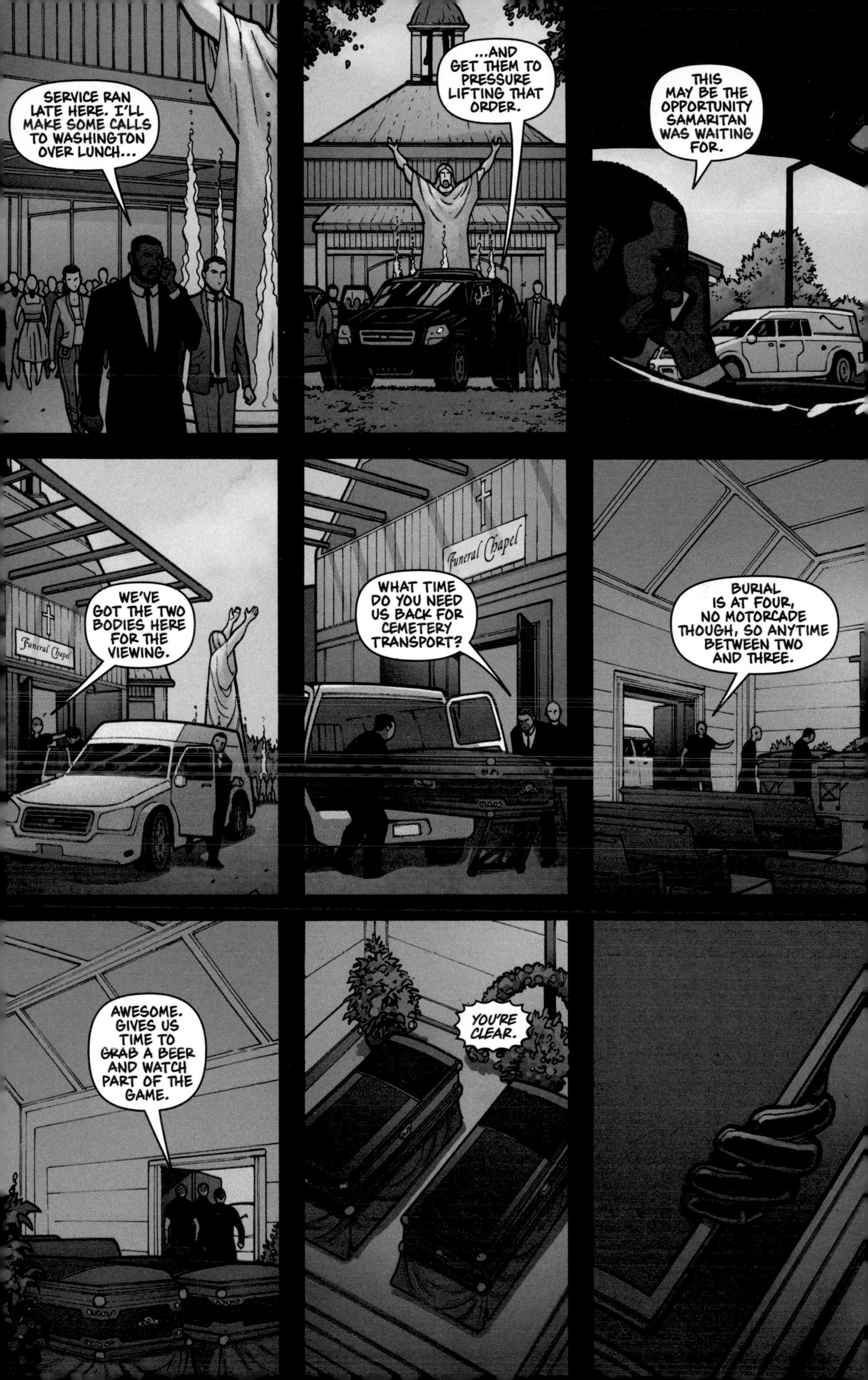
SERVICE RAN LATE HERE. I'LL MAKE SOME CALLS TO WASHINGTON OVER LUNCH...
...AND GET THEM TO PRESSURE LIFTING THAT ORDER.
THIS MAY BE THE OPPORTUNITY SAMARITAN WAS WAITING FOR.
Funeral Chapel
WE'VE GOT THE TWO BODIES HERE FOR THE VIEWING.
WHAT TIME DO YOU NEED US BACK FOR CEMETERY TRANSPORT?
BURIAL IS AT FOUR, NO MOTORCADE THOUGH, SO ANYTIME BETWEEN TWO AND THREE.
AWESOME. GIVES US TIME TO GRAB A BEER AND WATCH PART OF THE GAME.
YOU'RE CLEAR.

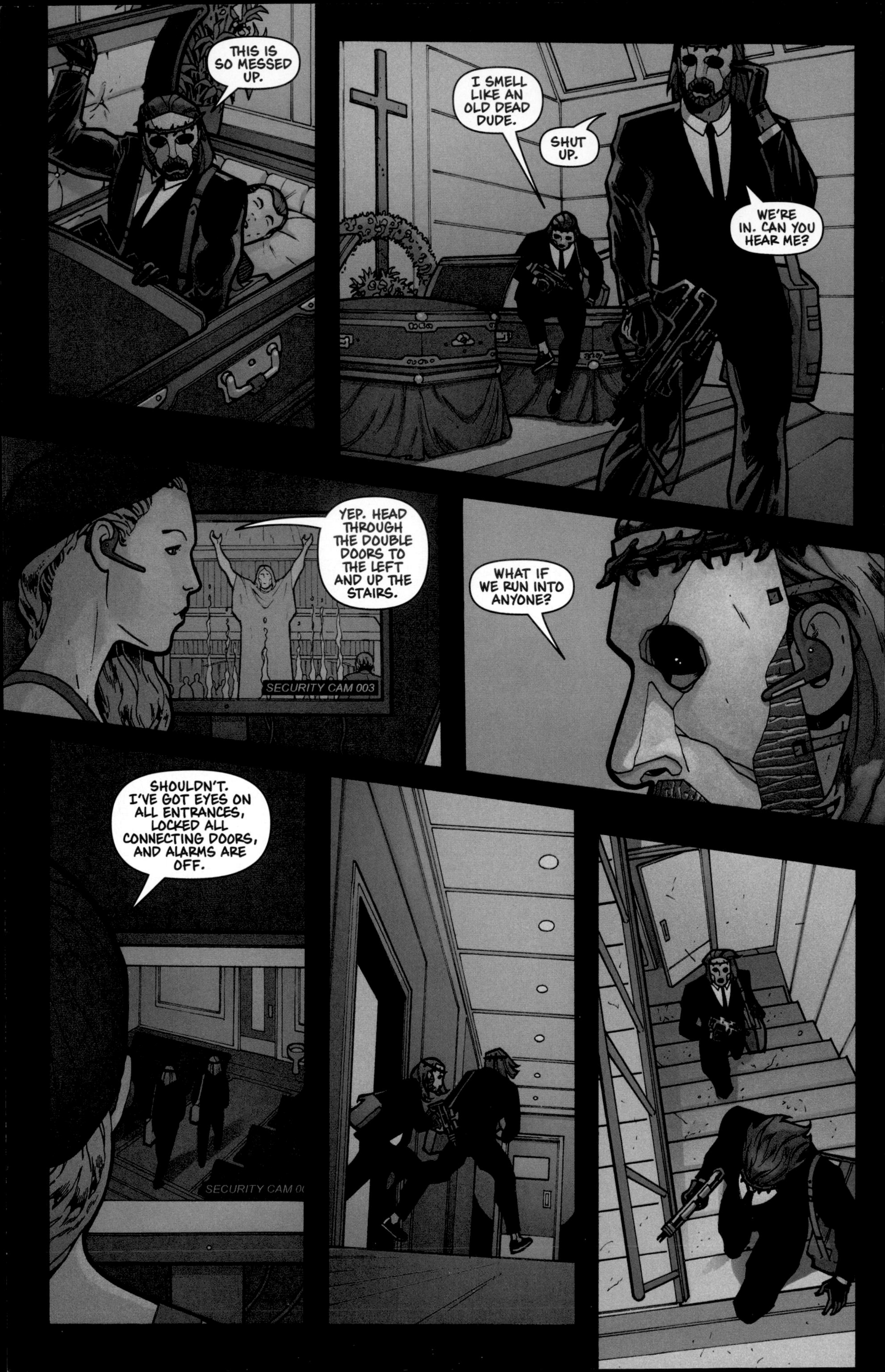
THIS IS SO MESSED UP.
I SMELL LIKE AN OLD DEAD DUDE.
SHUT UP.
WE'RE IN. CAN YOU HEAR ME?
YEP. HEAD THROUGH THE DOUBLE DOORS TO THE LEFT AND UP THE STAIRS.
SECURITY CAM 003
WHAT IF WE RUN INTO ANYONE?
SHOULDN'T. I'VE GOT EYES ON ALL ENTRANCES, LOCKED ALL CONNECTING DOORS, AND ALARMS ARE OFF.

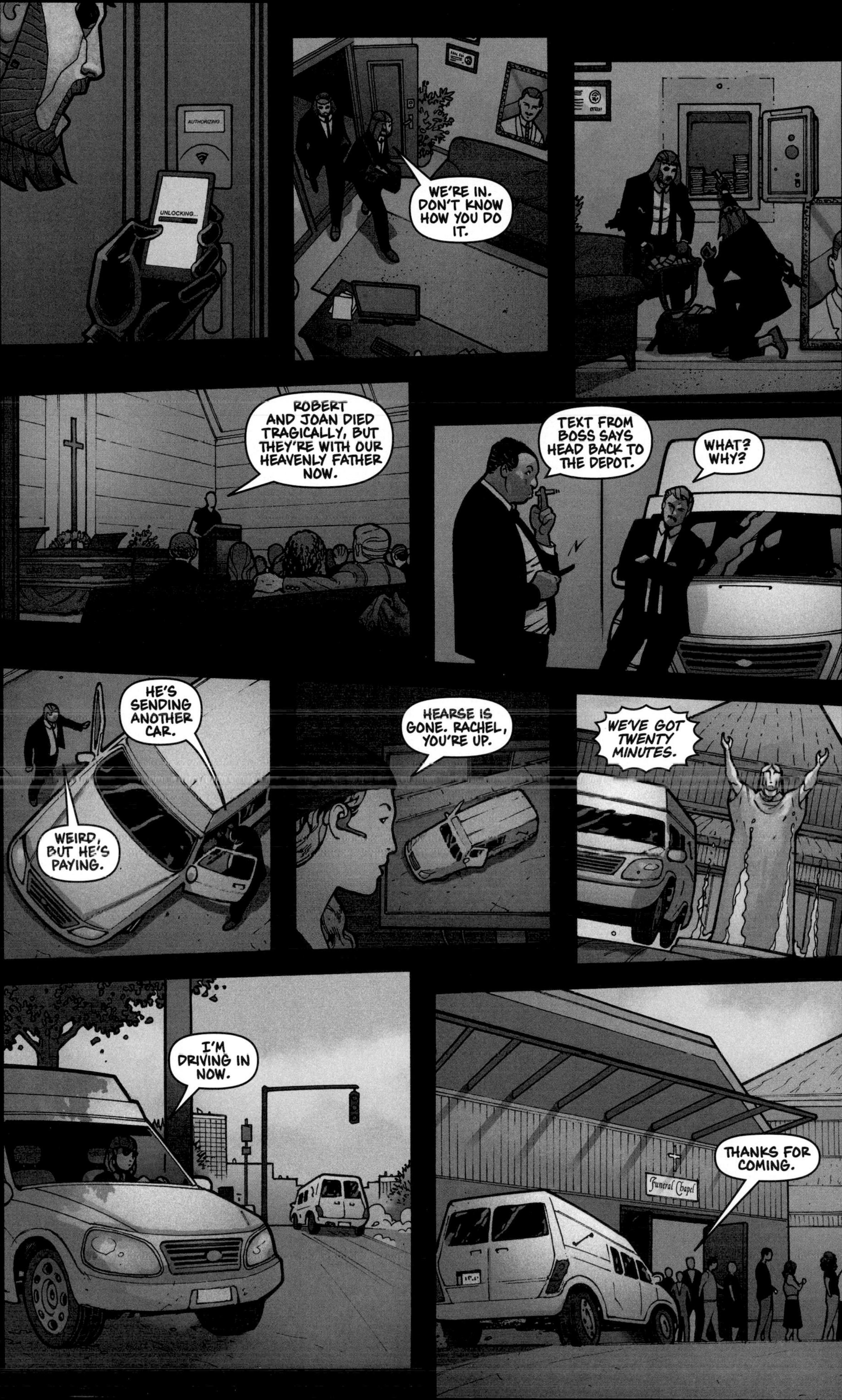
AUTHORIZING...
UNLOCKING...
WE'RE IN. DON'T KNOW HOW YOU DO IT.
ROBERT AND JOAN DIED TRAGICALLY, BUT THEY'RE WITH OUR HEAVENLY FATHER NOW.
TEXT FROM BOSS SAYS HEAD BACK TO THE DEPOT.
WHAT? WHY?
HE'S SENDING ANOTHER CAR.
WEIRD, BUT HE'S PAYING.
HEARSE IS GONE. RACHEL, YOU'RE UP.
WE'VE GOT TWENTY MINUTES.
I'M DRIVING IN NOW.
Funeral Chapel
THANKS FOR COMING.

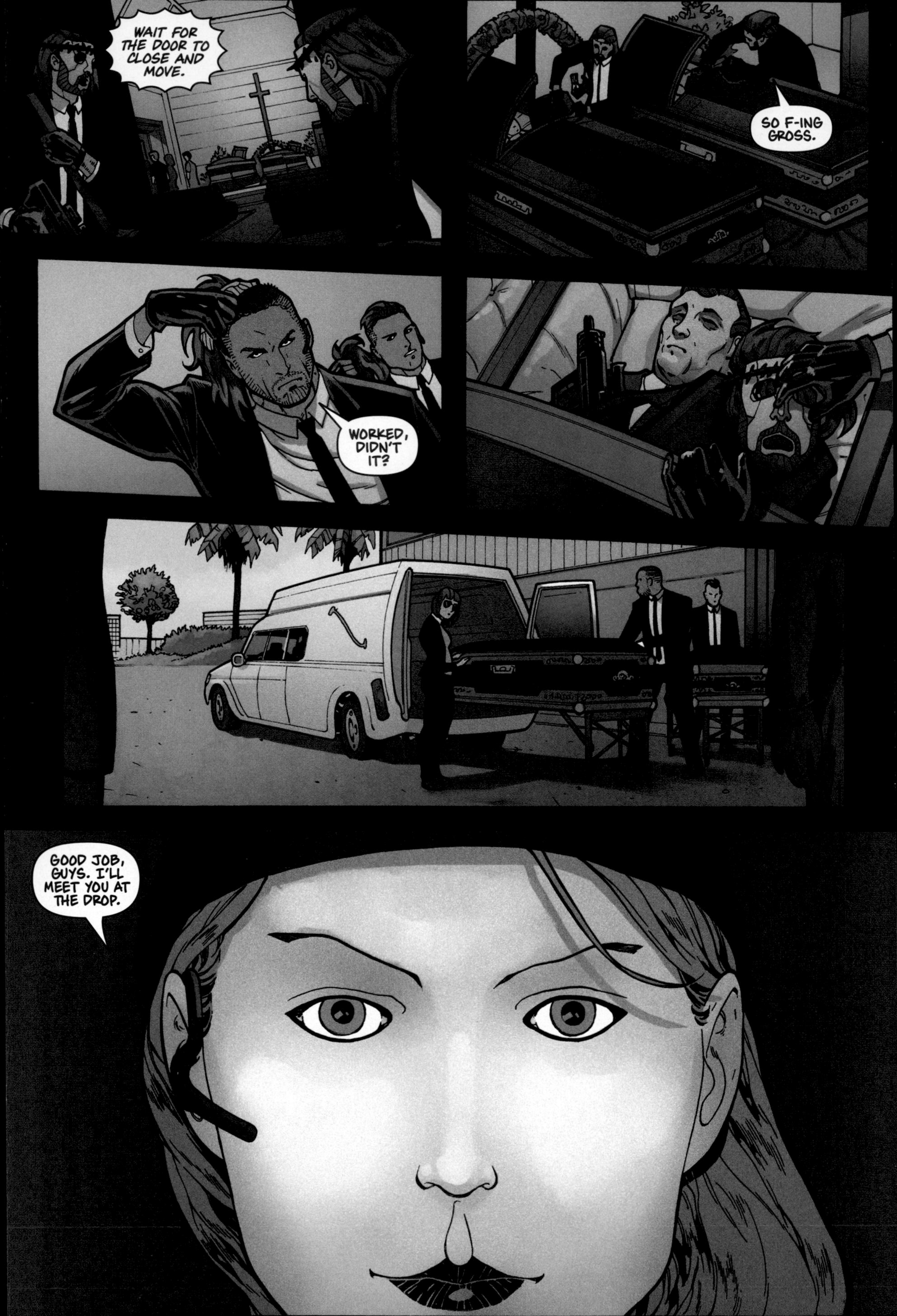
WAIT FOR THE DOOR TO CLOSE AND MOVE.
SO F-ING GROSS.
WORKED, DIDN'T IT?
GOOD JOB, GUYS. I'LL MEET YOU AT THE DROP.

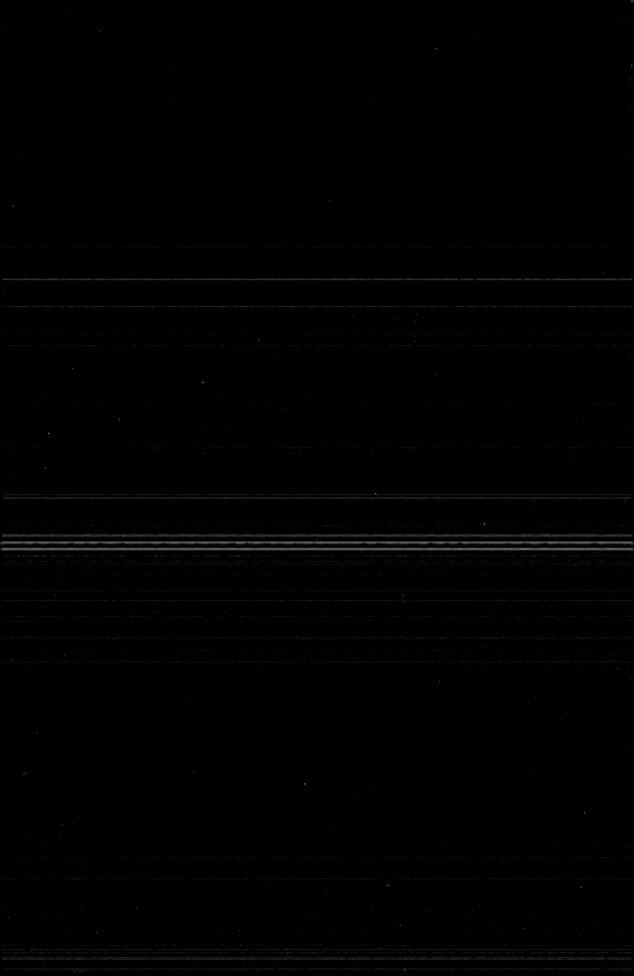

CHAPTER 3

IN *GOD'S WILL IS PROSPERITY,* GLORIA COPELAND WRITES OF THIS VERSE, "GIVE $10 AND RECEIVE $1,000; GIVE $1,000 AND RECEIVE $100,000... IN SHORT, **MARK 10:30** IS A VERY GOOD DEAL."

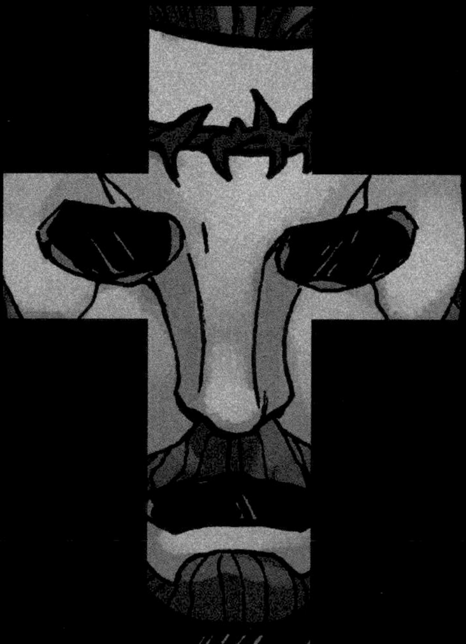

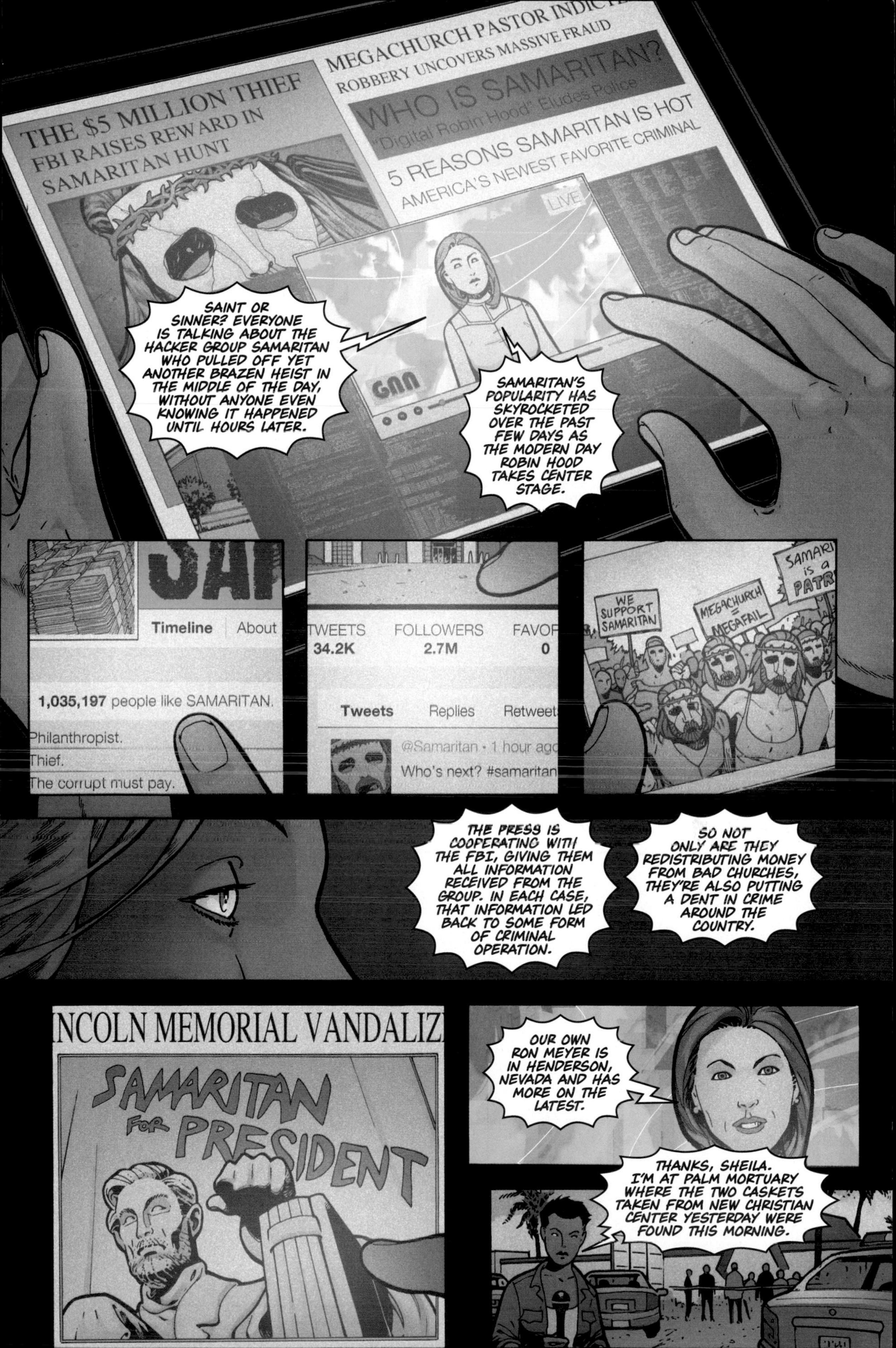
MEGACHURCH PASTOR INDICT
ROBBERY UNCOVERS MASSIVE FRAUD
THE $5 MILLION THIEF
FBI RAISES REWARD IN SAMARITAN HUNT
WHO IS SAMARITAN?
'Digital Robin Hood' Eludes Police
5 REASONS SAMARITAN IS HOT
AMERICA'S NEWEST FAVORITE CRIMINAL
LIVE
GNN
SAINT OR SINNER? EVERYONE IS TALKING ABOUT THE HACKER GROUP SAMARITAN WHO PULLED OFF YET ANOTHER BRAZEN HEIST IN THE MIDDLE OF THE DAY, WITHOUT ANYONE EVEN KNOWING IT HAPPENED UNTIL HOURS LATER.
SAMARITAN'S POPULARITY HAS SKYROCKETED OVER THE PAST FEW DAYS AS THE MODERN DAY ROBIN HOOD TAKES CENTER STAGE.
Timeline About
1,035,197 people like SAMARITAN.
Philanthropist.
Thief.
The corrupt must pay.
TWEETS 34.2K FOLLOWERS 2.7M FAVOR 0
Tweets Replies Retweets
@Samaritan • 1 hour ago
Who's next? #samaritan
WE SUPPORT SAMARITAN
MEGACHURCH = MEGAFAIL
SAMARI is a PATR
THE PRESS IS COOPERATING WITH THE FBI, GIVING THEM ALL INFORMATION RECEIVED FROM THE GROUP. IN EACH CASE, THAT INFORMATION LED BACK TO SOME FORM OF CRIMINAL OPERATION.
SO NOT ONLY ARE THEY REDISTRIBUTING MONEY FROM BAD CHURCHES, THEY'RE ALSO PUTTING A DENT IN CRIME AROUND THE COUNTRY.
INCOLN MEMORIAL VANDALIZ
SAMARITAN FOR PRESIDENT
OUR OWN RON MEYER IS IN HENDERSON, NEVADA AND HAS MORE ON THE LATEST.
THANKS, SHEILA. I'M AT PALM MORTUARY WHERE THE TWO CASKETS TAKEN FROM NEW CHRISTIAN CENTER YESTERDAY WERE FOUND THIS MORNING.

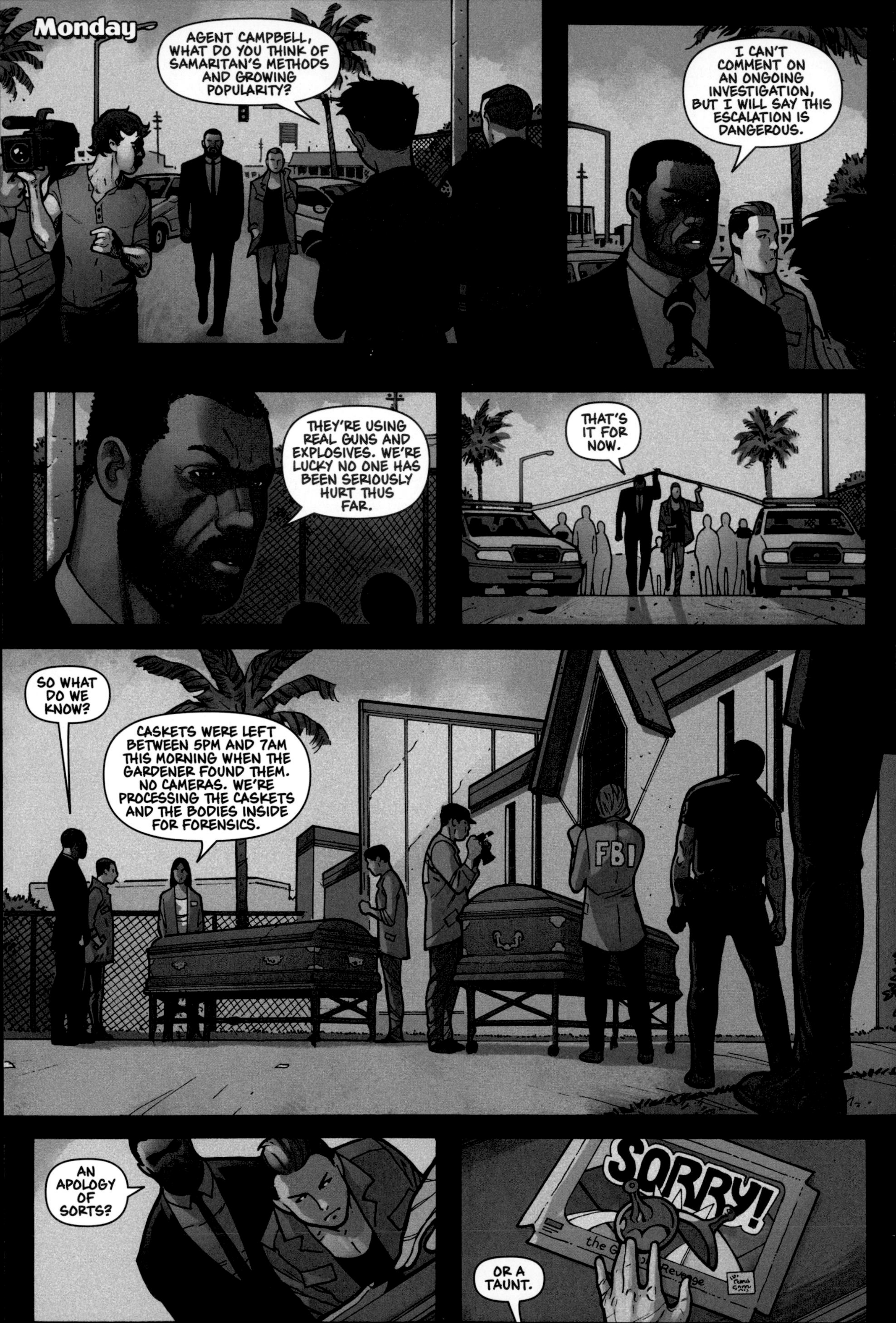
Monday
AGENT CAMPBELL, WHAT DO YOU THINK OF SAMARITAN'S METHODS AND GROWING POPULARITY?
I CAN'T COMMENT ON AN ONGOING INVESTIGATION, BUT I WILL SAY THIS ESCALATION IS DANGEROUS.
THEY'RE USING REAL GUNS AND EXPLOSIVES. WE'RE LUCKY NO ONE HAS BEEN SERIOUSLY HURT THUS FAR.
THAT'S IT FOR NOW.
SO WHAT DO WE KNOW?
CASKETS WERE LEFT BETWEEN 5PM AND 7AM THIS MORNING WHEN THE GARDENER FOUND THEM. NO CAMERAS. WE'RE PROCESSING THE CASKETS AND THE BODIES INSIDE FOR FORENSICS.
FBI
AN APOLOGY OF SORTS?
SORRY!
OR A TAUNT.

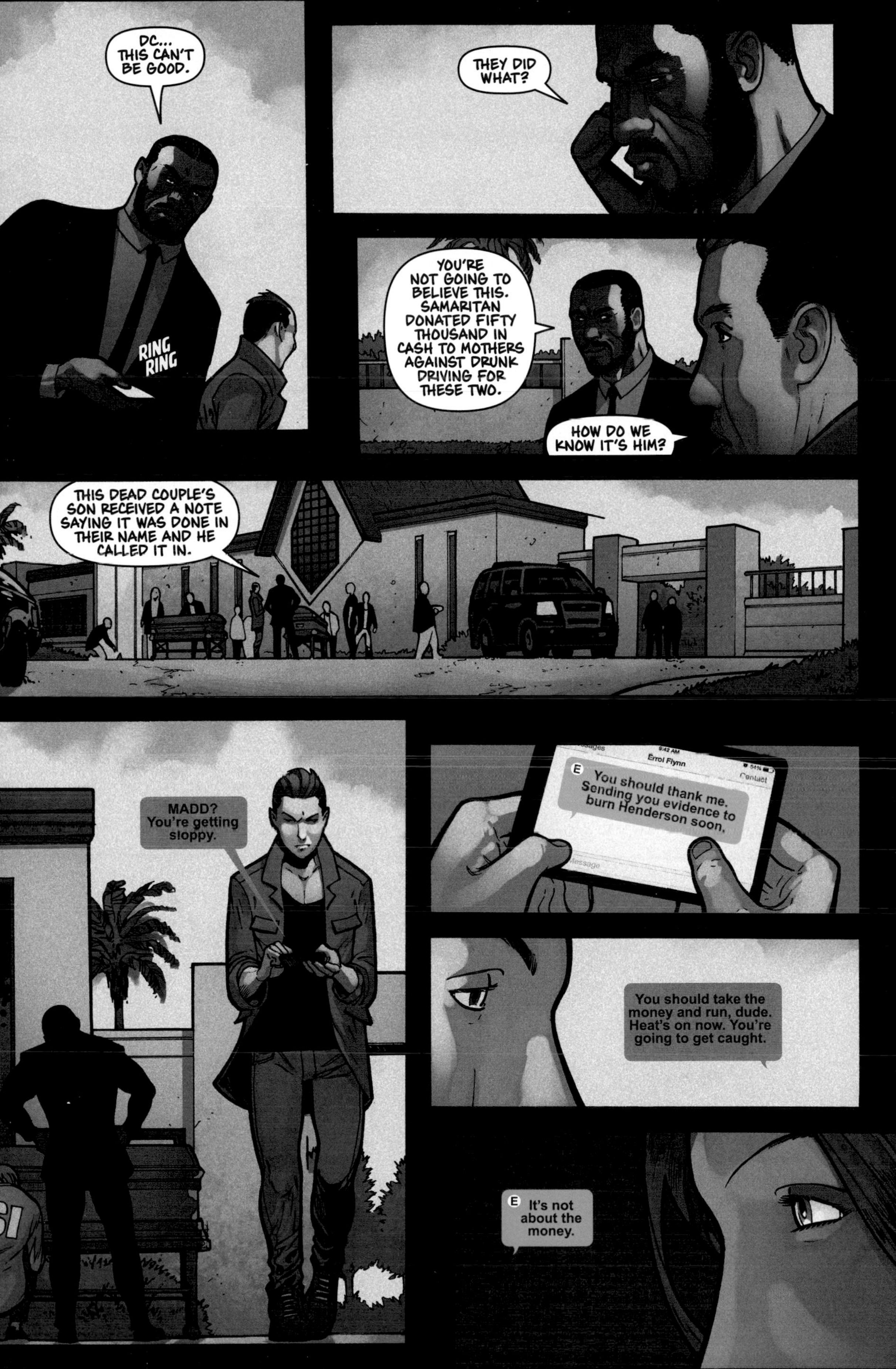
DC... THIS CAN'T BE GOOD.
RING RING
THEY DID WHAT?
YOU'RE NOT GOING TO BELIEVE THIS. SAMARITAN DONATED FIFTY THOUSAND IN CASH TO MOTHERS AGAINST DRUNK DRIVING FOR THESE TWO.
HOW DO WE KNOW IT'S HIM?
THIS DEAD COUPLE'S SON RECEIVED A NOTE SAYING IT WAS DONE IN THEIR NAME AND HE CALLED IT IN.
MADD? You're getting sloppy.
9:42 AM
Errol Flynn
Contact
E You should thank me. Sending you evidence to burn Henderson soon.
You should take the money and run, dude. Heat's on now. You're going to get caught.
E It's not about the money.

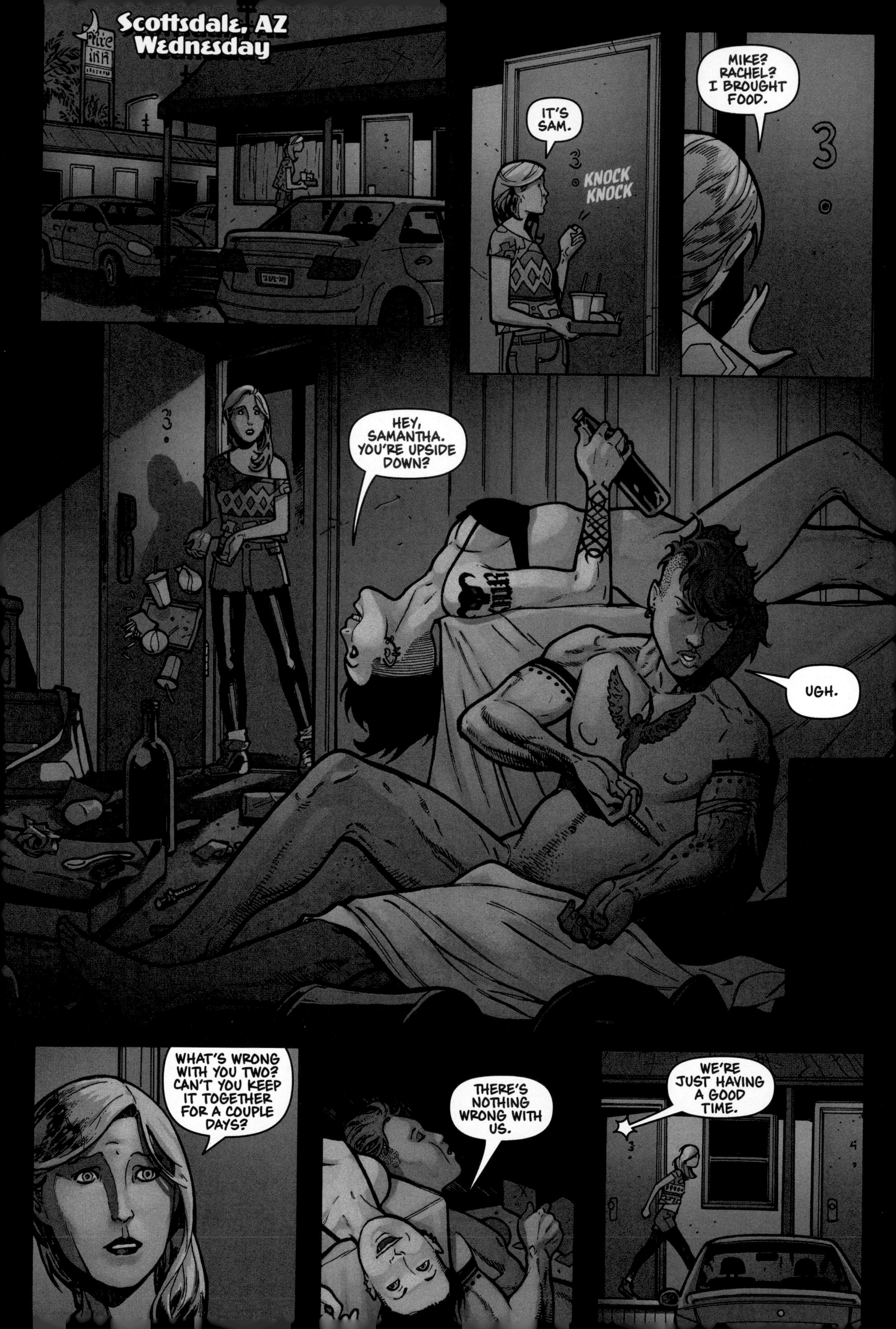

Scottsdale, AZ Wednesday
IT'S SAM.
KNOCK KNOCK
MIKE? RACHEL? I BROUGHT FOOD.
HEY, SAMANTHA. YOU'RE UPSIDE DOWN?
UGH.
WHAT'S WRONG WITH YOU TWO? CAN'T YOU KEEP IT TOGETHER FOR A COUPLE DAYS?
THERE'S NOTHING WRONG WITH US.
WE'RE JUST HAVING A GOOD TIME.

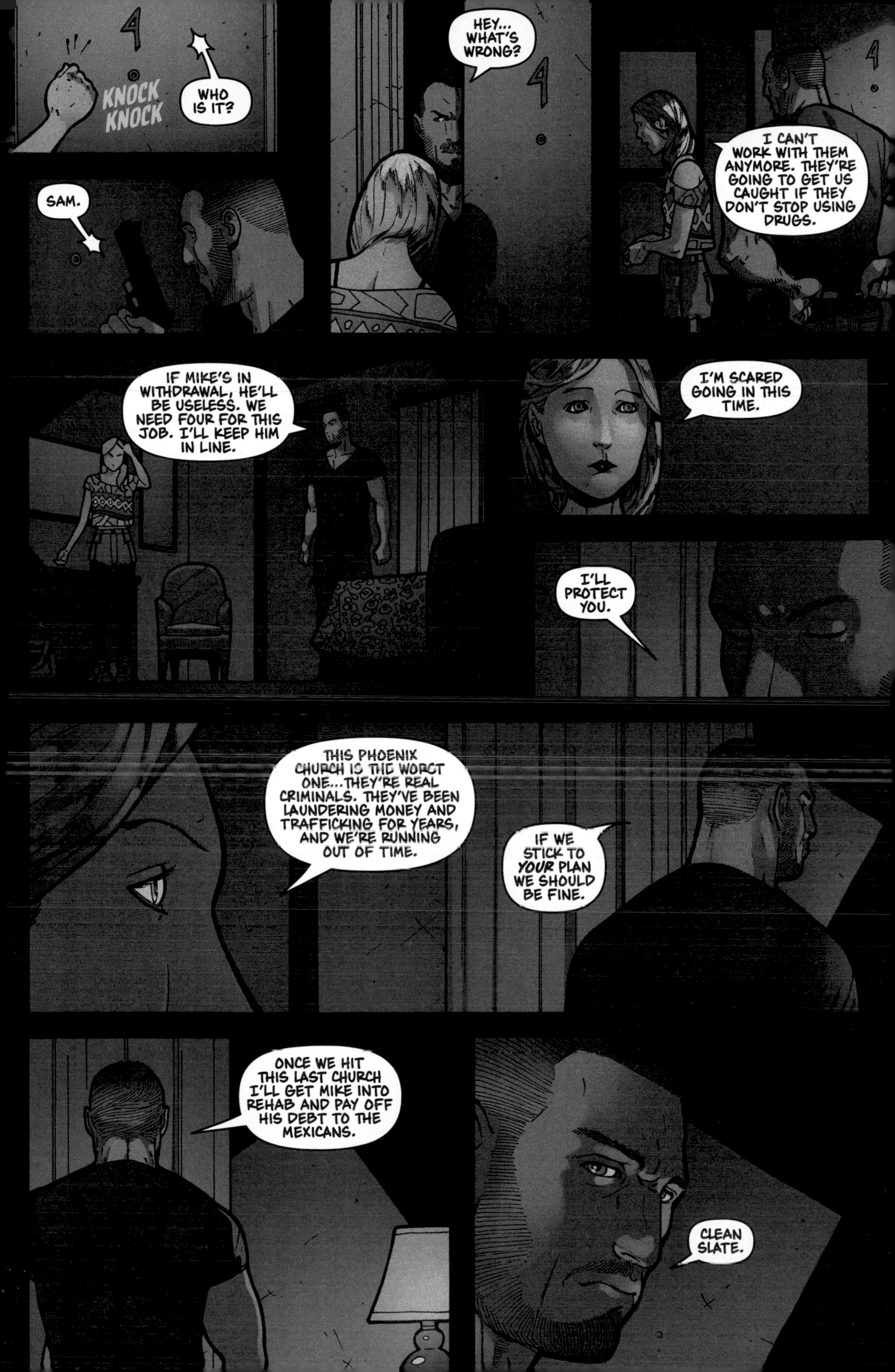
KNOCK KNOCK
WHO IS IT?
SAM.
HEY... WHAT'S WRONG?
I CAN'T WORK WITH THEM ANYMORE. THEY'RE GOING TO GET US CAUGHT IF THEY DON'T STOP USING DRUGS.
IF MIKE'S IN WITHDRAWAL, HE'LL BE USELESS. WE NEED FOUR FOR THIS JOB. I'LL KEEP HIM IN LINE.
I'M SCARED GOING IN THIS TIME.
I'LL PROTECT YOU.
THIS PHOENIX CHURCH IS THE WORST ONE...THEY'RE REAL CRIMINALS. THEY'VE BEEN LAUNDERING MONEY AND TRAFFICKING FOR YEARS, AND WE'RE RUNNING OUT OF TIME.
IF WE STICK TO YOUR PLAN WE SHOULD BE FINE.
ONCE WE HIT THIS LAST CHURCH I'LL GET MIKE INTO REHAB AND PAY OFF HIS DEBT TO THE MEXICANS.
CLEAN SLATE.

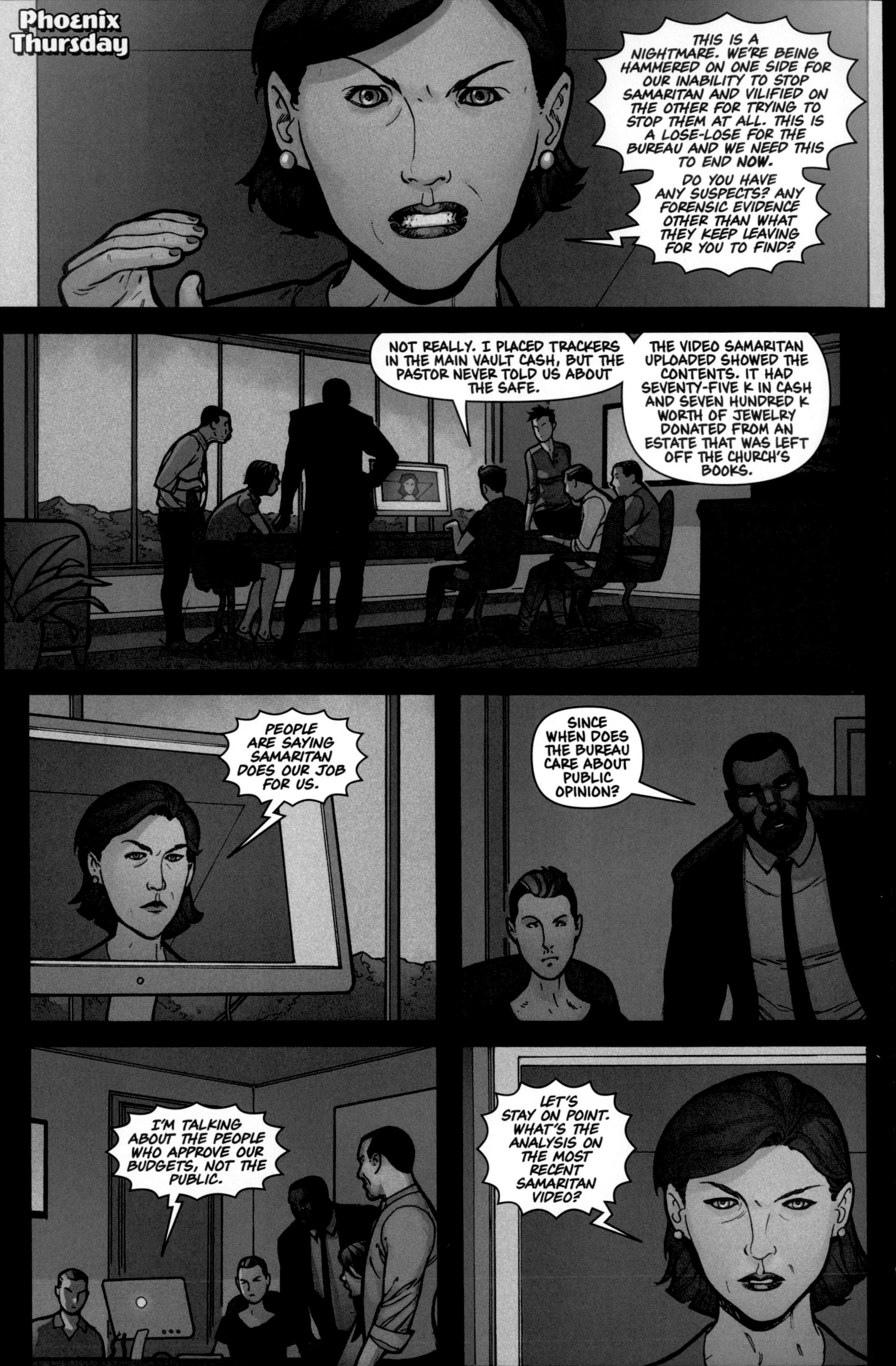

Phoenix Thursday
THIS IS A NIGHTMARE. WE'RE BEING HAMMERED ON ONE SIDE FOR OUR INABILITY TO STOP SAMARITAN AND VILIFIED ON THE OTHER FOR TRYING TO STOP THEM AT ALL. THIS IS A LOSE-LOSE FOR THE BUREAU AND WE NEED THIS TO END NOW.
DO YOU HAVE ANY SUSPECTS? ANY FORENSIC EVIDENCE OTHER THAN WHAT THEY KEEP LEAVING FOR YOU TO FIND?
NOT REALLY. I PLACED TRACKERS IN THE MAIN VAULT CASH, BUT THE PASTOR NEVER TOLD US ABOUT THE SAFE.
THE VIDEO SAMARITAN UPLOADED SHOWED THE CONTENTS. IT HAD SEVENTY-FIVE K IN CASH AND SEVEN HUNDRED K WORTH OF JEWELRY DONATED FROM AN ESTATE THAT WAS LEFT OFF THE CHURCH'S BOOKS.
PEOPLE ARE SAYING SAMARITAN DOES OUR JOB FOR US.
SINCE WHEN DOES THE BUREAU CARE ABOUT PUBLIC OPINION?
I'M TALKING ABOUT THE PEOPLE WHO APPROVE OUR BUDGETS, NOT THE PUBLIC.
LET'S STAY ON POINT. WHAT'S THE ANALYSIS ON THE MOST RECENT SAMARITAN VIDEO?

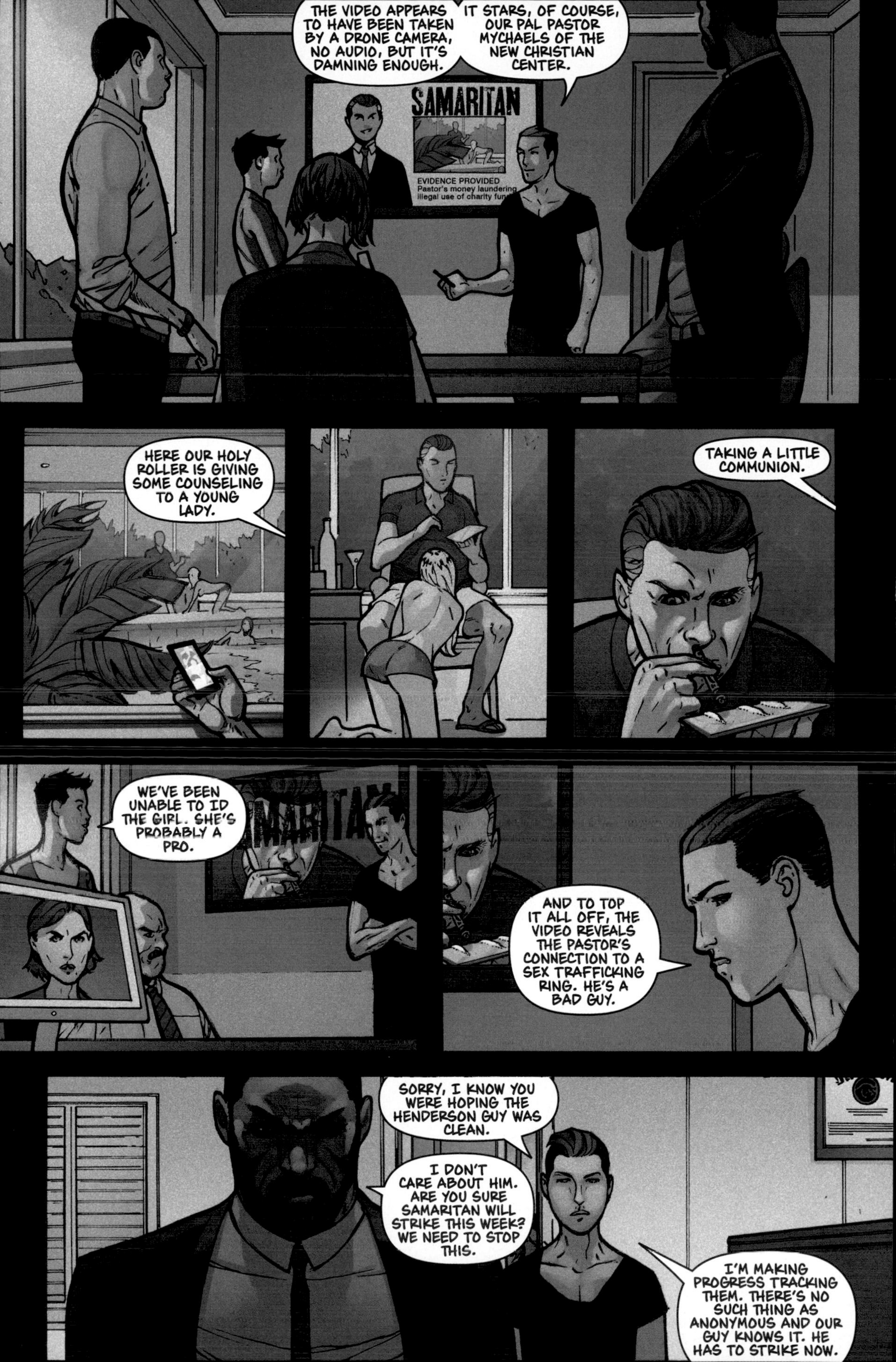
THE VIDEO APPEARS TO HAVE BEEN TAKEN BY A DRONE CAMERA, NO AUDIO, BUT IT'S DAMNING ENOUGH.
IT STARS, OF COURSE, OUR PAL PASTOR MYCHAELS OF THE NEW CHRISTIAN CENTER.
SAMARITAN
EVIDENCE PROVIDED
Pastor's money laundering
illegal use of charity fun
HERE OUR HOLY ROLLER IS GIVING SOME COUNSELING TO A YOUNG LADY.
TAKING A LITTLE COMMUNION.
WE'VE BEEN UNABLE TO ID THE GIRL. SHE'S PROBABLY A PRO.
AND TO TOP IT ALL OFF, THE VIDEO REVEALS THE PASTOR'S CONNECTION TO A SEX TRAFFICKING RING. HE'S A BAD GUY.
SORRY, I KNOW YOU WERE HOPING THE HENDERSON GUY WAS CLEAN.
I DON'T CARE ABOUT HIM. ARE YOU SURE SAMARITAN WILL STRIKE THIS WEEK? WE NEED TO STOP THIS.
I'M MAKING PROGRESS TRACKING THEM. THERE'S NO SUCH THING AS ANONYMOUS AND OUR GUY KNOWS IT. HE HAS TO STRIKE NOW.

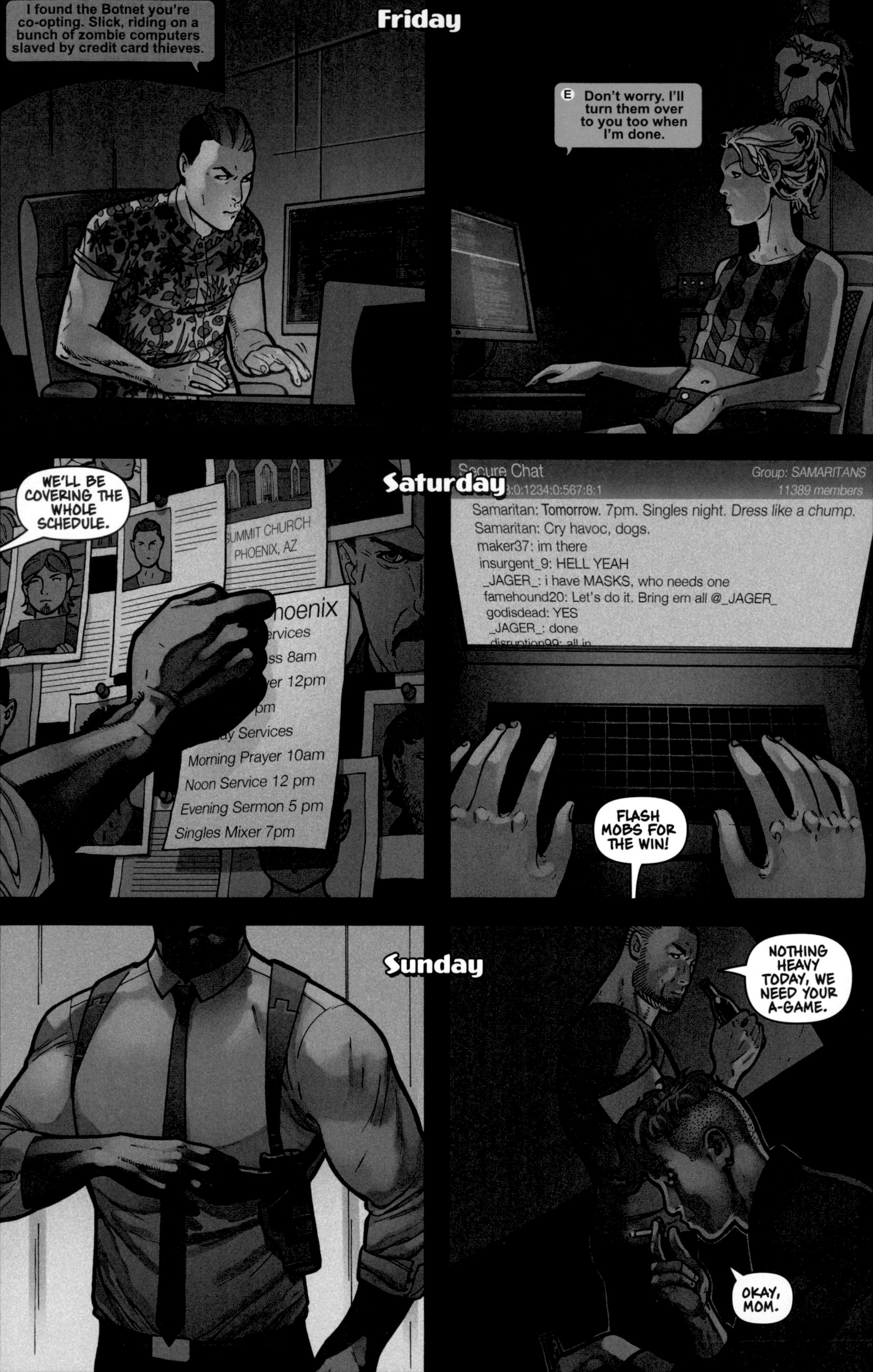
I found the Botnet you're co-opting. Slick, riding on a bunch of zombie computers slaved by credit card thieves.
Friday
Don't worry. I'll turn them over to you too when I'm done.
Saturday
WE'LL BE COVERING THE WHOLE SCHEDULE.
SUMMIT CHURCH
PHOENIX, AZ
Morning Prayer 10am
Noon Service 12 pm
Evening Sermon 5 pm
Singles Mixer 7pm
Group: SAMARITANS
11389 members
Samaritan: Tomorrow. 7pm. Singles night. Dress like a chump.
Samaritan: Cry havoc, dogs.
maker37: im there
insurgent_9: HELL YEAH
JAGER: i have MASKS, who needs one
famehound20: Let's do it. Bring em all @_JAGER_
godisdead: YES
JAGER: done
FLASH MOBS FOR THE WIN!
Sunday
NOTHING HEAVY TODAY, WE NEED YOUR A-GAME.
OKAY, MOM.

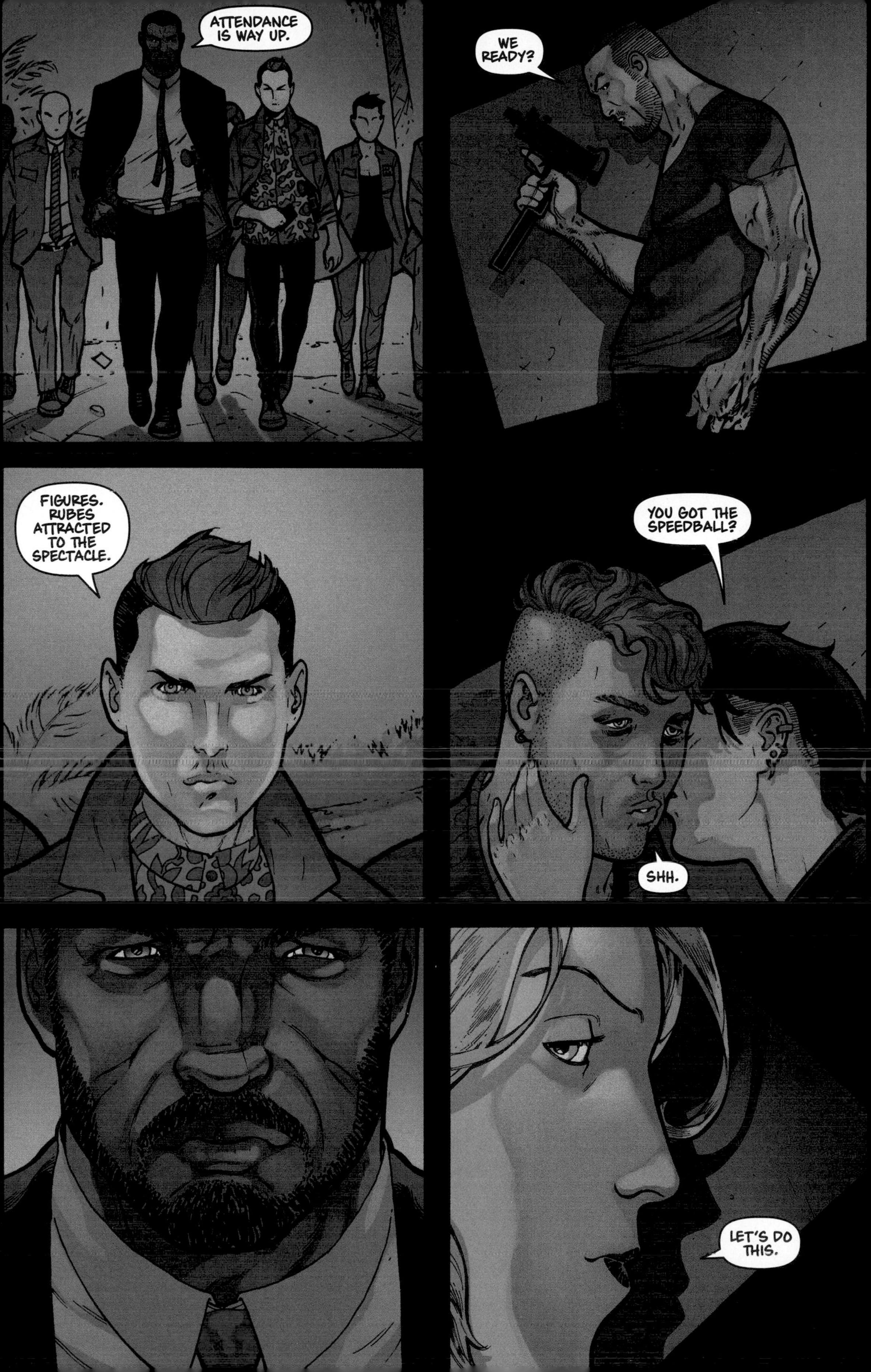
ATTENDANCE IS WAY UP.
WE READY?
FIGURES. RUBES ATTRACTED TO THE SPECTACLE.
YOU GOT THE SPEEDBALL?
SHH.
LET'S DO THIS.

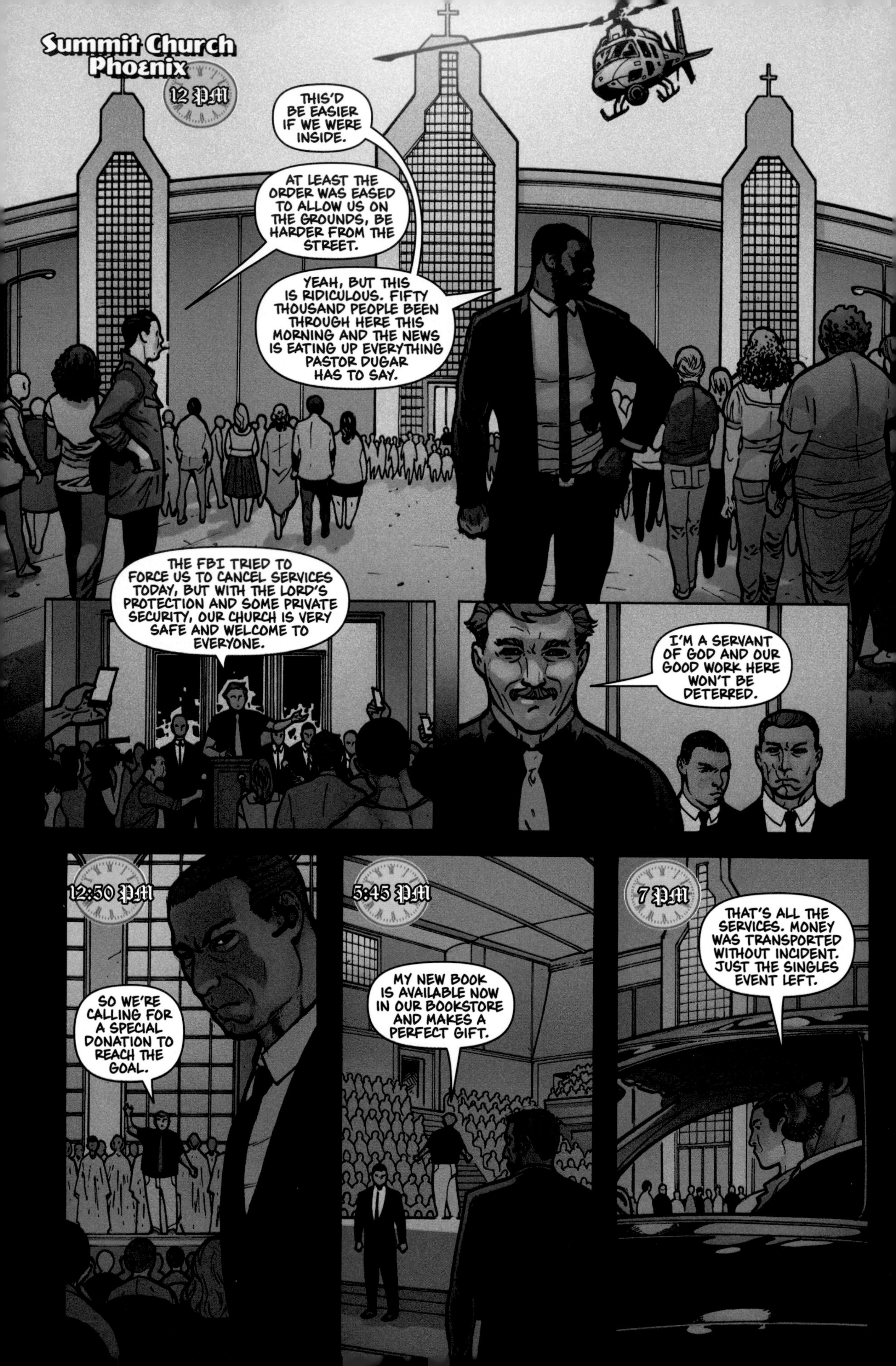
Summit Church Phoenix
12 PM
THIS'D BE EASIER IF WE WERE INSIDE.
AT LEAST THE ORDER WAS EASED TO ALLOW US ON THE GROUNDS, BE HARDER FROM THE STREET.
YEAH, BUT THIS IS RIDICULOUS. FIFTY THOUSAND PEOPLE BEEN THROUGH HERE THIS MORNING AND THE NEWS IS EATING UP EVERYTHING PASTOR DUGAR HAS TO SAY.
THE FBI TRIED TO FORCE US TO CANCEL SERVICES TODAY, BUT WITH THE LORD'S PROTECTION AND SOME PRIVATE SECURITY, OUR CHURCH IS VERY SAFE AND WELCOME TO EVERYONE.
I'M A SERVANT OF GOD AND OUR GOOD WORK HERE WON'T BE DETERRED.
12:50 PM
SO WE'RE CALLING FOR A SPECIAL DONATION TO REACH THE GOAL.
5:45 PM
MY NEW BOOK IS AVAILABLE NOW IN OUR BOOKSTORE AND MAKES A PERFECT GIFT.
7 PM
THAT'S ALL THE SERVICES. MONEY WAS TRANSPORTED WITHOUT INCIDENT. JUST THE SINGLES EVENT LEFT.

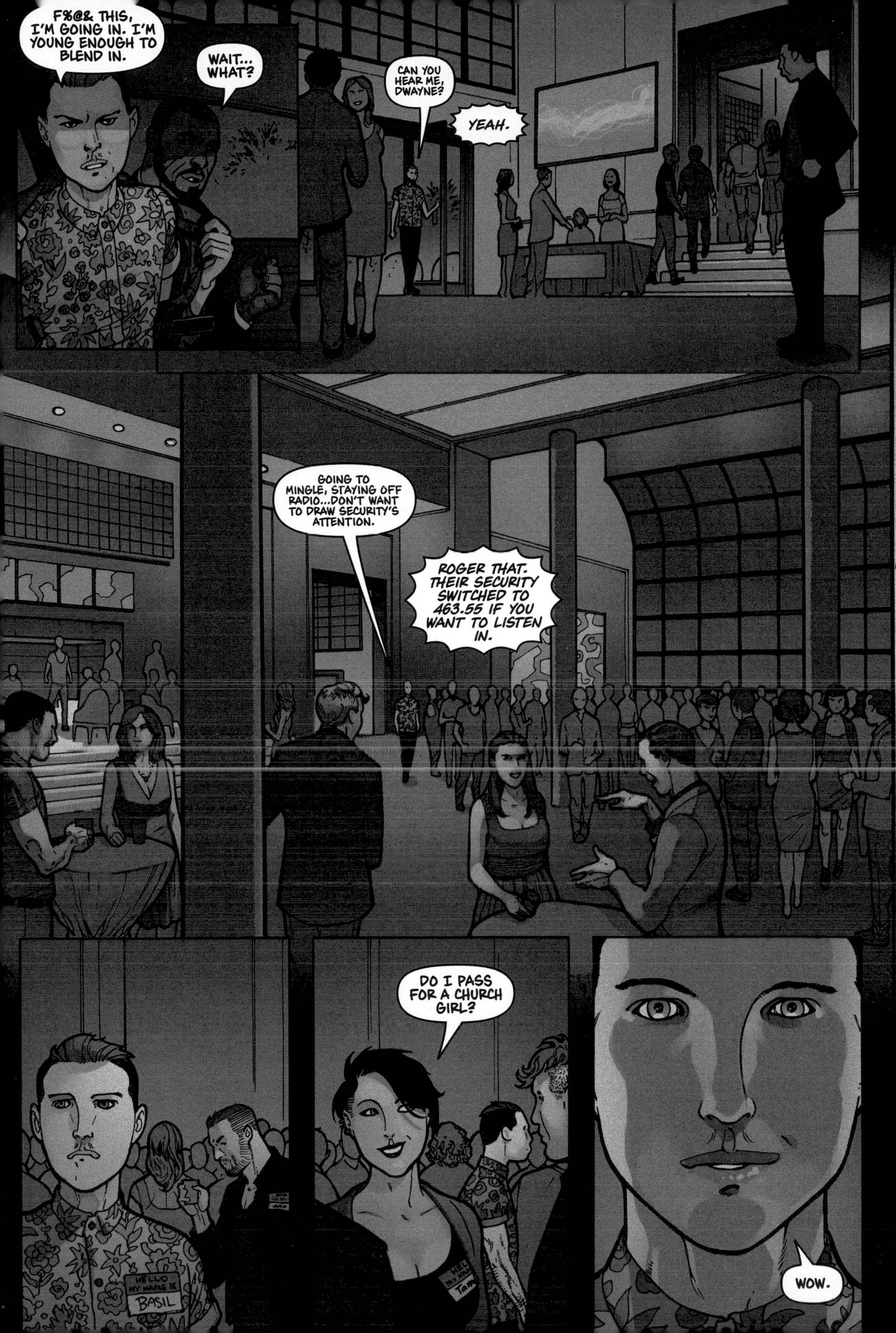
F%@& THIS, I'M GOING IN. I'M YOUNG ENOUGH TO BLEND IN.
WAIT... WHAT?
CAN YOU HEAR ME, DWAYNE?
YEAH.
GOING TO MINGLE, STAYING OFF RADIO...DON'T WANT TO DRAW SECURITY'S ATTENTION.
ROGER THAT. THEIR SECURITY SWITCHED TO 463.55 IF YOU WANT TO LISTEN IN.
HELLO MY NAME IS BASIL
DO I PASS FOR A CHURCH GIRL?
WOW.

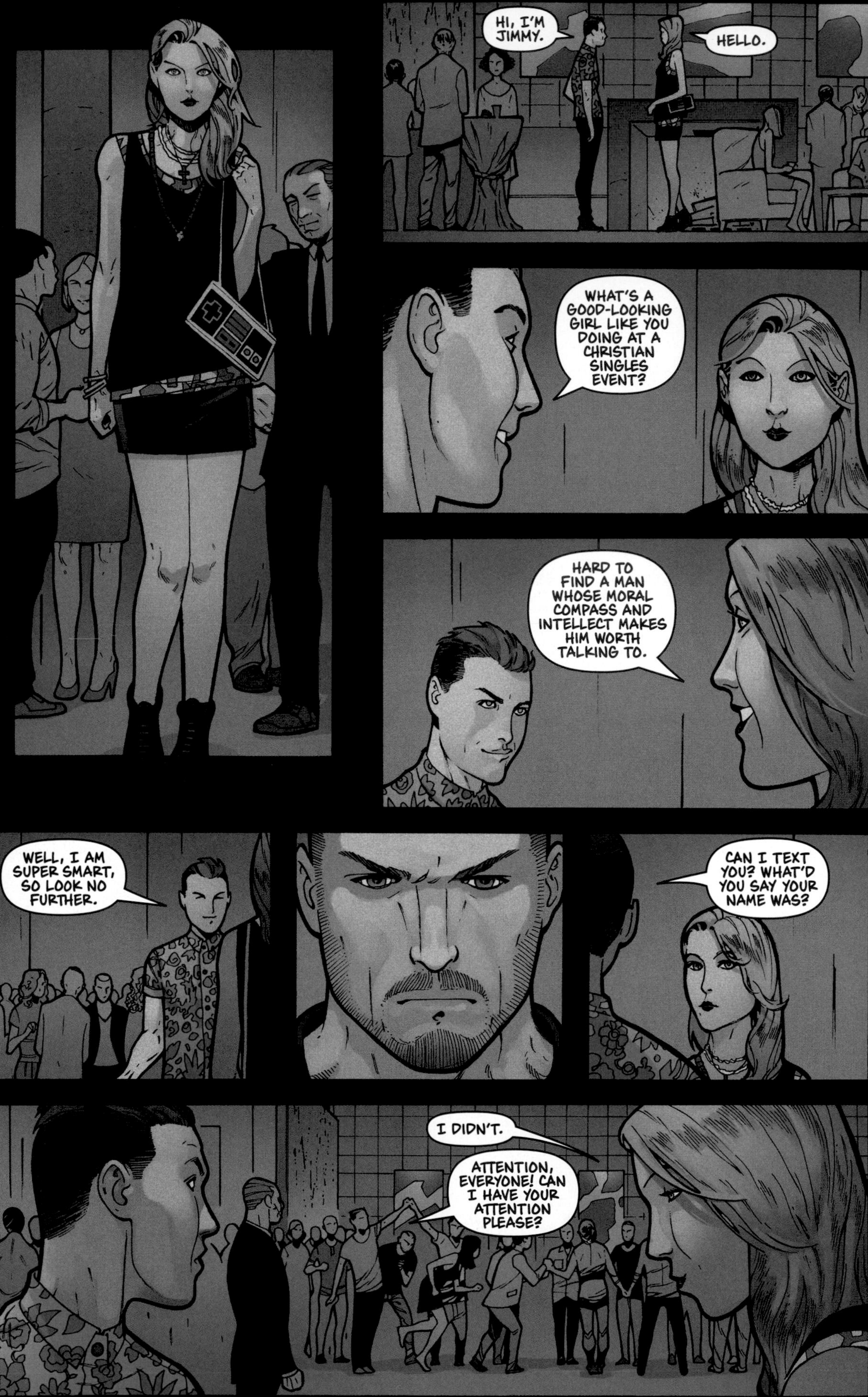
HI, I'M JIMMY.
HELLO.
WHAT'S A GOOD-LOOKING GIRL LIKE YOU DOING AT A CHRISTIAN SINGLES EVENT?
HARD TO FIND A MAN WHOSE MORAL COMPASS AND INTELLECT MAKES HIM WORTH TALKING TO.
WELL, I AM SUPER SMART, SO LOOK NO FURTHER.
CAN I TEXT YOU? WHAT'D YOU SAY YOUR NAME WAS?
I DIDN'T.
ATTENTION, EVERYONE! CAN I HAVE YOUR ATTENTION PLEASE?

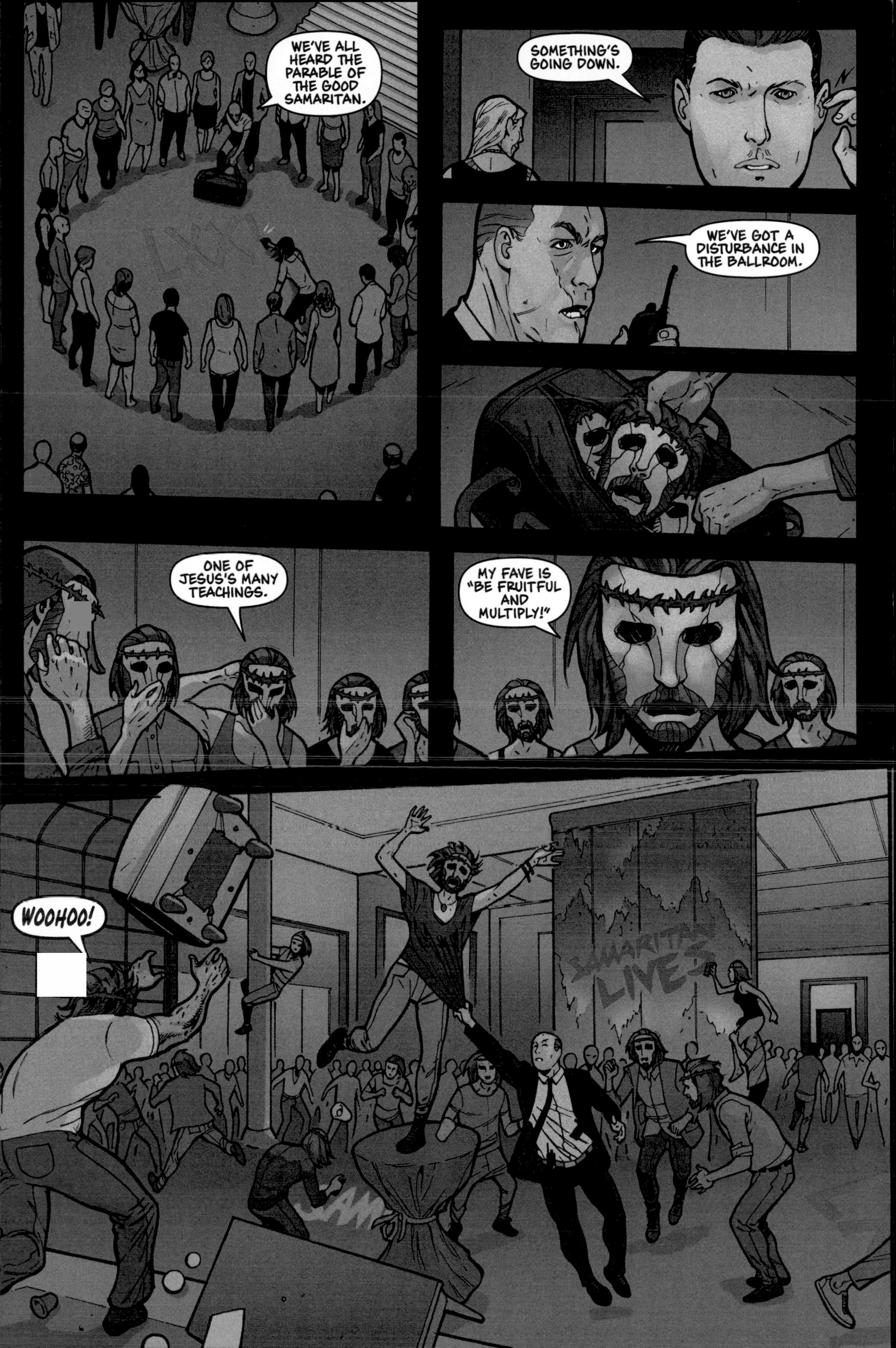
WE'VE ALL HEARD THE PARABLE OF THE GOOD SAMARITAN.
SOMETHING'S GOING DOWN.
WE'VE GOT A DISTURBANCE IN THE BALLROOM.
ONE OF JESUS'S MANY TEACHINGS.
MY FAVE IS "BE FRUITFUL AND MULTIPLY!"
WOOHOO!
LIVES

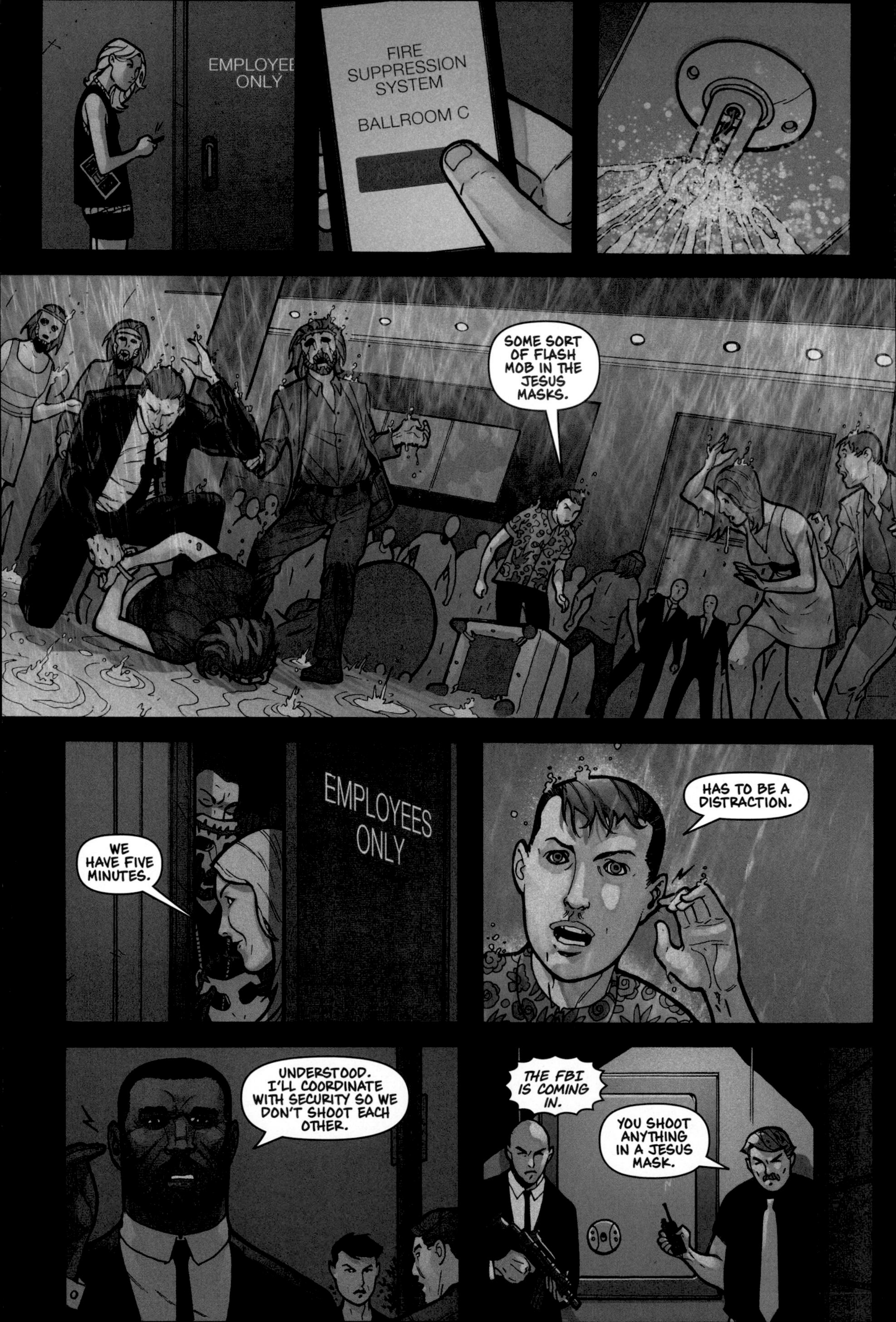
EMPLOYEES ONLY
FIRE SUPPRESSION SYSTEM
BALLROOM C
SOME SORT OF FLASH MOB IN THE JESUS MASKS.
EMPLOYEES ONLY
WE HAVE FIVE MINUTES.
HAS TO BE A DISTRACTION.
UNDERSTOOD. I'LL COORDINATE WITH SECURITY SO WE DON'T SHOOT EACH OTHER.
THE FBI IS COMING IN.
YOU SHOOT ANYTHING IN A JESUS MASK.

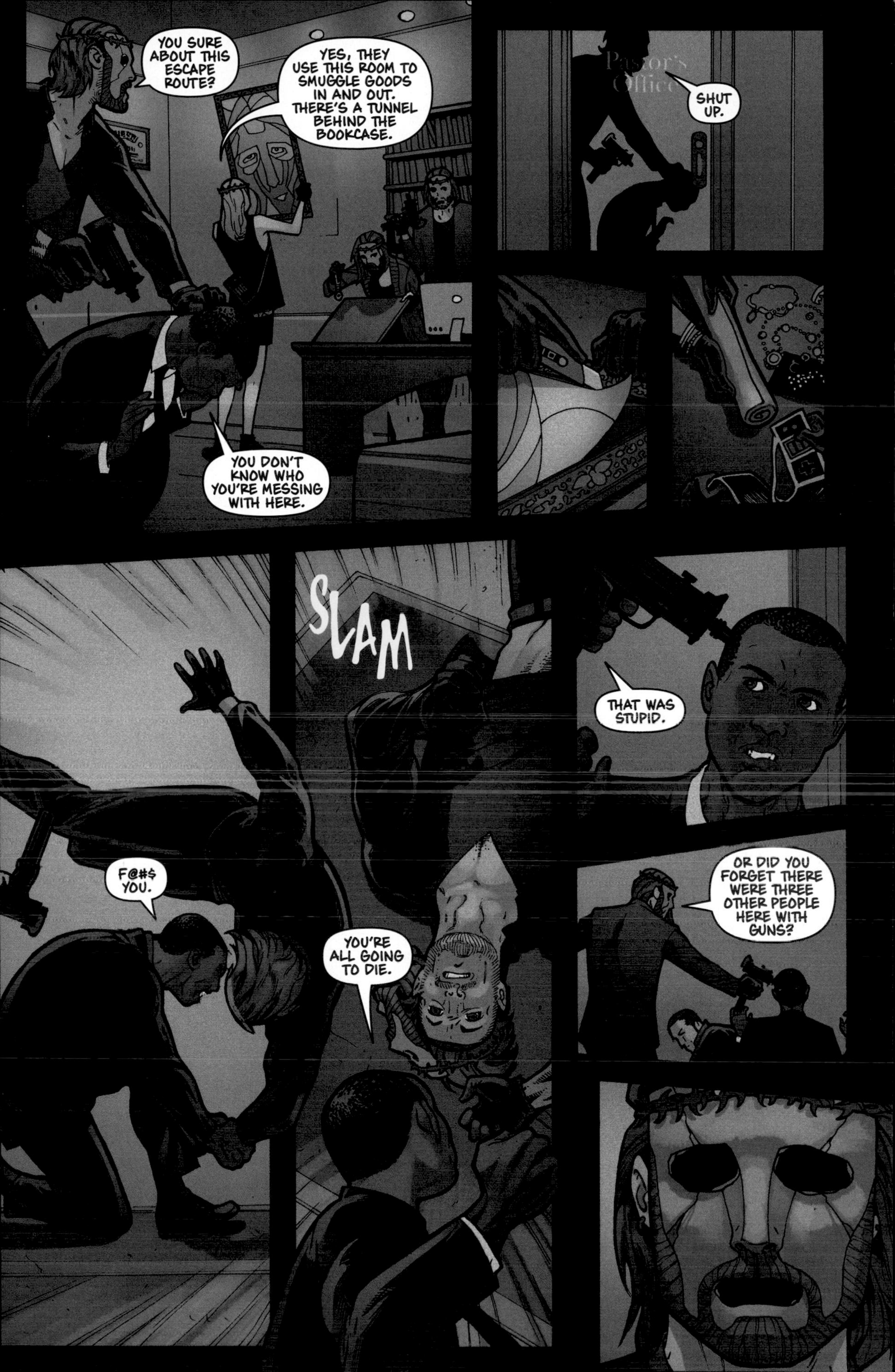
YOU SURE ABOUT THIS ESCAPE ROUTE?
YES, THEY USE THIS ROOM TO SMUGGLE GOODS IN AND OUT. THERE'S A TUNNEL BEHIND THE BOOKCASE.
YOU DON'T KNOW WHO YOU'RE MESSING WITH HERE.
Pastor's Office
SHUT UP.
SLAM
F@#$ YOU.
YOU'RE ALL GOING TO DIE.
THAT WAS STUPID.
OR DID YOU FORGET THERE WERE THREE OTHER PEOPLE HERE WITH GUNS?

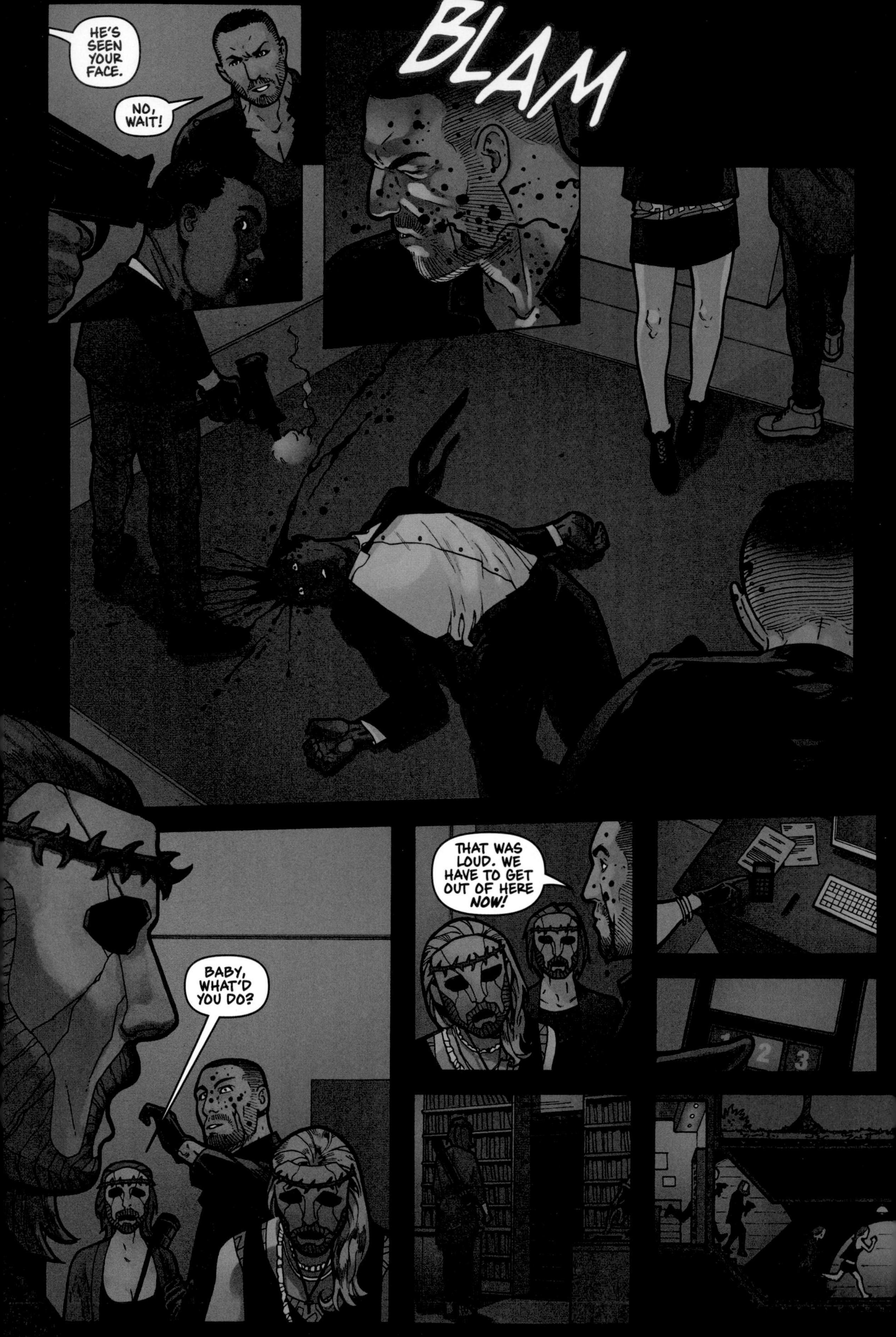
HE'S SEEN YOUR FACE.
NO, WAIT!
BLAM
BABY, WHAT'D YOU DO?
THAT WAS LOUD. WE HAVE TO GET OUT OF HERE NOW!
2
3

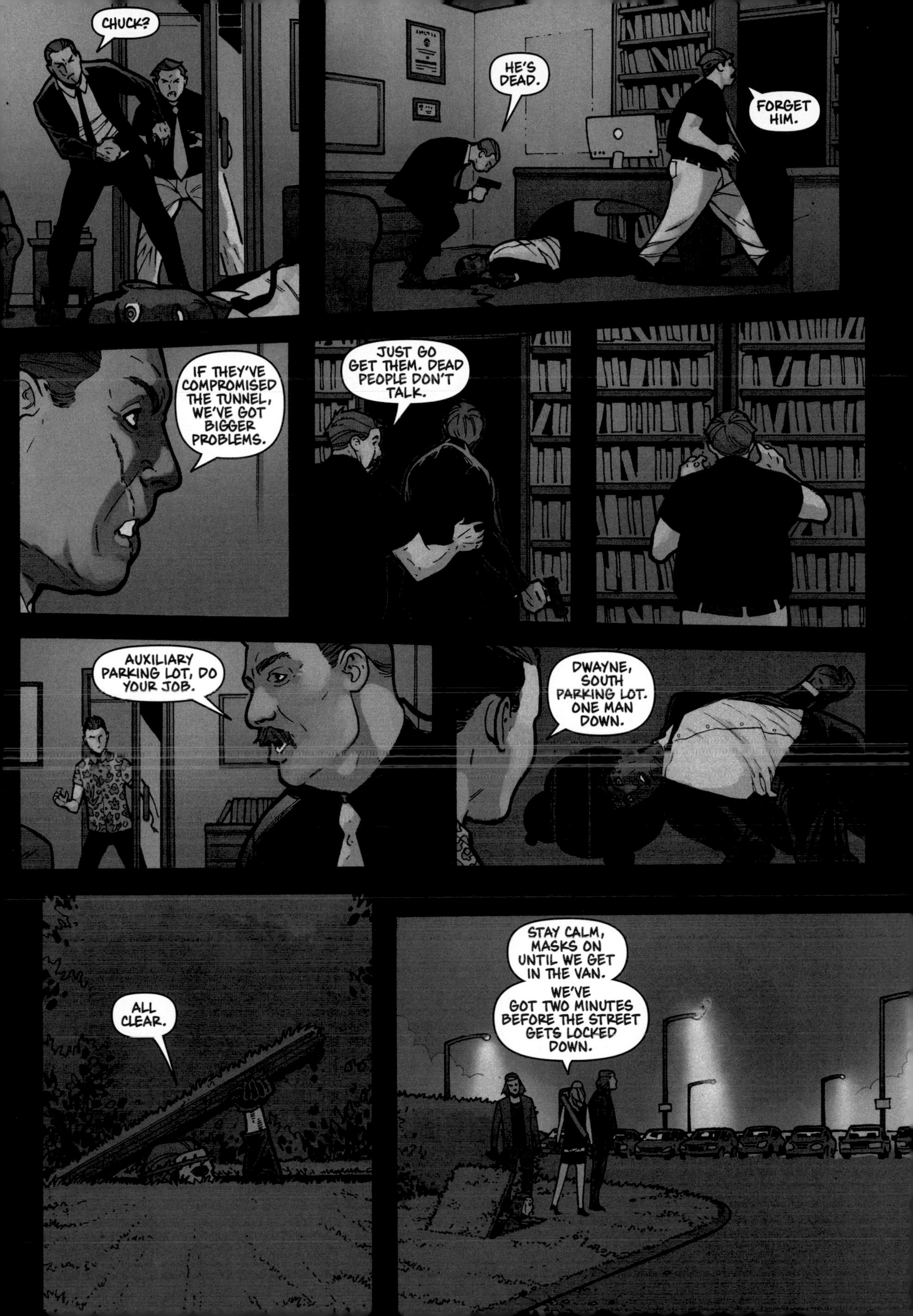
CHUCK?
HE'S DEAD.
FORGET HIM.
IF THEY'VE COMPROMISED THE TUNNEL, WE'VE GOT BIGGER PROBLEMS.
JUST GO GET THEM. DEAD PEOPLE DON'T TALK.
AUXILIARY PARKING LOT, DO YOUR JOB.
DWAYNE, SOUTH PARKING LOT. ONE MAN DOWN.
ALL CLEAR.
STAY CALM, MASKS ON UNTIL WE GET IN THE VAN.
WE'VE GOT TWO MINUTES BEFORE THE STREET GETS LOCKED DOWN.

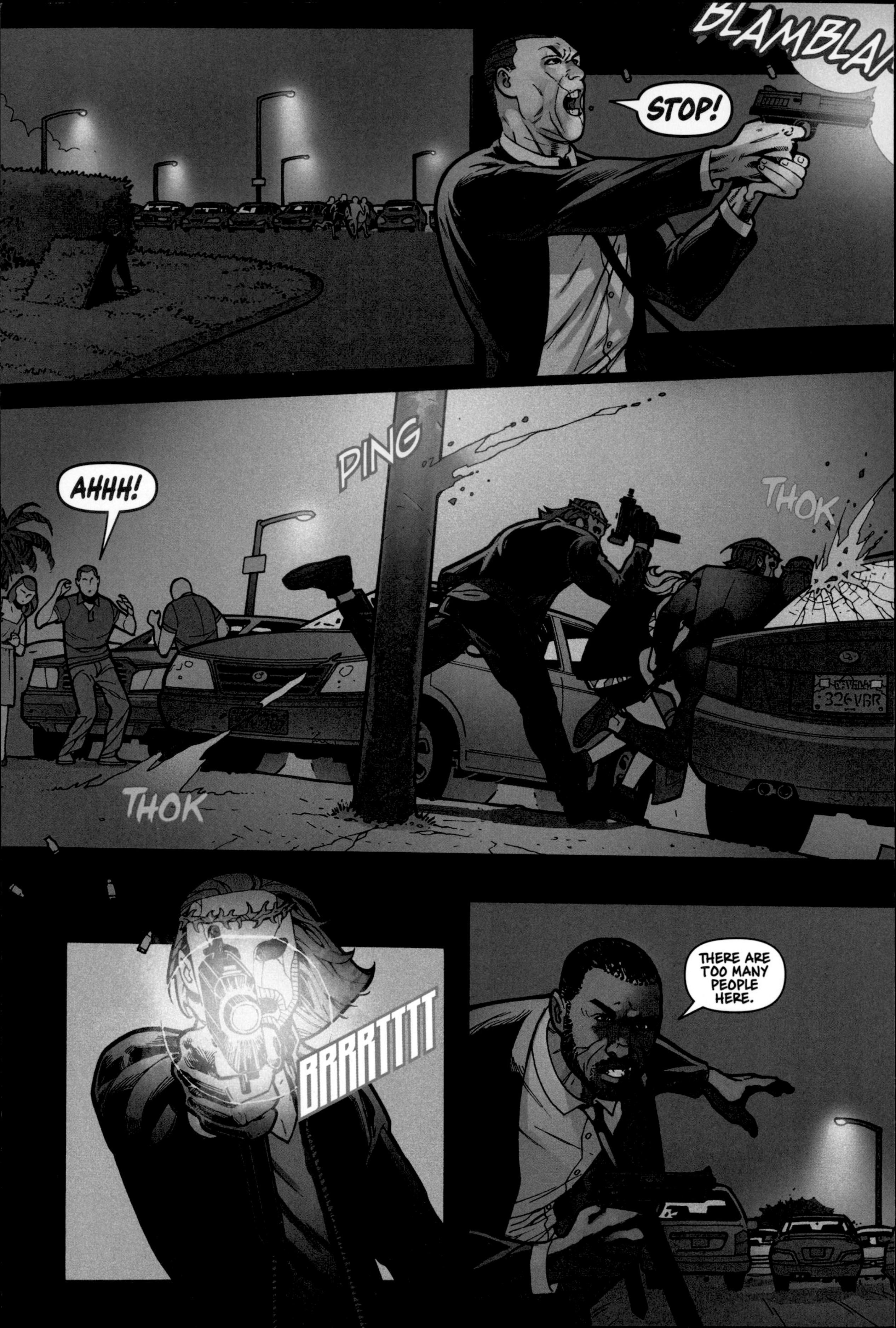

BLAMBLAM
STOP!
AHHH!
PING
THOK
THOK
BRRRTTTT
THERE ARE TOO MANY PEOPLE HERE.

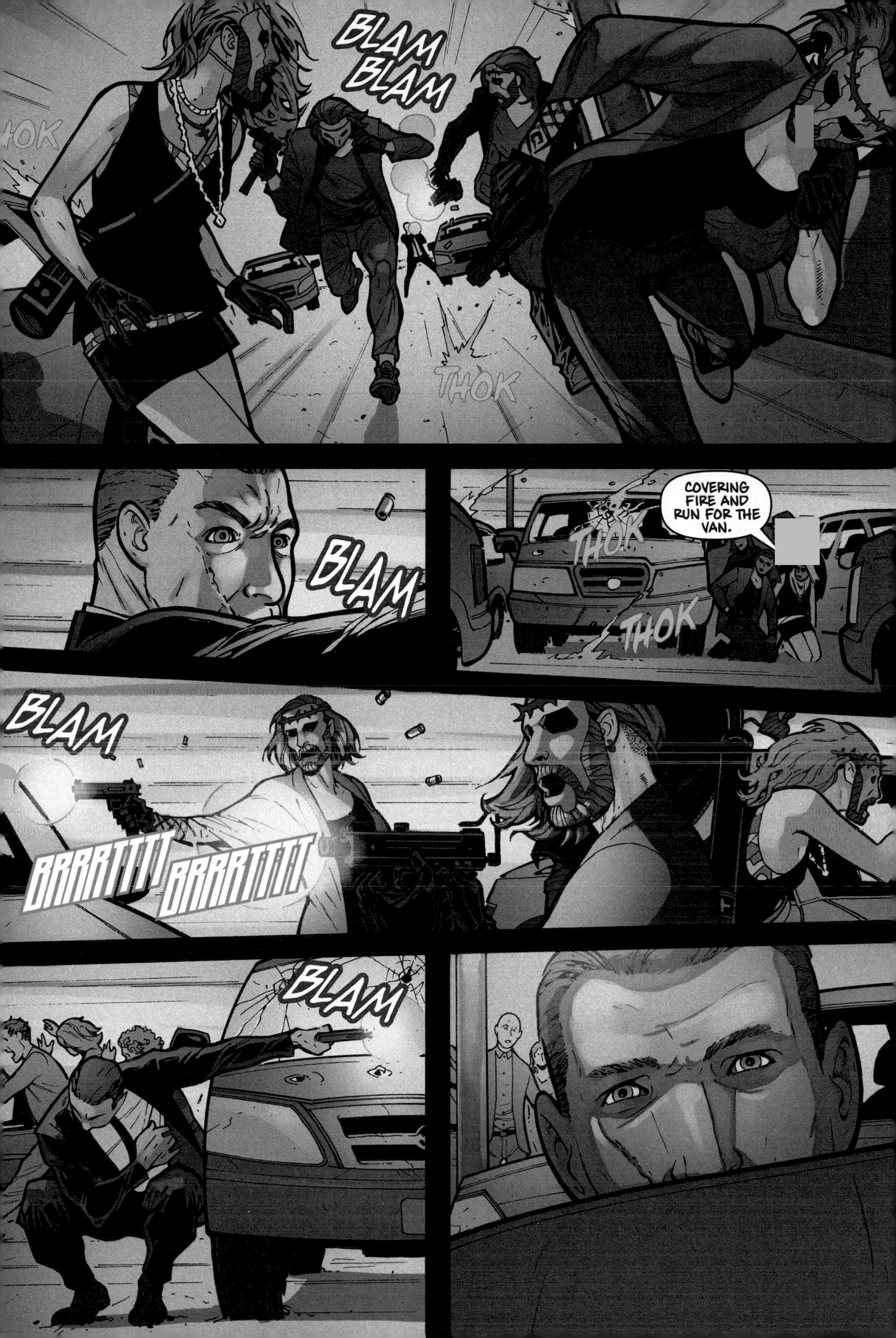
BLAM BLAM
THOK
BLAM
COVERING FIRE AND RUN FOR THE VAN.
THOK
THOK
BLAM
BRRRTTTT BRRRTTTT
BLAM

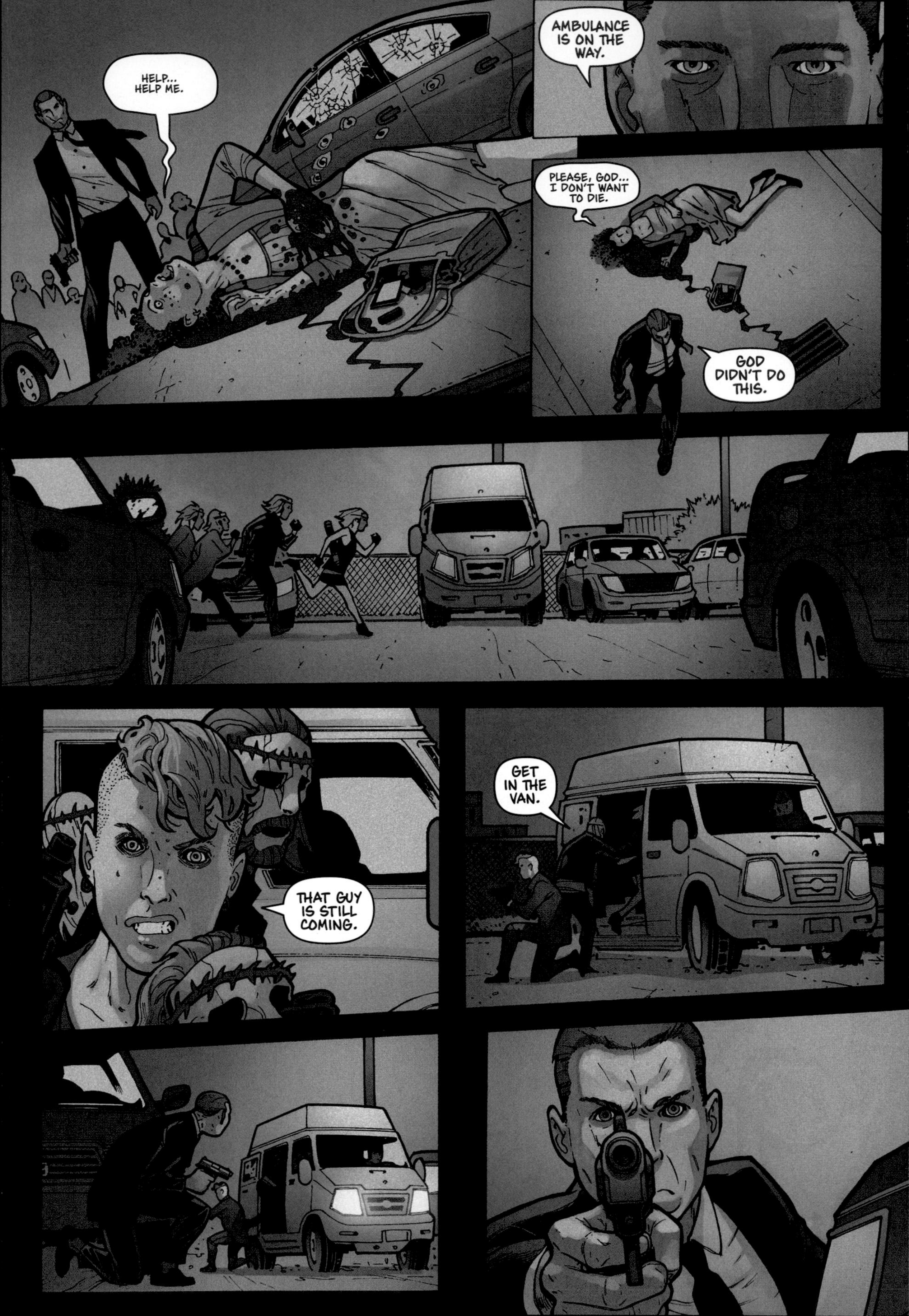
HELP... HELP ME.
AMBULANCE IS ON THE WAY.
PLEASE, GOD... I DON'T WANT TO DIE.
GOD DIDN'T DO THIS.
THAT GUY IS STILL COMING.
GET IN THE VAN.

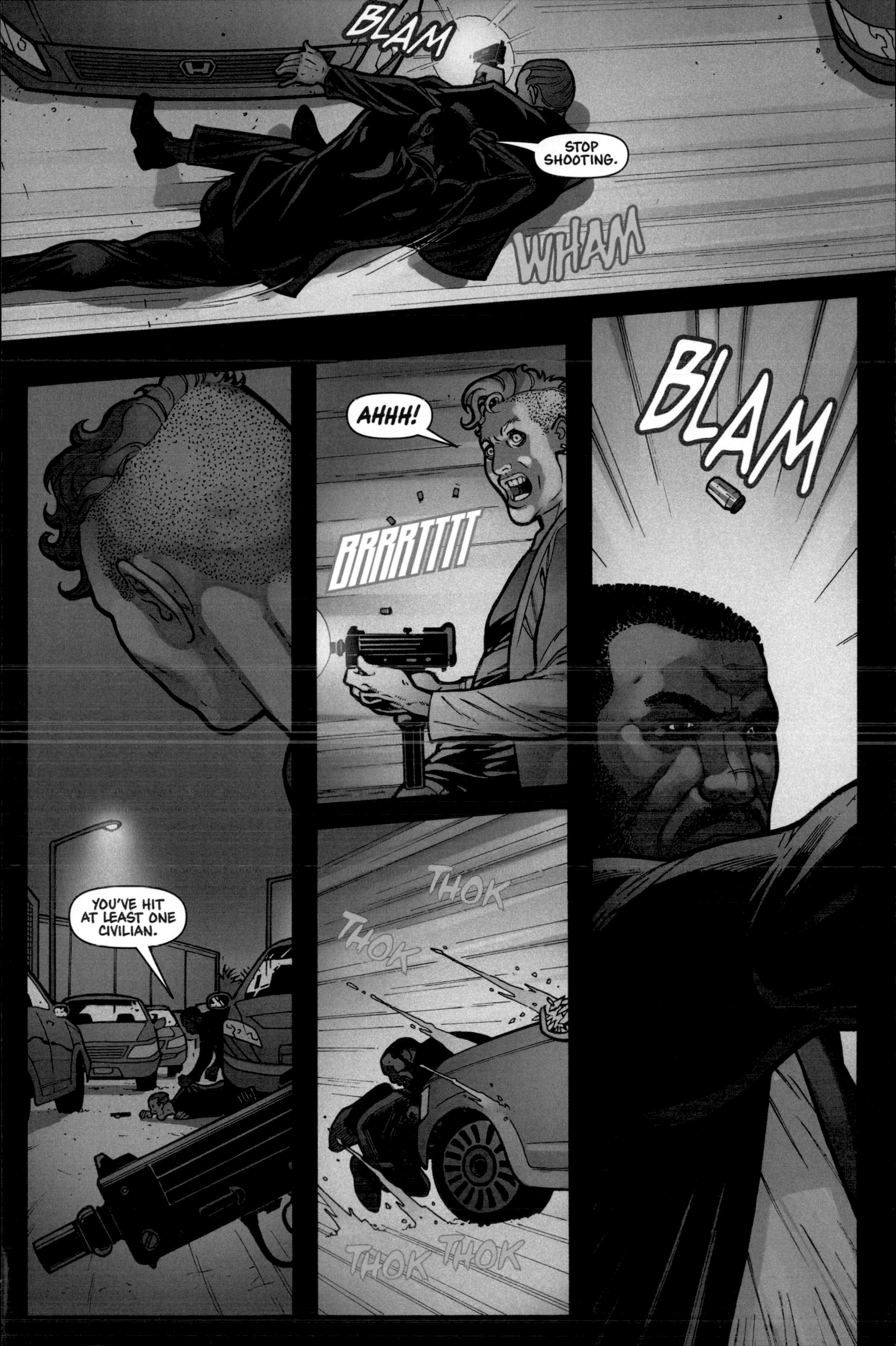
BLAM
STOP SHOOTING.
WHAM
AHHH!
BRRRTTTT
BLAM
YOU'VE HIT AT LEAST ONE CIVILIAN.
THOK
THOK
THOK
THOK

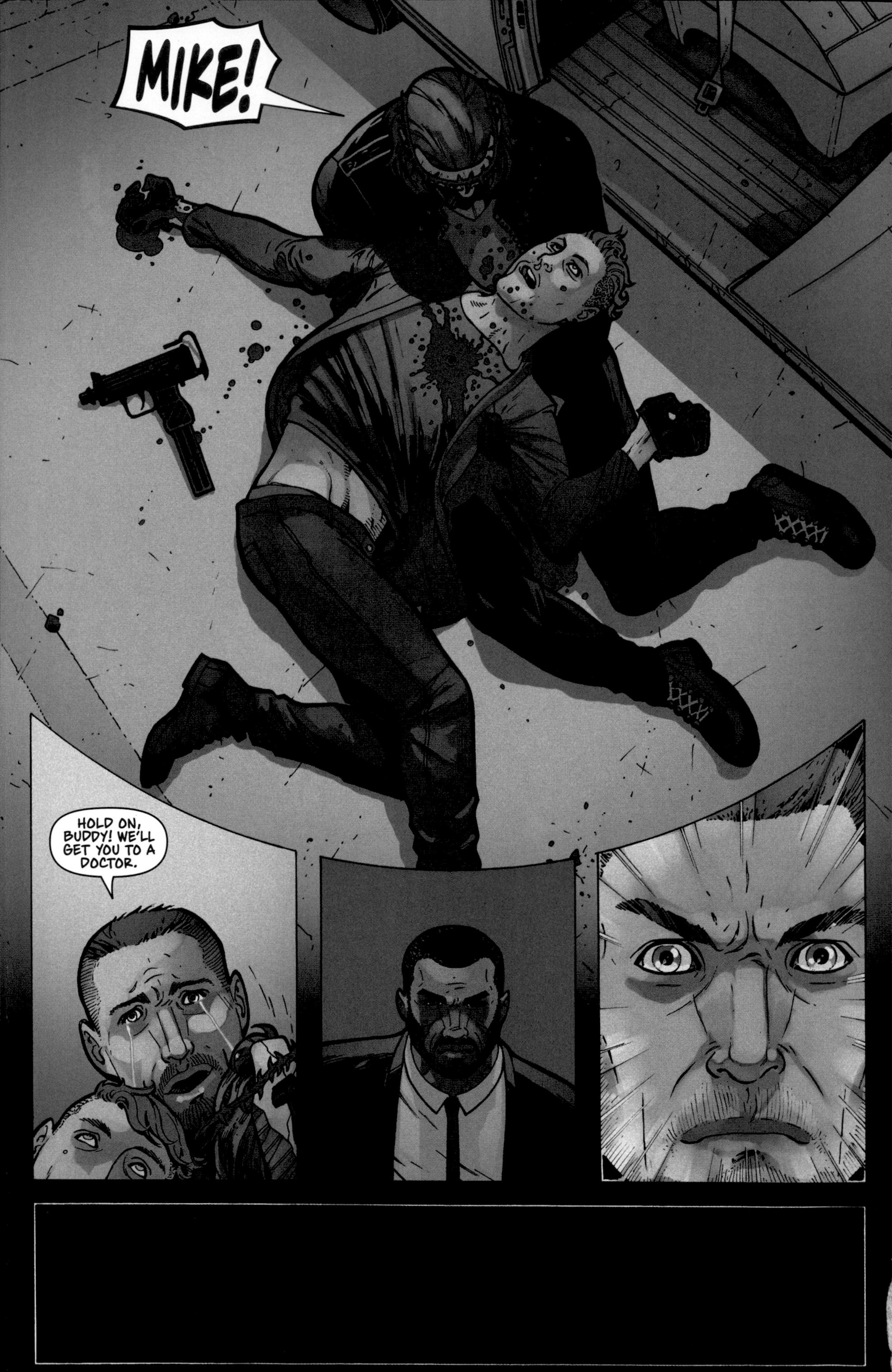
MIKE!
HOLD ON, BUDDY! WE'LL GET YOU TO A DOCTOR.

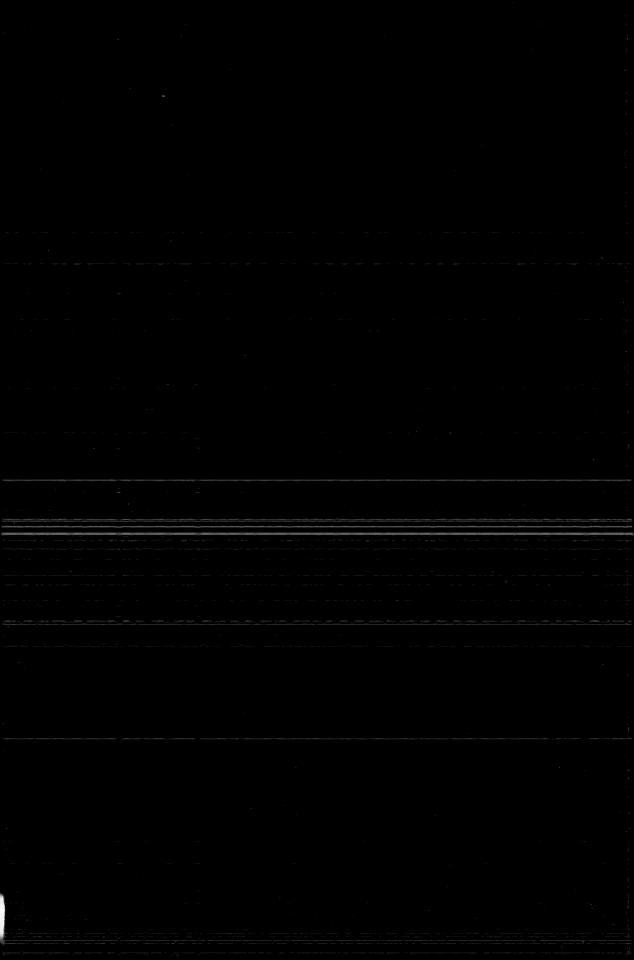

CHAPTER 4

PHILIPPIANS 4:13 (NKJV)

"I CAN DO ALL THINGS THROUGH CHRIST
WHO STRENGTHENS ME."

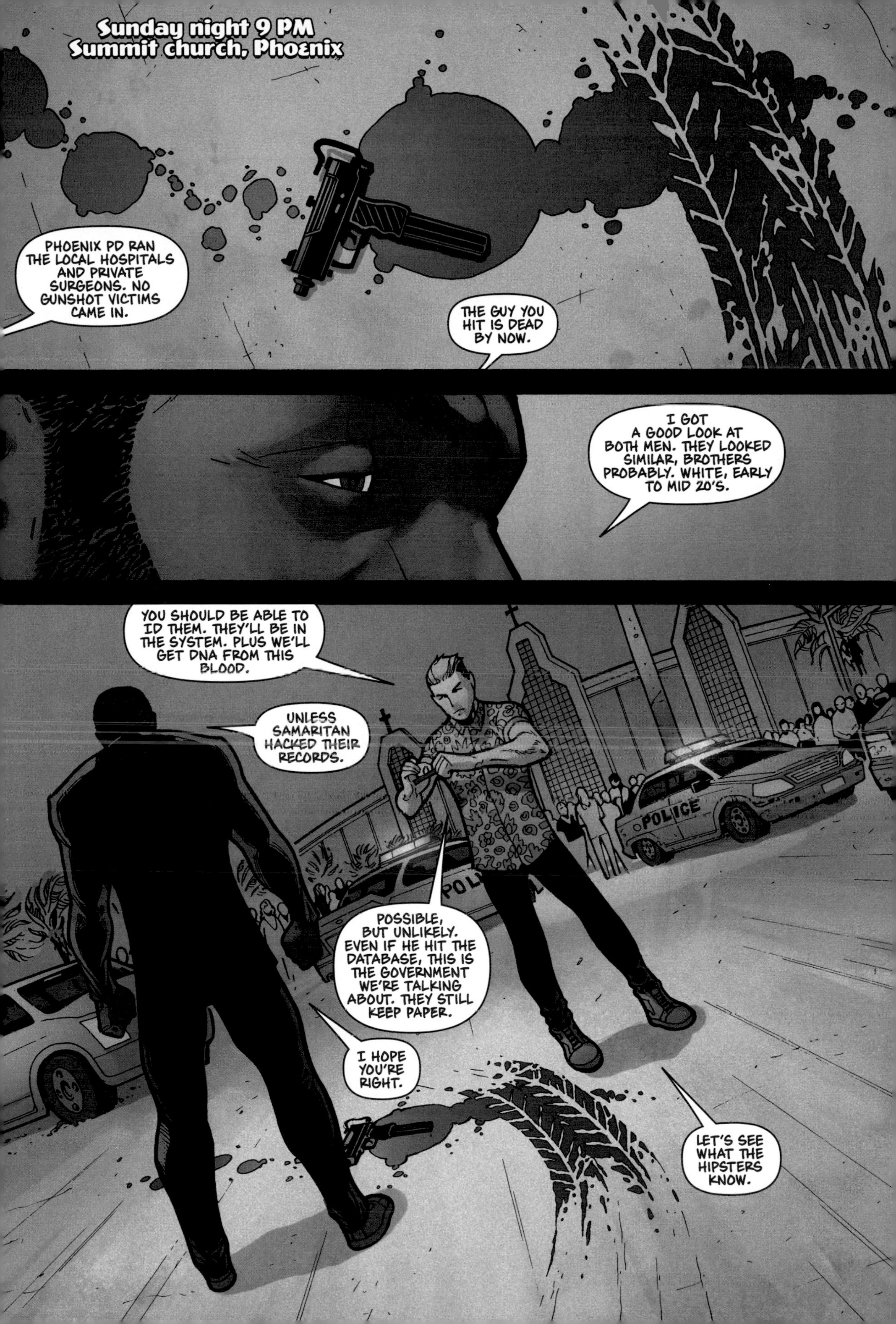
Sunday night 9 PM
Summit church, Phoenix
PHOENIX PD RAN THE LOCAL HOSPITALS AND PRIVATE SURGEONS. NO GUNSHOT VICTIMS CAME IN.
THE GUY YOU HIT IS DEAD BY NOW.
I GOT A GOOD LOOK AT BOTH MEN. THEY LOOKED SIMILAR, BROTHERS PROBABLY. WHITE, EARLY TO MID 20'S.
YOU SHOULD BE ABLE TO ID THEM. THEY'LL BE IN THE SYSTEM. PLUS WE'LL GET DNA FROM THIS BLOOD.
UNLESS SAMARITAN HACKED THEIR RECORDS.
POSSIBLE, BUT UNLIKELY. EVEN IF HE HIT THE DATABASE, THIS IS THE GOVERNMENT WE'RE TALKING ABOUT. THEY STILL KEEP PAPER.
I HOPE YOU'RE RIGHT.
LET'S SEE WHAT THE HIPSTERS KNOW.
POLICE

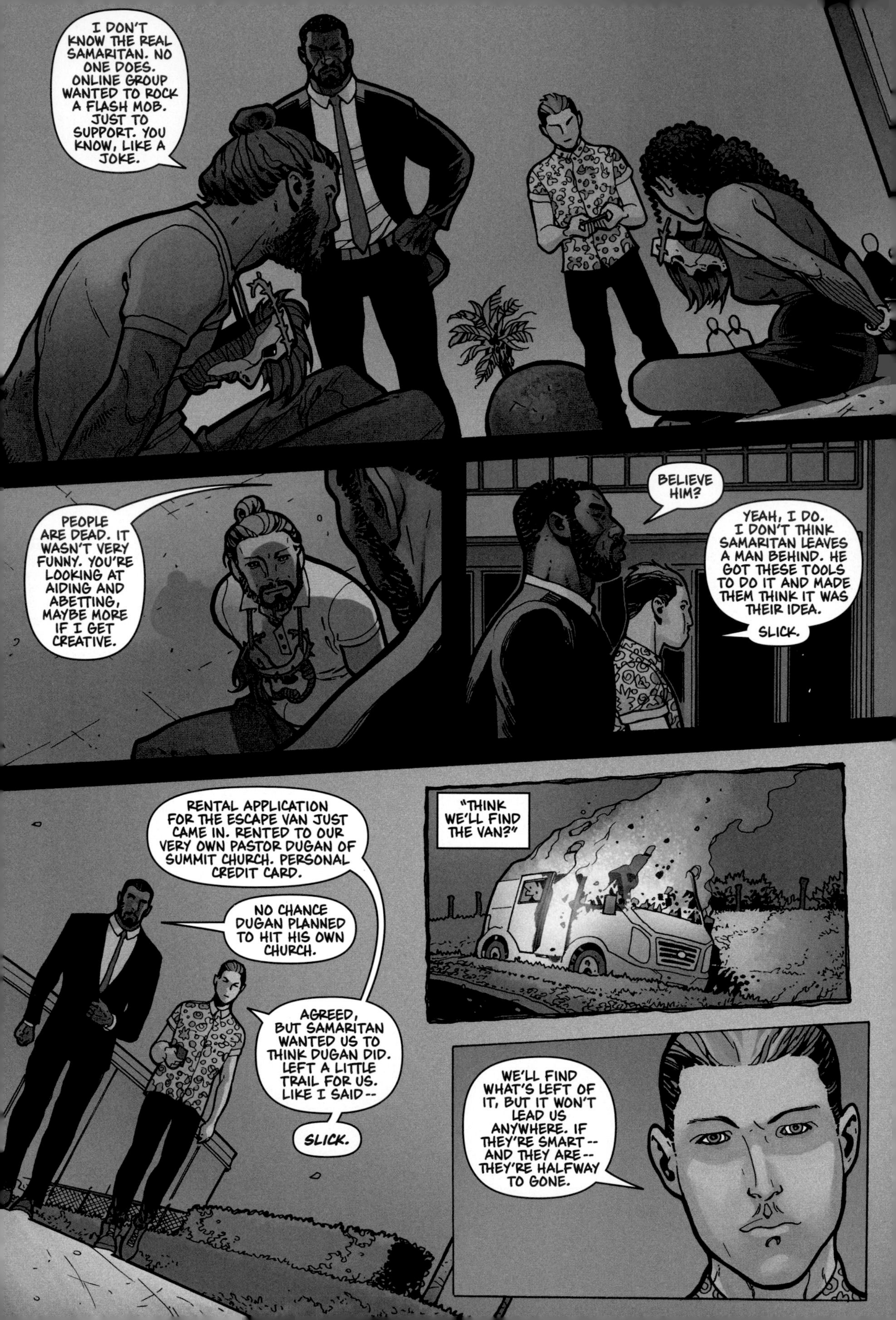
I DON'T KNOW THE REAL SAMARITAN. NO ONE DOES. ONLINE GROUP WANTED TO ROCK A FLASH MOB. JUST TO SUPPORT. YOU KNOW, LIKE A JOKE.
PEOPLE ARE DEAD. IT WASN'T VERY FUNNY. YOU'RE LOOKING AT AIDING AND ABETTING, MAYBE MORE IF I GET CREATIVE.
BELIEVE HIM?
YEAH, I DO. I DON'T THINK SAMARITAN LEAVES A MAN BEHIND. HE GOT THESE TOOLS TO DO IT AND MADE THEM THINK IT WAS THEIR IDEA.
SLICK.
RENTAL APPLICATION FOR THE ESCAPE VAN JUST CAME IN. RENTED TO OUR VERY OWN PASTOR DUGAN OF SUMMIT CHURCH. PERSONAL CREDIT CARD.
NO CHANCE DUGAN PLANNED TO HIT HIS OWN CHURCH.
AGREED, BUT SAMARITAN WANTED US TO THINK DUGAN DID. LEFT A LITTLE TRAIL FOR US. LIKE I SAID --
SLICK.
"THINK WE'LL FIND THE VAN?"
WE'LL FIND WHAT'S LEFT OF IT, BUT IT WON'T LEAD US ANYWHERE. IF THEY'RE SMART -- AND THEY ARE -- THEY'RE HALFWAY TO GONE.

WHOOPWHOOPWHOOPWHOOP
WHOOPWHOOPWHOOP

WHOOP WHOOP WHOOP WHOOP

WHAT?

THIS IS
A JOKE,
RIGHT?

BECAUSE IF IT'S NOT A JOKE
THEN I HAVE FOUR WOUNDED
CIVILIANS, A DEAD SECURITY
GUARD -- FATHER OF TWO, BY
THE WAY -- AND ANOTHER
SECURITY GUARD THAT SAYS YOU
SHOT A SINGLE MOM IN
A PARKING LOT.

I LIKE YOU, DWAYNE.
I KEPT QUANTICO OFF
YOU FOR THE LAST MONTH,
BECAUSE YOU WANTED
SAMARITAN AND I OWED
YOU THAT.

BUT I DO
NOT OWE YOU
THIS.

AH F#$@,
THIS CAN'T
BE GOOD.

THE GUARD
SHOT THE WOMAN.
I SHOT ONE OF
SAMARITAN'S. THE
BALLISTICS WILL
TRACK. GOT A GOOD
LOOK AT BOTH
MEN TOO.

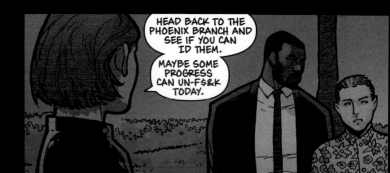

HEAD BACK TO THE
PHOENIX BRANCH AND
SEE IF YOU CAN
ID THEM.

MAYBE SOME
PROGRESS
CAN UN-F$&K
TODAY.

MIKE.

I CAN'T TAKE THIS.

WE'RE ALMOST TO THE CLINIC.

DON'T BOTHER. HE'S DEAD.

I'M SO SORRY, KYLE.

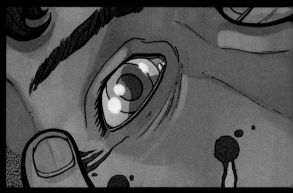

COME SIT UP HERE. TALK TO ME.

LEAVE ME ALONE.

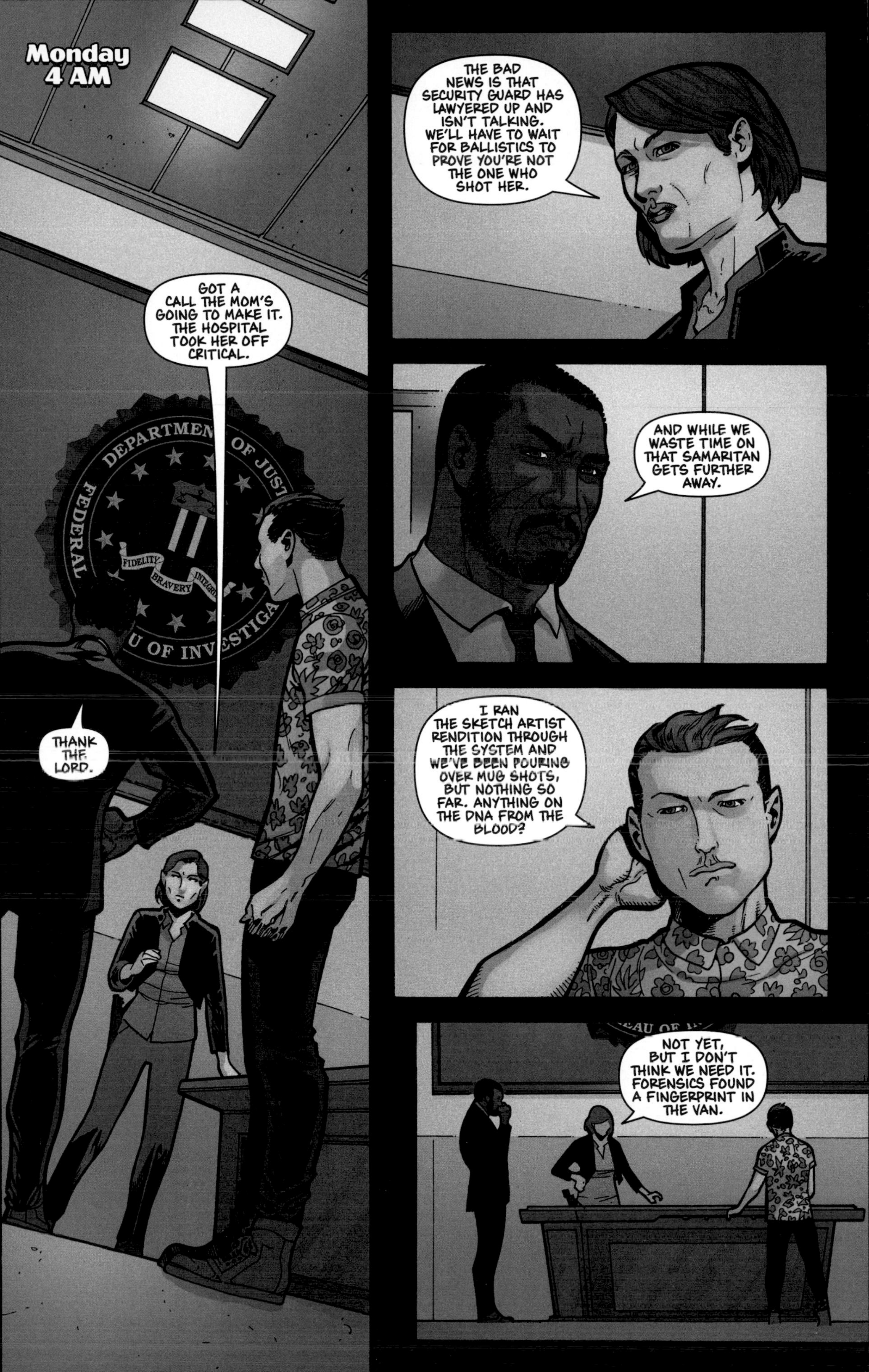

Monday 4 AM
GOT A CALL THE MOM'S GOING TO MAKE IT. THE HOSPITAL TOOK HER OFF CRITICAL.
THANK THE LORD.
DEPARTMENT OF JUSTICE FEDERAL BUREAU OF INVESTIGATION
FIDELITY BRAVERY INTEGRITY
THE BAD NEWS IS THAT SECURITY GUARD HAS LAWYERED UP AND ISN'T TALKING. WE'LL HAVE TO WAIT FOR BALLISTICS TO PROVE YOU'RE NOT THE ONE WHO SHOT HER.
AND WHILE WE WASTE TIME ON THAT SAMARITAN GETS FURTHER AWAY.
I RAN THE SKETCH ARTIST RENDITION THROUGH THE SYSTEM AND WE'VE BEEN POURING OVER MUG SHOTS, BUT NOTHING SO FAR. ANYTHING ON THE DNA FROM THE BLOOD?
NOT YET, BUT I DON'T THINK WE NEED IT. FORENSICS FOUND A FINGERPRINT IN THE VAN.

THEY TORCHED IT, BUT THEY WERE IN A HURRY AND F%$#ED UP. CAME BACK TO A RACHEL MARVIN.

RECOGNIZE HER?

NO.

ADOC Number: 43
SID Number: 23441H44
Name: MARVIN, RACHEL
Racial ID: Hispanic
Sex: Female
Hair: Black

ADOC RECORD

2008: Petty theft
2010: Driving under the influ
2011: Narcotics possession
2014: Disorderly Conduct

TWENTY-THREE, HISPANIC. MATCHES THE "MEXICAN GIRL" DESCRIPTION. LIST OF PETTY OFFENSES, MAINLY DRUG RELATED. STATE RAISED THROUGH PROGRAMS, BUT NO JAIL TIME.

THE BOYFRIEND'S NAME IS MICHAEL ARAMAN.

ADOC
SID N
Name
Racia
Sex:
Hair:
Eyes:
Heigh
Weigh
DOB:

AND HE'S GOT AN OLDER BROTHER KYLE.

A
S
N
R
S
H
E
H
W
D

THOSE ARE THE TWO GUYS I SAW. THE YOUNGER ONE IS THE ONE I SHOT.

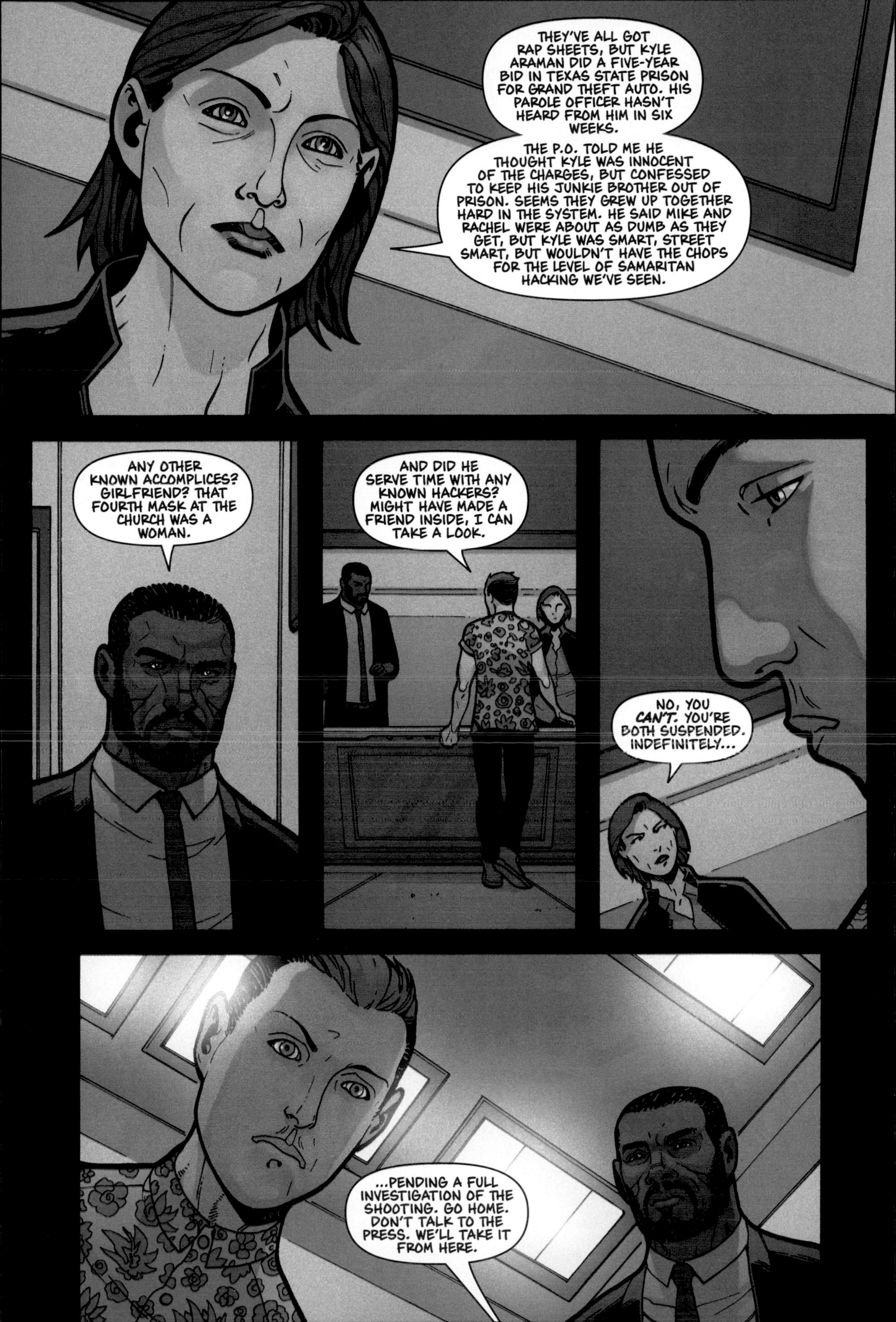
THEY'VE ALL GOT RAP SHEETS, BUT KYLE ARAMAN DID A FIVE-YEAR BID IN TEXAS STATE PRISON FOR GRAND THEFT AUTO. HIS PAROLE OFFICER HASN'T HEARD FROM HIM IN SIX WEEKS.
THE P.O. TOLD ME HE THOUGHT KYLE WAS INNOCENT OF THE CHARGES, BUT CONFESSED TO KEEP HIS JUNKIE BROTHER OUT OF PRISON. SEEMS THEY GREW UP TOGETHER HARD IN THE SYSTEM. HE SAID MIKE AND RACHEL WERE ABOUT AS DUMB AS THEY GET, BUT KYLE WAS SMART, STREET SMART, BUT WOULDN'T HAVE THE CHOPS FOR THE LEVEL OF SAMARITAN HACKING WE'VE SEEN.
ANY OTHER KNOWN ACCOMPLICES? GIRLFRIEND? THAT FOURTH MASK AT THE CHURCH WAS A WOMAN.
AND DID HE SERVE TIME WITH ANY KNOWN HACKERS? MIGHT HAVE MADE A FRIEND INSIDE, I CAN TAKE A LOOK.
NO, YOU *CAN'T.* YOU'RE BOTH SUSPENDED. INDEFINITELY...
...PENDING A FULL INVESTIGATION OF THE SHOOTING. GO HOME. DON'T TALK TO THE PRESS. WE'LL TAKE IT FROM HERE.

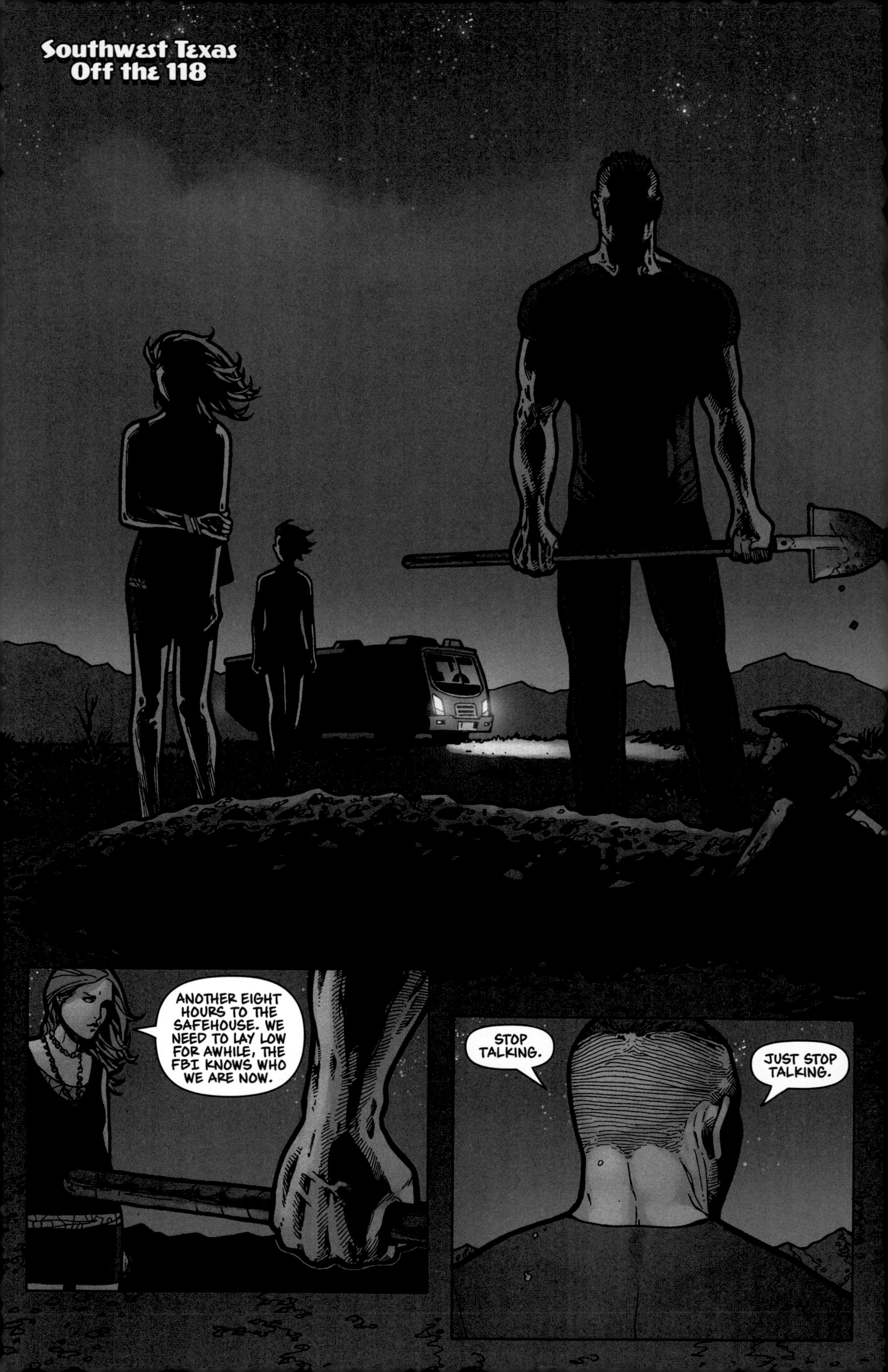
Southwest Texas
Off the 118
ANOTHER EIGHT HOURS TO THE SAFEHOUSE. WE NEED TO LAY LOW FOR AWHILE, THE FBI KNOWS WHO WE ARE NOW.
STOP TALKING.
JUST STOP TALKING.

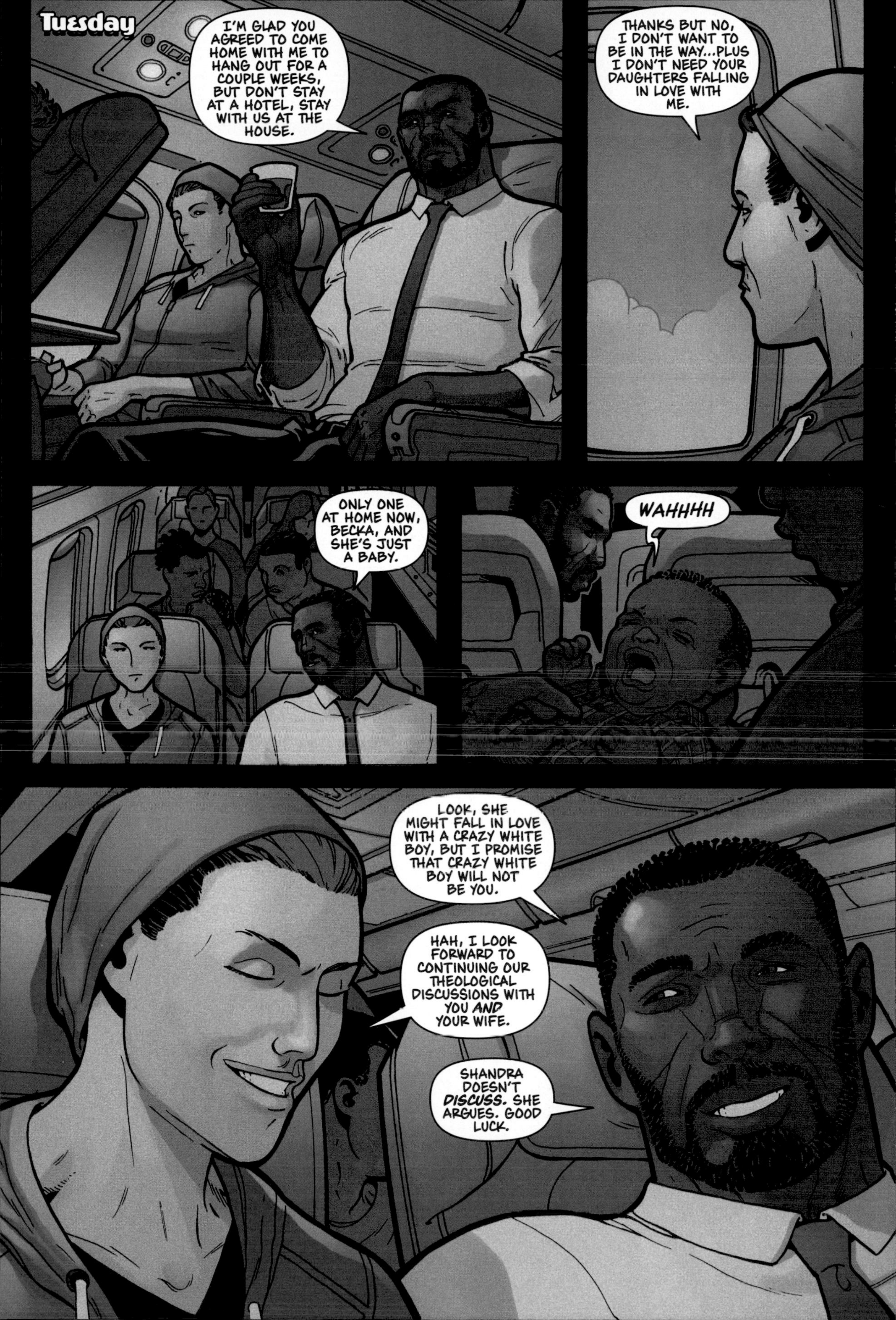
Tuesday
I'M GLAD YOU AGREED TO COME HOME WITH ME TO HANG OUT FOR A COUPLE WEEKS, BUT DON'T STAY AT A HOTEL, STAY WITH US AT THE HOUSE.
THANKS BUT NO, I DON'T WANT TO BE IN THE WAY...PLUS I DON'T NEED YOUR DAUGHTERS FALLING IN LOVE WITH ME.
ONLY ONE AT HOME NOW, BECKA, AND SHE'S JUST A BABY.
WAHHHH
LOOK, SHE MIGHT FALL IN LOVE WITH A CRAZY WHITE BOY, BUT I PROMISE THAT CRAZY WHITE BOY WILL NOT BE YOU.
HAH, I LOOK FORWARD TO CONTINUING OUR THEOLOGICAL DISCUSSIONS WITH YOU *AND* YOUR WIFE.
SHANDRA DOESN'T ***DISCUSS.*** SHE ARGUES. GOOD LUCK.

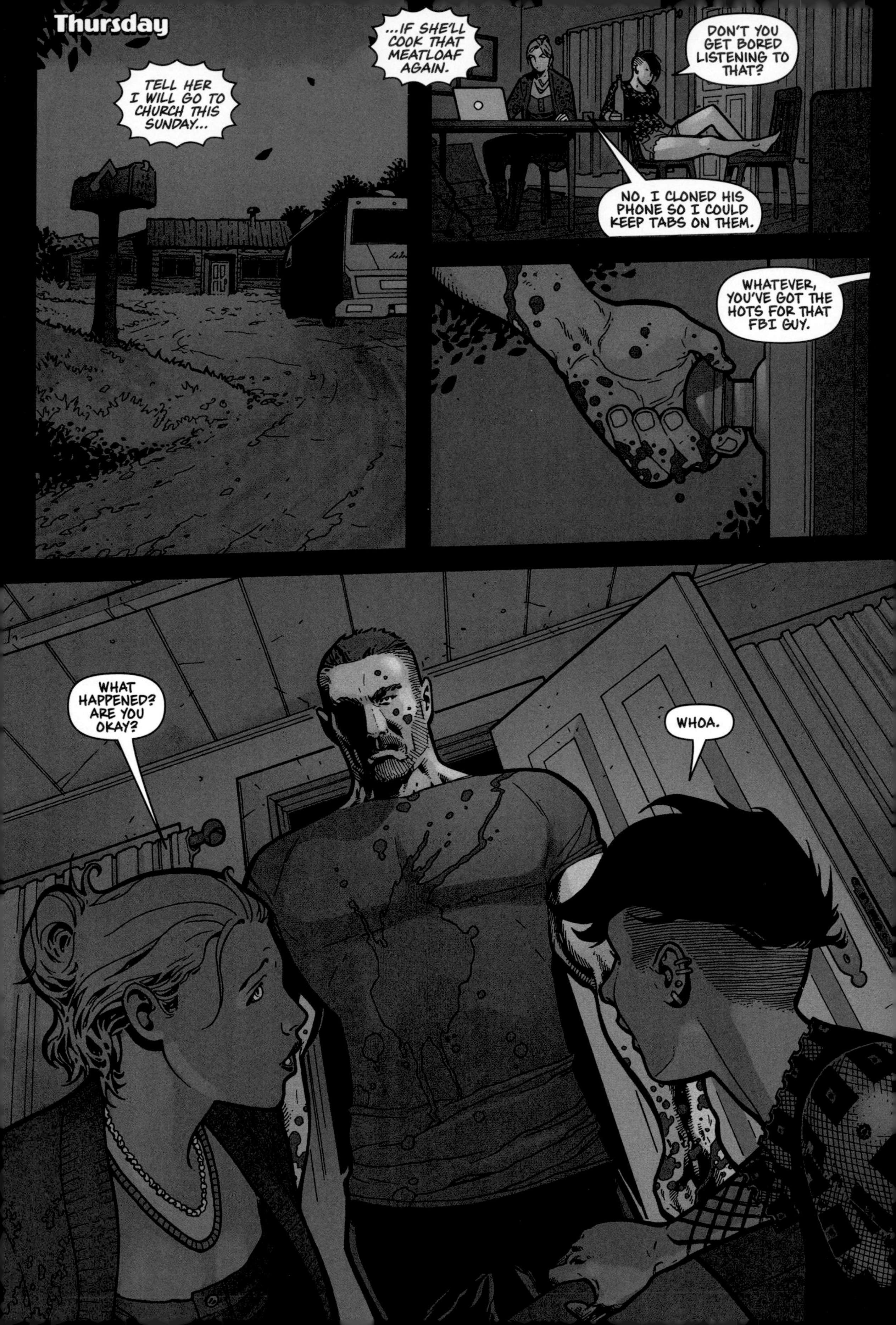
Thursday
TELL HER I WILL GO TO CHURCH THIS SUNDAY...
...IF SHE'LL COOK THAT MEATLOAF AGAIN.
DON'T YOU GET BORED LISTENING TO THAT?
NO, I CLONED HIS PHONE SO I COULD KEEP TABS ON THEM.
WHATEVER, YOU'VE GOT THE HOTS FOR THAT FBI GUY.
WHAT HAPPENED? ARE YOU OKAY?
WHOA.

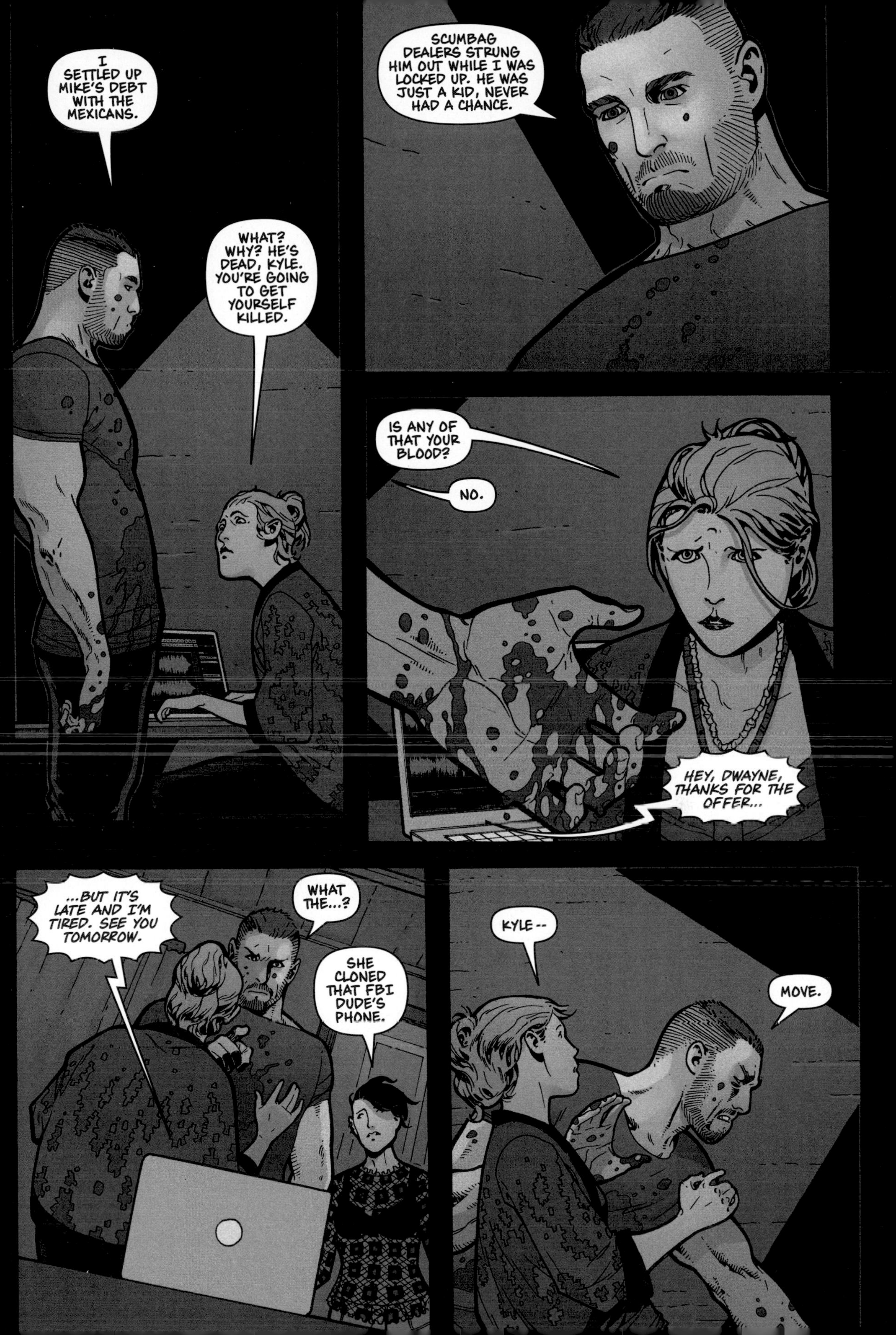
I SETTLED UP MIKE'S DEBT WITH THE MEXICANS.
SCUMBAG DEALERS STRUNG HIM OUT WHILE I WAS LOCKED UP. HE WAS JUST A KID, NEVER HAD A CHANCE.
WHAT? WHY? HE'S DEAD, KYLE. YOU'RE GOING TO GET YOURSELF KILLED.
IS ANY OF THAT YOUR BLOOD?
NO.
HEY, DWAYNE, THANKS FOR THE OFFER...
...BUT IT'S LATE AND I'M TIRED. SEE YOU TOMORROW.
WHAT THE...?
SHE CLONED THAT FBI DUDE'S PHONE.
KYLE --
MOVE.

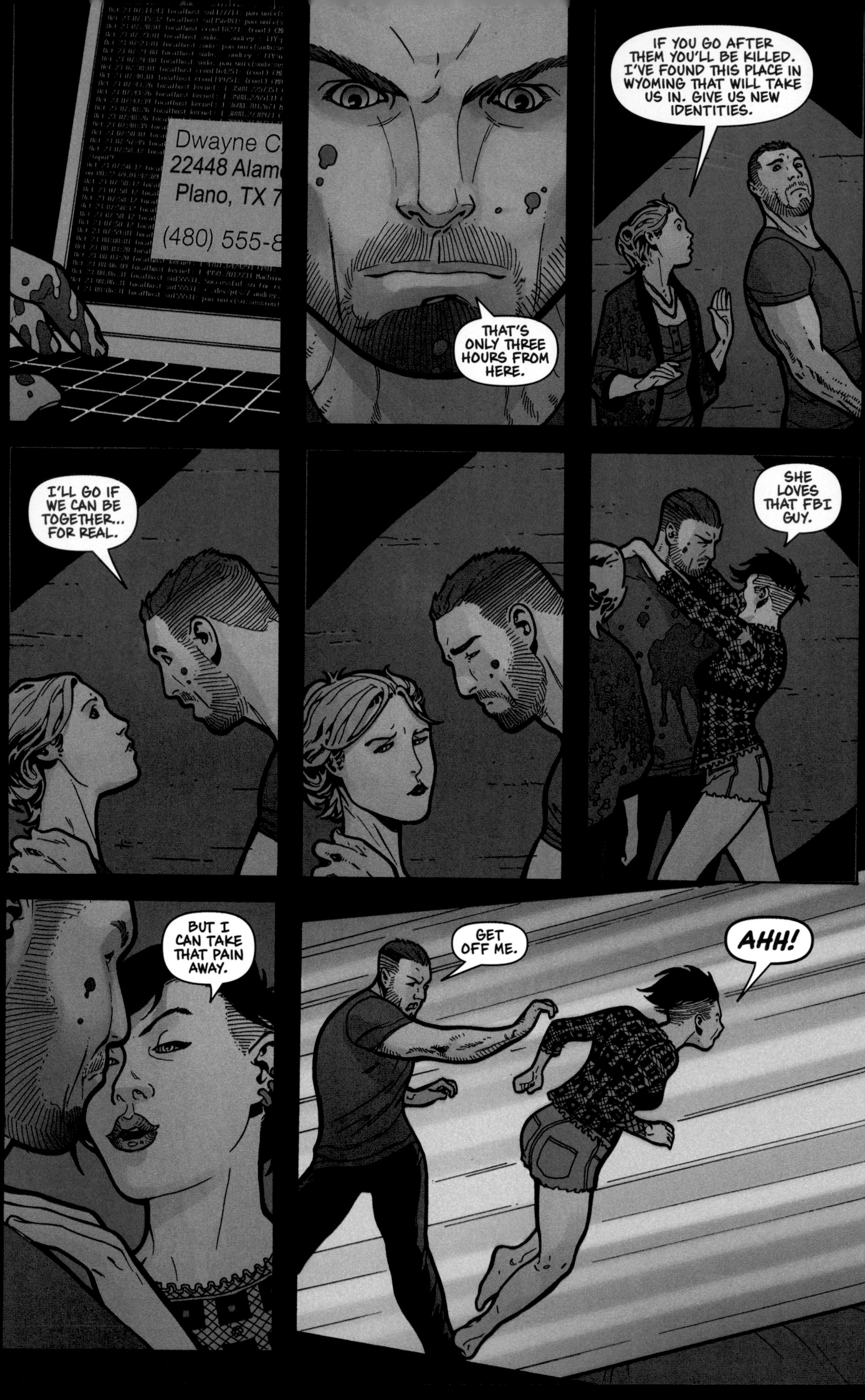
Dwayne C
22448 Alam
Plano, TX 7
(480) 555-8
THAT'S ONLY THREE HOURS FROM HERE.
IF YOU GO AFTER THEM YOU'LL BE KILLED. I'VE FOUND THIS PLACE IN WYOMING THAT WILL TAKE US IN. GIVE US NEW IDENTITIES.
I'LL GO IF WE CAN BE TOGETHER... FOR REAL.
SHE LOVES THAT FBI GUY.
BUT I CAN TAKE THAT PAIN AWAY.
GET OFF ME.
AHH!

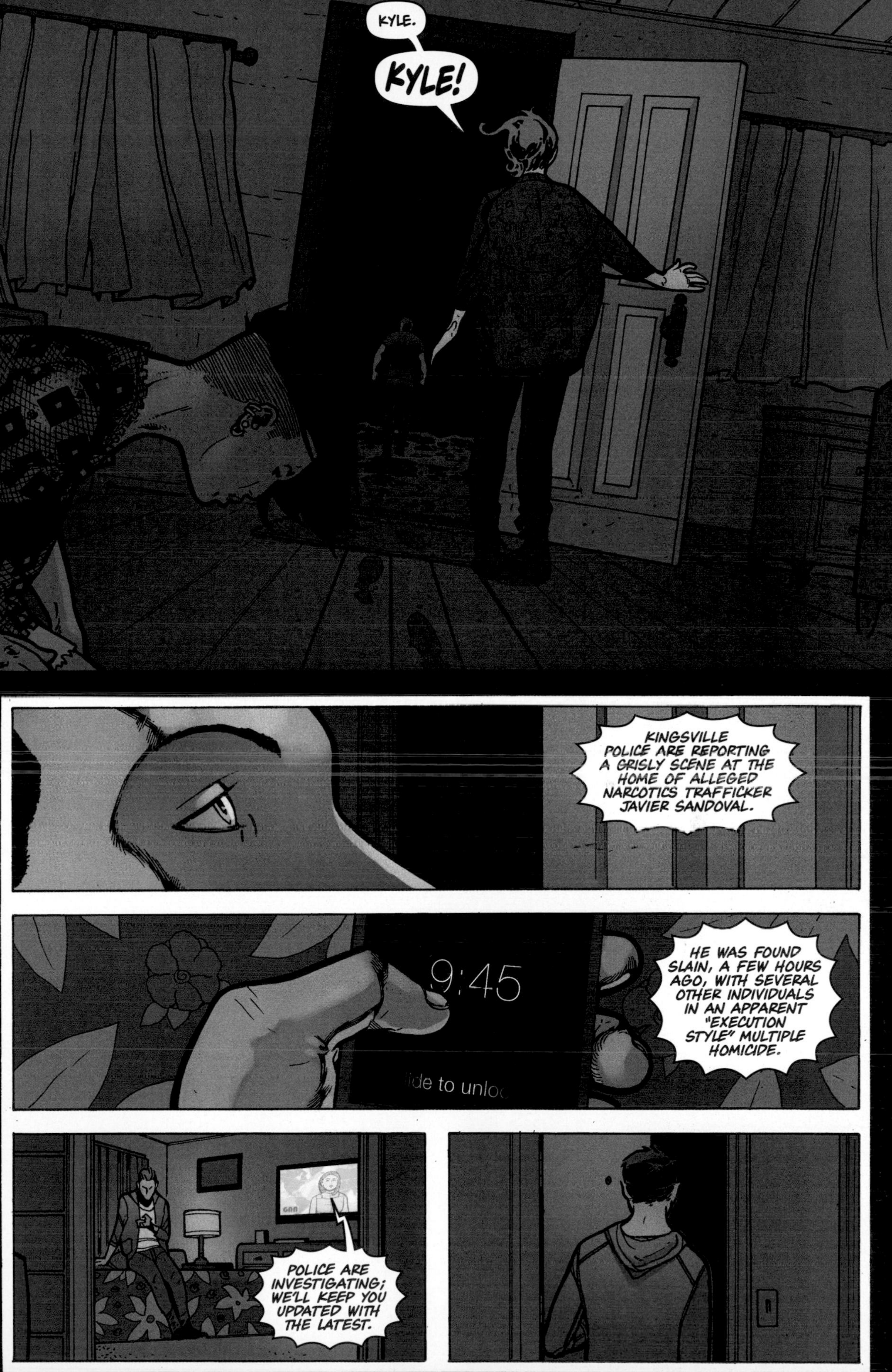
KYLE.
KYLE!
KINGSVILLE POLICE ARE REPORTING A GRISLY SCENE AT THE HOME OF ALLEGED NARCOTICS TRAFFICKER JAVIER SANDOVAL.
9:45
lide to unlo
HE WAS FOUND SLAIN, A FEW HOURS AGO, WITH SEVERAL OTHER INDIVIDUALS IN AN APPARENT "EXECUTION STYLE" MULTIPLE HOMICIDE.
POLICE ARE INVESTIGATING; WE'LL KEEP YOU UPDATED WITH THE LATEST.

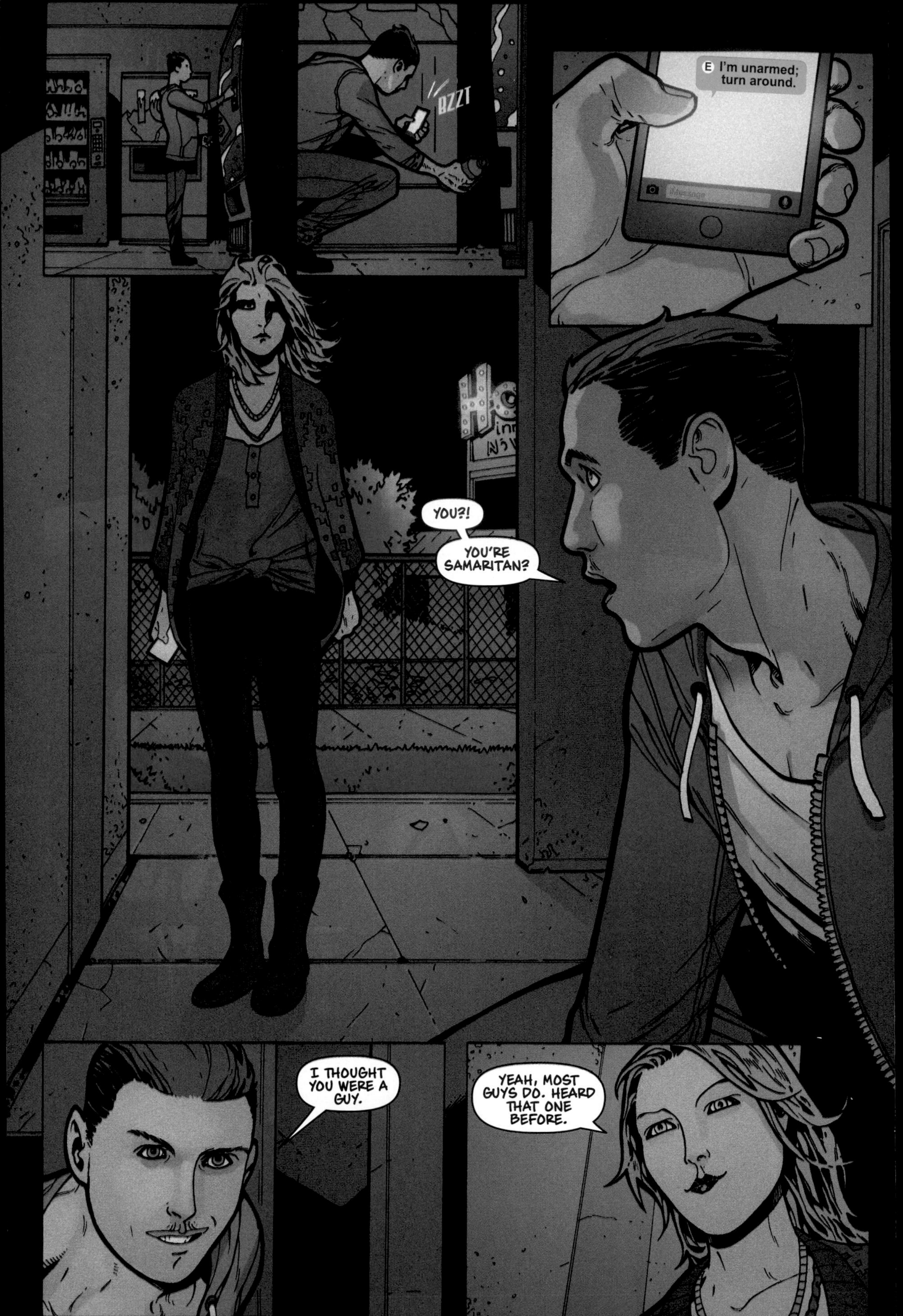
BZZT
E I'm unarmed; turn around.
iMessage
YOU?!
YOU'RE SAMARITAN?
I THOUGHT YOU WERE A GUY.
YEAH, MOST GUYS DO. HEARD THAT ONE BEFORE.

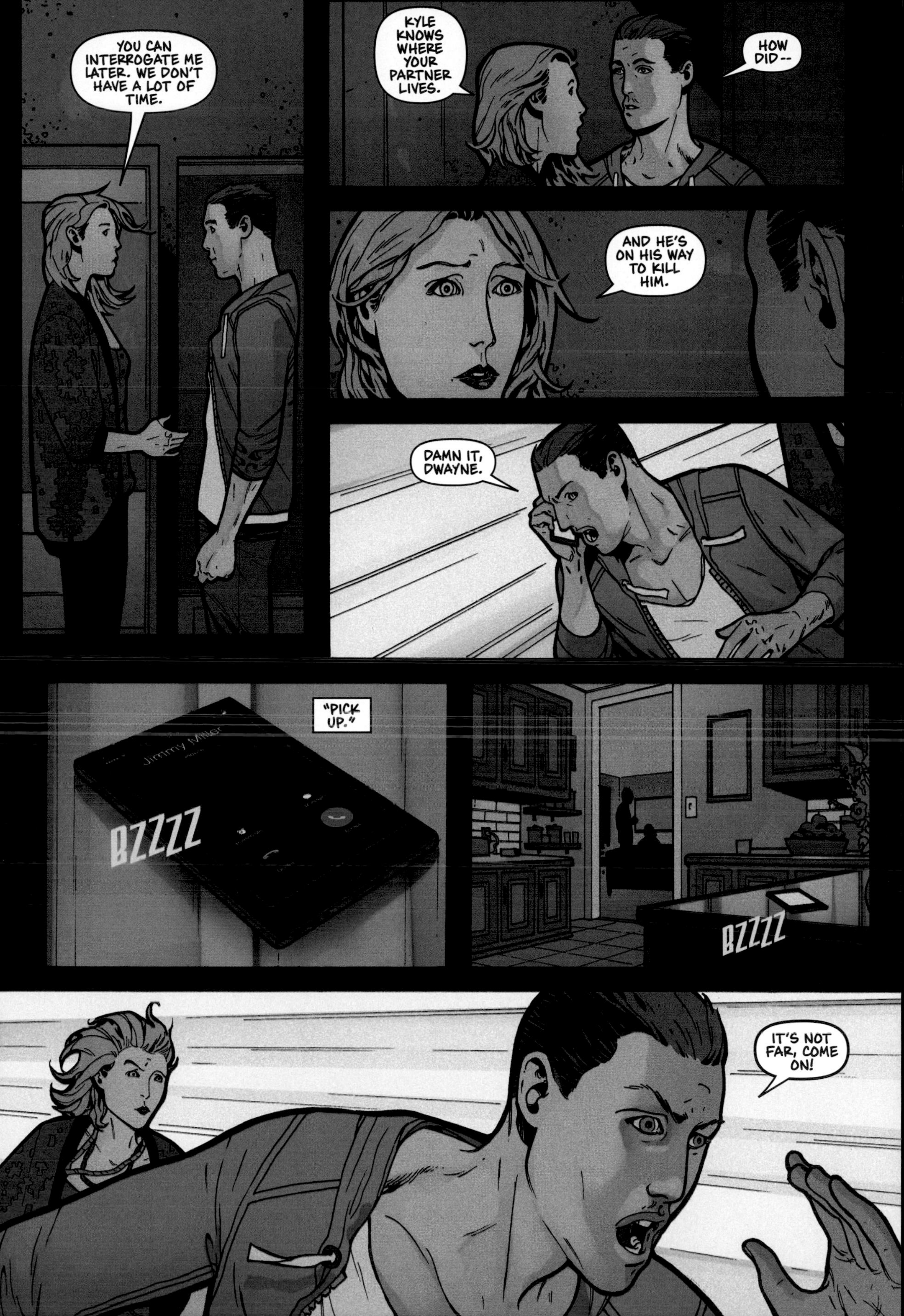
YOU CAN INTERROGATE ME LATER. WE DON'T HAVE A LOT OF TIME.
KYLE KNOWS WHERE YOUR PARTNER LIVES.
HOW DID--
AND HE'S ON HIS WAY TO KILL HIM.
DAMN IT, DWAYNE.
"PICK UP."
Jimmy Miller
BZZZZ
BZZZZ
IT'S NOT FAR, COME ON!

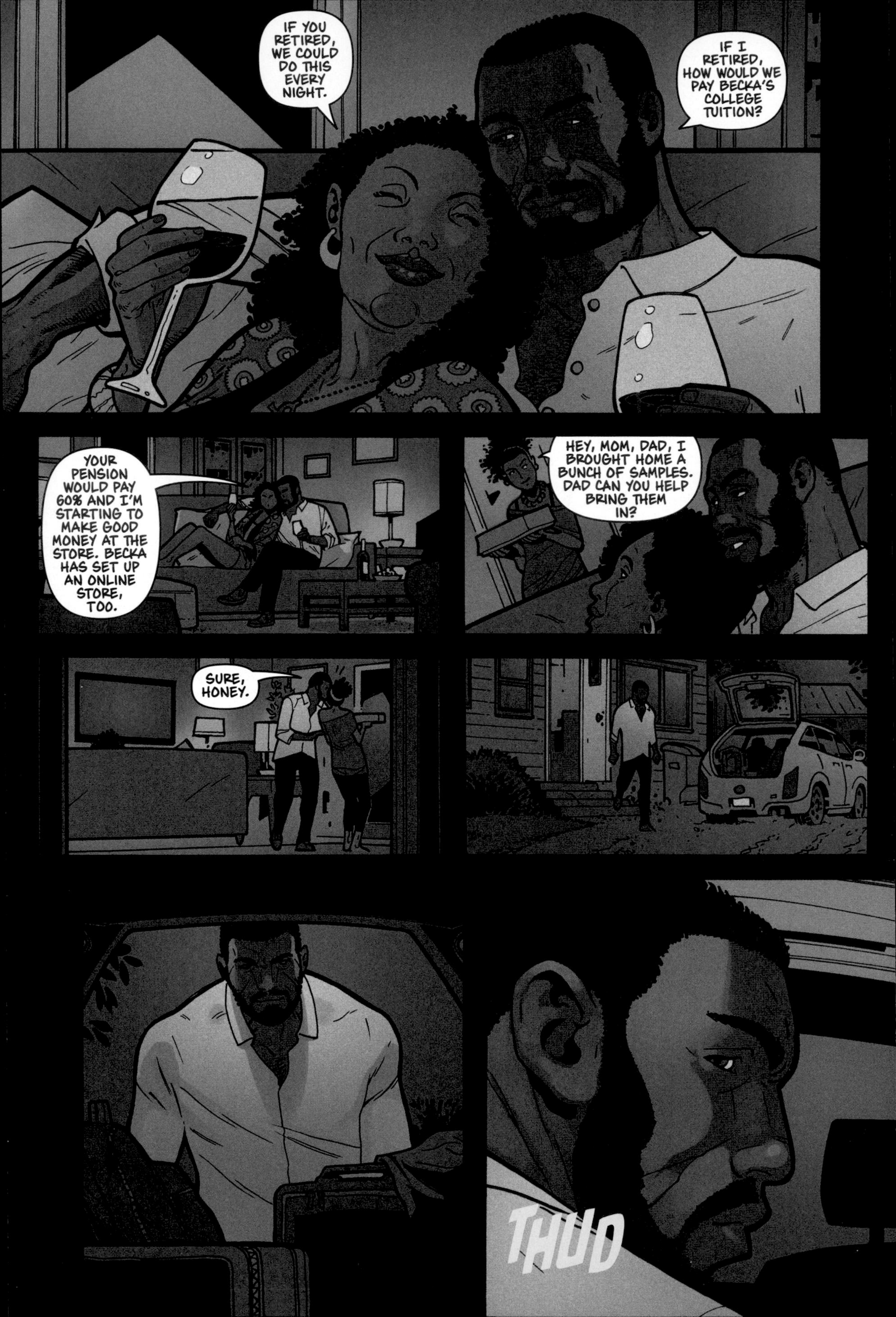
IF YOU RETIRED, WE COULD DO THIS EVERY NIGHT.
IF I RETIRED, HOW WOULD WE PAY BECKA'S COLLEGE TUITION?
YOUR PENSION WOULD PAY 60% AND I'M STARTING TO MAKE GOOD MONEY AT THE STORE. BECKA HAS SET UP AN ONLINE STORE, TOO.
HEY, MOM, DAD, I BROUGHT HOME A BUNCH OF SAMPLES. DAD CAN YOU HELP BRING THEM IN?
SURE, HONEY.
THUD

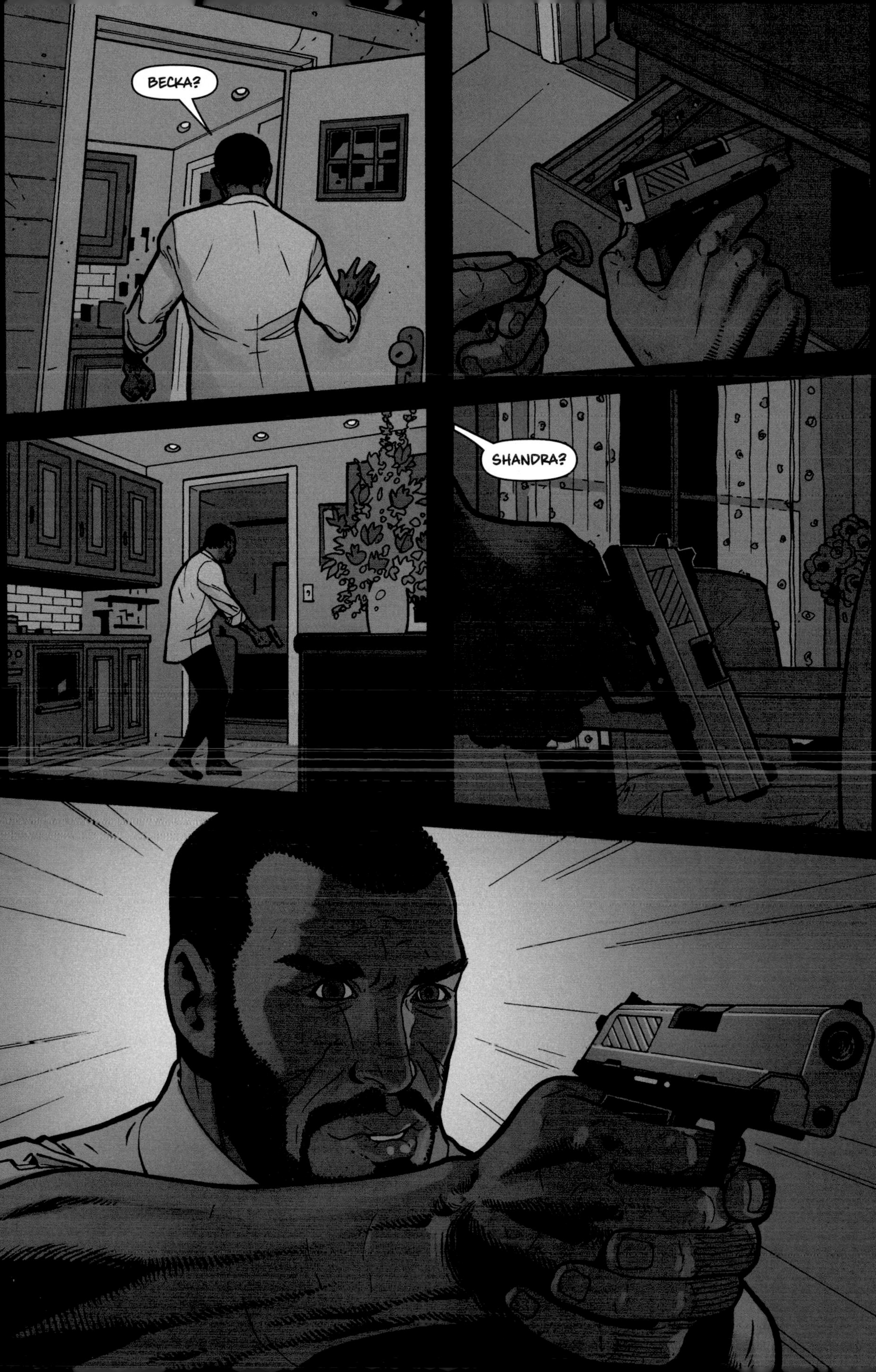
BECKA?
SHANDRA?

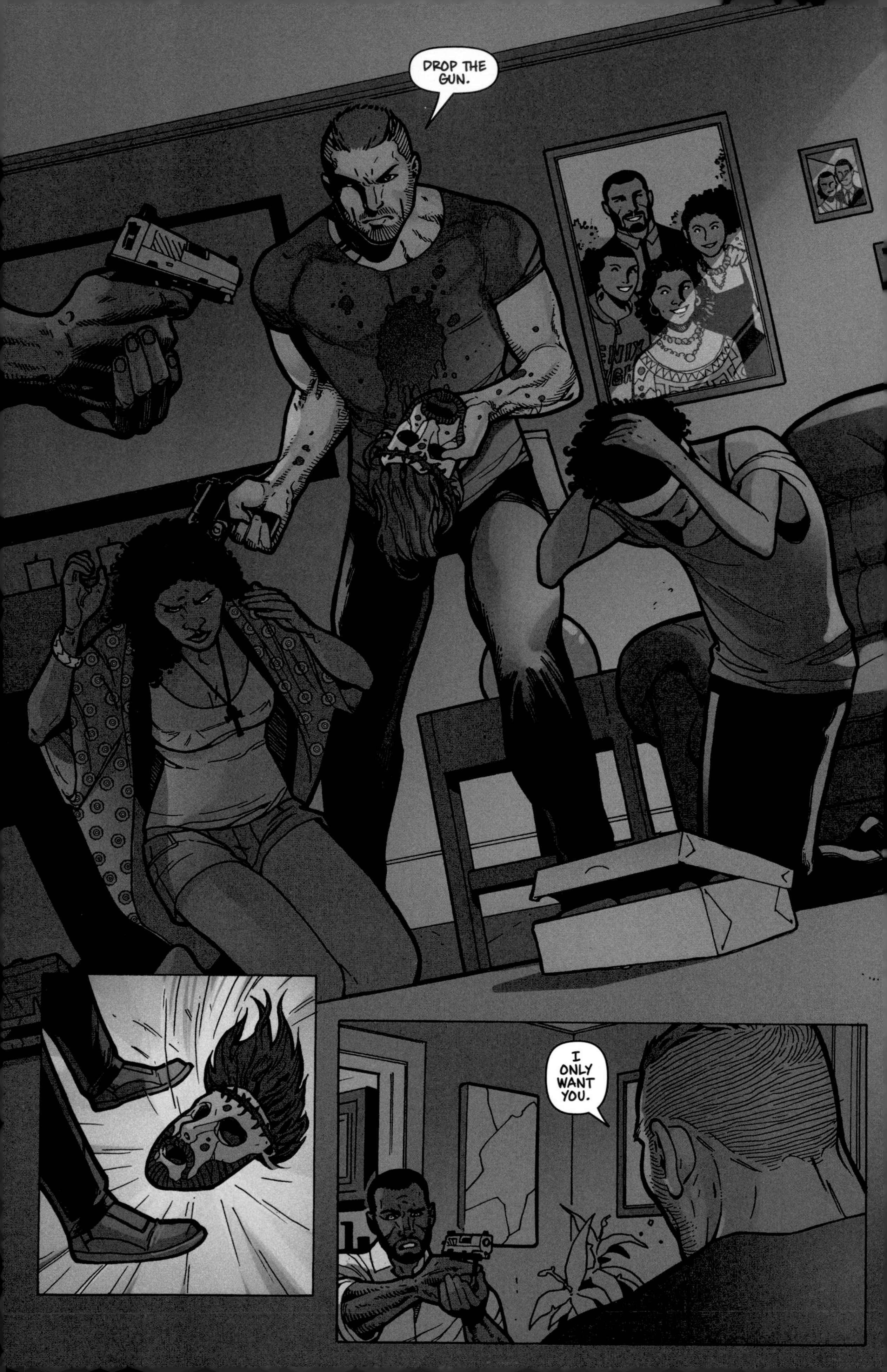
DROP THE GUN.
I ONLY WANT YOU.

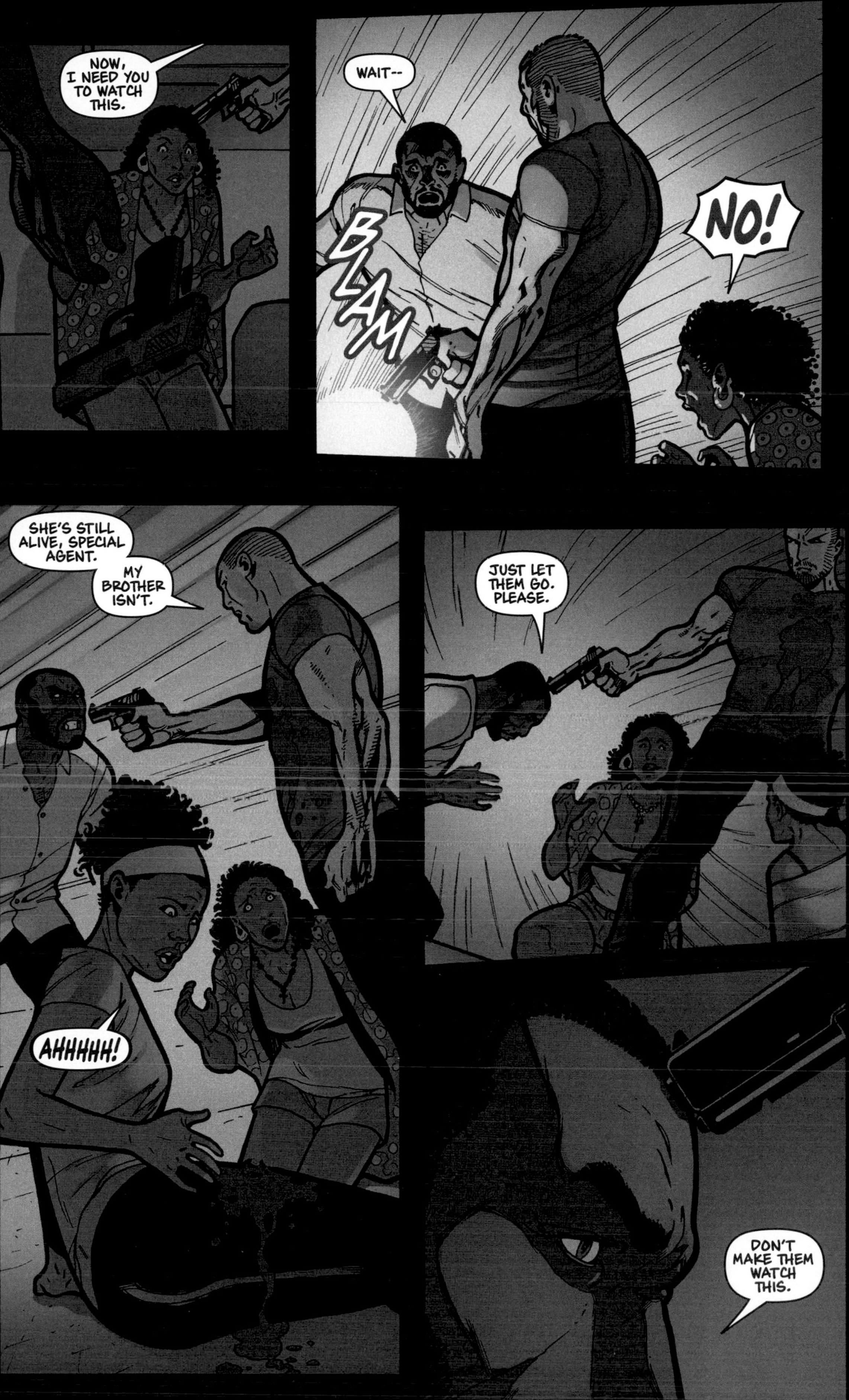
NOW, I NEED YOU TO WATCH THIS.
WAIT--
BLAM
NO!
SHE'S STILL ALIVE, SPECIAL AGENT.
MY BROTHER ISN'T.
AHHHHH!
JUST LET THEM GO. PLEASE.
DON'T MAKE THEM WATCH THIS.

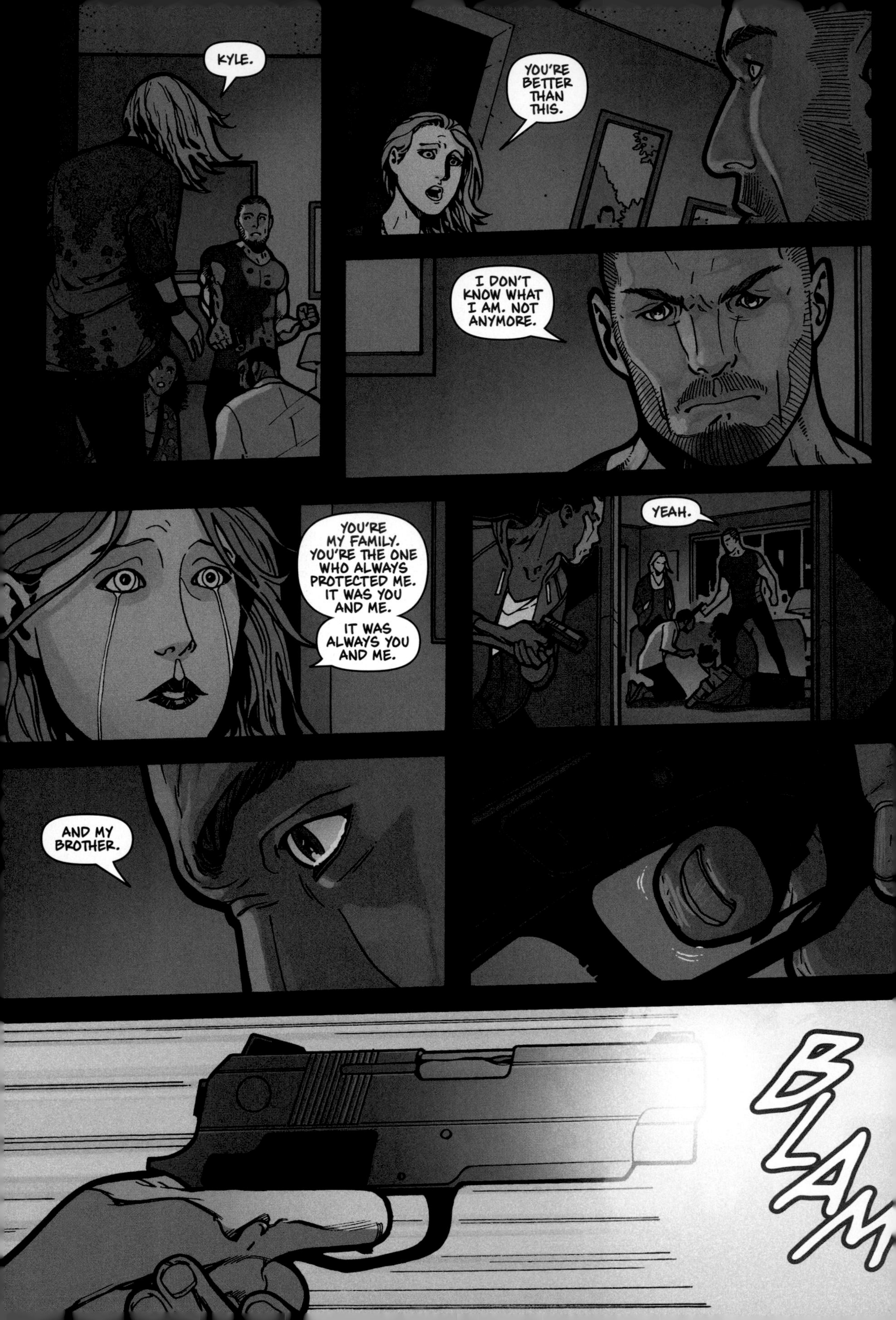
KYLE.
YOU'RE BETTER THAN THIS.
I DON'T KNOW WHAT I AM. NOT ANYMORE.
YOU'RE MY FAMILY. YOU'RE THE ONE WHO ALWAYS PROTECTED ME. IT WAS YOU AND ME.
IT WAS ALWAYS YOU AND ME.
YEAH.
AND MY BROTHER.
BLAM

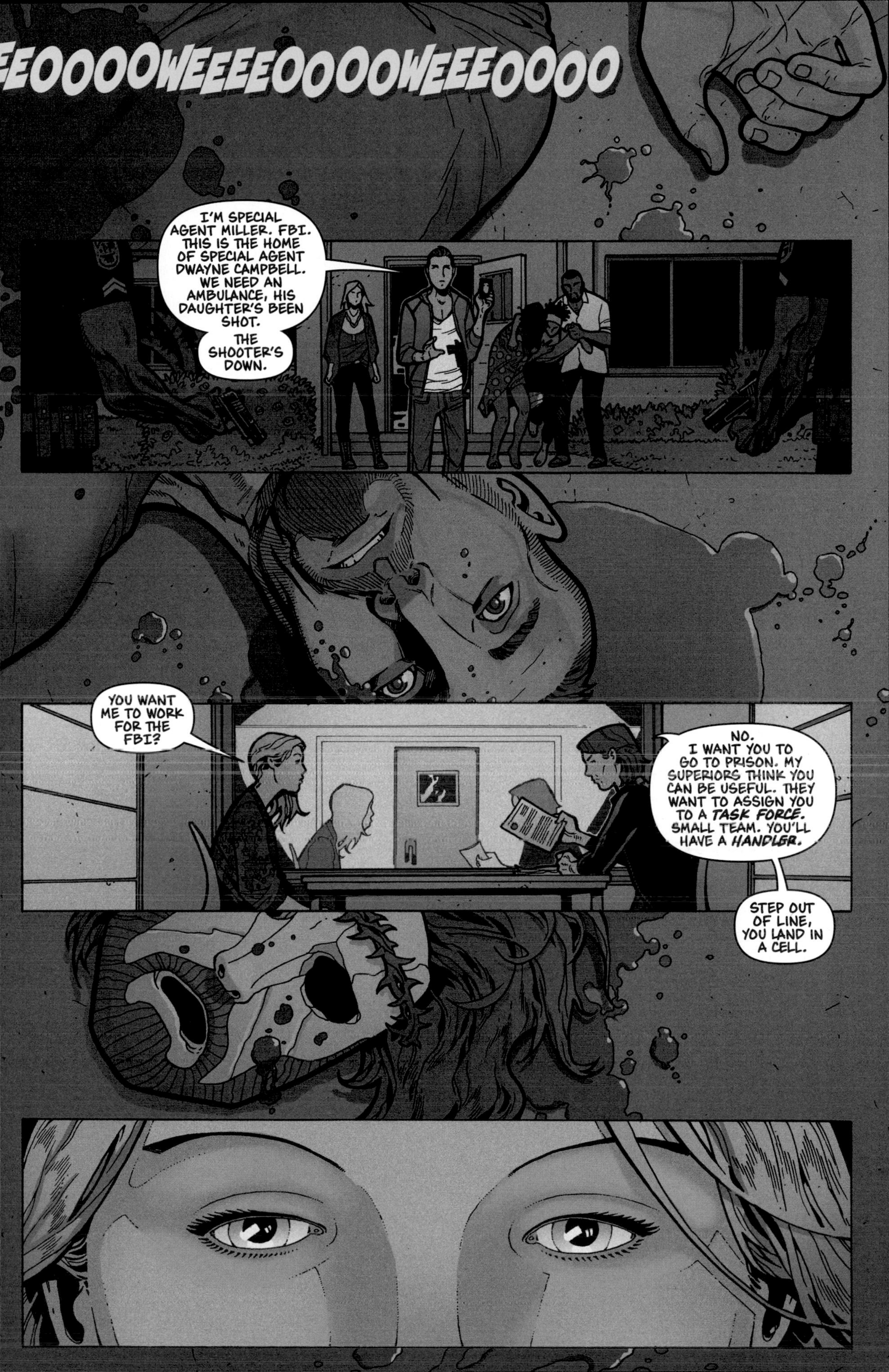
EEOOOOWEEEEOOOOWEEEOOOO
I'M SPECIAL AGENT MILLER. FBI. THIS IS THE HOME OF SPECIAL AGENT DWAYNE CAMPBELL. WE NEED AN AMBULANCE, HIS DAUGHTER'S BEEN SHOT.
THE SHOOTER'S DOWN.
YOU WANT ME TO WORK FOR THE FBI?
NO. I WANT YOU TO GO TO PRISON. MY SUPERIORS THINK YOU CAN BE USEFUL. THEY WANT TO ASSIGN YOU TO A *TASK FORCE.* SMALL TEAM. YOU'LL HAVE A *HANDLER.*
STEP OUT OF LINE, YOU LAND IN A CELL.

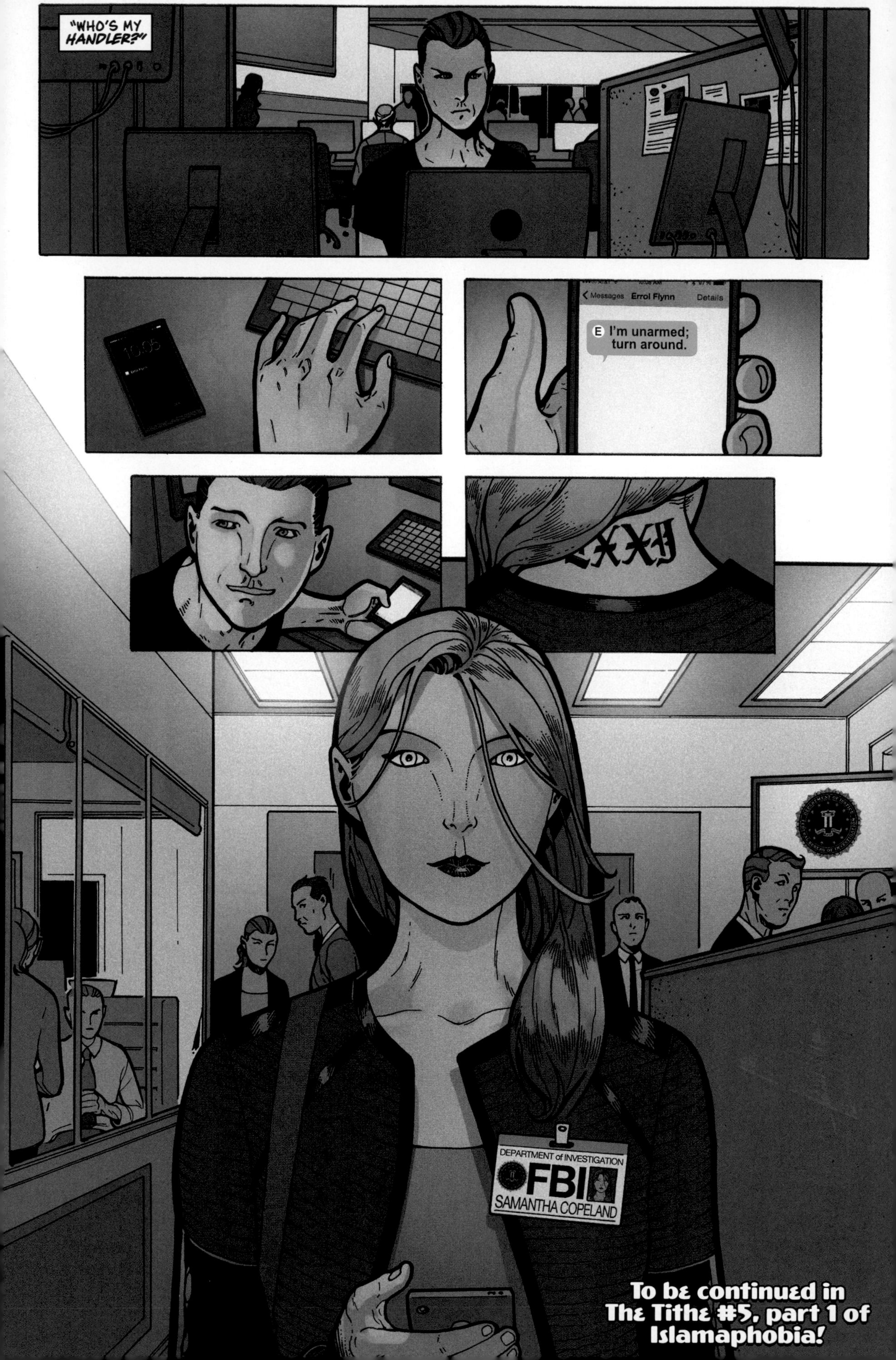
"WHO'S MY HANDLER?"
Messages Errol Flynn Details
I'm unarmed; turn around.
LXXI
DEPARTMENT of INVESTIGATION
FBI
SAMANTHA COPELAND
To be continued in The Tithe #5, part 1 of Islamaphobia!

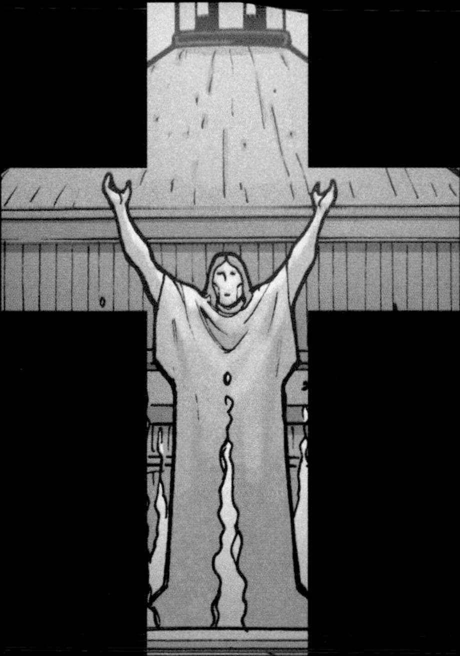

SUNDAY SCHOOL

Welcome to the first volume of *The Tithe*, thanks much for reading. If you enjoyed it, I'd ask that you please recommend the book to a friend - word of mouth means everything. I have Science Class in my *Think Tank*-y books; Sunday School seemed more appropriate for this one. Feel free to hit us up on social media or write to *The Tithe* at fanmail@topcow.com. If you want to click the links for this Sunday School instead of having to type them out, feel free to head on over to Matttalks.com (three t's in the middle there). By the time you read this, this Sunday School will be posted and you can just click on the links!

SOME PERSONAL HISTORY

I'm an atheist, but I wasn't always one. I was raised a Southern Baptist and went to church twice a week for the first 18 years of my life. I was "saved" at the age of about 8, baptized at 15. I sang in the choir, listened to Petra, Stryper and the Altar Boys, and worked with Pastor Greg Laurie as a counselor for the Harvest Crusade in the late 80s. I went to college and forgot about Church for a while like most do, but got back into it in my early 20s. In my late 20s, while doing research for *Lady Pendragon*, I read a book called *Holy Blood, Holy Grail*. It led to my reading a lot of other books, including the gnostic gospels and so many other books I doubt I could even name them all. I read Dawkins, Hitchens and others. This also led to an intensive study of the Bible and other religious texts. Within about a year of this intensive study, my faith in Christianity was completely gone.

That was a profound crisis in my life and once I started questioning and not simply following with blind faith, everything changed. Biblical passages I had read in the past that gave me hope now made me feel hopeless. Here's the thing; I want to believe. I really do. I just don't. I can't get my rational mind to accept it any longer. The biggest hurdle I have is when the literal fundamentalists try to say the Bible is the divinely inspired, absolutely flawless word of God. If people want to tell me they are allegories, parables and moral stories to learn from I can dig it. I no longer bother trying to talk to people that believe the world is less than 10,000 years old. There's a great documentary called *Understanding Darwin* where a Fundie woman says, "I don't care what science proves, if it conflicts with the Bible I won't believe it."

Would it be preferable for me to believe Christianity is true? Yes, of course, it's a far better consolation to believe than to not believe. The idea that there is indeed some sort of life after death is comforting. That desire for consolation and comfort, however, doesn't make it true.

Looking at it with skeptical glasses now it amazes me how Christians call Mormons a "cult" and their beliefs "crazy". I heard that a lot growing up. When you don't believe in either, they both seem equally far-fetched. I know many of you believe. I respect your beliefs and I'm not one of those militant atheists looking to unconvert you. Like I said, I have family and friends that are believers and I'm happy for them.

THE TITHE

The Tithe came about out of a love for heist movies. I love Michael Mann films and *The Town* is a recent favorite. There are so many movies with banks and art museums being robbed that I wanted to do that kind of a story but with a different setting. I started thinking about places with cash laying around and eventually thought about Megachurches. Rahsan Ekeda[redacted] my co-creator, collaborator, artist, and friend started doing some designs for the main characters. Here they are:

DWAYNE CAMPBELL

Dwayne Campbell (50s) -- Dwayne is a family man, loves his wife, has four daughters, only one[redacted]still at home the three oldest are educated, married professionals. He's dedicated to his job and attends a small Baptist church in a small Texas town. He wants to give his family everything he didn't have as a child. He's always wanted a son and Jimmy (the other agent) becomes a proxy of that for him. Raised in the foster system, Dwayne had no parents to speak of. In his job, he's smart, well respected, but considered a bit of a Luddite. He never advanced beyond his field agent status because of his unwillingness to sacrifice his family for career. Dwayne is a Baptist and a believer, which causes him[redacted]ome comedic friction with Jimmy. Despite his confident aura, he's never quite felt like he fit in the world, not comfortable in his own shoes. H[redacted]a[redacted]nightmares about his childhood, but he hides this and compartmentalizes it and has never sought therapy as an adult. He doesn't allow his family or work to see the weak side of him. Jimmy k[redacted]s more about his childhood than Dwayne's wife does.

FBI
CAMPBELL
THE TITHE

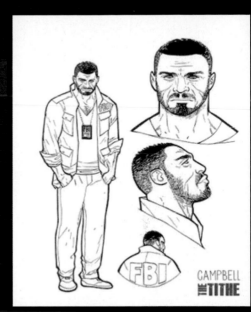

JAMES MILLER

James "Jimmy" Miller (late 20s) -- Jimmy is a hacker that was caught infiltrating the FBI database at age 14 and was recruited in lieu of going to jai[redacted]He's young, good-looking, smart, charming, likable and a bit of a womanizer. He has a bad boy image inside of the FBI, but most of it is a façade he continues to cultivate. When he applied to be an actual field agent instead of just in cyber crimes, Dwayne took him under his wing and has a soft spot for Jimmy. He's a genius level hacker but Samaritan is [redacted]ger/smarter and knows the new tricks -- this drives him nuts. He's our atheist.

JIMMY
THE TITHE

Definition: "One tenth of annual produce or earnings, formerly taken as a tax for the support of the church and clergy."

Pronunciation: TIE-THE. So think "TIE" fighter from Star Wars followed by a "THE" and run it together into one syllable.

So basically it's a 10% tax to keep the church going. If you believe in this stuff, 10% doesn't seem egregious, but it can also be a lot for someone who makes little money. Catholic and Protestant tithing are essentially the same. The Mormons are a little stricter, I'll discuss that below.

BIBLE VERSES ON TITHING

Malachi 3:10 ESV

Bring the full tithe into the storehouse, that there may be food in my house. And thereby put me to the test, says the Lord of hosts, if I will not open the windows of heaven for you and pour down for you a blessing until there is no more need.

Proverbs 11:24 ESV

One gives freely, yet grows all the richer; another withholds what he should give, and only suffers want.

There are a lot of verses with the Old Testament and the New Testament saying slightly different things. You can read a list of them at this link:

http://www.openbible.info/topics/tithes_and_offering

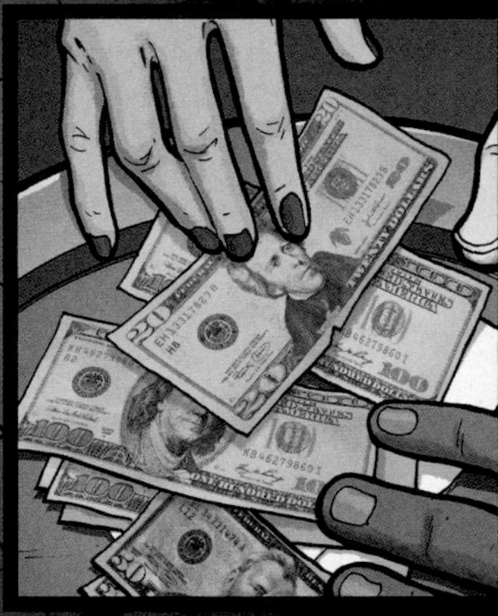

PROSPERITY THEOLOGY

This is essentially a doctrine that says financial blessing is the will of God for Christians and that donations to Christian ministries will increase one's wealth. So give money to the church and you'll get richer, get a promotion, and have better health. It's also how the pastors justify having multi-million dollar houses and private airplanes. Many of the evangelical mega-churches are Prosperity Doctrine churches. Creflo Dollar and many others espouse these principals and use this doctrine to justify aggressively pursuing donations.

From Wikipedia: "Based on non-traditional interpretations of the Bible, often with emphasis on the Book of Malachi, the doctrine views the Bible as a contract between God and humans: if humans have faith in God, he will deliver his promises of security and prosperity. Confessing these promises to be true is perceived as an act of faith, which God will honor."

https://www.faithstreet.com/onfaith/2014/05/09/ten-verses-prosperity-gospel-preachers-need-stop-misuising/32019

http://en.wikipedia.org/wiki/Prosperity_theology

JOEL OSTEEN CHURCH ROBBED

If you think these churches don't have tons of cash read this article. The ironic timing of this is the church was robbed on March 9, 2014. You can ask Rahsan Ekedal, I delivered the initial outline for this project literally THE DAY BEFORE. Weird timing.

http://www.christianpost.com/news/joel-osteens-lakewood-church-theft-still-a-mystery-25000-reward-offered-116688/

CREFLO DOLLAR PLANE

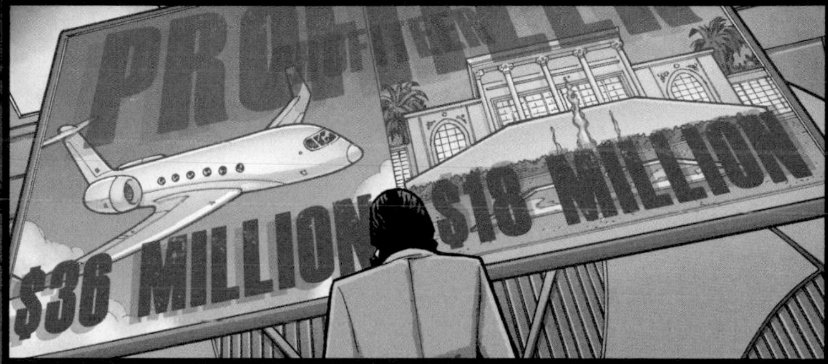
$36 MILLION
$18 MILLION

This Atlanta Pastor asked for $60 million in special donations so he could get a new private jet. Because, ya know, he needs a private jet and can't fly coach. Heh.

http://www.cnn.com/2015/03/13/living/creflo-dollar-jet-feat/

https://www.creflodollarministries.org/

MORMON TITHING

So despite aggressively pursuing money, the Protestant and Catholic ones don't limit access to anything when one doesn't tithe. The Mormons don't allow people that aren't paying 10% (of their gross, not their net, so pre-tax calculation) into the holiest areas. So either you pay or you don't go there. They actually have required annual meetings with a deacon to determine your tithing status.

http://mormonthink.com/tithing.htm

CHURCH SCANDAL

Should be an oxymoron, but it's not. Five million Google pages appear when you search church scandal. There are so many of these. I'm going to break some of the more entertaining ones down later on, but here's a taste:

http://atlantablackstar.com/2014/04/28/8-church-scandals-may-challenged-faith/

BIBLICAL KILLING AS A LAW MAN?

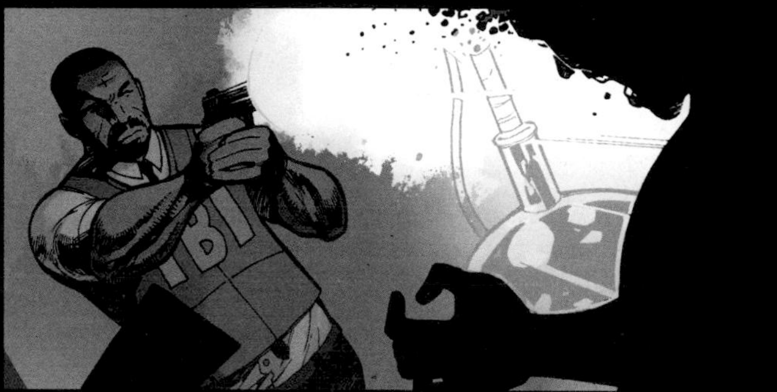
FBI

I was curious what the Bible said about self-defense or cops/military who kill, especially given Dwayne's killing in this issue. Check this link, it's worth reading:

http://www.biblicalselfdefense.com/

JOEL OSTEEN MINISTRIES/LAKEWOOD CHURCH

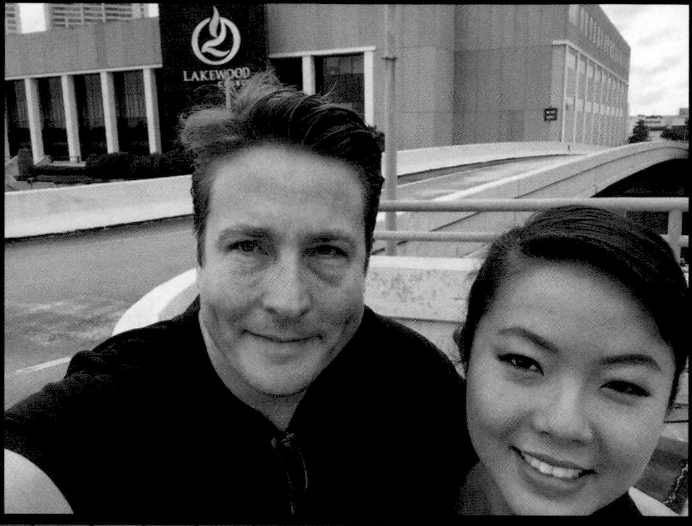
LAKEWOOD

I was just in Houston for Comicpalooza, and my wife and I went to Lakewood church for their 8:30 Sunday morning service. It was entertaining, quite a spectacle to behold. It reminds me of a concert with the lights, music, and the multi-ethnic attractive crowd leading the songs.

Joel Osteen is kind of like Tony Robbins with Christ mixed in. He has a very positive message, and regardless of my atheist views, I walked out of there feeling pretty good. One thing I noted was that there was not one cross or Jesus image depicted anywhere. If you find yourself in Houston, it's worth going just to check it out.

http://www.lakewoodchurch.com/Pages/Home.aspx

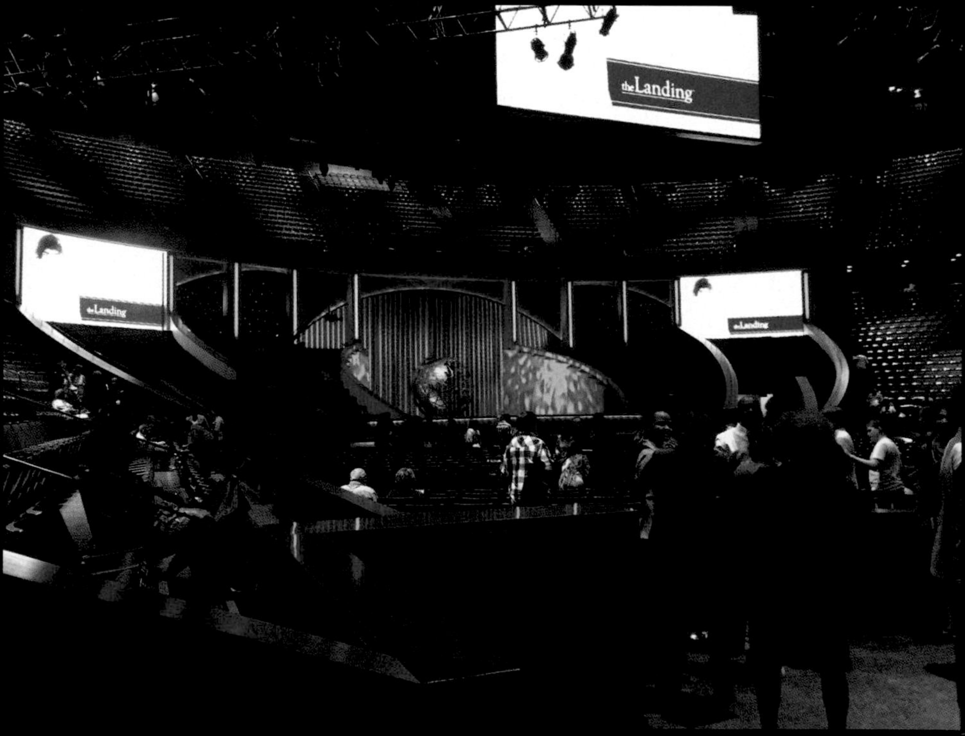
the Landing
the Landing
the Landing

As promised earlier, let's look at church scandals. Seems like it should be an oxymoron, but since there are so many, it's a testament to our inability to live "Christ-like" lives. They come in many forms: financial, sexual, doctrinal…the list goes on. There are so many of these it's disgusting, but I'll highlight a few.

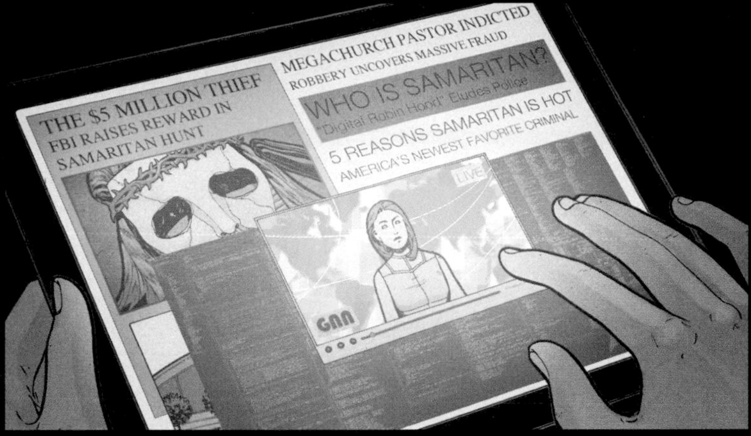
THE $5 MILLION THIEF
FBI RAISES REWARD IN SAMARITAN HUNT
MEGACHURCH PASTOR INDICTED
ROBBERY UNCOVERS MASSIVE FRAUD
WHO IS SAMARITAN?
"Digital Robin Hood" Eludes Police
5 REASONS SAMARITAN IS HOT
AMERICA'S NEWEST FAVORITE CRIMINAL
LIVE
GNN

SEX SCANDALS

The Catholic Church's nightmare has been dealing with the pedophile priests who like underage boys. In the U.S. alone the Vatican has paid out over $2.2 billion in settlements and has at least 100,000 victims. Think about that for a minute.

http://www.bishop-accountability.org/settlements/
http://ncronline.org/blogs/ncr-today/vatican-abuse-summit-22-billion-and-100000-victims-us-alone

Here is a complete list of sex scandals in the Catholic Church:

http://content.time.com/time/specials/packages/completelist/0,29569,1992502,00.html

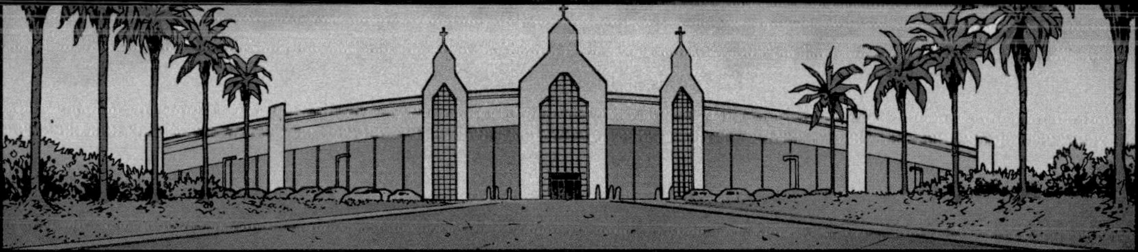

TED HAGGARD

Sex scandals aren't just for Catholics. Ted Haggard founded the New Life Church in Colorado Springs, an evangelical church that was very aggressive and strongly denounced immoral behavior (as most churches do). Ted blasted homosexuality as sin and then was caught having sex with male prostitutes allegedly while using crystal meth. He was booted from his New Life Church, but eventually asked for forgiveness and has started St. James Church. It conveniently leaves out his transgressions on the "about me" link on the sites I've linked below.

http://tedhaggard.com/

http://www.newlifechurch.org/

http://www.gq.com/news-politics/newsmakers/201102/pastor-ted-haggard

http://saintjameschurch.com/

Another gem that's still on the air now, Jim Bakker, became famous in the 80s with the 700 Club and the Praise the Lord (PTL) Club. He was convicted of financial fraud in 1989 and served five years of a forty-five year sentence. He was also involved in the Jessica Hahn scandal, in which he and another minister were accused of raping her (devil's three way anyone?). He started a new show and this headline says it all: "Jailed televangelist and accused rapist Jim Bakker is back in business hawking survivalist kits including everything from padded clothing to buckets of beans to enemas." If you want to gag, check your listings and watch him sell insanely overpriced "blessed" goods to senior citizens.

http://www.dailymail.co.uk/news/article-2752391/Jailed-televangelist-accused-rapist-Jim-Bakker-business-hawking-survivalist-kits-including-padded-clothing-buckets-beans-enemas.html#ixzz3bXF8YOGe

https://www.youtube.com/watch?v=VeA5ae2hkEo

https://www.youtube.com/watch?v=hd6813Zcp2s

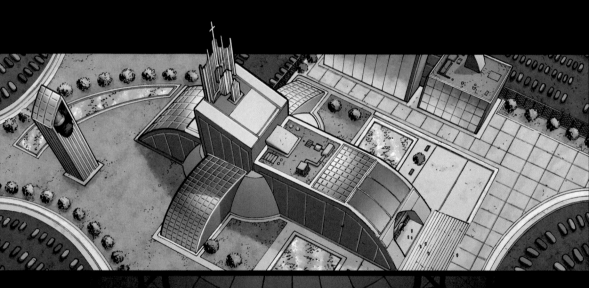

EDDIE LONG

Founder of the New Birth Missionary Baptist Church in Georgia, he was accused of abusive gay relationships with young members of his church who sought "counseling" from him and eventually settled so it never went to trial. I think they were looking for life advice not buggery, but hey, that may just be my opinion. He's still a pastor and his bio says it all:

"Apostle Eddie L. Long is known worldwide as a pioneering leader, revolutionary mind changer, a family man, and a caring and loving pastor. As a pioneering leader, Apostle Long is highly regarded for his vision, boldness, and unapologetic courage to walk in the supernatural."

I know Christians aren't fans of the gays, but calling them supernatural might be a bit much =P

http://www.newbirth.org/

http://www.christianpost.com/news/bishop-eddie-long-accused-of-abusive-gay-relationship-in-first-lady-book-90152/

99% FAITHFUL

For those of you who think I'm doing a hatchet job on Christianity and churches, it's not the intent. I'm all for churches and have been to half a dozen services over the past few months and enjoyed most of them. There are bad people and some of those bad people pretend to be Christians and profit off of well-intentioned people. The plot of this story was that the FBI had [redacted] ten churches they were investigating for fraud. There are approximately 350,000 religious churches in the U.S. So even if we took our ten bad churches and multiplied that by 350 you're still looking at less than 1%. So 99% of the churches are doing it the right way. It's the h[redacted]risy of that 1% that makes the fictional story so compelling. After reading the first arc i[redacted] STILL feel like I'm attacking your religion then I failed at what I was trying to do and accept my apology. This was never intended as an attack on religion.

Church statistics:

http://hirr.hartsem.edu/research/fastfacts/fast_facts.html
http://www.pewforum.org/religious-landscape-study/

LXXI

Sam's tattoo on her neck is symbolic of the Samaritan Pentateuch. We just used this because it looked cool and ties into her "name", but here's what it means:

"The Samaritan Pentateuch is not a version but a rival Hebrew text type to the Masoretic t[redacted]d. 90). It is an independent witness to Hebrew text types. In the fifth century b.c. the Samaritans adopted and adapted the Pentateuch alone as their sacred Scriptures. Since ther[redacted] were some changes in the extant Hebrew manuscripts during the later centuries, the Samaritan Pentateuch is an important tool for doing textual criticism, which tries to ascertain the probable original readings of the Masoretic text. It differs from the received Masoretic text in mostly minor ways. At times it agrees with the Septuagint, at times with the Masoretic text, at times with the manuscripts among the DSS."

https://www.biblegateway.com/resources/asbury-bible-commentary/Samaritan-Pentateuch

NARCISSISTS AND SOCIOPATHS

In the back of my head when writing this, both Sam and Jimmy have narcissistic tendencies. I see people equating narcissists with sociopaths all the time so I want to share the difference:

From the APA:

Narcissistic Personality Disorder (NPD)

THE NARCISSIST – This person is an elitist and exists to be adored and admired.
• A pervasive pattern of grandiosity, need for admiration, and a lack of empathy.
• Think *Wall Street* (Gordon Gekko) or *American Gigolo* (Richard Gere).

Anti-Social Personality Disorder (APD)

THE SOCIOPATH – This person is the con-artist who often exhibits more criminal and violent traits.
• A pervasive disregard for the law and the rights of others.
• Think *The Talented Mr. Ripley* (Matt Damon) or *American Psycho* (Christian Bale).

http://www.lisaescott.com/forum/2009/06/22/narcissist-or-sociopath-whats-difference

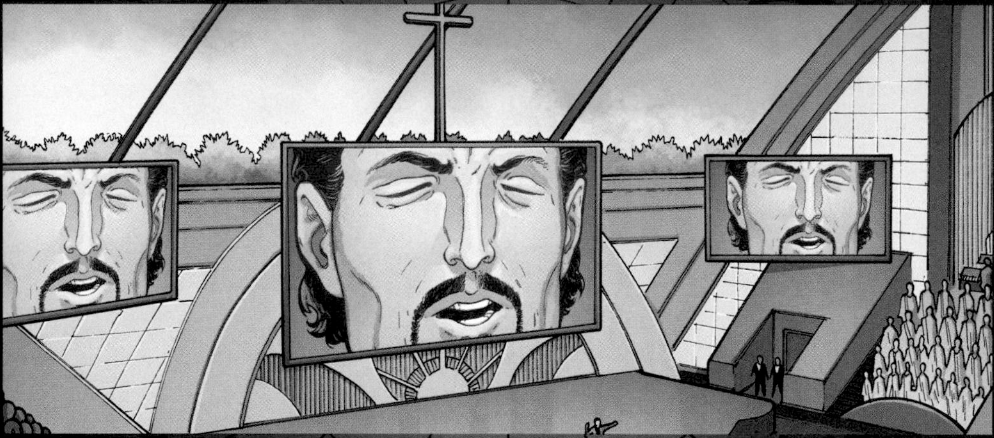

CORRECTION ON MORMON TITHING

From Gregory A. Swarthout's letter:

"In the back of this issue you have an informational section on tithing. I read all of it, but I wanted to point out that the 'Mormon Tithing' section has two factual errors in it. First, Mormons are not required to tithe on gross rather than net. Some do, but that is a matter of their personal choice. 2) Deacons in the Mormon churches are aged 12 & 13 years old so, no, you don't meet with one of them for your annual 'tithing settlement.' The link you provided actually gets that second point right in that it's the bishop (or, more correctly, a member of the bishopric) that you meet with instead of the youngster, but it doesn't even touch on the first point."

I got a few of these from the LDS faithful and did research this and found out that I was indeed wrong on these points. My apologies!

OTHER BOOKS BY ME:

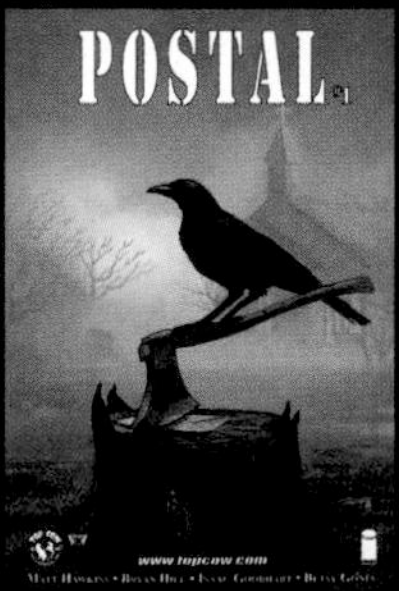
POSTAL
#1

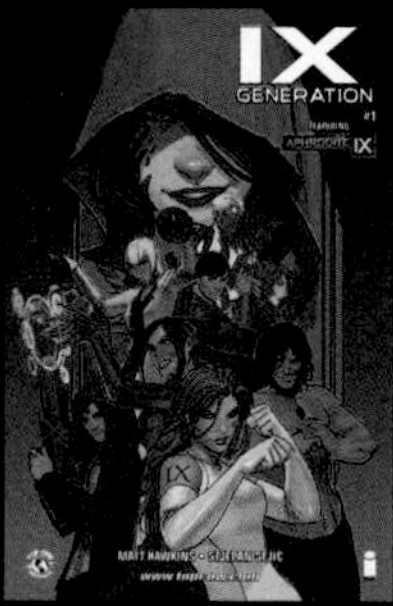
IX
GENERATION

LETTERS (some edited down for space and I corrected some of your grammar, sorry!)

Hey Matt Hawkins and the rest of *The Tithe* team!

I really loved the first issue of *The Tithe*. It was fresh and original and had a really nice drive to the story right from the get go. A lot of series these days like to start off slow and gradually reel you in, but I can tell this new series is gonna be exciting from beginning to end. It is a nice change of pace from some of the other series I read. Growing up in a very religious household (I would rather not post the name of the religion as I don't want to make anyone feel bad or give anyone a bad opinion of it) I was taught all about the bible and Jehovah along with his son Jesus Christ. I spent countless hours studying (not the bible so much but their literature) and going out door to door to share what I had learned. At 19 I went and served at the world headquarters in NYC and spent the next three and a half years of my life there, instead of furthering my education by going to college. Then all hell broke loose. My parents split up, as my dad had been cheating on my mom for some time, and he was excommunicated from the church meaning none of us could speak to him until he came back. My father was the man I was trying so hard to be so you can imagine this shook me to my very core. People told me to pray to God and share my feelings with him, but it didn't help. I kept thinking how could this happen to my dad? He was doing everything right; everything I believe, I took his word for and he was a liar all along. After a few months of this I turned to pain pills to find some relief and this quickly led to the worst years of my life. The world headquarters kicked me out with no remorse or offer of help, and the religion I gave my life to excommunicated me without any offer of sympathy. I spent the next 3 years on the streets trying to survive until one day I tried to take my own life with an overdose of heroin. When I came to in a hospital some days later, I found my dad sitting next to my bed crying uncontrollably. It was in that moment that I learned what true forgiveness is, and it wasn't this cruel hypocritical forgiveness I had been taught all my life in church. I didn't forgive him to save my "eternal soul" or because I was told to. I forgave him because I had messed up too, and I saw my father as just a man now. Men make mistakes, sometimes horrible mistakes.

I'm happy to say that I have been clean for 1 year now and have a wonderful relationship with my father again and the rest of my family for that matter. Religion can be great for some people, but in order for it to work you have to prove it to yourself. Don't let anyone else tell you what to believe, or else you may find yourself feeling as though your life doesn't even belong to you anymore. I really appreciate what you all are doing with this series and can't wait to see where it leads. Just out of curiosity what else have you worked on? Also if you don't mind me asking why did you say in the back of the last issue that you stop listening to anyone who says the bible is not older than 10,000 years old? Do we have any proof or examples of Bible's older than this? Just asking out of genuine curiosity. Thanks again!

Mark 9:3- "His clothing became glistening, exceedingly white, like snow, such as no launderer on earth can whiten them."

aylor, thanks for writing in. I've worked on Think Tank, Aphrodite IX, The Tales of Honor, and Vildfire in the last couple years. I'm glad things seem to be looking up for you. The 10,000 ear thing is a pet peeve of mine because there's so much evidence that the Earth and the niverse are far older than that. People who refuse to accept that, despite the overwhelming mount of evidence, are pointless to argue with. Check these links:

ttp://www.patheos.com/Resources/Additional-Resources/Debating-a-Young-Earth-Creationis tml

ttp://www.livescience.com/46123-many-americans-creationists.html

ttps://answersingenesis.org/age-of-the-earth/how-old-is-the-earth/

ttps://sensuouscurmudgeon.wordpress.com/2013/11/05/hey-young-earth-creationists-dig-this

)ear Mr. Matt Hawkins,

'his is my first time I've written fan mail to anyone, but after reading this comic I had to write n. I have been working in a Christian shop for over ten years, and today I joked with my vorkmates about stocking your comic in our store… teasingly. I argued the point there was nore biblical content in this comic than the majority of 'bestselling' Christian movies, music nd resources being sold today. We had a bit of a sadistic laugh about it and your wonderful omic didn't make it into our stock; but it did make it into the best comic I've read thus far for 2015!! I am very keen to learn where this story leads, I haven't been this excited with a comi ince the Walking Dead, keep up the brilliant work.

3lessings,
ohn L.

'hanks, John! I'd love to see **The Tithe** *in Christian book stores, if only to spark discussion, out you might be a rare individual willing to read my heretical works.*

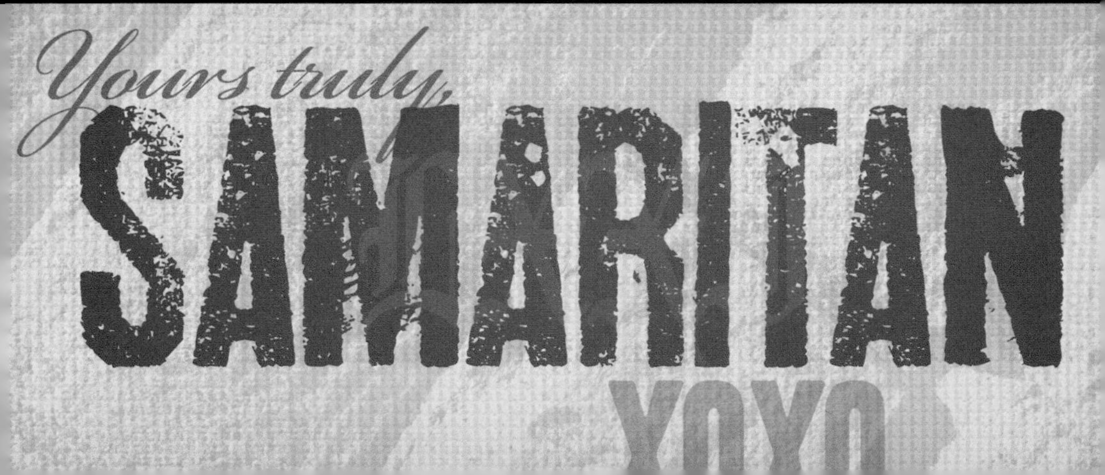
Yours truly,
SAMARITAN

Thanks Guys!

I figured that was the first thing I needed to say. Getting a comic like this in to the mainstream (Is Image mainstream now? Are comics mainstream? idk) is an absolute blessing ;p. It's great to see someone critical of faith-profiteering and create the role of a protagonist to be a complete skeptic. Other comics have touched on the topic I'm sure, but devoting a story-arc to it? Awesome. I'm very excited for the next issue and to watch its critical exposition develop on the pages.

P.S. I'm a Vegas local, most people that visit don't know Henderson is a place here. Shit, most tourists don't even know people live here. So I'm curious, is the next church going to be conveniently similar to one of our mega churches? "Central Christian" ((http://www.centralonline.tv/central-online/)) perhaps? That would be great. Friends and I used to throw eggs at the Maseratis in the parking lot after school some odd 10 years ago. hahah

Cheers Guys,
Fazz

Thanks, Fazz! As you can see from last issue, Samaritan did hit a church in Henderson. I've based none of the churches in **The Tithe** *on real churches, but I did look to see where they were located and used those areas.*

I was absolutely riveted while reading Tithe. It reads like a summer blockbuster with all the excitement and intrigue. I want to know more about Jimmy, will you be representing computer hacking and forensics realistically or will it be all super futuristic rather than watching a bar chase the screen and files compiling and sifting through data?

Mike E.

Thanks, Mike! Watching people hack is not all that interesting, as the makers of **Blackhat** *discovered. I certainly use hacking a lot in this book,* **Wildfire,** *and* **Think Tank,** *but I use a visual short hand to get the point across without (hopefully) making it too boring.*

LETTERS FROM PASTORS:

Matt (I assume you'll see this eventually), let me start by saying I love *The Tithe.* I opened my first comic book store when I was 16. I became a pastor when I was 22 (yes, you read that right).

I wasn't raised in church, gave my life to Christ at 20 and at 22 I was in ministry. At 27 I started a church called Revolution Church in Canton, Ga. We quickly became one of the fastest growing churches in America. We actually met in a movie theater and were running over 1000 ppl in a few years. While I wouldn't go as far as you do with the church about money, I preached money a lot because that is what I was taught. I actually know guys just like the guys in your story. I was literally a rock star. My ego got bigger, bigger, and bigger and eventually I thought I was above the rules. I had an affair and lost everything. The Church I started suddenly wanted nothing to do with me, forgot I existed and I never spoke to anyone there again. I was done with the "church."

Fast forward to 3 years ago. I had a group of people wanting to start a church and after much prayer I agreed. If they moved to the poorest part of our city, would feed the hungry, clothed the naked and provide shelter for the homeless I was in. Thirteen people agreed. Three years later Action Church (www.actionchurch.tv) is thriving in the poorest part of our city. It is literally a place of misfits and outcasts. We have the oddest mix of people. We have a large percent of bikers and homosexuals. I joke all the time what an odd mix that is. We run a huge food pantry, clothing closet and a homeless shelter in our building. I am broke and happier than ever. :)

I said all that to say this: I love you comics. The mega church needs to be exposed for what they are (not all, but most). But there are some of us broken, f'd up people out there still trying to minister to people.

I actually think that would be a good storyline: Former mega-pastor living out his second chance in the ghetto somehow helping Samaritan.

I also wanted you to know I'm not as far removed from that world as you are, so if you ever need help on making sure your details are accurate or want some good stories I'm you guy. I ran with some of the biggest names around in my previous life.
Keep up the good work!

Gary L.

Hi, Matt. I just picked up the first issue of your new book and I really like it. I'm a Presbyterian minister and have been a pastor for 25 years. Recently I've had my childhood love for comic books reignited and have been collecting stuff from the '80s and stuff I remember from when I was a kid, but haven't picked up much new material. I came across your book at a local store and the title really intrigued me. I love the story, but I also enjoyed reading your comments at the end.

I've been fascinated by atheism for awhile. I find I have a lot of affinity for the arguments atheists make. In college I wrote a paper on Nietzsche's "Twilight of the Gods" and "Anti-Christ." I found that I rejected the God he did. Much of my ministry has been spent searching for a way to reconcile that rejection with my vocation. I've discovered that the God of Church doctrine is not one I can affirm. And, frankly, I'm not convinced it's one Jesus affirmed. I've found Celtic Christian spirituality to be a great help, also meditation and Buddhism. It's made my preaching more interesting (at least to me!).

I don't know how interested you are in spirituality, but I've found the writings of Richard Rohr, John Philip Newell and Evelyn Underhill (more dated, but still very good) to be helpful. I think there is a shift occurring in our understanding of God, informed by physics, cosmology and evolutionary biology, that is changing Christianity in fundamental ways. That may be why we're hearing so many fundamentalist voices bemoaning the state of our culture and doing everything they can to pass judgment on LGBTQ people, Muslims, and, worst of all, atheists.

This is going longer than I intended. Thanks for your book and I'm looking forward to issue #2. (By the way, I downloaded the free pdf version of the first issue of Postal. It's awesome! Thanks a lot for yet another book I need to follow!)

Peace,
Bill H.

Thanks Bill and Gary, appreciate the letters.

That's all for The Tithe, Volume 1. The next arc will deal specifically with Islam and Christian relations in the U.S. Most Christians I know don't know any Muslims. I actually know quite a few. I've been to the Middle East a few times and have maintained relations with many there and opened dialogue with some on this side of the Atlantic. This isn't some pro-Islam propaganda piece; I wouldn't do that. I want people to think, that's it. Come to your own conclusions about things.

Carpe Diem!

Matt Hawkins
@topcowmatt | facebook.com/selfloathingnarcissist

POSTAL

CREATED BY MATT HAWKINS

ISSUE #1 PREVIEW

BRYAN HILL
MATT HAWKINS
WRITERS

ISAAC GOODHART
ARTIST

BETSY GONIA
COLORIST & EDITOR

TROY PETERI
LETTERER

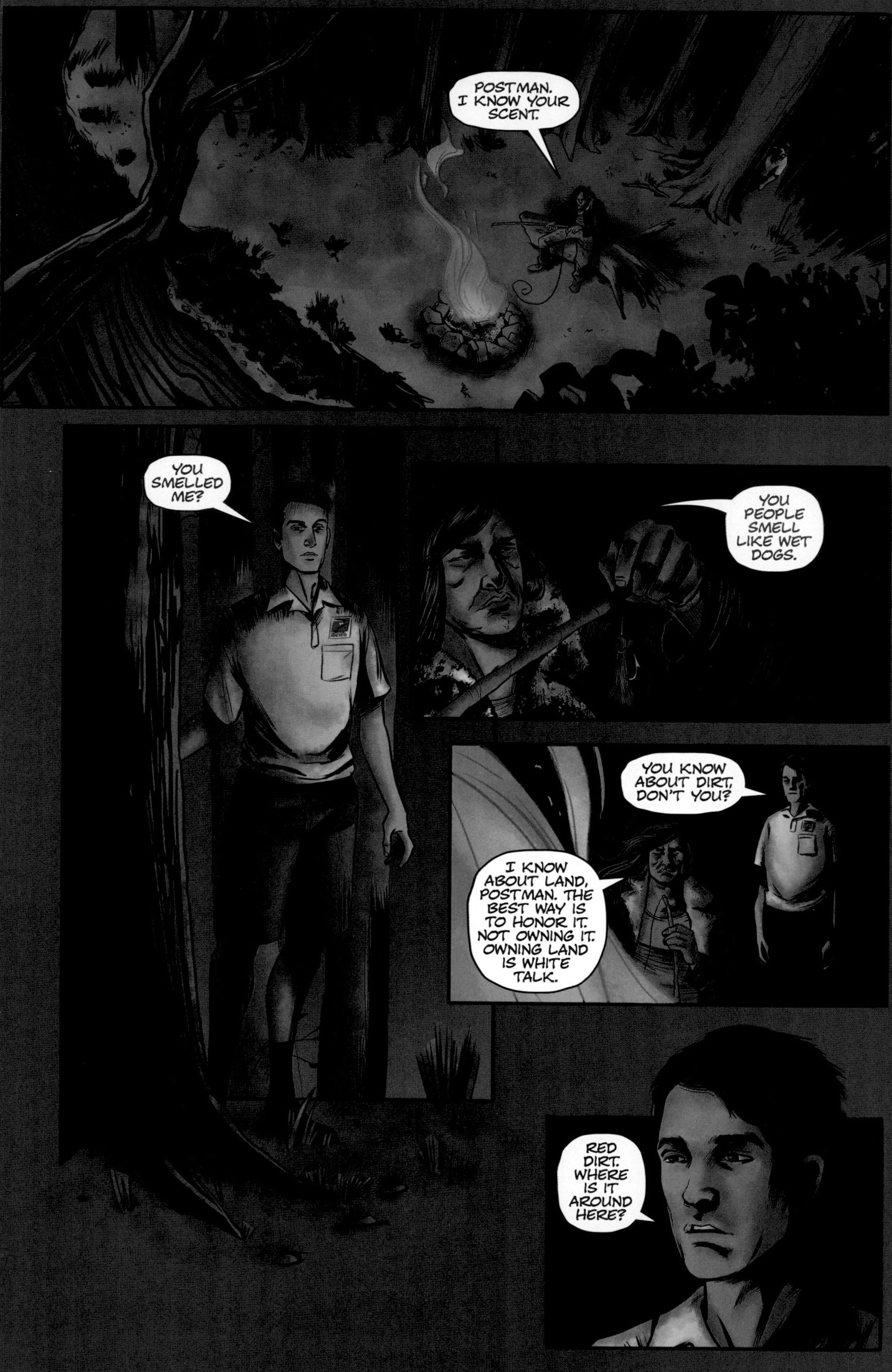
POSTMAN. I KNOW YOUR SCENT.
YOU SMELLED ME?
YOU PEOPLE SMELL LIKE WET DOGS.
YOU KNOW ABOUT DIRT, DON'T YOU?
I KNOW ABOUT LAND, POSTMAN. THE BEST WAY IS TO HONOR IT. NOT OWNING IT. OWNING LAND IS WHITE TALK.
RED DIRT. WHERE IS IT AROUND HERE?

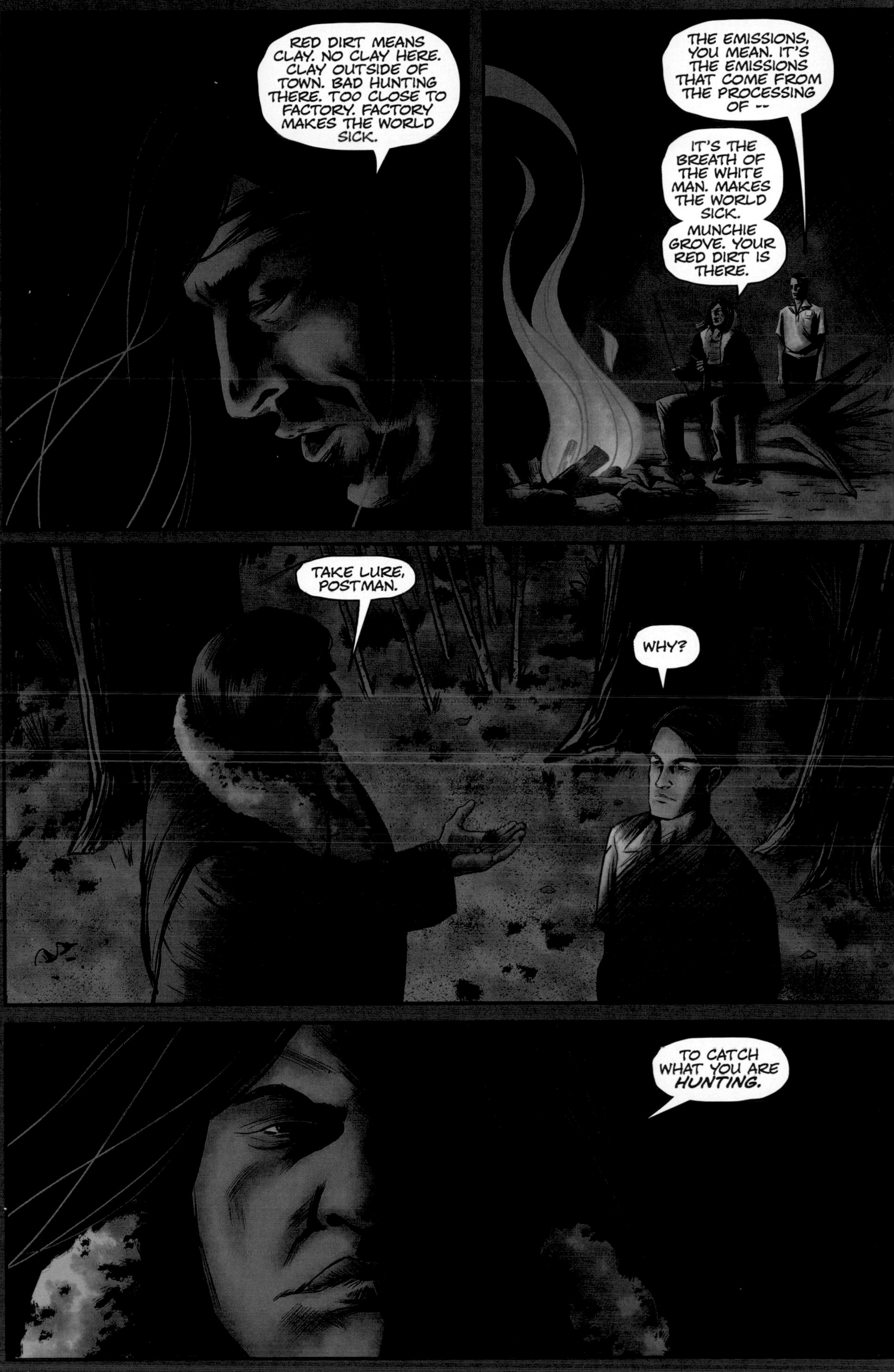
RED DIRT MEANS CLAY. NO CLAY HERE. CLAY OUTSIDE OF TOWN. BAD HUNTING THERE. TOO CLOSE TO FACTORY. FACTORY MAKES THE WORLD SICK.
THE EMISSIONS, YOU MEAN. IT'S THE EMISSIONS THAT COME FROM THE PROCESSING OF --
IT'S THE BREATH OF THE WHITE MAN. MAKES THE WORLD SICK.
MUNCHIE GROVE. YOUR RED DIRT IS THERE.
TAKE LURE, POSTMAN.
WHY?
TO CATCH WHAT YOU ARE *HUNTING.*

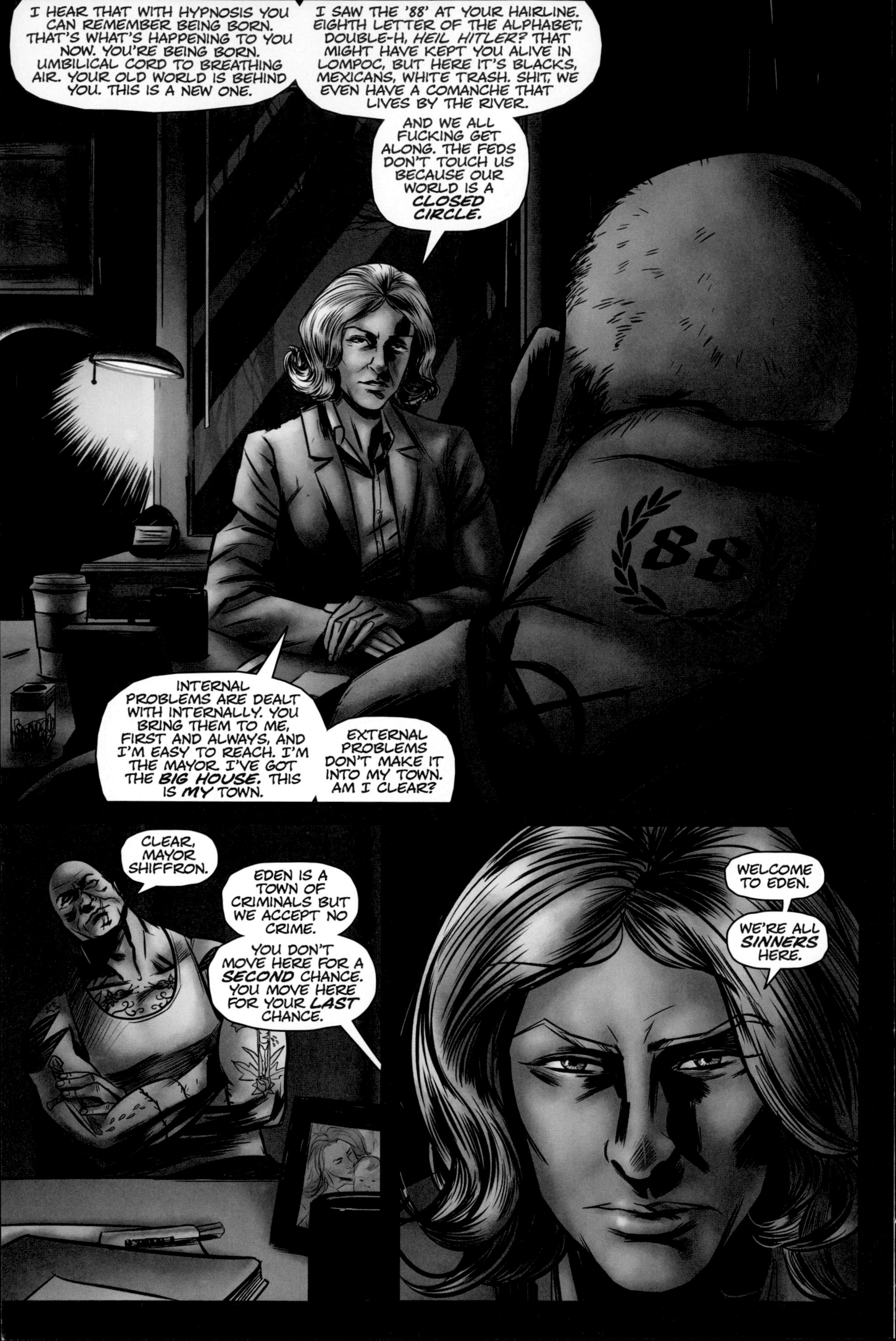
I HEAR THAT WITH HYPNOSIS YOU CAN REMEMBER BEING BORN. THAT'S WHAT'S HAPPENING TO YOU NOW. YOU'RE BEING BORN. UMBILICAL CORD TO BREATHING AIR. YOUR OLD WORLD IS BEHIND YOU. THIS IS A NEW ONE.
I SAW THE '88' AT YOUR HAIRLINE. EIGHTH LETTER OF THE ALPHABET, DOUBLE-H, *HEIL HITLER?* THAT MIGHT HAVE KEPT YOU ALIVE IN LOMPOC, BUT HERE IT'S BLACKS, MEXICANS, WHITE TRASH. SHIT, WE EVEN HAVE A COMANCHE THAT LIVES BY THE RIVER.
AND WE ALL FUCKING GET ALONG. THE FEDS DON'T TOUCH US BECAUSE OUR WORLD IS A ***CLOSED CIRCLE.***
88
INTERNAL PROBLEMS ARE DEALT WITH INTERNALLY. YOU BRING THEM TO ME, FIRST AND ALWAYS, AND I'M EASY TO REACH. I'M THE MAYOR I'VE GOT THE ***BIG HOUSE.*** THIS IS ***MY*** TOWN.
EXTERNAL PROBLEMS DON'T MAKE IT INTO MY TOWN. AM I CLEAR?
CLEAR, MAYOR SHIFFRON.
EDEN IS A TOWN OF CRIMINALS BUT WE ACCEPT NO CRIME.
YOU DON'T MOVE HERE FOR A ***SECOND*** CHANCE. YOU MOVE HERE FOR YOUR ***LAST*** CHANCE.
WELCOME TO EDEN.
WE'RE ALL ***SINNERS*** HERE.

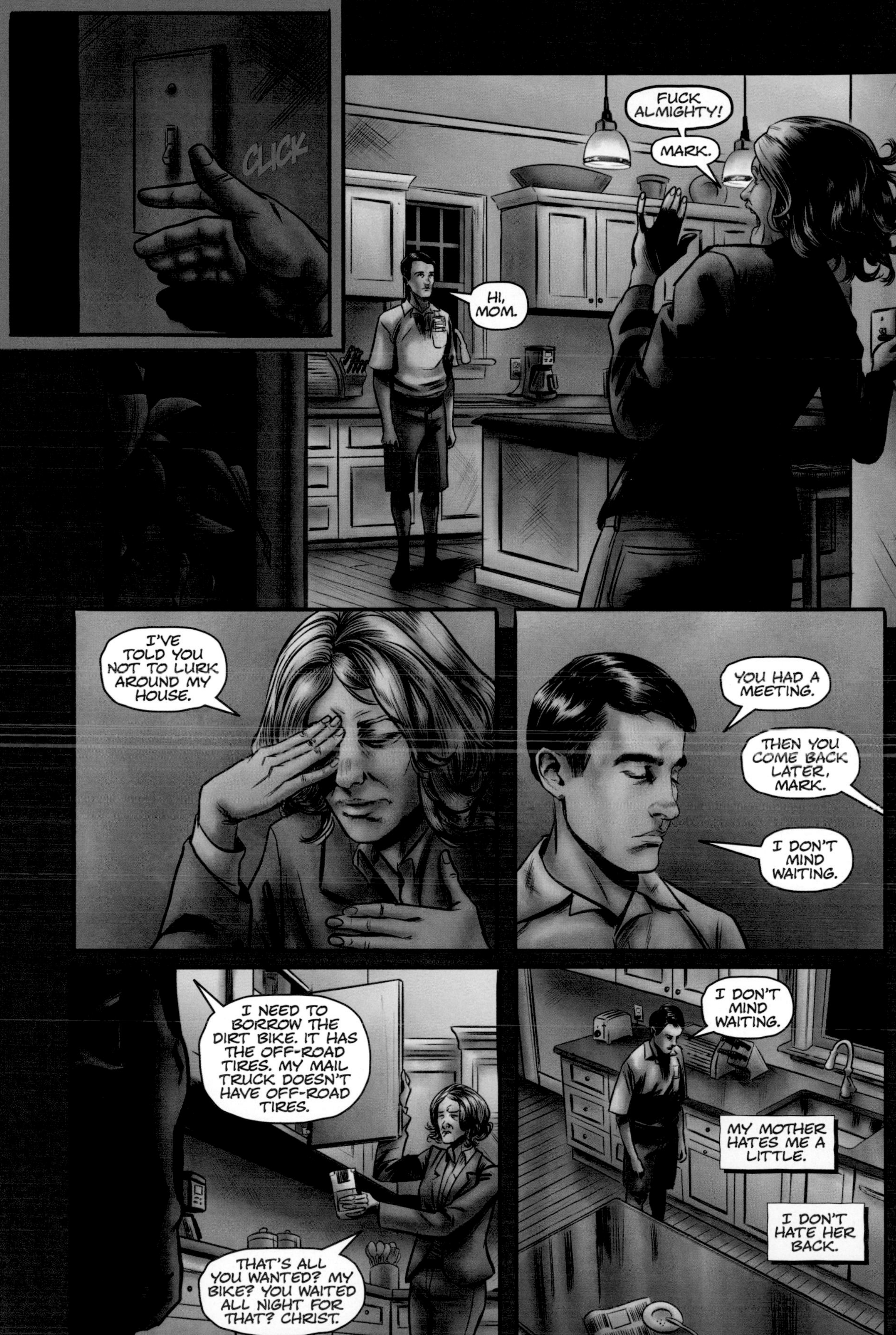
CLICK
FUCK ALMIGHTY!
MARK.
HI, MOM.
I'VE TOLD YOU NOT TO LURK AROUND MY HOUSE.
YOU HAD A MEETING.
THEN YOU COME BACK LATER, MARK.
I DON'T MIND WAITING.
I NEED TO BORROW THE DIRT BIKE. IT HAS THE OFF-ROAD TIRES. MY MAIL TRUCK DOESN'T HAVE OFF-ROAD TIRES.
THAT'S ALL YOU WANTED? MY BIKE? YOU WAITED ALL NIGHT FOR THAT? CHRIST.
I DON'T MIND WAITING.
MY MOTHER HATES ME A LITTLE.
I DON'T HATE HER BACK.

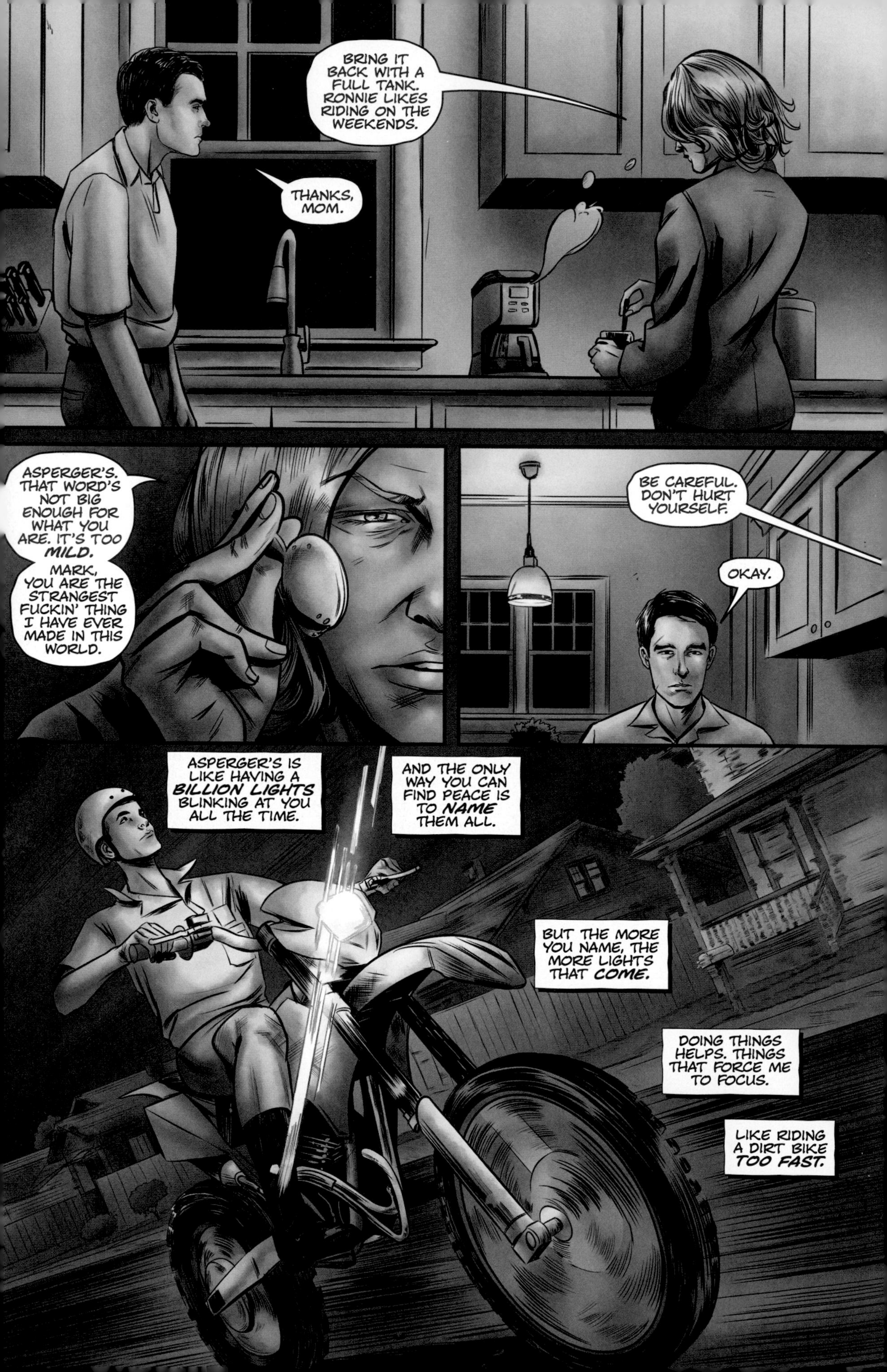
BRING IT BACK WITH A FULL TANK. RONNIE LIKES RIDING ON THE WEEKENDS.
THANKS, MOM.
ASPERGER'S. THAT WORD'S NOT BIG ENOUGH FOR WHAT YOU ARE. IT'S TOO MILD.
MARK, YOU ARE THE STRANGEST FUCKIN' THING I HAVE EVER MADE IN THIS WORLD.
BE CAREFUL. DON'T HURT YOURSELF.
OKAY.
ASPERGER'S IS LIKE HAVING A BILLION LIGHTS BLINKING AT YOU ALL THE TIME.
AND THE ONLY WAY YOU CAN FIND PEACE IS TO NAME THEM ALL.
BUT THE MORE YOU NAME, THE MORE LIGHTS THAT COME.
DOING THINGS HELPS. THINGS THAT FORCE ME TO FOCUS.
LIKE RIDING A DIRT BIKE TOO FAST.

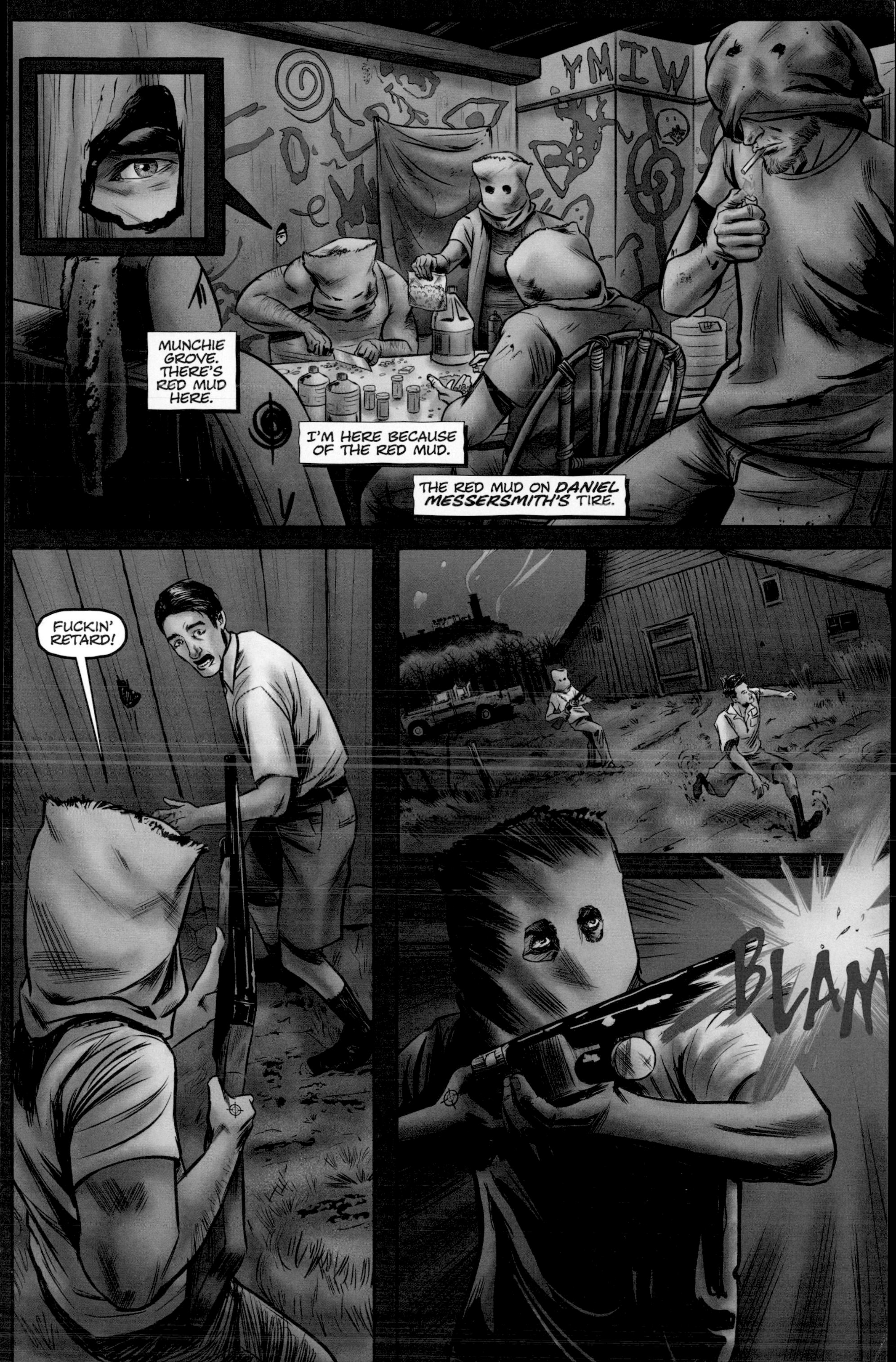

YMIW
MUNCHIE GROVE. THERE'S RED MUD HERE.
I'M HERE BECAUSE OF THE RED MUD.
THE RED MUD ON DANIEL MESSERSMITH'S TIRE.
FUCKIN' RETARD!
BLAM

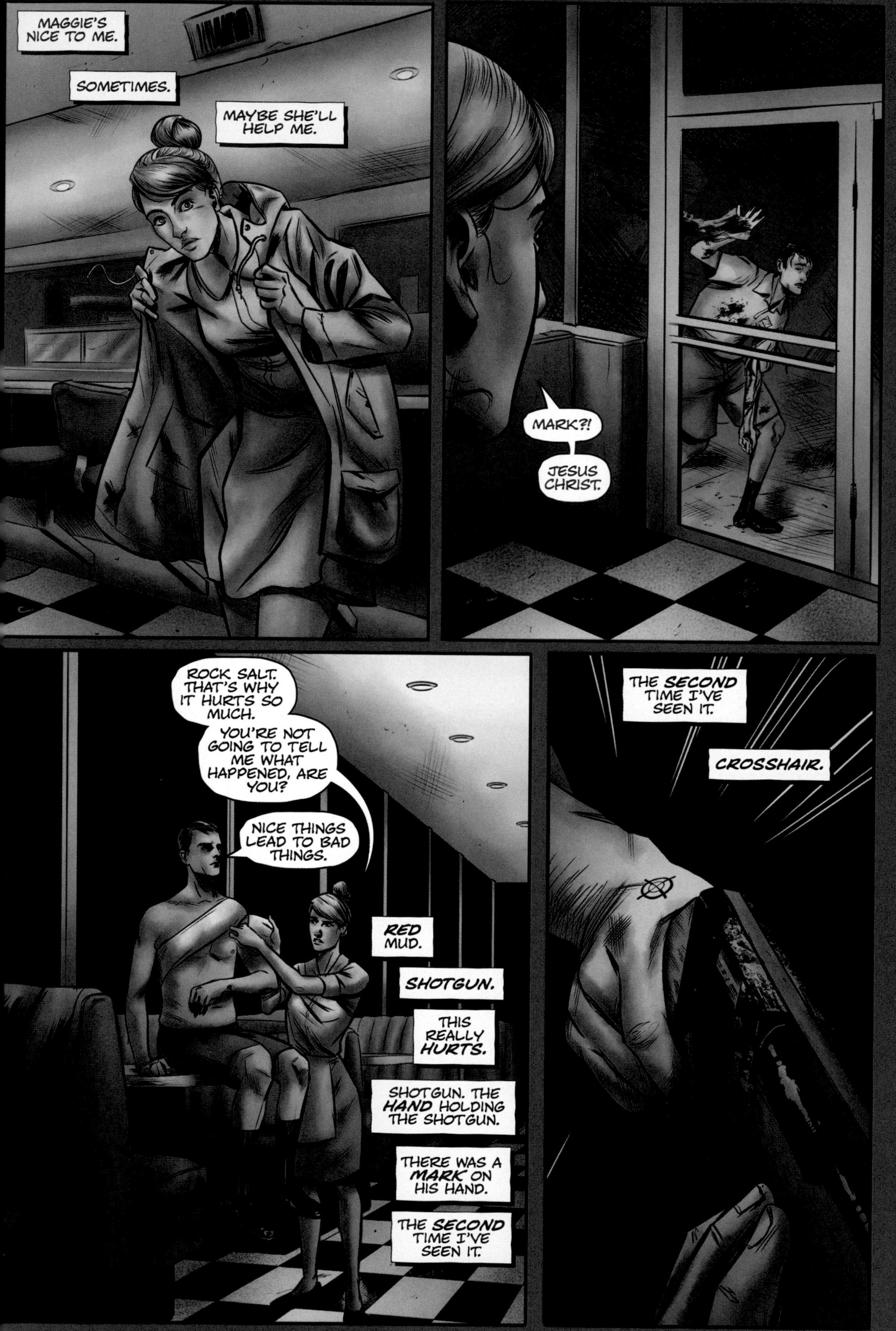
MAGGIE'S NICE TO ME.
SOMETIMES.
MAYBE SHE'LL HELP ME.
MARK?!
JESUS CHRIST.
ROCK SALT. THAT'S WHY IT HURTS SO MUCH.
YOU'RE NOT GOING TO TELL ME WHAT HAPPENED, ARE YOU?
NICE THINGS LEAD TO BAD THINGS.
RED MUD.
SHOTGUN.
THIS REALLY HURTS.
SHOTGUN. THE HAND HOLDING THE SHOTGUN.
THERE WAS A MARK ON HIS HAND.
THE SECOND TIME I'VE SEEN IT.
THE SECOND TIME I'VE SEEN IT.
CROSSHAIR.

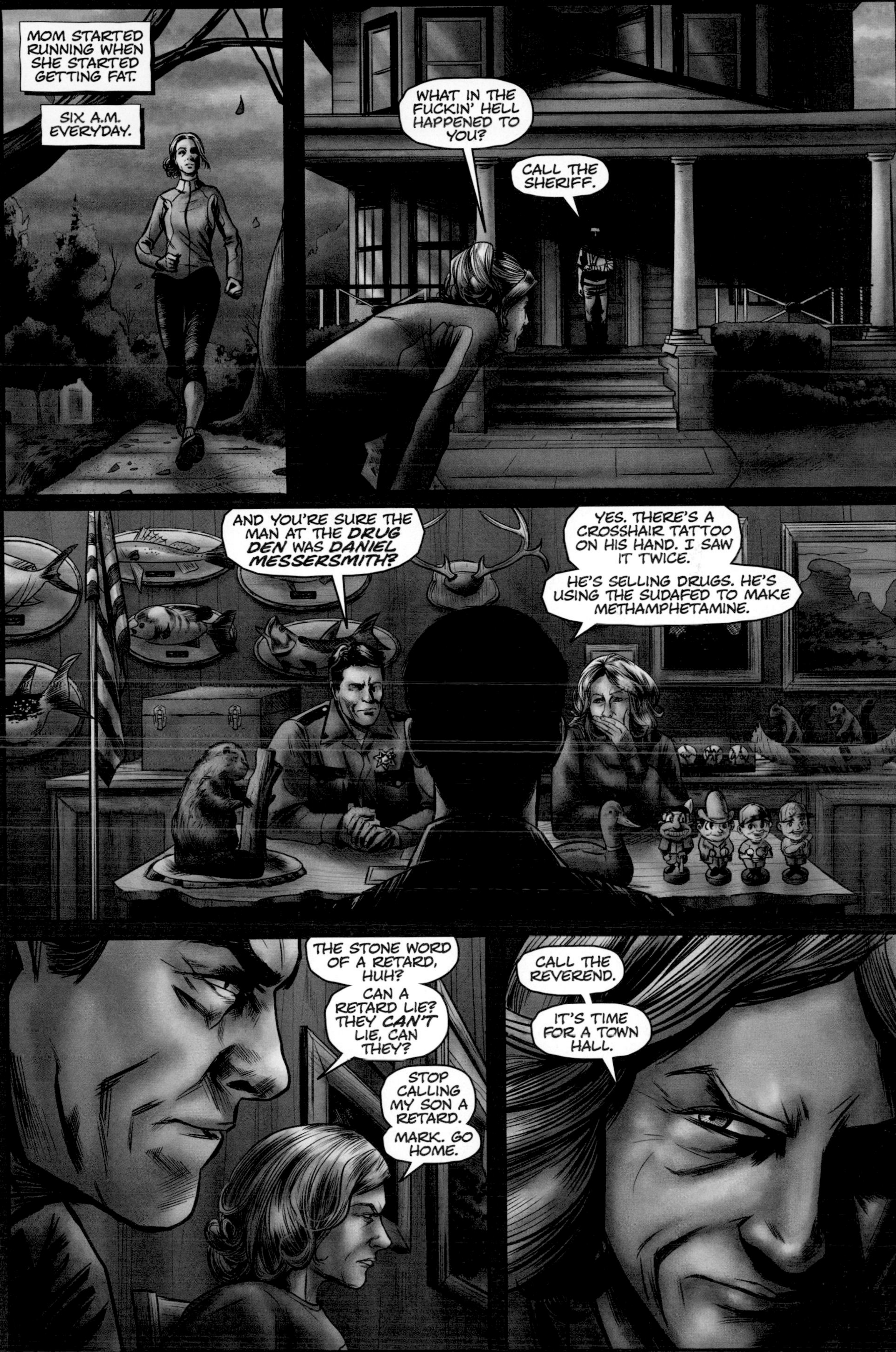
MOM STARTED RUNNING WHEN SHE STARTED GETTING FAT.
SIX A.M. EVERYDAY.
WHAT IN THE FUCKIN' HELL HAPPENED TO YOU?
CALL THE SHERIFF.
AND YOU'RE SURE THE MAN AT THE DRUG DEN WAS DANIEL MESSERSMITH?
YES. THERE'S A CROSSHAIR TATTOO ON HIS HAND. I SAW IT TWICE.
HE'S SELLING DRUGS. HE'S USING THE SUDAFED TO MAKE METHAMPHETAMINE.
THE STONE WORD OF A RETARD, HUH?
CAN A RETARD LIE? THEY CAN'T LIE, CAN THEY?
STOP CALLING MY SON A RETARD.
MARK. GO HOME.
CALL THE REVEREND.
IT'S TIME FOR A TOWN HALL.

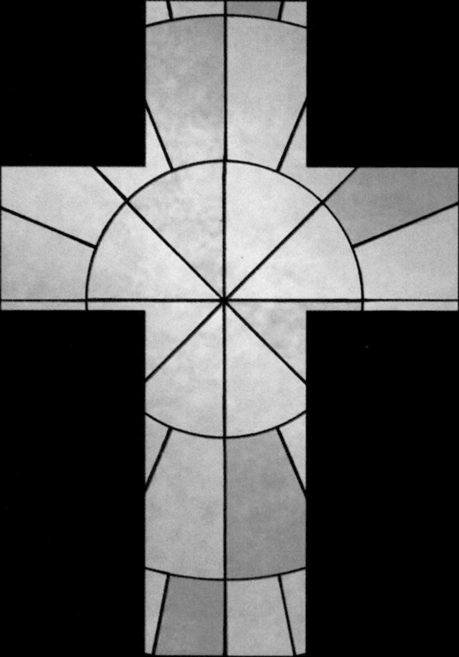

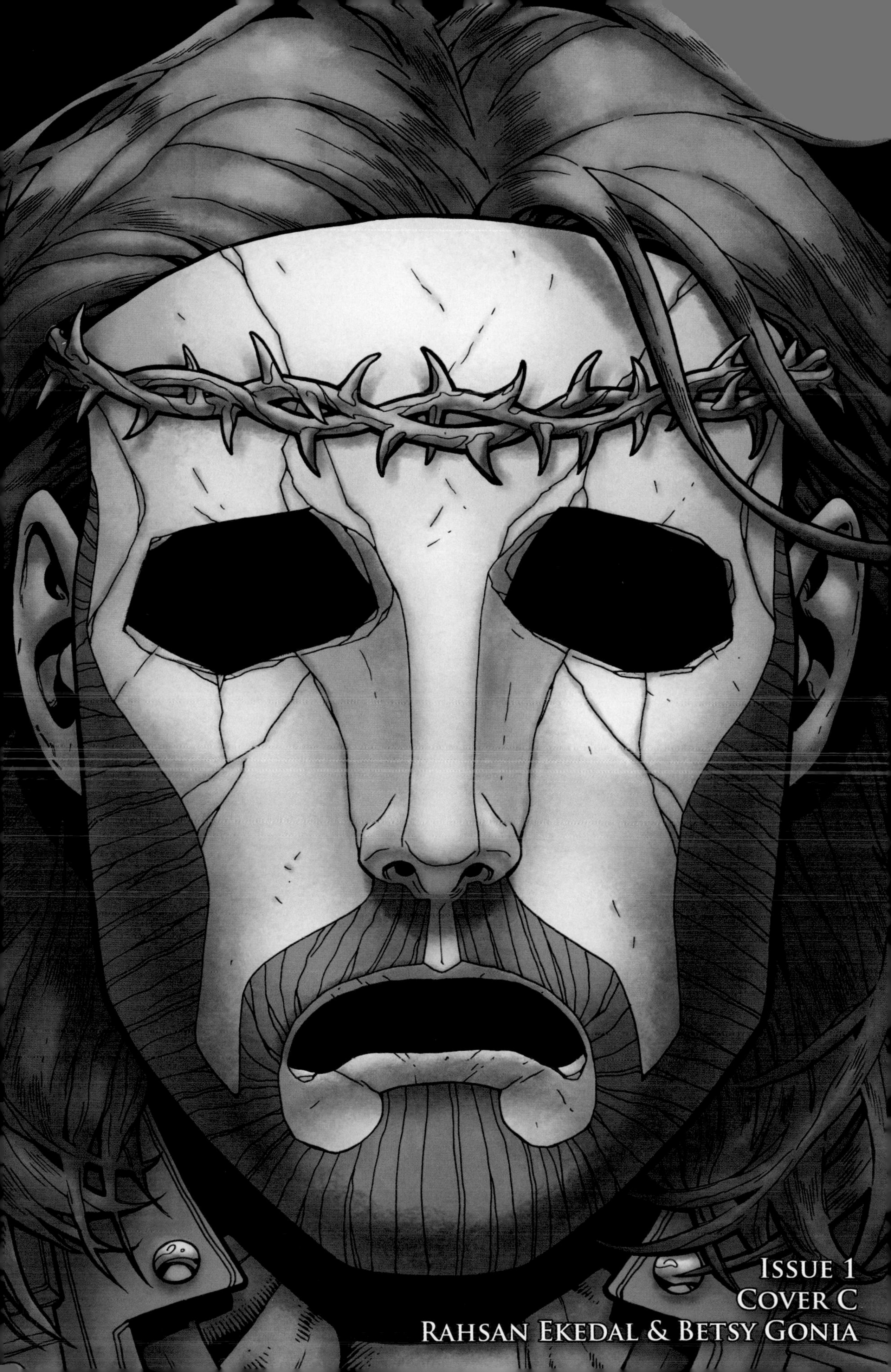

Issue 1
Cover C
Rahsan Ekedal & Betsy Gonia

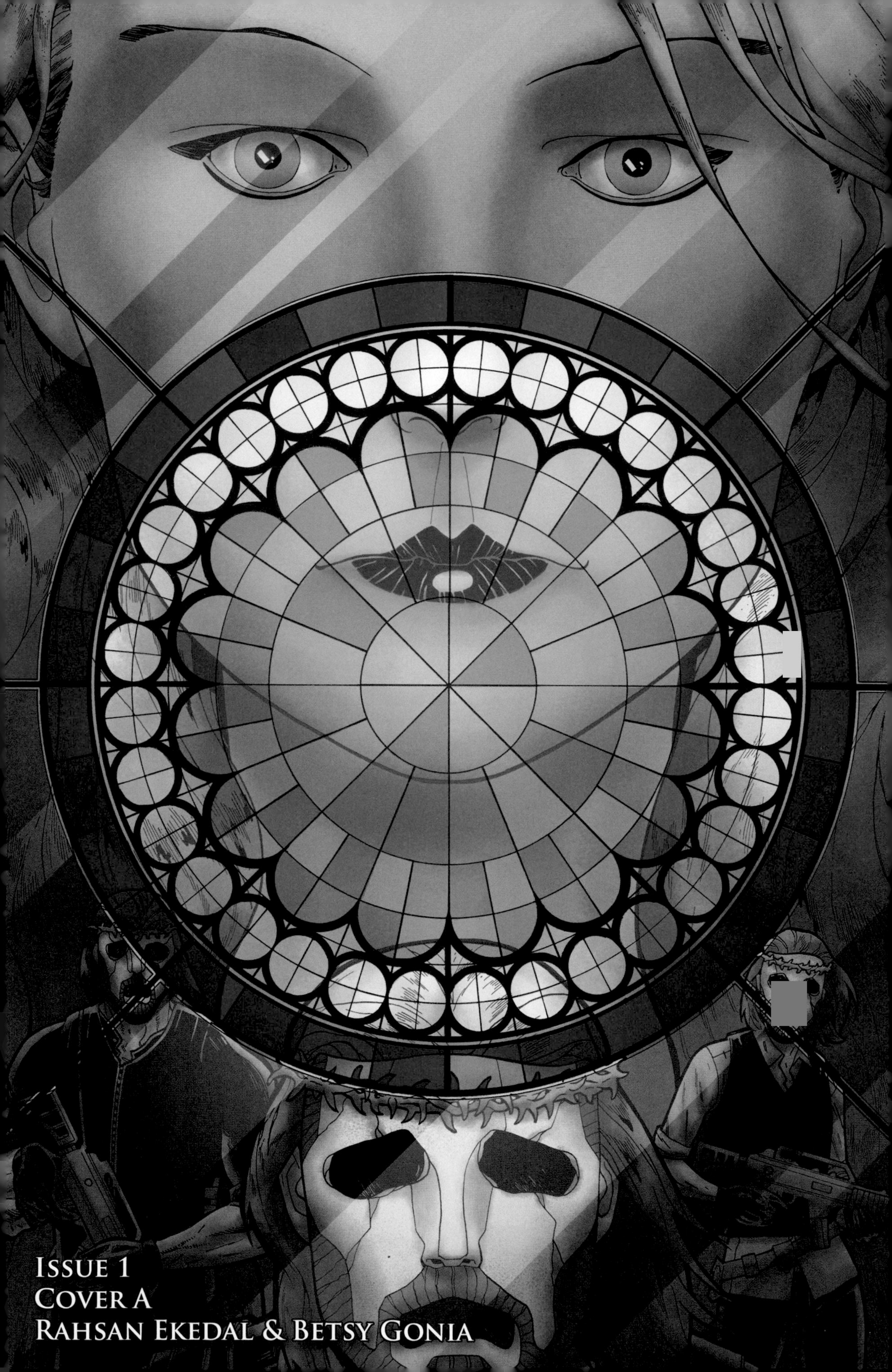
Issue 1
Cover A
Rahsan Ekedal & Betsy Gonia

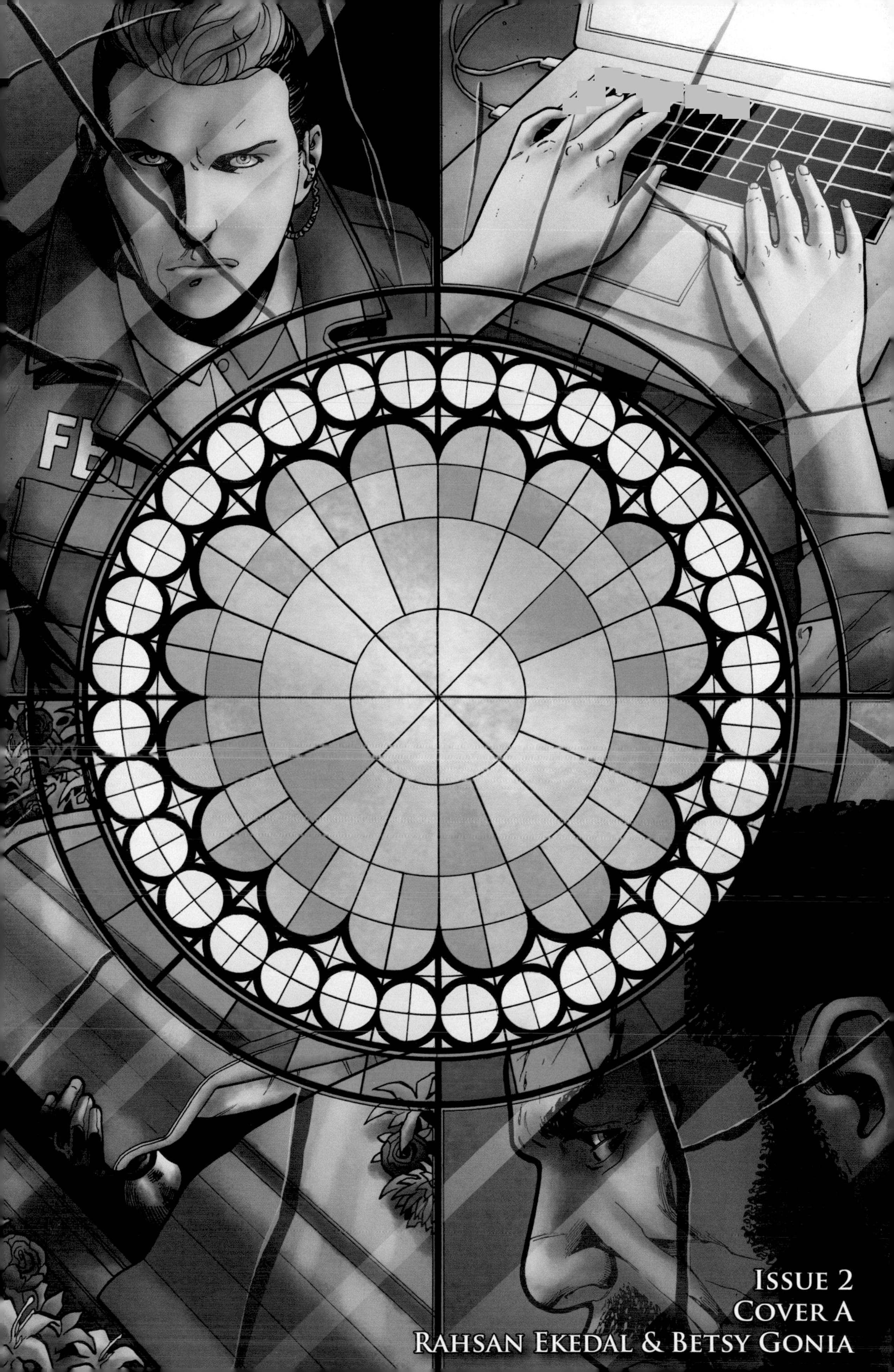

Issue 2
Cover A
Rahsan Ekedal & Betsy Gonia

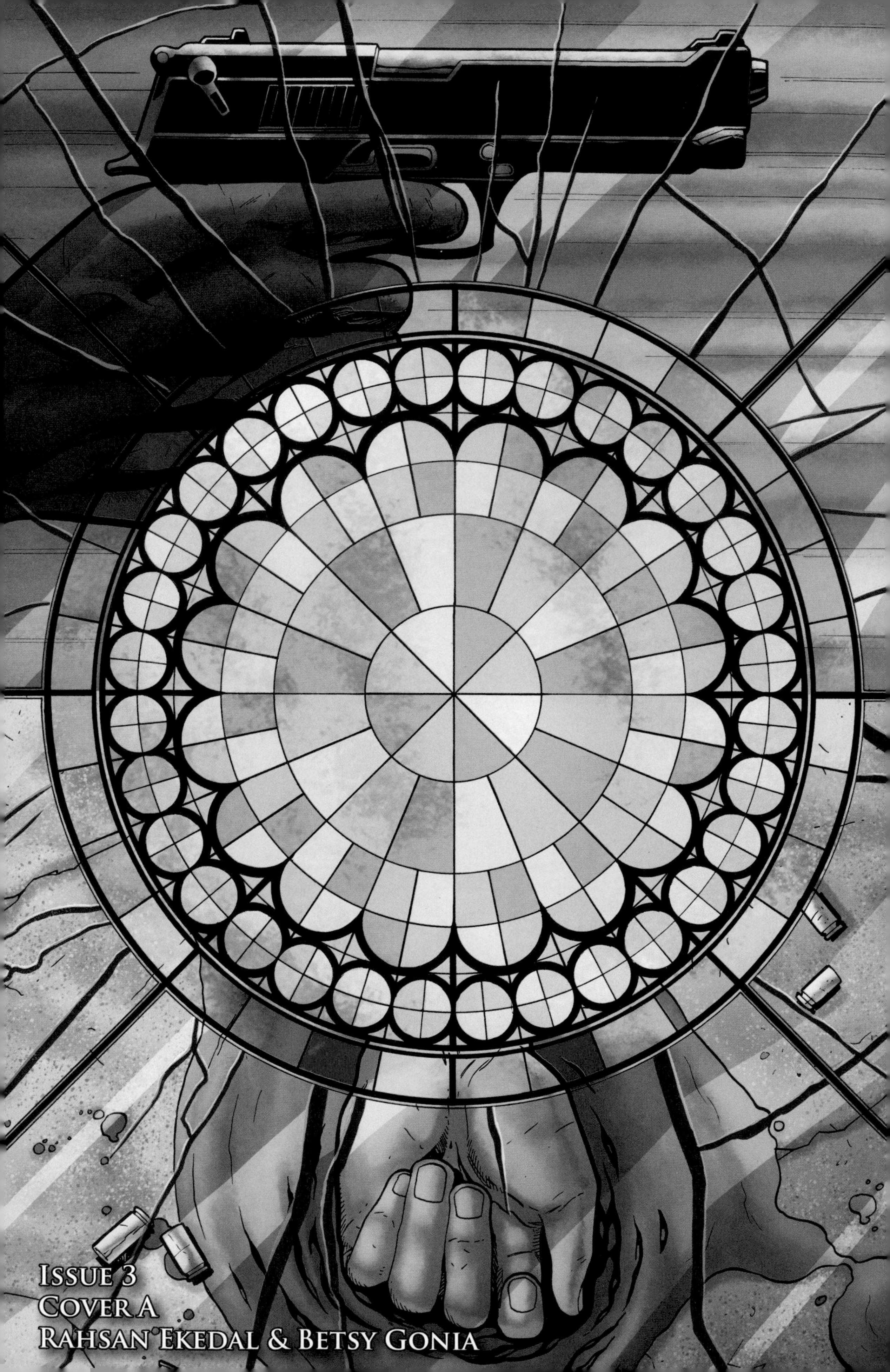

Issue 3
Cover A
Rahsan Ekedal & Betsy Gonia

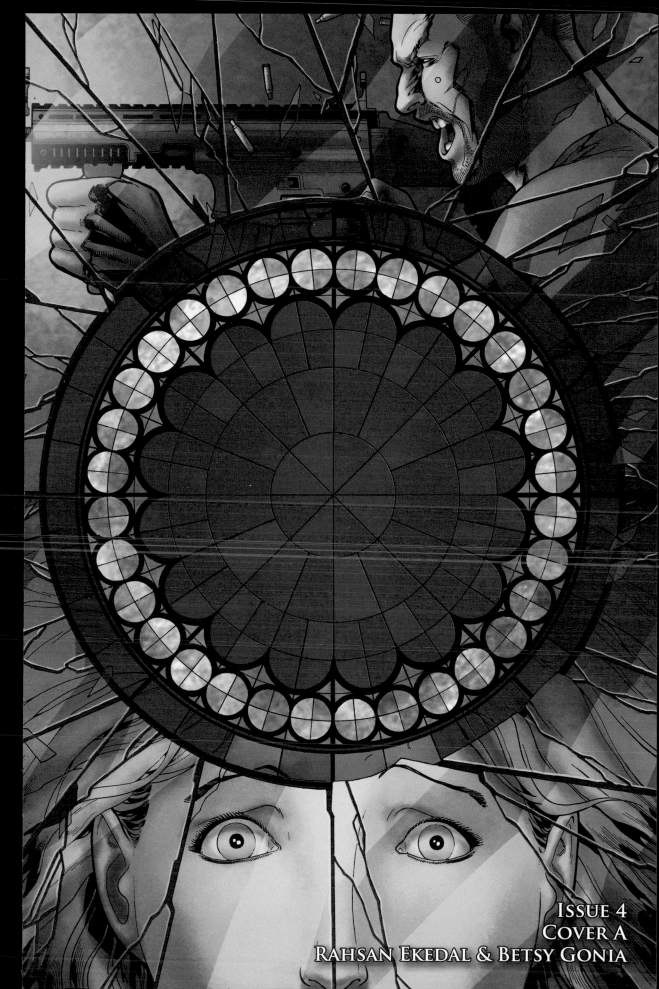

ISSUE 4
COVER A
RAHSAN EKEDAL & BETSY GONIA

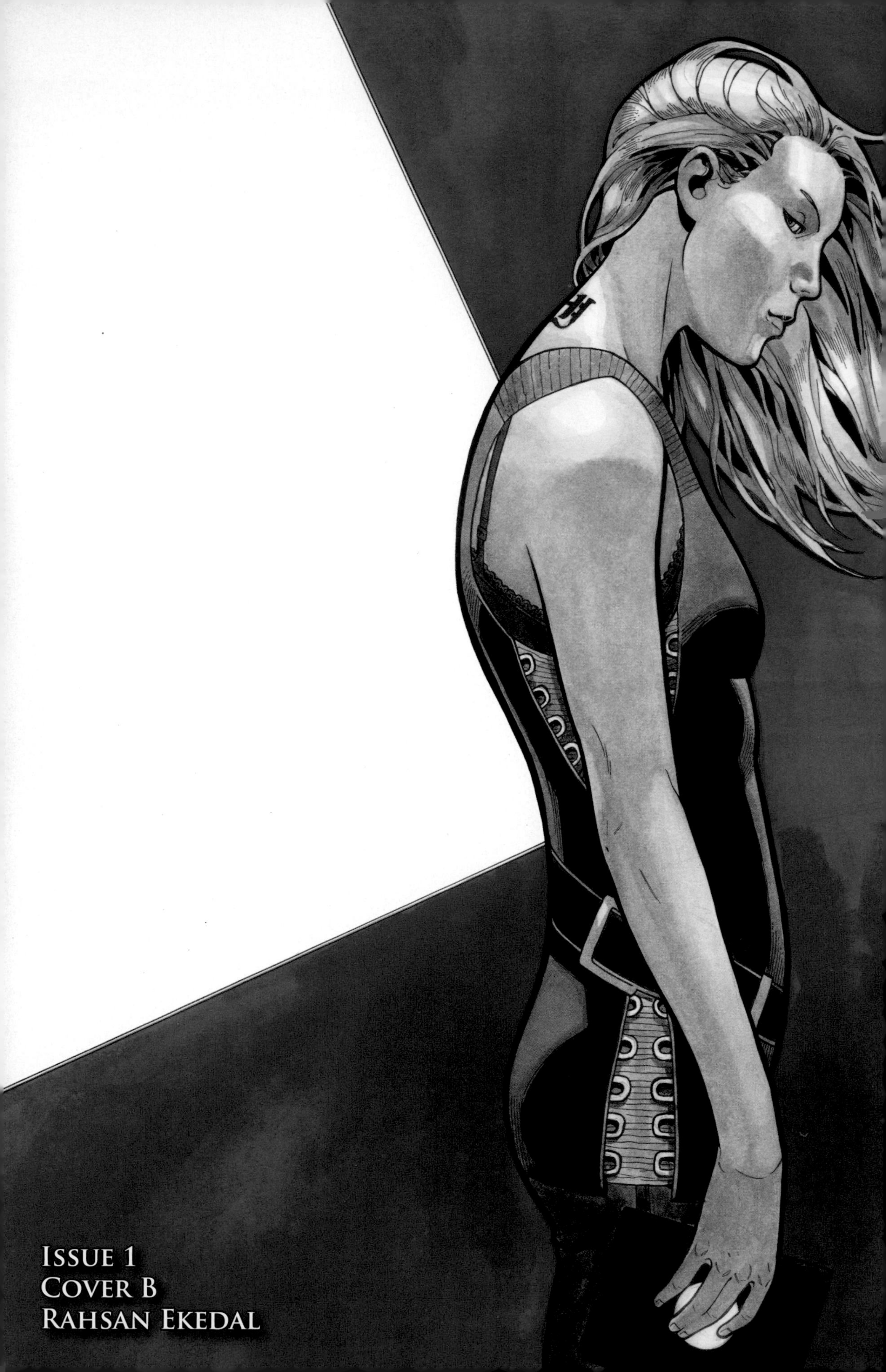

Issue 1
Cover B
Rahsan Ekedal

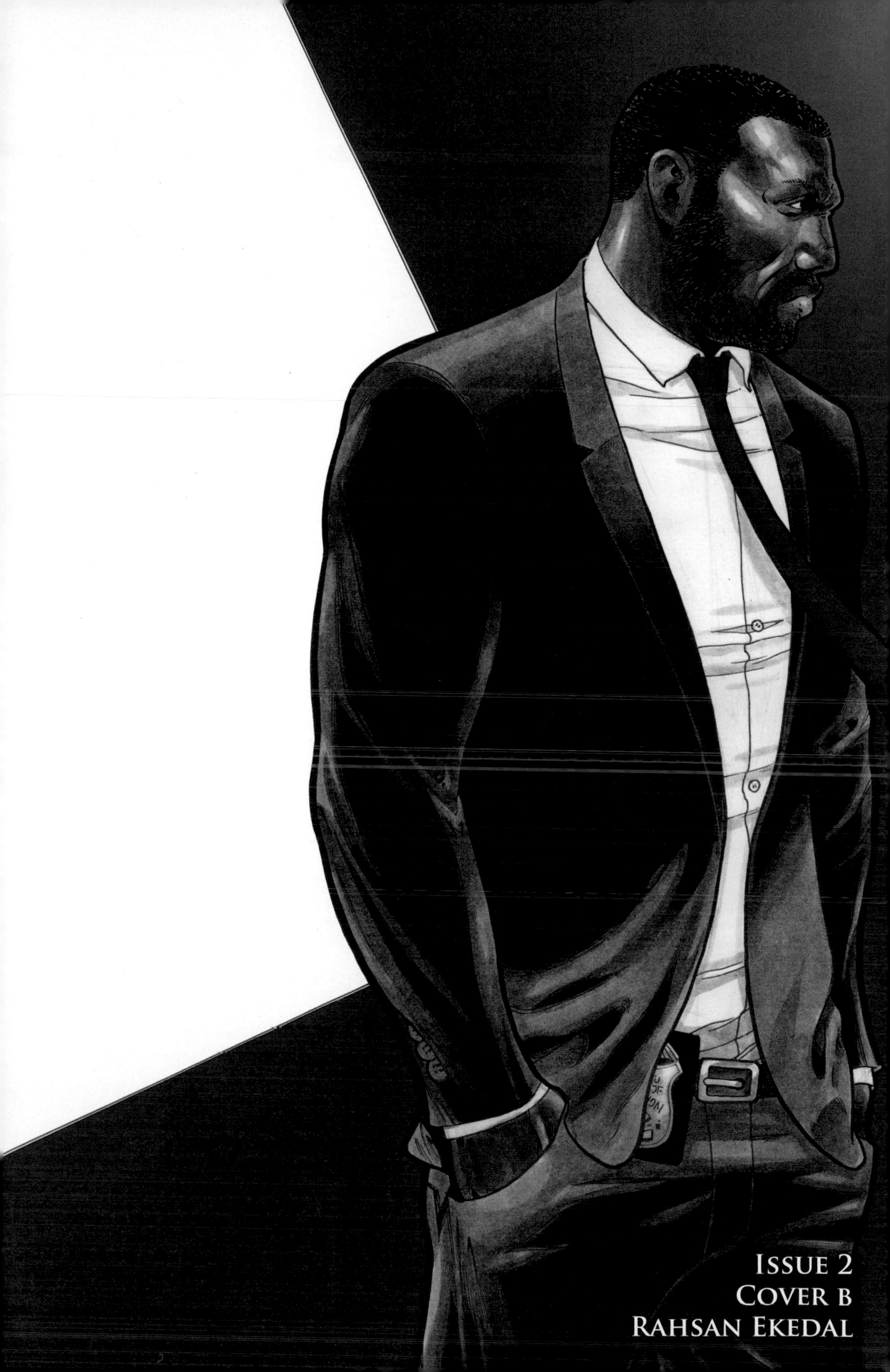
Issue 2
Cover B
Rahsan Ekedal

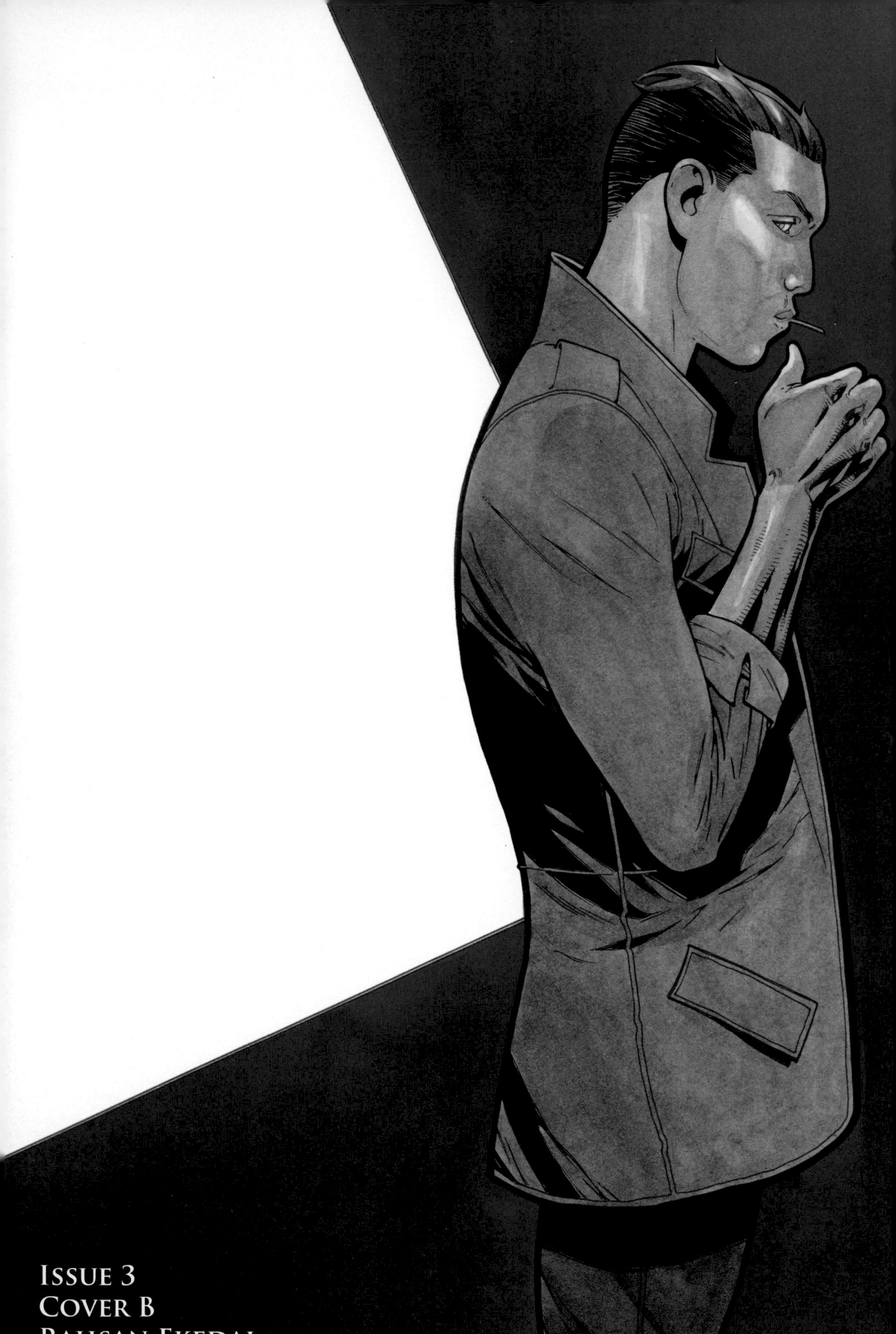

Issue 3
Cover B
Rahsan Ekedal

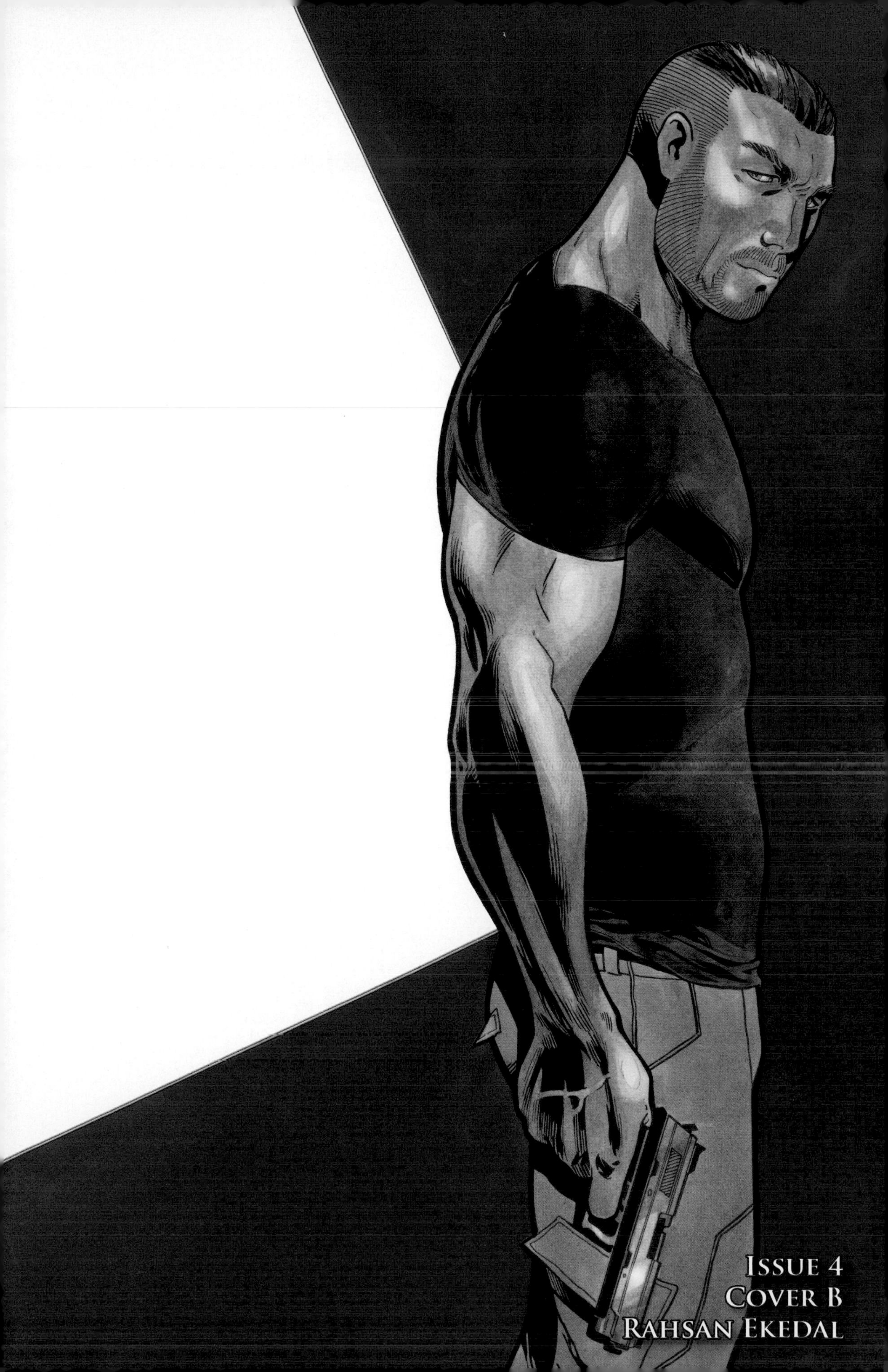

Issue 4
Cover B
Rahsan Ekedal

MEET THE CREATORS

MATT HAWKINS

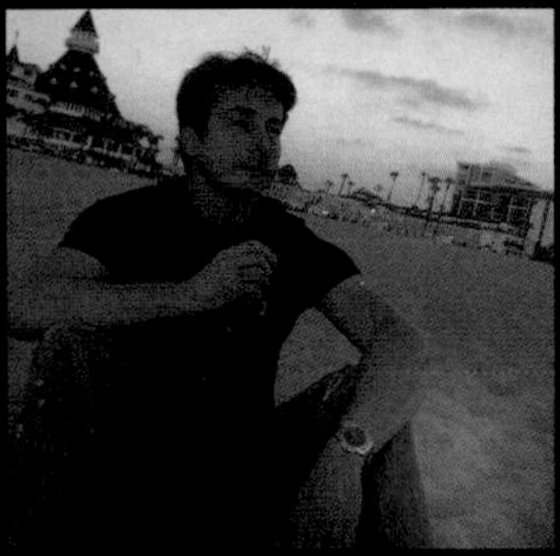

A veteran of the initial Image Comics launch, Matt started his career in comic book publishing in 1993 and has been working with Image as a creator, writer, and executive for over twenty years. President/COO of Top Cow since 1998, Matt has created and written over thirty new franchises for Top Cow and Image including ***Think Tank, Necromancer, VICE, Lady Pendragon, Aphrodite IX, IXth Generation*** as well as handling the company's business affairs.

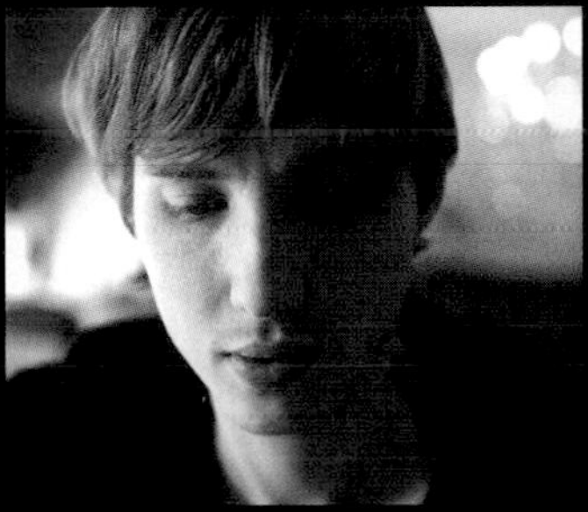

RAHSAN EKEDAL

Rahsan Ekedal is an artist best known for his work on ***Think Tank***, and the Harvey Award nominated graphic novel ***Echoes***. He has illustrated a variety of titles such as ***Solomon Kane, Creepy Comics, The Cleaners***, and ***Warhammer,*** and worked with many publishers including Top Cow, Dark Horse, DC/Vertigo, and Boom! Studios. He was born in California, and educated at the School of the Arts High School and the Academy of Art University, both in San Francisco. Rahsan currently lives in Berlin, Germany with his wife Shannon, and their big black cat, Flash.

BILL FARMER

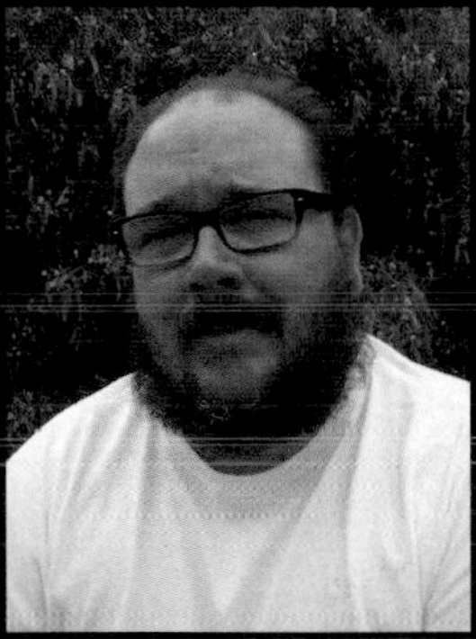

Bill Farmer is from Surprise, Arizona and has been coloring comics for about five years. He has colored Top Cow titles ***The Darkness, Witchblade, The Magdalena***, and ***Artifacts***.

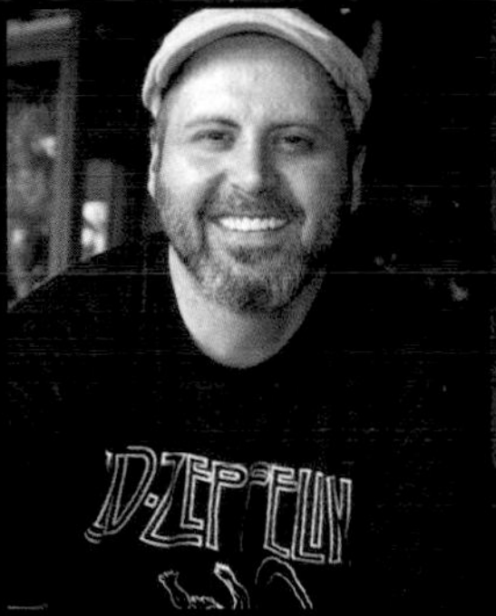

MIKE SPICER

Mike Spicer is a south Florida based artist. He's been working in comics since 2007. After almost entirely giving up on art, he was fortunate enough to be pulled back in, and into such a great community as comics. Mike is currently working on several titles, including *The Tithe*, *Mad Max*, *Mythic*, and *Dead Drop.*

TROY PETERI

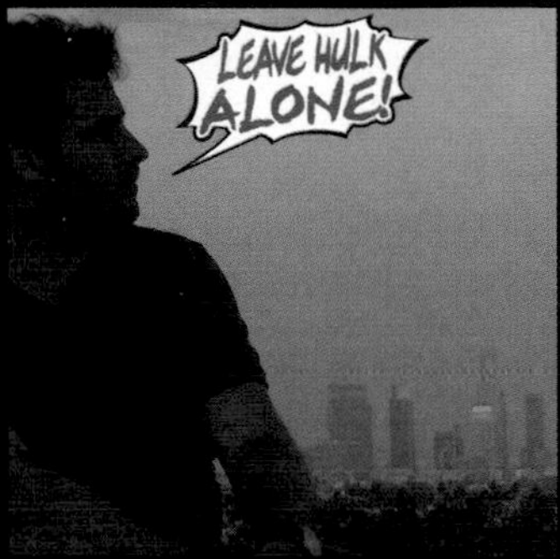
LEAVE HULK ALONE!

Starting his career at Comicraft, Troy Peteri lettered titles such as ***Iron Man, Wolverine***, and ***Amazing Spider-Man,*** among many others. He's been lettering roughly 97% of all Top Cow titles since 2005. In addition to Top Cow, he currently letters comics from multiple publishers and websites, such as Image Comics, Dynamite, and Archaia. He (along with co-writer Tom Martin and artist Dave Lanphear) is currently writing (and lettering) ***Tales of Equinox***, a webcomic of his own creation for www.Thrillbent.com. (Once again, www.Thrillbent.com.) He's still bitter about no longer lettering ***The Darkness*** and wants it back on stands immediately.

The Top Cow essentials checklist:

Aphrodite IX: The Complete Series
(ISBN: 978-1-63215-368-5)

Artifacts Origins: First Born
(ISBN: 978-1-60706-506-7)

Broken Trinity, Volume 1
(ISBN: 978-1-60706-051-2)

Cyber Force: Rebirth, Volume 1
(ISBN: 978-1-60706-671-2)

The Darkness: Accursed, Volume 1
(ISBN: 978-1-58240-958-0)

The Darkness: Rebirth, Volume 1
(ISBN: 978-1-60706-585-2)

Impaler, Volume 1
(ISBN: 978-1-58240-757-9)

Postal, Volume 1
(ISBN: 978-1-63215-342-5)

Rising Stars Compendium
(ISBN: 978-1-63215-246-6)

Sunstone, Volume 1
(ISBN: 978-1-63215-212-1)

Think Tank, Volume 1
(ISBN: 978-1-60706-660-6)

Wanted
(ISBN: 978-1-58240-497-4)

Wildfire, Volume 1
(ISBN: 978-1-63215-024-0)

Witchblade: Redemption, Volume 1
(ISBN: 978-1-60706-193-9)

Witchblade: Rebirth, Volume 1
(ISBN: 978-1-60706-532-6)

Witchblade: Borne Again, Volume 1
(ISBN: 978-1-63215-025-7)

For more ISBN and ordering information on our latest collections go to:
www.topcow.com
Ask your retailer about our catalogue of collected editions,
digests, and hard covers or check the listings at:
Barnes and Noble, Amazon.com,
and other fine retailers.

To find your nearest comic shop go to:
www.comicshoplocator.com